T0110838

THE PENGUIN BOOK OF VICTORIAN WOMEN IN CRIME

MICHAEL SIMS is the author of several nonfiction books, including *Apollo's Fire: A Day on Earth in Nature and Imagination, Adam's Navel: A Natural and Cultural History of the Human Form*, and most recently *In the Womb: Animals*, a companion book to a National Geographic Channel TV series. For Penguin Classics he has edited *The Annotated Archy and Mehitabel*; *Arsène Lupin, Gentleman-Thief;* and *The Penguin Book of Gaslight Crime;* and he introduced *The Leavenworth Case* by Anna Katherine Green. He is also the editor of *Dracula's Guest: A Connoisseur's Collection of Victorian Vampire Stories*. His work has appeared in the *Washington Post*, *Orion*, the *Times of London*, *New Statesman*, and *Chronicle of Higher Education*. Learn more at www.michaelsimsbooks.com.

The Penguin Book of Victorian Women in Crime

FORGOTTEN COPS AND PRIVATE EYES FROM THE TIME OF SHERLOCK HOLMES

Edited with an Introduction
by MICHAEL SIMS

PENGUIN BOOKS

PENGUIN BOOKS

Published by the Penguin Group
Penguin Group (USA) Inc., 375 Hudson Street,
New York, New York 10014, U.S.A.
Penguin Group (Canada), 90 Eglinton Avenue East, Suite 700, Toronto,
Ontario, Canada M4P 2Y3 (a division of Pearson Penguin Canada Inc.)
Penguin Books Ltd, 80 Strand, London WC2R 0RL, England
Penguin Ireland, 25 St Stephen's Green, Dublin 2,
Ireland (a division of Penguin Books Ltd)
Penguin Group (Australia), 250 Camberwell Road,
Camberwell, Victoria 3124, Australia
(a division of Pearson Australia Group Pty Ltd)
Penguin Books India Pvt Ltd, 11 Community Centre,
Panchsheel Park, New Delhi - 110 017, India
Penguin Group (NZ), 67 Apollo Drive, Rosedale, North Shore 0632,
New Zealand (a division of Pearson New Zealand Ltd)
Penguin Books (South Africa) (Pty) Ltd, 24 Sturdee Avenue,
Rosebank, Johannesburg 2196, South Africa

Penguin Books Ltd, Registered Offices:
80 Strand, London WC2R 0RL, England

First published in Penguin Books 2011

Selection, introduction and notes copyright © Michael Sims, 2011
All rights reserved

LIBRARY OF CONGRESS CATALOGING IN PUBLICATION DATA
The Penguin book of Victorian women in crime : forgotten cops and private eyes from the time of Sherlock Holmes / edited with an introduction by Michael Sims.
p. cm.—(Penguin classics)
ISBN 978-0-14-310621-0
1. Women detectives—England—Fiction. 2. Women private investigators—England—Fiction.
3. Detective and mystery stories, English. 4. English fiction—19th century. I. Sims, Michael.
PR1309.D4P45 2011
823'.0872083522—dc22 2010040866

Printed in the United States of America
Set in Sabon

Except in the United States of America, this book is sold subject to the condition that it shall not, by way of trade or otherwise, be lent, resold, hired out, or otherwise circulated without the publisher's prior consent in any form of binding or cover other than that in which it is published and without a similar condition including this condition being imposed on the subsequent purchaser.

The scanning, uploading and distribution of this book via the Internet or via any other means without the permission of the publisher is illegal and punishable by law. Please purchase only authorized electronic editions and do not participate in or encourage electronic piracy of copyrighted materials. Your support of the author's rights is appreciated.

146122990

Contents

Acknowledgments

Once again I thank the admirable team at Penguin Classics, who have been a dream to work with, and who even sent care packages of books and cookies while I recovered from a car wreck. My thanks to editorial director Elda Rotor, who is helpful and patient and who wears great colors; her intrepid and eagle-eyed assistant, Lorie Napolitano; publicity director Maureen Donnelly; publicists Meghan Fallon and Courtney Allison; Bennett Petrone, associate director of publicity; cover designer Jaya Miceli; and production editor Jennifer Tait.

I welcome this opportunity to thank Elizabeth Carolyn Miller, assistant professor of English at the University of California at Davis, for her generosity in providing copies of her insightful articles and for her critique of my introduction to this volume as well as my introduction to Penguin's edition of Anna Katharine Green's novel *The Leavenworth Case* (and thanks for tea at MLA). Thank you also to Arlene Young, assistant professor of English at the University of Manitoba, for her critiques and advice and her generosity in sending her own article. Several people generously provided sources, suggested authors or books, discussed issues, or otherwise assisted: Jon Erickson, Michele Flynn, Collier Goodlett, Michele B. Slung, John Spurlock, Art Taylor, and Mark Wait. Once again Karissa Kilgore proved invaluable. Perpetual gratitude goes to the staff of the Greensburg Hempfield Area Library, especially Cindy Dull and Linda Matey, those book detectives extraordinaire, and library director (and good friend) Cesare Muccari. And always, my thanks to Laura Sloan Patterson, my wife and in-house literary scholar and the most entertaining traveling companion I could imagine. She would have made a great detective but I'm glad she chose teaching instead.

Introduction

Intimate Watching

> The reader will comprehend that the woman detective has far greater opportunities than a man of intimate watching, and of keeping her eye upon matters near where a man could not conveniently play the eavesdropper.
>
> —MRS. G., IN *The Female Detective* (1864)

One aspect of the Victorian era that captivated and energized many of its fiction writers was the chaotic bustle of the London streets. Crowds featured not only ladies crowned in velveteen and feathers, strolling arm in arm with waistcoated men in sugarloaf top hats, but also their social inferiors. The jostling hoards included bootblacks and chimney sweeps, urchins selling crude little boxes of lucifer matches, knife grinders at their humming whetstone wheels and strops. Street entrepreneurs hawked everything from ballads to puppies to those quintessential items of Englishness even today: umbrellas. Buskers sang or played the fiddle before their upended cap; vendors sold lemonade, pastries, and milk so fresh it might still be warm. Carriages and bicycles threaded among pedestrians as nearby trains belched smoke.

Not surprisingly, such crowds drew all species of cutpurse and brigand. Every kind of crime, from a team of pickpockets' choreographed three-way lift to a brutish smash-and-grab, could be found on the streets. Private homes, from mansion to tenement, were less secure then than now, and nighttime alleys were not for the faint of heart. Burglary, armed robbery, assault, murder, infanticide, spousal abuse, racially motivated hate crimes—the whole menu of depravity could be found. It was a time much like our own.

From the earliest stories in the genre, urban bustle has been the backdrop of most detective fiction, as many stories in this anthology demonstrate. Although some of the stories occur in the United States, most take place in England, which is why I use the term *Victorian* in the anthology's title. The chronological progression of stories extends into World War I. This range gives us an opportunity to see how times were changing in the generation following Queen Victoria's death. During her reign, which comprised two-thirds of the nineteenth century, the detective story was born and bolted through its rowdy youth into maturity—or at least into young adulthood. Nowadays we think of its celebrity sleuths as strolling down crowded streets in London or New York or Paris, and it's true that from its inception the detective story was largely an urban art. Although each detective ventures out to the country as well, Loveday Brooke and Dorcas Dene and their colleagues, like Sherlock Holmes and Martin Hewitt—and like Philip Marlowe and Cordelia Grey after them—are headquartered in, and operate largely within, cities.

Now we can revise our opening crowd scene, with its thieves plucking the innocent, and restore a comforting sense of order by placing detectives on the trail of the miscreants. But wait—the setting is real but the sleuths are fictional. I raise this seemingly obvious point for a reason. Most of us, even fans of Victorian detective fiction, know little about the actual investigative work of the era. Before we bring out the brave and resourceful women who are waiting backstage, let's glance briefly at their real-life contemporaries to see how much (or how little) the fiction in these pages resembled reality. Many of the female detectives in this anthology have a curious trait in common: they are employed by, or at least consulted by, the official police. Only with a look at their historical context can I demonstrate the revolutionary nature of the early debut of fictional female detectives. I first yearned to edit this anthology after I discovered how early in the genre female detectives emerged.

When we go back to the genesis of modern police work, we find ourselves—appropriately for a genre that has always intertwined fact and fiction—in the presence of an author. In 1749, the year he published his picaresque novel *Tom Jones*, the English novelist Henry Fielding launched an organization that came to be called the Bow Street Runners. Working out of Fielding's Bow Street office in London, where he served as chief magistrate, the Runners traveled far and wide to arrest offenders and serve subpoenas and other writs. Originally there were only eight Runners. Although in some respects they were more like private detectives than our contemporary notion of cops, many historians consider them the first modern police force. They were paid out of allocated government funds, a kind of payment that separates them from their juridical ancestors. Before the Runners, many crime victims had recourse only to thief-takers. These shady characters weren't precisely bounty hunters, most of whom were paid by bail bondsmen; thief-takers were usually in the employ of those few victims who could afford them. Naturally such an arrangement lent itself to chicanery. Some thief-takers acted as go-betweens, returning goods that their partners had stolen.

What was needed was an official police department, despite such an institution's own fertile ground for corruption. In 1829, eight years before the reign of Victoria began, Parliament passed the Metropolitan Police Act, which replaced the antique plexus of watchmen and parish constables with a reasonably organized force. Soon London saw a bold new figure striding down the street. These constables were a tough-looking lot—tall, sturdy, dressed in blue top hat and tailcoat to make them look as different as possible from the red-coated and metal-helmeted soldiers who had often served as military police on the streets. They were armed with only a wooden truncheon and a pair of handcuffs. At first they carried a wooden rattle to summon other officers, but it turned out to be too cumbersome and not loud enough; a whistle replaced it. Because the police force was launched by popular home secretary Robert Peel, they were nicknamed *peelers* in Ireland and *bobbies* in England. Peel had earned his reputation while launching the Royal Irish Constabulary during his tenure as chief secretary for Ireland, in which his job was to maintain "order"—as defined, we must remember, by the English occupying force.

Within a decade of the bobbies' founding, the Bow Street Runners were gone. But bobbies were there to prevent crimes or to respond to them immediately, not to solve them. They were not detectives. Not until 1842 was there a detective bureau—the ancestor of the Criminal Investigation Department (CID) that still exists in England—to decipher clues and investigate the crimes discovered or interrupted by uniformed officers.

Missing from the new detective bureau, of course, were women. It would take four more decades, until 1883, before women were employed in even the most menial of police jobs—the searching of female prisoners upon their arrest. In 1905 a woman was hired in a position that seems to have merged truant officer, prison warder, and counselor. Not until 1918 did the London police hire the first women as officers. As late as 1924, the Joint Central Committee of the Police Federation of England and Wales issued a public statement in opposition to this idea: "[T]he very nature of the duties of a police constable is contrary to that which is finest and best in women . . . it is purely a man's job alone." Women's law enforcement work, in the eyes of the police administration, included such domestic tragedies as spousal abuse and child prostitution, but larceny and homicide remained for many more years the purview of men only.

The kinds of glamorous jewel theft and high-society murder that appear in these pages have always existed mostly in fiction, and in made-up worlds other strange things could happen. "The representation of a woman engaging in detection during the nineteenth century," writes Joseph A. Kestner, "constituted a profound fantasy of female empowerment." It was a fantasy because fiction was decades ahead of reality. The first stories about female detectives appeared in the early 1860s. I'm imprecise about the year because critics aren't sure. They argue over whether W. S. Hayward anonymously published *Revelations of a Lady Detective* in 1864 or if the 1864 edition was a reprint of an 1861 edition barely mentioned but otherwise unknown. From this collection, whatever its birth date, comes a fine story, "The Mysterious Countess," which you will find herein. And it was definitely 1864 when Andrew Forrester published *The Female Detective*, from which I have chosen the longest story in the anthology: an extraordinary novella entitled "The Unknown Weapon." These two stories present the first female professional investigators diligently pursuing their careers. There are moments in literature so far ahead of their time they seem almost science-fictional. Not even Captain Nemo's electrical submarine in *Twenty Thousand Leagues Under the Sea* was more futuristic than the representation of "lady" detectives that you will encounter in the pages ahead.

Why did female characters show up in crime fiction several decades ahead of their appearance in the real world? Probably every author had a different reason for deciding to write about a female protagonist. "That so many male writers . . . created women sleuths may say something about their feminist sympathies," writes Laura Marcus, "but it also suggests that female characters allowed for quite specific kinds of detective work and detective narrative." Whatever the progressive sensibilities of the author, the creation of a female detective instantly provided a number of narrative possibilities that were unavailable to male heroes—as my title for this introduction implies. Sometimes, to be observant, all a lady detective had to do to was remain silent and be carried along by the authoritarian assumptions of the men in the case, including their belief that she was unlikely to be either intelligent or brave. A female detective would notice different clues and be welcomed behind doors closed to her male counterparts. She could disguise herself and become even less noticeable than the postman in G. K. Chesterton's famous Father Brown story "The Invisible Man." Many of the heroines in this anthology employ disguises, but Loveday Brooke is particularly good at turning herself into an unseen housemaid or overlooked governess, placing herself in a position that permits intimate watching.

As you will observe in these stories, one of the most important questions to be settled by each author is how the character came to find herself working in such an unladylike profession. Dorcas Dene begins as an actress and moves into investigation only after her artist husband loses his sight and thus his ability to support her; young socialite Violet Strange needs money to secretly assist a disowned sister; Mrs. Paschal's husband dies and leaves her penniless. Therefore outraged readers could see these women's transgressions beyond Victorian norms as nobly heroic efforts to preserve the sacred family.

The phrase "Victorian detective story" sparks a particular image in my mind. It's the old Sherlock Holmes vignette—nighttime in London, fog rolling in off the Thames, the wheels of a hansom cab clattering across the cobblestones. I don't find it any less evocative for its being a cliché. I enjoy the era's texture and, in the better works, its precise and vivid language. Surely we return to a favorite genre in quest of a predictable experience. That's why most genres are described by the primary emotion sought by the reader who picks them up for diversion: horror, thrills, humor, adventure, love, mystery.

But when we say "detective story" instead of "mystery," we reveal a distinct aspect of this genre—its emphasis not on a particular emotion, because detective stories may be suspenseful or humorous or adventurous, but on a particular kind of character. Like many other readers, I revel in the investigative routine that reveals glimpses of many lives, in the puzzle that motivates the action, in the deciphering of clues and pursuit of the malefactor. (Based upon an extremely unscientific poll of friends of mine, I suggest that a Venn diagram of Mystery Readers would reveal blank areas in which the readership of detective stories doesn't overlap with the readership of thrillers that focus on the abominable behavior of the miscreants instead of on the detective's efforts to find or stop them.) Most detective stories are part of a series, as well, so we have the pleasure of returning to the company of an already familiar character, usually someone intelligent and courageous, even heroic. No wonder psychologists describe detective stories, especially the early ones, as cathartic and often conservative—portraying an initial threat to the social order combated and vanquished by the investigator.

Here we come to the unique pleasures of the book you hold in your hands: the characters, the detectives themselves. You will meet the dashing young Dora Myrl and the sardonic old Amelia Butterworth. You will encounter a thoughtful tragedy that young socialite Violet Strange uncovers, the professional routine of policewomen such as Mrs. Paschal, and the adventures of that indefatigable private detective Loveday Brooke. Among the protagonists in this book, only Sarah Fairbanks, the observant narrator of Mary E. Wilkins's story "The Long Arm," is not a series character. Only one character, Anna Katharine Green's Amelia Butterworth, is truly an amateur detective, allied with neither police nor a private inquiry agency—although in her later outings she becomes ever more respected by Ebenezer Gryce, Green's already famous detective whom she had introduced in 1878 in *The Leavenworth Case.*

In most cases I have read every story in each series in order to choose the best. In a couple of instances I found two or three nominees equally strong, and chose the one that had previously been anthologized least often. You will also find the first chapter of Anna Katharine Green's important and highly amusing 1897 novel *That Affair Next Door*, the debut of her spinster snoop Amelia Butterworth, clearly the direct ancestor of Agatha Christie's Miss Marple although a more three-dimensional and believable character. In this selection you won't be able to follow the mystery to its denouement, but you will see why the quick and vivid Green was one of the most influential writers in the genre. In each story's individual introduction, I describe in detail its author and characters and historical context, so I won't clutter this overview with biographical or bibliographical details.

How did this anthology come about? My first foray into editing a collection of crime stories was *Arsène Lupin, Gentleman-Thief*, a selection of the best of Maurice Leblanc's tales about the suave and vainglorious French master criminal, which Penguin published in 2007. My survey of Lupin's ancestors, descendants, and context directly inspired *The Penguin Book of Gaslight Crime: Con Artists, Burglars, Rogues, and Scoundrels from the Time of Sherlock Holmes*, which Penguin published in 2009. My wide reading for this book, in turn, reminded me how few of the great women detectives and criminals of the Victorian and Edwardian eras are remembered today. Although they show up here and there, I could find no collection devoted strictly to these pioneer characters. I thought this absence a shame, and the opportunity to fill the gap exciting; and Elda Rotor, the editorial director of Penguin Classics, agreed on both points. So here we are.

In this as in my previous collections, I have faced the anthologist's sweet dilemma: How many of the usual suspects ought to be included and how many omitted to make room for lesser-known characters? This problem results from an embarrassment of riches, so it isn't exactly a burden, but space limitations demand triage. In order to make room for unfamiliar authors such as W. S. Hayward and Andrew Forrester, I left out several stories that are already widely available. "The Diary of Anne Rodway," for example, which Wilkie Collins published in 1856, is often described as starring the first female detective. It's an interesting story and the narrator is sharp and courageous; but she is not a professional, the primary clue simply falls into her lap, and the adventure as a whole is not quite a detective story. One anthology favorite, Clarence Rook's brief 1898 story "The Stir Outside the Cafe Royal," although it involves the police and a criminal, isn't really a detective story.

For various reasons, I have refused admittance to several female series detectives. Space is an issue, of course. So is boredom, an emotion that every anthologist must employ as doorkeeper. I exclude, for example, Fergus Hume's stories about Hagar Stanley, as well as a series about criminal-turned-detective Constance Dunlap, written by Arthur B. Reeve, creator of the popular scientific detective Craig Kennedy. I never found copies of books that supposedly would have introduced me to Marie Connor Leighton's Lucille Dare and Beatrice Heron-Maxwell's Mollie Delamere, but these both live in longer works unlikely to lend themselves to coherent excerpts. We wanted to include a Lady Molly story by L. T. Meade and Robert Eustace, but reprint rights proved outrageously expensive.

Many of the stories I include first appeared as part of a progressive series, one in which each story stands alone but also moves toward a denouement, like TV series such as *Veronica Mars* or *Lost*. In these cases I carefully chose a story that stood on its own legs. Any necessary background information from earlier stories or chapters I provide in my introduction to the selection. Because not every first story is the best in its series, I often choose a later one for inclusion and simply preface it with the relevant passage from the origin story. Whenever I do so, I specify the nature of this merger in the story's introduction; I hate to be misled by invisible editorial tinkering and I assume that you do too.

One author appears more than once. Anna Katharine Green shows up with one story from her series about the young socialite detective Violet Strange and also with the first chapter of the novel that introduced Amelia Butterworth. Our eleven authors have produced stories about murder, theft, swindling, impersonation, kidnapping, and other antisocial entertainments. Within such a seemingly narrow focus as Victorian female detectives, the variety is highly enjoyable.

This collection concentrates on female *characters*. Many of the authors are female as well, but not all. To honor this premise, I omit the first known detective story by a woman, because her protagonist was a man. In early 1866 the *Australian Journal* published a story entitled "The Dead Witness," a suspenseful tale of an outback manhunt by Irish-born Mary Fortune, who wrote under the nom de plume W.W., which represented her poignant nickname for herself—Waif Wander. Obviously many of the pioneer writers in the field were women, but at first few of them wrote about female protagonists. But it's fun to see that they were on board so early. When W.W. published her first detective story, it had been only a quarter century since the genre's birth.

In 1841, a year before the founding of the first detective bureau in England, an oddball American poet, fiction writer, and critic scribbled a story entitled "The Murders in the Rue Trianon" and signed it Edgar A. Poe. Before he published it in the Philadelphia-based *Graham's Magazine,* of which he had just become editor, Poe changed the street to Rue Morgue—a great editorial decision, adding that chilling whiff of death in the title. Unquestionably Poe was the father of the detective story. "The Murders in the Rue Morgue" was the first of three stories about an amateur French detective named C. Auguste Dupin, a highborn melancholic whose spirit has been broken by his clan's pecuniary fall from grace. Arthur Conan Doyle purloined many of the stories' idiosyncrasies for Sherlock Holmes: an admiring narrator, an egocentric genius, and official police almost addle-brained enough to audition for the Keystone Kops. "The time of the professional police detective had barely begun," as Kate Summerscale wrote in her recent nonfiction book *The Suspicions of Mr. Whicher*, but "the era of the amateur was already in full flower."

None of Poe's grotesques and arabesques was more influential than this clever and revolutionary tale that, however outrageous its premise, nonetheless eschews the supernatural in deciphering the mystery at its core. It was the first detective story—that is, the first fiction in which the focus of the plot is the unraveling of a crime by investigative methods. Poe also wrote the first impossible-crime murder story ("Rue Morgue" again), the first in which a detective springs a surprise on a murderer to elicit a confession ("Thou Art the Man"), and the first in which a suspect is unknowingly shadowed by a detective ("The Man of the Crowd").

Some critics argue that Poe was in turn inspired by such works as "Mademoiselle de Scuderi," by the brilliant German fabulist E. T. A. Hoffmann, and that those tales ought to be regarded as protodetective stories. As much as I would like to bring one of my favorite writers into this genesis myth, I have to disagree with critics who consider Mlle Scuderi a detective. She is not an investigator by trade, neither amateur nor professional; nor does she launch anything approaching an investigation. The violent outrages of the Inquisition show up at her door in eighteenth-century Paris, and she proves smart and brave. But ratiocination is not her forte and most of the solution falls into her lap. Calling the tale a detective story is similar to borrowing noble ancestors for the luster they add to the family tree. Surely Poe is exotic enough.

Poe did have predecessors in the crime story, of course, including a long-winded, not-quite-detective-novel from 1794—*Things As They Are; or, The Adventures of Caleb Williams*, by the English radical William Godwin. Dupin had ancestors of sorts in other genres, including Voltaire's novel *Zadig*, which briefly features ratiocinative work performed in a different context entirely. Also, alongside the first police department had come the first subgenre of detective fiction—the "casebook" phenomenon. These books and stories recounted adventures that were sometimes true, sometimes a hybrid of truth and fantasy, and sometimes avowedly fictional. Casebook works included *Richmond: or, Scenes in the Life of a Bow Street Officer*, published in 1827; and, two years later, about the time the first bobbies hit the street, *Memoirs of Vidocq, Principal Agent of the French Police*, by Eugène François Vidocq, a criminal who became a detective and founded the Paris Sûreté. There were also American dime novels that included policemen and fugitives from justice, but they were seldom carefully plotted or featured anything approaching actual detective work. In 1853, twelve years after Dupin's debut, Charles Dickens was the first writer to prominently feature a detective in a serious novel, *Bleak House,* but the book is not a detective story. Sly Inspector Bucket is a prominent and memorable figure, but he is not the book's protagonist and his investigation of Lady Dedlock is not its primary feature.

In 1866, the same year that Mary Fortune published "The Dead Witness," Emile Gaboriau published in France *L'Affaire Lerouge,* which introduced both an amateur detective and a policeman named Monsieur Lecoq, who became a series character. Gaboriau merged fact and fiction by basing Lecoq upon the half-real, half-legendary exploits of Vidoq. Many critics call this the first detective novel. The very next year an American dime novelist named Metta Victoria Fuller Victor published, under the pseudonym Seeley Regester, a novel that some critics cite as the first detective novel by a woman, *The Dead Letter.* But in fact the story depends heavily upon psychic visions and coincidence. Earning ancestor status at best, it can't qualify as a legitimate detective story.

Dickens's friend Wilkie Collins featured the next famously memorable detective, the sedate and rose-loving Sergeant Cuff, in *The Moonstone,* published in 1868. Despite its outrageous plot, T. S. Eliot called this irresistible story "the first, the longest, and the best of modern English detective novels." An interesting sidelight in literary history is that the characters of both Bucket and Cuff seem to have been inspired by the real-life adventures of the same London detective, Inspector Charles Field, whom Dickens accompanied on his police rounds and wrote about in his journalism, and who later became a friend of both Dickens and Collins.

The first legitimate detective novel by a woman turned out to be one of the great bestsellers of the nineteenth century and one of the earliest important books in the genre—*The Leavenworth Case,* which Anna Katharine Green published in 1878. (Penguin Classics published a new edition in 2010.) Soon it was required reading at Yale's school of law. It introduced the sardonic and oblique Ebenezer Gryce of the New York City police, who would reappear in all three novels about her later detective Amelia Butterworth. *Leaven-*

worth was a locked-room murder and its construction founded the English country-house style of murder—revolving around a discrete set of suspects enclosed within a fixed area—even though it was set in a big city in the United States. It also founded the now iconic climax of the detective's unraveling of the mystery in the presence of a roomful of suspects. It is impossible to overstate the importance of Anna Katharine Green in the early history of the detective story. No wonder she shows up in this anthology twice.

The rapid rate of change during the Victorian era, like that of our own new millennium, can be graphed in part by the evolution of its vehicles—in particular those featured in the following stories about women: hansom cab, bicycle, and train. Often such background textures become plot elements. A glance at them will also address a complaint from some readers of Victorian fiction that they get lost amid the background detail.

Plowing through the crowds of jostling pedestrians, many species of carriage jammed the cobblestone streets and country thoroughfares of the nineteenth century—elegant enclosed broughams and landaus, sporty little phaetons on four high wheels, six-horse mail coaches with room for passengers on top. A pedestrian would have to dodge eye-catching rented post chaises called "yellow bounders," driven by a postilion astride one of the horses, or even the smart but unstable two-horse curricle memorably driven by dashing young Henry Tilney in *Northanger Abbey*.

Probably the iconic vehicle for fans of detective fiction is the two-wheeled hansom cab that seated a pair of passengers behind a low double door that guarded their shoes and clothes from mud and excrement flung up by the horse's rear hooves; the top-hatted driver stood outside at the back, holding the reins through a loop on the roof. These vehicles were so popular that Fergus Hume worked them into the title of the hottest nineteenth-century bestseller in the crime genre, *The Mystery of the Hansom Cab*, set in Gold Rush–era Australia. During the heyday of Sherlock Holmes, more than eight thousand hansom cabs served London and its environs—and the last was gone by 1933. Among the early stories in this volume, it is the hansom that most often bears Loveday Brooke and Dorcas Dene on their investigations.

Such variety in transportation testifies to changes in the rising middle class and the bustling urban workforce, innovations that in their own way helped prepare society for women who worked and voted. Like the twentieth century, the nineteenth was a period of almost constant change in the material world, thanks primarily to the Industrial Revolution's innovations in travel and communication. The queen herself changed greatly over those decades, but not as much as the world around her. Victoria reigned for a record-breaking sixty-four years, from 1837 to 1901—from the year that Dickens began serializing *Oliver Twist* to the year that Gary Cooper was born. When she acceded to the throne at the age of eighteen, Samuel Morse was patenting the telegraph; she died a few months after Guglielmo Marconi received the first transatlantic radio signal—in, appropriately, the first year of a new century. This was the lively era in which our stories take place.

The queen's own century rode in behind horses and rode out behind a smoke-coughing, coal-driven engine. In the first decade of Victoria's reign, Charles Dickens in *Dombey and Son* was already comparing the vast excavations and construction on the Camden Town rail tracks to "the first shock of a great earthquake." With a little jaunt from Slough to Paddington in 1842, Victoria became the first British monarch to travel by rail; one of the earliest regularly operating trains was a royal coach for her aunt, Queen Adelaide. By the late 1860s, trains were omnipresent. While Victoria floated along in a luxurious coach with yellow satinwood trim and a quilted ceiling of moiré silk, the homespun poor crowded into hard wooden seats or stood gripping a railing.

During Victoria's reign, horse-drawn carriages went through considerable evolution before surrendering to trains and, eventually, automobiles. Along the way, as you will see in some of these stories, England fell in love with bicycling. "Get a bicycle," advised Mark Twain in 1884. "You will not regret it, if you live." Safety was a key issue and intimately related to female freedom. As early as 1880, the penny weekly *Girl's Own Paper* was running—alongside articles on "Lissome Hands and Pretty Feet" and "Female Clerks and Book-Keepers (Earning One's Living)"—reminders that when dressing for tricycling a girl must omit trailing garments that might catch in the wheels. At first it was common to see a frilled and furbelowed woman perched on the carriage seat of a high-wheeled tricycle, with her suited husband astride a unicycle nearby. But traditional dress hampered exercise. This point was publicly demonstrated by the many accident reports that soon filled newspapers—to be gleefully cited by conservatives as proving the dangers of innovation. Feminist reformer Ada Ballin, author of the popular child-care manual *From Cradle to School*, wrote rather grandly in *The Science of Dress* that "tight lacing must be banished from the mind and body of the woman who would ride the steel horse."

This remark encapsulates one of the era's deepest fears: that as women's clothes became less straitlaced, so might their morals. What was England coming to, with all these uppity women propelling themselves around on newfangled contraptions, in charge of their own unpredictable mobility? Bicycles—which soon replaced their three-wheeled ancestor—quickly became emblematic of the New Woman. They show up often within the pages of this anthology, as the cover suggests, and play a key role in a couple of stories. By 1897, the cover of the *Girl's Own Paper* was portraying a female cyclist wearing the baggy, trouserlike fashion named for the American suffragist Amelia Jenks Bloomer, who argued that women ought to replace their layered petticoats with something resembling Turkish pants. It was Bloomer who wrote the revolutionary sentence, "The costume of women should be suited to her wants and necessities." Many disagreed. No less a personage than Lady Harberton was famously refused admittance to the Hautboy Hotel because she showed up at the door in the kind of divided skirt and long coat she recommended for cyclists. An 1894 *Punch* cartoon satirized the New Woman as "Donna Quixote."

The conservatives were right to be worried. As you will see in this book, bicycling was both a new adventure and an eagerly embraced symbol for the New Woman. Instead of chatting about fashion in the parlor while their men smoked after-dinner cigars, these women are out in the London fog, shadowing suspects, crawling through secret passages, and even fingerprinting corpses.

Like Arthur Conan Doyle and G. K. Chesterton, the creators of the pioneer female detectives don't hesitate to stack the deck for their protagonist, but you didn't have to be Sherlock Holmes to observe a lot about the people on the street. In this period there really were many clues visible about a stranger's profession and place in the world. Remember that this was before a millionaire might wear jeans or a college student dress like a lumberjack. A man's detachable collar spoke volumes about his status. No clubbable dandy would have been caught dead in the kind of low St. Leger collar worn by grooms, any more than a county gentlemen would have traded his tweed and gaiters for tenant homespun or the corduroy that replaced it. Yet even fashion, especially women's, was evolving. Neither the wasp waist nor the leg-of-mutton sleeve proved immortal. Everything was changing. These are the kinds of details not lost upon our intrepid heroines—Loveday Brooke and Madelyn Mack, Judith Lee and Mrs. Paschal and their colleagues—those invisible women whose livelihood and excitement in life depended upon the accuracy of their intimate watching.

MICHAEL SIMS

Suggestions for Further Reading

This bibliography includes all sources cited in, or useful in the writing of, this book's introductory essay or its individual story introductions. It also includes certain biographies, general introductions to the topics of detective fiction or female detectives, and other commentaries on particular authors and themes. It excludes works by those authors whose stories or excerpts appear in this anthology and thus receive attention in the biographical note that introduces their contribution. Web sites appear separately at the end.

Bargainnier, Earl F., ed. 10 *Women of Mystery*. Bowling Green, Ohio: Bowling Green State University Popular Press, 1981.

Beckson, Karl. *London in the 1890s: A Cultural History*. New York: Norton, 1992.

Bentley, Nicolas. *The Victorian Scene: 1837–1901*. London: Weidenfeld and Nicolson, 1968.

Chesterton, G. K. *A Century of Detective Stories*. London: Hutchinson, 1935.

Clodd, Edward. *Grant Allen: A Memoir*. London: Grant Richards, 1900.

Corey, Melinda, and George Ochoa. *The Encyclopedia of the Victorian World*. New York: Henry Holt, 1996.

Cornillon, John. "A Case for Violet Strange," in *Images of Women in Fiction: Feminist Perspectives*. Bowling Green, Ohio: Bowling Green University Popular Press, 1972.

Craig, Patricia, and Mary Cadogan. *The Lady Investigates: Women Detectives and Spies in Fiction*. New York: St. Martin's, 1981.

Cunningham, Gail. *The New Woman and the Victorian Novel*. New York: Barnes & Noble, 1979.

Dictionary of Literary Biography, various volumes, and the numerous sources listed therein.

Ensor, Sir Robert. *England 1870–1914*. London: Oxford University Press, 1936.

Flanders, Judith. *The Victorian House: Domestic Life from Childbirth to Deathbed*. London: HarperCollins, 2003.

Garforth, John. *A Day in the Life of a Victorian Policeman*. London: Allen Unwin, 1974.

Hadfield, John. *Victorian Delights*. London: Herbert Press, 1987.

Haycraft, Howard. *Murder for Pleasure: The Life and Times of the Detective Story*. 1941, rev. 1951. Reprint, New York: Carroll & Graf, 1984.

Kestner, Joseph A. *The Edwardian Detective, 1901–1915*. Aldershot: Ashgate, 2000.

———. *Sherlock's Sisters: The British Female Detective, 1864–1913*. Aldershot: Ashgate, 2003.

Klein, Kathleen Gregory. *The Woman Detective: Gender and Genre*. Urbana and Chicago: University of Illinois Press, 2nd ed., 1995. See especially chapter 3, "Britain's Turn-of-the-Century 'Lady Detective': 1891–1910," and chapter 4, "The Lady Detective's Yankee Cousin: 1906–15."

Knight, Stephen. *Crime Fiction, 1800–2000*. London: Palgrave Macmillan, 2003.

La Cour, Tage, and Harald Mogensen. *The Murder Book: An Illustrated History of the Detective Story*. New York: Herder & Herder, 1971.

Lock, Joan. *The British Policewoman: Her Story*. London: Robert Hale, 1979.

Maida, Patricia D. *Mother of Detective Fiction: The Life and Works of Anna Katharine Green*. Bowling Green, Ohio: Bowling Green State University Popular Press, 1989.

Marcus, Laura, with Chris Willis. *12 Women Detective Stories*. Oxford: Oxford University Press, 1997. See Marcus's introduction.

Miller, Elizabeth Carolyn. *Framed: The New Woman Criminal in British Culture at the Fin de Siècle*. Ann Arbor: University of Michigan Press, 2008.

———. "Trouble with She-Dicks: Private Eyes and Public Women in *The Adventures of Loveday Brooke, Lady Detective*." *Victorian Literature and Culture* 33 (2005): 47–65.

Murch, Alma E. *The Development of the Detective Novel*. Westport, Conn.: Greenwood, 1981.

Nickerson, Catherine Ross. *The Web of Iniquity: Early Detective Fiction by American Women*. Chapel Hill: Duke University Press, 1998.

Panek, LeRoy Lad. *The Origins of the American Detective Story*. Jefferson, NC: McFarland & Co., 2006.

Sims, Michael. Introduction to *The Leavenworth Case*, by Anna Katharine Green. New York: Penguin Classics, 2010.

———. Introduction to *The Penguin Book of Gaslight Crime: Con Artists, Burglars, Rogues, and Scoundrels from the Time of Sherlock Holmes*. New York: Penguin Classics, 2009.

Slung, Michele B. Introduction to *Crime on Her Mind: Fifteen Stories of Female Sleuths from the Victorian Era to the Forties*. New York: Pantheon, 1975.

Steinbrunner, Chris, and Otto Penzler. *Encyclopedia of Mystery and Detection*. New York: McGraw-Hill, 1976.

Summerscale, Kate. *The Suspicions of Mr. Whicher: A Shocking Murder and the Undoing of a Great Victorian Detective*. New York: Walker, 2008.

Watson, Colin. *Snobbery with Violence: English Crime Stories and Their Audience*. Rev. ed., London: Macmillan, 1979.

Winn, Dilys. *Murder Ink: The Mystery Reader's Companion*. New York: Workman, 1977.

———. *Murderess Ink: The Better Half of the Mystery*. New York: Workman, 1979.

Young, Arlene. "'Petticoated Police': Propriety and the Lady Detective in Victorian Fiction." *Clues: A Journal of Detection* 26 (Spring 2008): 3.

WEB SITES

www.classiccrimefiction.com/history-articles.htm
http://gadetection.pbwiki.com
http://motherofmystery.com/articles/plots
www.mysterylist.com
www.philsp.com/homeville/CrFiwww.wilkiecollins.com

The Penguin Book of Victorian Women in Crime

W. S. HAYWARD

(DATES UNKNOWN)

Little is known about William Stephens Hayward, who published *Revelations of a Lady Detective* anonymously. Even the initial publication date is uncertain, with some sources arguing for 1864 and others insisting that the 1864 edition was a reprint of an otherwise unknown 1861 edition. Yet either date establishes the book as the first to feature a female professional detective. This historic development in the field came along only two decades after Edgar Allan Poe launched the genre with his story "The Murders in the Rue Morgue." During the next twenty years, Stephens would also publish several other books, including *Hunted to Death* and *The Stolen Will,* but he is remembered only for this collection, especially for the first story, "The Mysterious Countess." In a vivid but eccentric style, replete with lyrical asides about train journeys and quotations from Sir Walter Scott, Hayward narrates a tale of disguised countesses and secret underground passages.

The adventures are narrated by Mrs. Paschal, a fortyish woman who turns to detective work despite being "well born and well educated." (She admits casually that her brain is "vigorous and subtle.") Her boss is Colonel Warner, "head of the Detective Department of the Metropolitan Police." However pacifying Mrs. Paschal's attitude toward him may be, however much she tries to behave appropriately in his presence, from the first she subverts one aspect of the usual male/female relationships in fiction at the time. She is not one to cower before male authority: "I met the glance of Colonel Warner and returned it unflinchingly; he liked people to stare back again at him, because it betokened confidence in themselves, and evidenced that they would not shrink in the hour of peril." The unwavering gaze inspired by confidence is a unifying trait among lady detectives. Warner expects Mrs. Paschal to rely upon her own wits; "he was a man who always made you find your own tools, and do your work with as little assistance as possible from him." Determined and resourceful, she compares herself to Nemesis.

Mrs. Paschal, like so many other female detectives of the era, winds up in this socially unsavory profession because of trouble that prevents her from leading a "normal" feminine existence. "It is hardly necessary to refer," she says, "to the circumstances which led me to embark in a career at once strange, exciting, and mysterious, but I may say that my husband died suddenly, leaving me badly off." Despite this misfortune, she certainly lands on her feet.

THE MYSTERIOUS COUNTESS

I

The Chief of the Detective Police

I turned a familiar corner, and was soon threading the well-known avenues of Whitehall. It was in a small street, the houses in which cover the site of the once splendid palace of the Stuarts, where one king was born and another lost his head, that the head-quarters of the London Detective Police were situated. I stopped at a door of modest pretensions, and knocked three times. I was instantly admitted. The porter bowed when he saw who I was, and at once conducted me into a room of limited dimensions. I had not to wait long. Coming from an inner room, a man of spare build, but with keen searching eyes, like those of a ferret, shook me, in a cold, businesslike way, by the hand, and desired me to be seated. His forehead bulged out a little, indicating the talent of which he was the undoubted possessor. All who knew him personally, or by reputation, admired him; he performed the difficult duties of an arduous position with untiring industry and the most praiseworthy skill and perseverance. He left nothing to others, except, of course, the bare execution. This man with the stern demeanour and the penetrating glance was Colonel Warner—at the time of which I am writing, head of the Detective Department of the Metropolitan Police. It was through his instigation that women were first of all employed as detectives. It must be confessed that the idea was not original, but it showed him to be a clever adapter, and not above imitating those whose talent led them to take the initiative in works of progress. Fouché, the great

Frenchman, was constantly in the habit of employing women to assist him in discovering the various political intrigues which disturbed the peace of the first empire. His petticoated police were as successful as the most sanguine innovator could wish; and Colonel Warner, having this fact before his eyes, determined to imitate the example of a man who united the courage of a lion with the cunning of a fox, culminating his acquisitions with the sagacity of a dog.

"Sit down, Mrs. Paschal," exclaimed the colonel, handing me a chair.

I did so immediately, with that prompt and passive obedience which always pleased him. I was particularly desirous at all times of conciliating Colonel Warner, because I had not long been employed as a female detective, and now having given up my time and attention to what I may call a new profession, I was anxious to acquit myself as well and favourably as I could, and gain the goodwill and approbation of my superior. It is hardly necessary to refer to the circumstances which led me to embark in a career at once strange, exciting, and mysterious, but I may say that my husband died suddenly, leaving me badly off. An offer was made me through a peculiar channel. I accepted it without hesitation, and became one of the much-dreaded, but little-known people called Female Detectives, at the time I was verging upon forty. My brain was vigorous and subtle, and I concentrated all my energies upon the proper fulfilment and execution of those duties which devolved upon me. I met the glance of Colonel Warner and returned it unflinchingly; he liked people to stare back again at him, because it betokened confidence in themselves, and evidenced that they would not shrink in the hour of peril, when danger encompassed them and lurked in front and rear. I was well born and well educated, so that, like an accomplished actress, I could play my part in any drama in which I was instructed to take a part. My dramas, however, were dramas of real life, not the mimetic representations which obtain on the stage. For the parts I had to play, it was necessary to have nerve and strength, cunning and confidence, resources unlimited, confidence and numerous other qualities of which actors are totally ignorant. They strut, and talk, and give expression to the thoughts of others, but it is such as I who really create the incidents upon which their dialogue is based and grounded.

"I have sent for you," exclaimed the colonel, "to entrust a serious case to your care and judgement. I do not know a woman more fitted for the task than yourself. Your services, if successful, will be handsomely rewarded, and you shall have no reason to complain of my parsimony in the matter of your daily expenses. Let me caution you about hasting—take time—elaborate and mature your plans; for although the hare is swift, the slow and sure tortoise more often wins the race than its fleet opponent. I need hardly talk to you in this way, but advice is never prejudicial to anyone's interests."

"I am very glad, I am sure," I replied, "to hear any suggestions you are good enough to throw out for my guidance."

"Quite so," he said; "I am aware that you possess an unusual amount of common sense, and consequently are not at all likely to take umbrage at what is kindly meant."

"Of what nature is the business?" I asked.

"Of a very delicate one," answered Colonel Warner; "you have heard of the Countess of Vervaine?"

"Frequently; you mean the lady who is dazzling all London at the present moment by the splendour of her equipage and her diamonds, and the magnificent way in which she spends what must be a colossal fortune."

"That's her," said the colonel. "But I have taken great pains to ascertain what her fortune actually consists of. Now, I have been unable to identify any property as belonging to her, nor can I discern that she has a large balance in the hands of any banker. From what source, then, is her income derived?"

I acknowledged that I was at a loss to conjecture.

"Very well," cried Colonel Warner, "the task I propose for you is to discover where, and in what way, Lady Vervaine obtains the funds which enable her to carry on a career, the splendour and the profuseness of which exceed that of a prince of the blood royal during the Augustan age of France, when Louis XIV set an example of extravagance which was pursued to ruination by the dissolute nobility, who surrounded the avenues of his palaces, and thronged the drawing-rooms of his country seats. Will it be an occupation to your mind, do you think? If not, pray decline it at once. It is always bad to undertake a commission when it involves a duty which is repugnant to you."

"Not at all," I replied; "I should like above all things to unravel the secrets of the mysterious countess, and I not only undertake to do so, but promise to bring you the tidings and information you wish for within six weeks."

"Take your own time," said the colonel; "anyone will tell you her ladyship's residence; let me see or hear from you occasionally, for I shall be anxious to know how you are getting on. Once more, do not be precipitate. Take this cheque for your expenses. If you should require more, send to me. And now, good morning, Mrs. Paschal. I hope sincerely that your endeavours may be crowned with the success they are sure to merit."

I took the draft, wished Colonel Warner goodbye, and returned to my own lodgings to ruminate over the task which had just been confided to me.

II

The Black Mask

I imagined that the best and surest way of penetrating the veil of secrecy which surrounded the Countess of Vervaine would be to obtain a footing in her household, either as a domestic servant, or in some capacity such as would enable me to play the spy upon her actions, and watch all her movements with the greatest care and closeness. I felt confident that Colonel Warner had some excellent motive for having the countess unmasked; but he was a man who always made you find your own tools, and do your work with as little assistance as possible from him. He told you what he wanted done, and nothing remained but for you to go and do it. The Countess of Vervaine was the young and lovely widow of the old earl of that name. She was on the stage when the notorious and imbecile nobleman made her his wife. His extravagance and unsuccessful speculations in railway shares, in the days when Hudson was king, ruined him, and it was well known that, when he died broken-hearted, his income was very much reduced—so much so, that when his relict began to lead the gay and luxurious life she did, more than one head was gravely shaken, and people wondered how she did it. She thought nothing of giving a thousand pounds for a pair of carriage horses, and all enterprising tradesmen were only too rejoiced when anything rare came in their way, for the Countess of Vervaine was sure to buy it. A rare picture, or a precious stone of great and peculiar value, were things that she would buy without a murmur, and pay the price demanded for them without endeavouring to abate the proprietor's price the value of a penny piece. Personally, she was a rare combination of loveliness and accomplishments. Even the women admitted that she was beautiful, and the men raved about her. She went into the best society, and those of the highest rank and the most exalted social position in London were very glad to be asked to her magnificent and exclusive parties. Fanny, Countess of Vervaine, knew very well that if you wish to become celebrated in the gay and giddy world of fashion, you must be very careful who you admit into your house. It may be convenient, and even necessary, to ask your attorney to dine with you occasionally; but forbear to ask a ducal friend on the same day, because his grace would never forgive you for making so great a blunder. The attorney would go about amongst his friends and tell them all in what company he had been. Your house would acquire the reputation of being an "easy" one, and your acquaintances who were really worth knowing would not any more visit at a house where "anybody" was received with the same cordiality that they had themselves met with. The Countess of Vervaine lived in a large mansion in one of the new, but aristocratic squares in Belgravia. A huge towering erection it was to look at—a corner house with many windows and balconies and verandahs and conservatories. It had belonged to the earl, and he bequeathed it to her with all its wealth of furniture, rare pictures, and valuable books. It was pretty well all he had to leave her, for his lands were all sold, and the amount of ready money standing to his credit at his banker's was lamentably small—so small, indeed, as to be almost insignificant. The earl had been dead a year and a half now. She had mourned six months for him, and at the expiration of that time she cast off her widow's weeds—disdaining the example of royalty to wear them for an indefinite period—and launched into all the gaiety and dissipation that the Babylon of the moderns could supply her with. Very clever and versatile was her ladyship, as well able to talk upon abstruse subjects with a member of a scientific society as to converse with one of her patrician friends upon the merits of the latest fashions which the Parisians had with their usual taste designed.

I dressed myself one morning, after having gained the information I have just detailed, and put on the simplest things I could find in my wardrobe, which was as extensive and as full of disguises as that of a costumier's shop. I wished to appear like a servant out of place. My idea was to represent myself as a lady's-maid or under housekeeper. I did not care what situation I took as long as I obtained a footing in the household. When I approached Lady Vervaine's house, I was very much struck by its majestic and imposing appearance. I liked to see the porcelain boxes in the windows filled with the choicest flowers, which a market gardener and floriculturist undertook by contract to change twice a week, so that they should never appear shabby or out of season. I took a delight in gazing at the trailing creepers running in a wild, luxuriant, tropical manner, all over the spacious balconies, and I derived especial pleasure from the contemplation of the orange trees growing in large wooden tubs, loaded with their yellow fruit, the sheen and glimmer of which I could faintly see through the well-cleaned windows of the conservatory, which stood over the porch protecting the entrance to the front door.

I envied this successful actress all the beautiful things she appeared to have in her possession, and wondered why she should be so much more fortunate than myself; but a moment afterwards, I congratulated myself that I was not, like her, an object of suspicion and mistrust to the police, and that a female detective, like Nemesis, was not already upon my track. I vowed that all her splendour should be short-lived, and that in those gilded saloons and lofty halls, where now all was mirth and song and gladness, there should soon be nothing but weeping and gnashing of teeth. I descended the area steps, and even here there was a trace of refinement and good taste, for a small box of mignonette was placed on the sill of each window, and a large Virginia creeper reared its slender limbs against the stuccoed wall.

A request to see the housekeeper brought me into the presence of that worthy. I stated my business to her, and asked her favourable consideration of my case. She shook her head, and said she was afraid that there was no vacancy just at present, but if I would call again, she might perhaps be able to give me a more encouraging reply. I knew perfectly well how to treat a lady of her calibre. Servants in gentlemen's families are generally engaged in making a purse, upon the proceeds of which they are enabled to retire when the domestic harness begins to gall their necks, and they sigh for rest after years of hard work and toil. They either patronize savings' banks, where they get their two and a half per cent, on the principle that every little helps, although they could at the same time obtain six per cent in foreign guaranteed government stock; but those who work hard, know how to take care of their money, because they understand its value, and they distrust speculative undertakings, as it is the duty of all prudent people to do; or if they distrust the parochial banks, they have a stocking which they keep carefully concealed, the contents of which are to help their possessors to furnish a lodging-house, or take a tavern, when the time arrives at which they think fit to assert their independence and retire from the servitude which they have all along tolerated for a purpose. Armed with a thorough knowledge of the class, I produced a five-pound note, and said that it was part of my savings from my last place, and that I should be happy to make her a present of it, if she would use the influence I was sure she possessed to procure me the situation I was so desirous of obtaining.

This offer produced a relaxation of the housekeeper's sternness. She asked for a reference, which I gave her; we always knew how to arrange those little matters, which were managed without any difficulty; and the result of our interview was, that I was engaged as third lady's-maid at a salary of fifteen pounds a year, and to find myself in tea and sugar. I entered my new place in less than a week, and soon had an opportunity of observing the demeanour of the Countess of Vervaine; at times it was restless and excited. Her manner was frequently preoccupied, and she was then what is called absent. You might speak to her three or four times before you obtained an answer. She did not appear to hear you. Some weighty matter was occupying her attention, and she was so engrossed by its contemplation that she could not bestow a single thought on external objects. She was very young—scarcely five-and-twenty, and not giving evidence of being so old as that. She was not one of those proud, stern, and haughty aristocrats whom you see in the Park, leaning back in their open carriages as if they were casting their mantle of despisal and scorn to those who are walking. She was not pale, and fagged, and bilious-looking; on the contrary, she was fat and chubby, with just the smallest tinge of rose-colour on her cheek—natural colour, I mean, not the artificial hue which pernicious compounds impart to a pallid cheek.

Now and then there was an air of positive joyousness about her, as if she was enamoured of life and derived the most intense pleasure from existence in this world below, where most of us experience more blows and buffets than we do occurrences of a more gratifying nature. Although not pretending to do so, I studied her with great care, and the result of my observations was, that I could have sworn before any court of justice in the world that to the best of my belief, she had a secret—a secret which weighed her down and crushed her young, elastic spirit, sitting on her chest like a nightmare, and spoiling her rest by hideous visions. In society she showed nothing of this. It was in the company of others that she shone; at home, in her bedroom, with her attendant satellites about her, whom she regarded as nobodies, she gave way to her fits of melancholy, and showed that every shining mirror has its dull side and its leaden reverse. There are some people who are constituted in such a manner by nature, that though they may be standing upon the crater of a volcano given to chronic eruptions, and though they are perfectly cognizant of the perilous position in which they are, will not trouble themselves much about it. It was my private opinion that the ground under the feet of the Countess of Vervaine was mined, and that she knew it, but that she had adopted that fallacious motto which has for its burden "a short life and a merry one." There was something very mysterious about her, and I made the strongest resolution that I ever made in my life that I would discover the nature of the mystery before many days had passed over my head. The countess had not the remotest idea that I was in any way inimical to her. She regarded me as something for which she paid, and which was useful to her on certain occasions. I believe she looked upon me very much as a lady in the Southern States of America looks upon a slave—a thing to minister to her vanity and obey her commands. Lady Vervaine was one of those fascinating little women who charm you by their simple, winning ways, and you do not dream for a moment that they are not terrestrial angels; did you know them intimately, however, you would discover that they have a will and a temper of their own, such as would render the life of a husband miserable and unhappy if he did succumb to her slightest wish and put up with her most frivolous caprice. She was frequently tyrannical with her servants, and would have her most trivial command obeyed to the letter, under pain of her sovereign displeasure. One day she struck me on the knuckles with a hairbrush, because I ran a hairpin into her head by the merest accident in the world. I said nothing, but I cherished an idea of retaliation nevertheless. We had dressed her on a particular evening for the Opera. She looked very charming; but so graceful was her manner, so pleasant was her bearing, and so unexceptionable her taste, that she could never look anything else.

"Paschal," she said to me.

"Yes, my lady," I replied.

"I shall come home a little before twelve; wait up for me."

"Yes, my lady," I replied again, in the monotonous, parrot-like tone that servants are supposed to make use of when talking to those who have authority over them.

It was a long, dreary evening; there was not much to do, so I took up a book and tried to read; but although I tried to bring my attention upon the printed page, I was unable to succeed in doing so. I was animated with a conviction that I should make some important discovery that night. It is a singular thing, but in my mind coming events always cast their shadows before they actually occurred. I invariably had an intuition that such and such a thing would happen before it actually took place. It was considerably past twelve when the mysterious countess came home; the charms of the Opera and the Floral Hall must have detained her until the last moment, unless she had met with some entertaining companion who beguiled the hours by soft speeches and tender phrases, such as lovers alone know how to invent and utter. I began to unrobe her, but after I had divested her of her cloak, she called for her dressing-gown, and told me to go and bring her some coffee. The cook was gone to bed, and I found some difficulty in making the water boil, but at last I succeeded in brewing the desired beverage, and took it upstairs. The countess was, on my return, industriously making calculations, at least so it seemed to me, in a little book bound in morocco leather, and smelling very much like a stationer's shop. She might have been making poetry, or concerting the plot of a drama, but she stopped every now and then, as if to "carry" something, after the manner of mathematicians who do not keep a calculating machine on the premises.

After I had put down the coffee, she exclaimed—

"You can go. Goodnight."

I replied in suitable terms, and left her, but not to go to my room or to sleep. I hung about the corridor in a stealthy way, for I knew very well that no one else was likely to be about, and I wanted to watch my lady that night, which I felt convinced was going to be prolific of events of a startling nature. The night was a little chilly, but I did not care for that. Sheltering myself as well as I could in the shadow of a doorway, I waited with the amount of resignation and patience that the occasion required. In about half an hour's time the door of the Countess of Vervaine's apartment opened. I listened breathlessly, never daring to move a muscle, lest my proximity to her should be discovered. What was my surprise and astonishment to see a man issue from the room! He held a light in his hand, and began to descend a flight of stairs by its aid.

I rubbed my eyes to see whether I had not fallen asleep and dreamed a dream; but no, I was wide awake. The man must, I imagined, have been concealed somewhere about the apartment, for I saw no trace of him during the time that I was in the room. He was a person of small size, and dressed in an odd way, as if he was not a gentleman, but a servant out of livery. This puzzled me more than ever, but I had seen a few things in my life which appeared scarcely susceptible of explanation at first, but which, when eliminated by the calm light of reason and dissected by the keen knife of judgement, were in a short time as plain as the sun at noonday. I thought for a brief space, and then I flattered myself that I had penetrated the mystery. I said to myself, *It is a disguise.* The Countess of Vervaine was a little woman. She would consequently make a very small man. The one before me, slowly and with careful tread going down the staircase, was a man of unusually small stature. You would call him decidedly undersized. There was a flabbiness about the clothes he wore which seemed to indicate that they had not been made for him. The coat-sleeves were especially long. This gave strength to the supposition that the countess had assumed male attire for purposes of her own. She could not possibly have had herself measured for a suit of clothes. No tailor in London would have done such a thing. She had probably bought the things somewhere—picking them up at random without being very particular as to their size or fit. I allowed the man to reach the bottom of the staircase before I followed in pursuit. Gliding stealthily along with a care and precision I had often practised in the dead of night at home in order that I might become well versed and experienced in an art so useful to a detective, I went down step by step and caught sight of the man turning an angle which hid him from my view, but as he did so I contrived to glance at his features. I started and felt inclined to shriek. Every lineament of his face was concealed by a hideous black mask. My sensations were not enviable for many a long night afterwards; that dark funereal face-covering was imprinted in an almost indelible manner upon my mind, and once or twice I awoke in bed shivering all over in a cold perspiration, fancying that the Black Mask was standing over me, holding a loaded pistol at my head, and threatening my life if I did not comply with some importunate demand which I felt I could not pay the slightest attention to. Recovering myself as best I could, I raised my dress, and stepping on my toes, followed the Black Mask. He descended to the lower regions. He held the light before him, occasionally looking around to see if any one were behind him. I contrived whenever he did this to vanish into some corner or fall in a heap so that the rays of the lamp should not fall upon my erect form. We passed the kitchens, from which the stale cabbage-watery smell arose which always infests those interesting domestic offices after their occupants have retired to rest. I could hear the head cook snoring. He slept in a small room on the basement, and was, I have no doubt, glad to go to bed after the various onerous duties that he had to perform during the day, for the office of cook in a good family is by no means a sinecure. Aristocratic birth does not prevent the possessor from nourishing a somewhat plebeian appetite, which must be satisfied at least four or five times a day. A plain joint is not sufficient, a dozen messes called *entrées* must accompany it, composed of truffles and other evil-smelling abominations, such as are to be met with at the shop of a Parisian *épicier*. I had not searched the rooms on the basement very closely, but during the cursory investigation I had made, I noticed that there was one which was always kept locked. No one ever entered it. Some said the key was lost, but none of the servants seemed to trouble themselves much about it. It was an empty room, or it was a lumber room. They did not know, neither did they care. This being the state of things existent respecting that room, I was astonished to see the man in the black mask produce a key well oiled so as to make it facile of turning, put it in the lock, turn it, open the door, enter and disappear, shutting the door after him. It did not take me long to reach the keyhole, to which I applied my eye. The key was not in it, but whether the Black Mask had secured the door inside or not, I could not tell. The time had not then arrived at which it was either necessary or prudent to solve the riddle. I could see inside the room with the greatest ease. The lamp was on the floor, and the Black Mask was on his knees engaged in scrutinizing the flooring. The apartment was utterly destitute of furniture, not even a chair or a common deal table adorned the vacant space, but a few bricks piled on the top of one another lay in one corner. Near them was a little mound of dry mortar, which, from its appearance, had been made and brought there months ago. A trowel such as bricklayers use was not far off. While I was noticing these things the man in the black mask had succeeded in raising a couple of planks from the floor. These he laid in a gentle way on one side. I could perceive that he had revealed a black yawning gulf such as the entrance to a sewer might be. After hesitating a moment to see if his lamp was burning brightly and well, he essayed the chasm and disappeared in its murky depths, as if he had done the same thing before and knew very well where he was going. Perfectly amazed at the discoveries I was making, I looked on in passive wonderment. I was, as may be supposed, much pleased at what I saw, because I felt that I had discovered the way to unravel a tangled skein. Queen Eleanor, when she found out the clue which led her through the maze to the bower of fair Rosamond, was not more delighted than myself, when I saw the strange and mystic proceeding on the part of the Black Mask. When I had allowed what I considered a sufficient time to elapse, I tried the handle of the door—it turned. A slight push and the door began to revolve on its hinges; another one, and that more vigorous, admitted me to the room. All was in darkness. Sinking on my hands and knees, I crawled with the utmost caution in the direction of the hole in the floor. Half a minute's search brought me to it. My hand sank down as I endeavoured to find a resting-place for it. I then made it my business to feel the sides of the pit to discover if there was any ladder, through the instrumentality of whose friendly steps I could follow the Black Mask. There was. Having satisfied myself of this fact, I with as much rapidity as possible took off the small crinoline I wore, for I considered that it would very much impede my movements. When I had divested myself of the obnoxious garment, and thrown it on the floor, I lowered myself into the hole and went down the ladder. Four or five feet, I should think, brought me to the end of the flight of steps. As well as I could judge I was in a stone passage. The air was damp and cold. The sudden chill made me shudder. It was evidently a long way underground, and the terrestrial warmth was wanting. It had succumbed to the subterraneous vapours, which were more searching than pleasant. A faint glimmer of light some distance up the passage showed me that the Black Mask had not so much the best of the chase. My heart palpitated, and I hastened on at the quickest pace I considered consistent with prudence.

III

Bars of Gold and Ingots

I could see that the passage I was traversing had been built for some purpose to connect two houses together. What the object of such a connection was it was difficult to conceive. But rich people are frequently eccentric, and do things that those poorer and simpler than themselves would never dream of. The Black Mask had discovered the underground communication, and was making use of it for the furtherance of some clandestine operation. The passage was not of great length. The Black Mask stopped and set the light upon the ground. I also halted, lest the noise of my footsteps might alarm the mysterious individual I was pursuing. I had been in many perplexities and exciting situations before, and I had taken a prominent part in more than one extremely perilous adventure, but I do not think that I was ever, during the whole course of my life, actuated by so strong a curiosity, or animated with so firm a desire to know what the end would be, as I was on the present occasion. In moments such as those which were flitting with the proverbial velocity of time, but which seemed to me very slow and sluggish, the blood flows more quickly through your veins, your heart beats with a more rapid motion, and the tension of the nerves becomes positively painful. I watched the movements of the Black Mask with the greatest care and minuteness. He removed, by some means with which he was acquainted, half a dozen good-sized bricks from the wall, revealing an aperture of sufficient dimensions to permit the passage of a human body. He was not slow in passing through the hole. The light he took with him. I was in darkness. Crawling along like a cat about to commit an act of feline ferocity upon some musipular abortion, I reached the cavity and raised my eyes to the edge, so as to be able to scrutinize the interior of the apartment into which the Black Mask had gone. It was a small place, and more like a vault than anything else. The light had been placed upon a chest, and its flickering rays fell around, affording a sickly glare very much like that produced on a dark afternoon in a shrine situated in a Roman Catholic Continental church. The sacred edifice is full of darkening shadows, but through the bronzed railings which shut off egress to the shrine, you can see the long wax tapers burning, emitting their fiery tribute to the manes of the dead. The Black Mask had fallen on his knees before a chest of a peculiar shape and make; it was long and narrow. Shooting back some bolts, the lid flew open and disclosed a large glittering pile of gold to my wondering gaze. There was the precious metal, not coined and mixed with alloy, but shining in all the splendour of its native purity. There were bars of gold and ingots, such as Cortez and Pizarro, together with their bold followers, found in Peru, when the last of the Incas was driven from his home, his kingdom, and his friends, after many a sanguinary battle, after many a hard-fought fray. The bars were heavy and valuable, for they were pure and unadulterated. There were many chests, safes, and cases, in the vault. Were they all full of gold? If so, what a prize had this audacious robber acquired! He carefully selected five of the largest and heaviest ingots. Each must have been worth at least a thousand pounds. It was virgin gold, such as nuggets are formed of, and, of course, worth a great deal of money. After having made his choice, it was necessary to place the bars in some receptacle. He was evidently a man of resources, for he drew a stout canvas bag from his pocket, and, opening it, placed them inside; but, as he was doing so, the mask fell from his face. Before he could replace the hideous facial covering, I made a discovery, one I was not altogether unprepared for. The black mask—ungainly and repulsive as it was—had hitherto concealed the lovely features of the Countess of Vervaine. With a tiny exclamation of annoyance she replaced the mask and continued her task. I smiled grimly as I saw who the midnight robber was, whose footsteps I had tracked so well, whose movements I had watched so unerringly. It would take but few visits to this treasure vault, I thought to myself, to bring in a magnificent income; and then I marvelled much what the vault might be, and how the vast and almost countless treasure got there. Questions easy to propound, but by no means so facile of reply. At present my attention was concentrated wholly and solely upon the countess. It would be quite time enough next morning to speculate upon the causes which brought about effects of which I was the exultant witness. Having stowed away the ingots in the canvas bag, the mysterious countess rose to her feet, and made a motion indicative of retiring. At this juncture I was somewhat troubled in my mind. Would it be better for me to raise an alarm or to remain quiet? Supposing I were to cry out, who was there to hear my exclamation or respond to my earnest entreaty for help and assistance. Perhaps the countess was armed. So desperate an adventuress as she seemed to be would very probably carry some offensive weapon about her, which it was a fair presumption she would not hesitate to use if hard pressed, and that lonely passage, the intricacies of which were in all probability known but to herself and me, would for ever hide from prying eyes my blanching bones and whitening skeleton. This was not a particularly pleasant reflection, and I saw that it behoved me to be cautious. I fancied that I could regain the lumber room before the countess could overtake me, because it would be necessary for her to shut down and fasten the chest, and when she had done that she would be obliged to replace the bricks she had removed from the wall, which proceeding would take her some little time and occupy her attention while I made my escape. I had gained as much information as I wished, and I was perfectly satisfied with the discovery I had made. The countess was undoubtedly a robber, but it required some skill to succeed in bringing her to justice. In just that species of skill and cunning I flattered myself I was a proficient. Hastily retreating, I walked some distance, but to my surprise did not meet with the ladder. Could I have gone wrong? Was it possible that I had taken the wrong turning? I was totally unacquainted with the ramifications of these subterranean corridors. I trembled violently, for a suspicion arose in my breast that I might be shut in the vault. I stopped a moment to think, and leaned against the damp and slimy wall in a pensive attitude.

IV

In the Vault

Without a light I could not tell where I was, or in which direction it would be best for me to go. I was in doubt whether it would be better to go steadily on or stay where I was, or retrace my steps. I had a strong inclination to do the latter. Whilst I was ruminating a light appeared to the left of me. It was that borne by the Countess of Vervaine. I had then gone wrong. The passage prolonged itself, and I had not taken the right turning. The countess was replacing the bricks, so that it was incumbent upon me to remain perfectly still, which I did. Having accomplished her task, she once more took up her bag, the valuable contents of which were almost as much as she could carry. I was in the most critical position. She would unquestionably replace the planks, and perhaps fasten them in some way so as to prevent my escaping as she had done. My only chance lay in reaching the ladder before her, but how was it possible to do so when she was between myself and the ladder? I should have to make a sudden attack upon her, throw her down, and pass over her prostrate body,—all very desirable, but totally impossible. I was defenceless. I believed her to be armed. I should run the risk of having a couple of inches of cold steel plunged into my body, or else an ounce of lead would make a passage for itself through the ventricles of my heart, which were not at all desirous of the honour of being pierced by a lady of rank. I sighed for a Colt's revolver, and blamed myself for not having taken the precaution of being armed. Although I wished to capture Lady Vervaine above all things, I was not tired of my life. Once above ground again and in the house I should feel myself more of a free agent than I did in those dreary vaults, where I felt sure I should fall an easy prey to the attacks of an unscrupulous woman. Lady Vervaine pursued her way with a quick step, which showed that she had accomplished her object, and was anxious to get to her own room again, and reach a haven of safety. As for me, I resigned myself to my fate. What could I do? To attack her ladyship would, I thought, be the forerunner of instant death. It would be like running upon a sword, or firing a pistol in one's own mouth. She would turn upon me like a tiger, and in order to save herself from the dreadful consequences of her crime, she would not hesitate a moment to kill me. Serpents without fangs are harmless, but when they have those obnoxious weapons it is just as well to put your iron heel upon their heads and crush them, so as to render them harmless and subservient to your sovereign and conquering will. I followed the Countess of Vervaine slowly, and at a distance, but I dared not approach her. I was usually fertile in expedients, and I thought I should be able to find my way out of the dilemma in some way. I was not a woman of one idea, and if one dart did not hit the mark I always had another feathered shaft ready for action in my well-stocked quiver. Yet it was not without a sickening feeling of uncertainty and doubt that I saw her ladyship ascend the ladder and vanish through the opening in the flooring. I was alone in the vault, and abandoned to my own resources. I waited in the black darkness in no enviable frame of mind, until I thought the countess had had sufficient time to evacuate the premises, then I groped my way to the ladder and mounted it. I reached the planks and pushed against them with all my might, but the strength I possessed was not sufficient to move them. My efforts were futile. Tired and exhausted, I once more tried the flags which paved the passage, and cast about in my mind for some means of escape from my unpleasant position. If I could find no way of extrication it was clear that I should languish horribly for a time, and ultimately perish of starvation. This was not an alluring prospect, nor did I consider it so. I had satisfied myself that it was impossible to escape through the flooring, as the Countess of Vervaine had in some manner securely fastened the boards. Suddenly an idea shot through my mind with the vivid quickness of a flash of lightning. I could work my way back through the passage, and by feeling every brick as I went, discover those which gave her ladyship admittance into the vault where the massive ingots of solid bullion were kept. I had no doubt whatever that so precious a hoard was visited occasionally by those it belonged to, and I should not only be liberated from my captivity, but I should discover the mystery which was at present perplexing me. Both of these were things I was desirous of accomplishing, so I put my shoulder to the wheel, and once more threaded the circumscribed dimensions of the corridor which led to the place in which such a vast quantity of gold was concealed. I took an immense deal of trouble, for I felt every brick singly, and after passing my fingers over its rough surface gave it a push to see if it yielded. At last, to my inexpressible joy, I reached one which "gave," another vigorous thrust and it fell through with a harsh crash upon the floor inside. The others I took out more carefully. When I had succeeded in removing them all I entered the bullion vault in the same way in which her ladyship had, and stopped to congratulate myself upon having achieved so much. The falling brick had made a loud noise, which had reverberated through the vault, producing cavernous echoes; but I had not surmised that this would be productive of the consequences that followed it. Whilst I was considering what I should do or how I should dispose myself to sleep for an hour or so—for, in nursery parlance, the miller had been throwing dust in my eyes, and I was weary—I heard a noise in one corner of the vault, where I afterwards found the door was situated. A moment of breathless expectation followed, and then dazzling blinding lights flashed before me and made me close my shrinking eyes involuntarily. Harsh voices rang in my ears, rude hands grasped me tightly, and I was a prisoner. When I recovered my power of vision, I was surrounded by three watchmen, and as many policemen. They manacled me. I protested against such an indignity, but appearances were against me.

"I am willing to come with you," I exclaimed, in a calm voice, because I knew I had nothing to fear in the long run. "But why treat me so badly?"

"Only doing my duty," replied one of the police, who seemed to have the command of the others.

"Why do you take me in custody?" I demanded.

"Why? Come, that's a good joke," he replied.

"Answer my question."

"Well, if you don't know, I'll tell you," he answered, with a grin.

"I have an idea, but I want to be satisfied about the matter."

"We arrest you for *robbing the bank*," he replied, solemnly.

My face brightened. So it was a bank, and the place we were in was the bullion vault of the house. The mystery was now explained. The Countess of Vervaine had by some means discovered her proximity to so rich a place, and had either had the passage built, or had been fortunate enough to find it ready-made to her hand. This was a matter for subsequent explanation.

"I am ready to go with you," I said; "when we arrive at the station-house I shall speak to the inspector on duty."

The man replied in a gruff voice, and I was led from the vault, happy in the reflection that I had escaped from the gloom and darkness of the treasure house.

V

Hunted Down

"Glad to see you, Mrs. Paschal," exclaimed Colonel Warner when I was ushered into his presence. "I must congratulate you upon your tact, discrimination, and perseverance, in running the Countess of Vervaine to earth as cleverly as you did. Rather an unpleasant affair, though, that of the subterranean passage."

"I am accustomed to those little dramatic episodes," I replied: "when I was taken to the station-house by the exultant policeman, the inspector quickly released me on finding who I was. I always carry my credentials in my pocket, and your name is a tower of strength with the executive."

"We must consider now what is to be done," said the colonel; "there is no doubt whatever that the South Belgrave Bank has been plundered to a great extent, and that it is from that source that our mysterious countess has managed to supply her extravagant habits and keep up her transitory magnificence, which she ought to have seen would, from its nature, be evanescent. I am only surprised to think that her depredations were not discovered before; she must have managed everything in a skilful manner, so skilful indeed as to be worthy of the expertest burglar of modern times. I have had the manager of the bank with me this morning, and he is desirous of having the matter hushed up if possible; but I told him frankly that I could consent to nothing of the kind. One of the watchmen or policemen who took you into custody must have gone directly to a newspaper office, and have apprised the editor of the fact, because here is a statement of the circumstance in a daily paper, which seems to have escaped the manager's notice. Newspapers pay a small sum for information, and that must have induced the man to do as he apparently has done. The astute Countess of Vervaine has, I may tell you, taken advantage of this hint, and gone away from London, for I sent to her house this morning, which was shut up. The only reply my messengers could get was that her ladyship had gone out of town, owing to the illness of a near relation; which is, of course, a ruse."

"Clearly," I replied, "she has taken the alarm, and wishes to throw dust in our eyes."

"What do you advise?" asked Colonel Warner, walking up and down the room.

"I should say, leave her alone until her fears die away and she returns to town. It is now the height of the season, and she will not like to be away for any great length of time."

"I don't agree with you, Mrs. Paschal," returned the colonel, testily.

"Indeed, and why not?"

"For many reasons. In the first place, she may escape from the country with the plunder. What is to prevent her from letting her house and furniture in London, and going abroad with the proceeds?"

"There is some truth in that," I said, more than half convinced that the colonel took the correct view of the case.

"Very well; my second reason is, that a bird in the hand is worth two in the bush."

Proverbial, but true, I thought to myself.

"Thirdly, I wish to recover as much of the stolen property as I can. A criminal with full hands is worth more than one whose digits are empty."

"Do you propose that I shall follow her up?" I demanded.

"Most certainly I do."

"In that case, the sooner I start the better it will be."

"Start at once, if your arrangements will permit you to do so. Servants are not immaculate, and by dint of enquiry at her ladyship's mansion, I have little doubt you will learn something which you will find of use to you."

"In less than a week, colonel," I replied, confidently, "the Countess of Vervaine shall be in the hands of the police."

"In the hands of the police!" What a terrible phrase!—full of significance and awful import—redolent of prisons and solitary confinement—replete with visions of hard-labour and a long and weary imprisonment—expressive of a life of labour, disgrace, and pain—perhaps indicative of summary annihilation by the hands of the hangman.

"I rely upon you," said Colonel Warner, shaking my hand. "In seven days from this time I shall expect the fulfilment of your promise."

I assented, and left the office in which affairs of so much importance to the community at large were daily conducted, and in nine cases out of ten brought to a successful issue.

Yet the salary this man received from a grateful nation, or more strictly speaking from its Government, was a bare one thousand a year, while many sinecurists get treble that sum for doing nothing at all. My first care was to return to the Countess of Vervaine's house. It was shut up, but that merely meant that the blinds were down and the shutters closed in the front part. The larger portion of the servants were still there and glad to see me. They imagined that I had been allowed a holiday, or that I had been somewhere on business for her ladyship. I at once sought the housekeeper.

"Well, Paschal," she said, "what do you want?"

"I have been to get some money for the countess, who sent me into the City for that purpose, ma'am," I boldly replied, "and she told me I was to come to you, give you ten pounds, and you would give me her address, for she wished me to follow her into the country."

"Oh! indeed. Where is the money?"

I gave the housekeeper ten sovereigns, saying—

"You can have five more if you like, I dare say she wont miss it."

"Not she. She has plenty."

The five additional portraits of Her Majesty were eagerly taken possession of by the housekeeper, who blandly told me that the countess would be found at Blinton Abbey, in Yorkshire, whither she had gone to spend a fortnight with some aristocratic acquaintançe. I always made a point of being very quiet, civil, and obliging when in the presence of the housekeeper, who looked upon me as remarkably innocent, simple, and hardworking. After obtaining the information I was in search of I remained chatting in an amicable and agreeable manner for a short time, after which I took my leave. When, ho! for the night mail, north. I was accompanied by a superintendent, to whom I invariably intrusted the consummation of arduous enterprises which required masculine strength. He was a sociable man, and we might between us have proved a match for the cleverest thieves in Christendom. In fact we frequently were so, as they discovered to their cost. There is to me always something very exhilarating in the quickly rushing motion of a railway carriage. It is typical of progress, and raises my spirits in proportion to the speed at which we career along, now through meadow and now through woodland, at one time cutting through a defile and afterwards steaming through a dark and sombre tunnel. What can equal such magical travelling?

It was night when we reached Blinton. The Abbey was about a mile and a half from the railway station. Neither the superintendent or myself felt inclined to go to rest, for we had indulged in a nap during the journey, from which we awoke very much invigorated. We left our carpet bags in the care of a sleepy railway porter who had only awaited the arrival of the night mail north, and at half-past one o'clock set out to reconnoitre the position of Blinton Abbey. The moon was shining brightly. We pursued a bridle path and found little difficulty in finding the Abbey as we followed the porter's instructions to the letter. All was still as we gazed undisturbed upon the venerable pile which had withstood the blasts of many a winter and reflected the burning rays of innumerable summer suns. I was particularly struck with the chapel, which was grey and sombre before us; the darkened roof, the lofty buttresses, the clustered shafts, all spoke of former grandeur. The scene forcibly recalled Sir Walter Scott's lines,

> "If thou would'st view fair Melrose aright,
> Go visit it by the pale moonlight;
> For the gay beams of lightsome day
> Gild but to flout the ruins grey.
> When the broken arches are black in night,
> And each shafted oriel glimmers white;
> When the cold light's uncertain shower
> Streams on the ruined central tower;
> When buttress and buttress alternately
> Seem framed of ebon and ivory—

Then go, but go alone the while,
And view St. David's sacred pile."

We halted, inspired with a sort of sacred awe. The chapel, the turreted castle, the pale and silvery moonlight, the still and witching time of night, the deep castellated windows, the embrasures on the roof from which, in days gone by, many a sharp-speaking culverin was pointed against the firm and lawless invader, all conspired to inspire me with sadness and melancholy. I was aroused from my reverie by the hand of the Superintendent which sought my arm. Without speaking a word he drew me within the shadow of a recess, and having safely ensconced me together with himself, he whispered the single word, "Look!" in my ear. I did as he directed me, and following the direction indicated by his outstretched finger saw a dark figure stealing out of a side door of Blinton Abbey. Stealthily and with cat-like tread did that sombre figure advance until it reached the base of a spreading cedar tree whose funereal branches afforded a deathlike shade like that of yew trees in a churchyard, when the figure produced a sharp-pointed instrument and made a hole as if about to bury something. I could scarcely refrain a hoarse cry of delight, for it seemed palpable to me that the Countess of Vervaine was about to dispose of her ill-gotten booty. I blessed the instinct which prompted me to propose a visit to the Abbey in the night-time, although I invariably selected the small hours for making voyages of discovery. I have generally found that criminals shun the light of day and seek the friendly shelter of a too often treacherous night. In a low voice I communicated my suspicions to the superintendent, and he concurred with me. I suggested the instant arrest of the dark figure. The lady was so intently engaged that she did not notice our approach; had she done so she might have escaped into the Abbey. The strong hand of the superintendent was upon her white throat before she could utter a sound. He dragged her remorselessly into the moonlight, and the well-known features of the Countess of Vervaine were revealed indisputably.

"What do you want of me, and why am I attacked in this way?" she demanded in a tremulous voice as soon as the grasp upon her throat was relaxed.

I had meanwhile seized a bag, the same canvas bag which had contained the ingots on the night of the robbery. They were still there. When I heard her ladyship's enquiry, I replied to it. "The directors of the South Belgravia Bank are very anxious to have an interview with your ladyship," I said.

She raised her eyes to mine, and an expression of anguish ran down her beautiful countenance. She knew me, and the act of recognition informed her that she was hunted down. With a rapid motion, so swift, so quick, that it resembled a sleight-of-hand, the Countess of Vervaine raised something to her mouth; in another moment her hand was by her side again, as if nothing had happened. Something glittering in the moonlight attracted my attention. I stooped down and picked it up. It was a gold ring of exquisite workmanship. A spring lid revealing a cavity was open. I raised it to my face. A strong smell of bitter almonds arose. I turned round with a flushed countenance to her ladyship. She was very pale. The superintendent was preparing to place handcuffs around her slender wrists; he held the manacles in his hand and was adjusting them. But she was by her own daring act spared this indignity. A subtle poison was contained in the secret top of her ring, and she had with a boldness peculiar to herself swallowed it before we could anticipate or prevent her rash act. The action of the virulent drug was as quick as it was deadly. She tottered. A smile which seemed to say, the battle is over, and I soon shall be at rest, sat upon her lips. Then she fell heavily to the ground with her features convulsed with a hard spasm, a final pain; her eyes were fixed, her lips parted, and Fanny, the accomplished, lovely, and versatile Countess of Vervaine was no more. I did not regret that so young and fair a creature had escaped the felon's dock, the burglar's doom. The affair created much excitement at the time, and the illustrated papers were full of pictures of Blinton Abbey, but it has long since passed from the public mind, and hundreds of more sensations have cropped up since then. The South Belgravian Bank recovered its ingots, but it was nevertheless a heavy loser through the former depredations of the famous Countess of Vervaine.

ANDREW FORRESTER

(DATES UNKNOWN)

Andrew Forrester Jr. is another author about whom little is known. The great crime fiction scholar and anthologist E. F. Bleiler suggests that the name "was a pseudonym chosen to capitalize on the fame of the historical Forrester brothers, who served as detectives for the City of London and were pioneers in the application of scientific methods to detection." Given or assumed, the name Andrew Forrester shows up as author of three books (not counting two later rearrangements of the same work), including *The Revelations of a Private Detective* from 1863 and *Secret Service* from the following year. Also in 1864—the year in which Mrs. Paschal made her appearance—Ward Lock in London published *The Female Detective*. It was a milestone year in the history of women detectives.

"My trade is a necessary one, but the world holds aloof my order." These words by Mrs. G——, the narrator of *The Female Detective*, summarize much of the real-world attitude toward detectives in the mid-nineteenth century. Many newspaper commentators and lawmakers worried about the idea of unidentified, uniformless "spies" infiltrating respectable English households. But detectives soon caught the public imagination and newspapers couldn't supply enough tales of their adventures.

In "Arrested on Suspicion," a story from *Revelations of a Private Detective*, the narrator explains that his admiration for Edgar Allan Poe's detective stories is what inspired him to investigate the crime for which his sister is wrongly accused. How apt that Forrester was aware of and explicit about his debt to Poe, because Forrester was himself one of the next great innovators. He cites Poe in the following story as well. Forrester takes the popular "Waters" Casebook school—the collections of informal reminiscences, usually at least semifictional, of a police officer—and transforms them into a well-organized, plot-driven narrative built around investigative methods. Forrester simply had more talent than most of his colleagues. "The Unknown Weapon" is driven by character-revealing dialogue, especially in great inquest and interrogation scenes, and Mrs. G. has an appealingly observant and ironic narrative voice. She begins by recounting the facts of the case as they are known before she herself becomes involved, and she makes even this summary lively and entertaining. And when she enters the scene herself, the action never flags until she solves the crime. Periodically she also summarizes the evidence gathered thus far. This method would reach its peak during the genre's so-called golden age of the early twentieth century, when many puzzle-driven detective stories included murder-scene diagrams, train timetables, and other clues for the wary reader, culminating in Ellery Queen's famous gimmick of a "Challenge to the Reader."

This entertaining and influential novella had never been reprinted after its first publication until an edition that E. F. Bleiler published in the 1970s. We are indebted to Bleiler for its resurrection. (It is his initials, E.F.B., that appear in a bracketed aside in the story.) Police casebook stories didn't disappear because Forrester surpassed them, but a new way of doing things had been established and would soon find its followers. Mrs. G. relies upon forensic evidence from footprints and coroner's reports to microscopic examination of "fluff." This is a very forward-looking story.

THE UNKNOWN WEAPON

I am about to set out here one of the most remarkable cases which have come under my actual observation.

I will give the particulars, as far as I can, in the form of a narrative.

The scene of the affair lay in a midland county, and on the outskirts of a very rustic and retired village, which has at no time come before the attention of the world.

Here are the exact preliminary facts of the case. Of course I alter names, for as this case is now to become public, and as the inquiries which took place at the time not only ended in disappointment, but by some inexplicable means did not arrest the public curiosity, there can be no wisdom in covering the names and places with such a thin veil of fiction as will allow of the truth being seen below that literary gauze. The names and places here used are wholly fictitious, and in no degree represent or shadow out the actual personages or localities.

The mansion at which the mystery which I am about to analyse took place was the manor-house, while its occupant, the squire of the district, was also the lord of the manor. I will call him Petleigh.

I may at once state here, though the fact did not come to my knowledge till after the catastrophe, that the squire was a thoroughly mean man, with but one other passion than the love of money, and that was a greed for plate.

Every man who has lived with his eyes open has come across human beings who concentrate within themselves the most wonderful contradictions. Here is a man who lives so scampishly that it is a question if ever he earnt an honest shilling, and yet he would firmly believe his moral character would be lost did he enter a theatre; there is an individual who never sent away a creditor or took more than a just commercial discount, while any day in the week he may be arrested upon a charge which would make him a scandal to his family.

So with Squire Petleigh. That he was extremely avaricious there can be no doubt, while his desire for the possession and display of plate was almost a mania.

His silver was quite a tradition in the county. At every meal—and I have heard the meals at Petleighcote were neither abundant nor succulent—enough plate stood upon the table to pay for the feeding of the poor of the whole county for a month. He would eat a mutton chop off silver.

Mr. Petleigh was in parliament, and in the season came up to town, where he had the smallest and most miserable house ever rented by a wealthy county member.

Avaricious, and therefore illiberal, Petleigh would not keep up two establishments; and so, when he came to town for the parliamentary season, he brought with him his country establishment, all the servants composing which were paid but third-class fares up to town.

The domestics I am quite sure, from what I learnt, were far from satisfactory people; a condition of things which was quite natural, seeing that they were not treated well, and were taken on at the lowest possible rate of wages.

The only servitor who remained permanently on the establishment was the housekeeper at the manor-house, Mrs. Quinion.

It was whispered in the neighbourhood that she had been the foster-sister ("and perhaps more") of the late Mrs. Petleigh; and it was stated with sufficient openness, and I am afraid also with some general amount of chuckling satisfaction, that the squire had been bitten with his lady.

The truth stood that Petleigh had married the daughter of a Liverpool merchant in the great hope of an alliance with her fortune, which at the date of her marriage promised to be large. But cotton commerce, even twenty-five years ago, was a risky business, and to curtail here particulars which are only remotely essential to the absolute comprehension of this narrative, he never had a penny with her, and his wife's father, who had led a deplorably irregular life, started for America and died there.

Mrs. Petleigh had but one child, Graham Petleigh, and she died when he was about twelve years of age.

During Mrs. Petleigh's life, the housekeeper at Petleighcote was the foster-sister to whom reference has been made. I myself believe that it would have been more truthful to call Mrs. Quinion the natural sister of the squire's wife.

Be that as it may, after the lady's death Mrs. Quinion, in a half-conceded, and after an uncomfortable fashion, became in a measure the actual mistress of Petleighcote.

Possibly the squire was aware of a relationship to his wife at which I have hinted, and was therefore not unready in recognising that it was better she should be in the house than any other woman. For, apart from his avariciousness and his mania for the display of plate, I found beyond all dispute that he was a man of very estimable judgment.

Again, Mrs. Quinion fell in with his avaricious humour. She shaved down his household expenses, and was herself contented with a very moderate remuneration.

From all I learnt, I came to the conclusion that Petleighcote had long been the most uncomfortable house in the county, the display of plate only tending to intensify the general barrenness.

Very few visitors came to the house, and hospitality was unknown; yet, notwithstanding these drawbacks, Petleigh stood very well in the county, and indeed, on the occasion of one or two charitable collections, he had appeared in print with sufficient success.

Those of my readers who live in the country will comprehend the style of the squire's household when I say that he grudged permission to shoot rabbits on his ground. Whenever possible, all the year round, specimens of that rather tiring food were to be found in Squire Petleigh's larder. In fact, I learnt that a young curate who remained a short time at Tram (the village), in gentle satire of this cheap system of rations, called Petleighcote the "Warren."

The son, Graham Petleigh, was brought up in a deplorable style, the father being willing to persuade himself, perhaps, that as he had been disappointed in his hopes of a fortune with the mother, the son did not call for that consideration to which he would have been entitled had the mother brought her husband increased riches. It is certain that the boy roughed life. All the schooling he got was that which could be afforded by a foundation grammar school, which happened fortunately to exist at Tram.

To this establishment he went sometimes, while at others he was off with lads miserably below him in station, upon some expedition which was not perhaps, as a rule, so respectable an employment as studying the humanities.

Evidently the boy was shamefully ill-used; for he was neglected.

By the time he was nineteen or twenty (all these particulars I learnt readily after the catastrophe, for the townsfolk were only too eager to talk of the unfortunate young man)—by the time he was nineteen or twenty, a score of years of neglect bore their fruit. He was ready, beyond any question, for any mad performance. Poaching especially was his delight, perhaps in a great measure because he found it profitable; because, to state the truth, he was kept totally without money, and to this disadvantage he added a second, that of being unable to spread what money he did obtain over any expanse of time.

I have no doubt myself that the depredations on his father's estate might have with justice been put to his account, and, from the inquiries I made, I am equally free to believe that when any small article of the mass of plate about the premises was missing, that the son knew a good deal more than was satisfactory of the lost valuables.

That Mrs. Quinion, the housekeeper, was extremely devoted to the young man is certain; but the money she received as wages, and whatever private or other means she had, could not cover the demands made upon them by young Graham Petleigh, who certainly spent money, though where it came from was a matter of very great uncertainty.

From the portrait I saw of him, he must have been of a daring, roving, jovial disposition—a youngster not inclined to let duty come between him and his inclinations; one, in short, who would get more out of the world than he would give it.

The plate was carried up to town each year with the establishment, the boxes being under the special guardianship of the butler, who never let them out of his sight between the country and town houses. The man, I have heard, looked forward to those journeys with absolute fear.

From what I learnt, I suppose the convoy of plate boxes numbered well on towards a score.

Graham Petleigh sometimes accompanied his father to town, and at other times was sent to a relative in Cornwall. I believe it suited father and son better that the latter should be packed off to Cornwall in the parliamentary season, for in town the lad necessarily became comparatively expensive—an objection in the eyes of the father, while the son found himself in a world to which, thanks to the education he had received, he was totally unfitted.

Young Petleigh's passion was horses, and there was not a farmer on the father's estate, or in the neighbourhood of Tram, who was not plagued for the loan of this or that horse—for the young man had none of his own.

On my part, I believe if the youth had no self-respect, the want was in a great measure owing to the father having had not any for his son.

I know I need scarcely add, that when a man is passionately fond of horses generally he bets on those quadrupeds.

It did not call for many inquiries to ascertain that young Petleigh had "put" a good deal of money upon horses, and that, as a rule, he had been lucky with them. The young man wanted some excitement, some occupation, and he found it in betting. Have I said that after the young heir was taken from the school he was allowed to run loose? This was the case. I presume the father could not bring his mind to incurring the expense of entering his son at some profession.

Things then at Petleighcote were in this condition; the father neglectful and avaricious; the son careless, neglected, and daily slipping down the ladder of life; and the housekeeper, Mrs. Quinion, saying nothing, doing nothing, but existing, and perhaps showing that she was attached to her foster-sister's son. She was a woman of much sound and discriminating sense, and it is certain that she expressed herself to the effect that she foresaw the young man was being silently, steadfastly, unceasingly ruined.

All these preliminaries comprehended, I may proceed to the action of this narrative.

It was the 19th of May (the year is unimportant), and early in the morning when the discovery was made, by the gardener to Squire Petleigh—one Tom Brown.

Outside the great hall-door, and huddled together in an extraordinary fashion, the gardener, at half-past five in the morning (a Tuesday), found lying a human form. And when he came to make an examination, he discovered that it was the dead body of the young squire.

Seizing the handle of the great bell, he quickly sounded an alarm, and within a minute the housekeeper herself and the one servant, who together numbered the household which slept at Petleighcote when the squire was in town, stood on the threshold of the open door.

The housekeeper was half-dressed, the servant wench was huddled up in a petticoat and a blanket.

The news spread very rapidly, by means of the gardener's boy, who, wondering where his master was stopping, came loafing about the house, quickly to find the use of his legs.

"He must have had a fit," said the housekeeper; and it was a flying message to that effect carried by the boy into the village, which brought the village doctor to the spot in the quickest possible time.

It was then found that the catastrophe was due to no *fit*.

A very slight examination showed that the young squire had died from a stab caused by a rough iron barb, the metal shaft of which was six inches long, and which still remained in the body.

At the inquest, the medical man deposed that very great force must have been used in thrusting the barb into the body, for one of the ribs had been half severed by the act. The stab given, the barb had evidently been drawn back with the view of extracting it—a purpose which had failed, the flanges of the barb having fixed themselves firmly in the cartilage and tissue about it. It was impossible the deceased could have turned the barb against himself in the manner in which it had been used.

Asked what this barb appeared like, the surgeon was unable to reply. He had never seen such a weapon before. He supposed it had been fixed in a shaft of wood, from which it had been wrenched by the strength with which the barb, after the thrust, had been held by the parts surrounding the wound.

The barb was handed round to the jury, and every man cordially agreed with his neighbour that he had never seen anything of the kind before; it was equally strange to all of them.

The squire, who took the catastrophe with great coolness, gave evidence to the effect that he had seen his son on the morning previous to the discovery of the murder, and about noon—seventeen and a half hours before the catastrophe was discovered. He did not know his son was about to leave town, where he had been staying. He added that he had not missed the young man; his son was in the habit of being his own master, and going where he liked. He could offer no explanation as to why his son had returned to the country, or why the materials found upon him were there. He could offer no explanation in any way about anything connected with the matter.

It was said, as a scandal in Tram, that the squire exhibited no emotion upon giving his evidence, and that when he sat down after his examination he appeared relieved.

Furthermore, it was intimated that upon being called upon to submit to a kind of cross-examination, he appeared to be anxious, and answered the few questions guardedly.

These questions were put by one of the jurymen—a solicitor's clerk (of some acuteness it was evident), who was the Tram oracle.

It is perhaps necessary for the right understanding of this case, that these questions should be here reported, and their answers also.

They ran as follows:

"Do you think your son died where he was found?"

"I have formed no opinion."

"Do you think he had been in your house?"

"Certainly not."

"Why are you so certain?"

"Because had he entered the house, my housekeeper would have known of his coming."

"Is your housekeeper here?"

"Yes."

"Has it been intended that she should be called as a witness?"

"Yes."

"Do you think your son attempted to break into your house?"

[The reason for this question I will make apparent shortly. By the way, I should, perhaps, here at once explain that I obtained all these particulars of the evidence from the county paper.]

"Do you think your son attempted to break into your house?"

"Why should he?"

"That is not my question. Do you think he attempted to break into your house?"

"No, I do not."

"You swear that, Mr. Petleigh?"

[By the way, there was no love lost between the squire and the Tram oracle, for the simple reason that not any existed that could be spilt.]

"I do swear it."

"Do you think there was anybody in the house he wished to visit clandestinely?"

"No."

"Who were in the house?"

"Mrs. Quinion, my housekeeper, and one servant woman."

"Is the servant here?"

"Yes."

"What kind of a woman is she?"

"Really Mr. Mortoun you can see her and judge for yourself."

"So we can. I am only going to ask one question more."

"I reserve to myself the decision whether I shall or shall not answer it."

"I think you will answer it, Mr. Petleigh."

"It remains, sir, to be seen. Put your question."

"It is very simple—do you intend to offer a reward for the discovery of the murderer of your son?"

The squire made no reply.

"You have heard my question, Mr. Petleigh."

"I have."

"And what is your answer?"

The squire paused for some moments. I should state that I am adding the particulars of the inquest I picked up, or detected if you like better, to the information afforded by the county paper to which I have already referred.

"I refuse to reply," said the squire.

Mortoun thereupon applied to the coroner for his ruling.

Now it appears evident to me that this juryman had some hidden motive in thus questioning the squire. If this were so, I am free to confess I never discovered it beyond any question of doubt. I may or I may not have hit on his motive. I believe I did.

It is clear that the question Mr. Mortoun urged was badly put, for how could the father decide whether he would offer a reward for the discovery of a murderer who did not legally exist till after the finding of the jury? And indeed it may furthermore be added that this question had no bearing upon the elucidation of the mystery, or at all events it had no apparent bearing upon the facts of the catastrophe.

It is evident that Mr. Mortoun was actuated in all probability by one of two motives, both of which were obscure. One might have been an attempt really to obtain a clue to the murder, the other might have been the endeavour to bring the squire, with whom it has been said he lived bad friends, into disrespect with the county.

The oracle-juryman immediately applied to the coroner, who at once admitted that the question was not pertinent, but nevertheless urged the squire as the question had been put to answer it.

It is evident that the coroner saw the awkward position in which the squire was placed, and spoke as he did in order to enable the squire to come out of the difficulty in the least objectionable manner.

But as I have said, Mr. Petleigh, all his incongruities and faults apart, was a clear-seeing man of a good and clear mind. As I saw the want of consistency in the question, as I read it, so he must have remarked the same failure when it was addressed to him.

For after patiently hearing the coroner to the end of his remarks, Petleigh said, quietly,——

"How can I say I will offer a reward for the discovery of certain murderers when the jury have not yet returned a verdict of murder?"

"But supposing the jury do return such a verdict?" asked Mortoun.

"Why then it will be time for you to ask your question."

I learnt that the juryman smiled as he bowed and said he was satisfied.

It appears to me that at that point Mr. Mortoun must have either gained that information which fitted in with his theory, or, accepting the lower motive for his question, that he felt he had now sufficiently damaged the squire in the opinion of the county. For the reporters were at work, and every soul present knew that not a word said would escape publication in the county paper.

Mr. Mortoun however was to be worsted within the space of a minute.

"Have you ceased questioning me, gentlemen?" asked the squire.

The coroner bowed, it appeared.

"Then," continued the squire, "before I sit down—and you will allow me to remain in the room until the inquiry is terminated—I will state that of my own free will which I would not submit to make public upon an illegal and a totally uncalled for attempt at compulsion. Should the jury bring in a verdict of murder against unknown persons, I shall *not* offer a reward for the discovery of those alleged murderers."

"Why not?" asked the coroner, who I learnt afterwards admitted that the question was utterly unpardonable.

"Because," said Squire Petleigh, "it is quite my opinion that no *murder* has been committed."

According to the newspaper report these words were followed by "sensation."

"No murder?" said the coroner.

"No; the death of the deceased was, I am sure, an accident."

"What makes you think that, Mr. Petleigh?"

"The nature of the death. Murders are not committed, I should think, in any such extraordinary manner as that by which my son came to his end. I have no more to say."

"Here," says the report, "the squire took his seat."

The next witness called—the gardener who had discovered the body had already been heard, and simply testified to the finding of the body—was Margaret Quinion, the housekeeper.

Her depositions were totally valueless from my point of view, that of the death of the young squire. She stated simply that she had gone to bed at the usual time (about ten) on the previous night, and that Dinah Yarton retired just previously, and to the same room. She heard no noise during the night, was disturbed in no way whatever until the alarm was given by the gardener.

In her turn Mrs. Quinion was now questioned by the solicitor's clerk, Mr. Mortoun.

"Do you and this—what is her name?—Dinah Yarton; do you and she sleep alone at Petleighcote?"

"Yes—when the family is away."

"Are you not afraid to do so?"

"No."

"Why?"

"Why should I be?"

"Well—most women are afraid to sleep in large lonely houses by themselves. Are you not afraid of burglars?"

"No."

"Why not?"

"Simply because burglars would find so little at Petleighcote to steal that they would be very foolish to break into the house."

"But there is a good deal of plate in the house—isn't there?"

"It all goes up to town with Mr. Petleigh."

"All, ma'am?"

"Every ounce—as a rule."

"You say the girl sleeps in your room?"

"In my room."

"Is she an attractive girl?"

"No."

"Is she unattractive?"

"You will have an opportunity of judging, for she will be called as a witness, sir."

"Oh; you don't think, do you, that there was anything between this young person and your young master?"

"Between Dinah and young Mr. Petleigh?"

"Yes."

"I think there could hardly be any affair between them, for [here she smiled] they have never seen each other—the girl having come to Petleighcote from the next county only three weeks since, and three months after the family had gone to town."

"Oh; pray have you not expected your master's son home recently?"

"I have not expected young Mr. Petleigh home recently—he never comes home when the family is away."

"Was he not in the habit of coming to Petleighcote unexpectedly?"

"No."

"You know that for a fact?"

"I know that for a fact."

"Was the deceased kept without money?"

"I know nothing of the money arrangements between the father and son."

"Well—do you know that often he wanted money?"

"Really—I decline to answer that question."

"Well—did he borrow money habitually from you?"

"I decline also to answer that question."

"You say you heard nothing in the night?"

"Not anything."

"What did you do when you were alarmed by the gardener in the morning?"

"I am at a loss to understand your question."

"It is very plain, nevertheless. What was your first act after hearing the catastrophe?"

[After some consideration.] "It is really almost impossible, I should say, upon such terrible occasions as was that, to be able distinctly to say what is one's first act or words, but I believe the first thing I did, or the first I remember, was to look after Dinah."

"And why could she not look after herself?"

"Simply because she had fallen into a sort of epileptic fit—to which she is subject—upon seeing the body."

"Then you can throw no light upon this mysterious affair?"

"No light: all I know of it was the recognition of the body of Mr. Petleigh, junior, in the morning."

The girl Dinah Yarton was now called, but no sooner did the unfortunate young woman, waiting in the hall of the publichouse at which the inquest was held, hear her name, than she swooped into a fit which totally precluded her from giving any evidence "except," as the county paper facetiously remarked, "the proof by her screams that her lungs were in a very enviable condition."

"She will soon recover," said Mrs. Quinion, "and will be able to give what evidence she can."

"And what will that be, Mrs. Quinion?" asked the solicitor's clerk.

"I am not able to say, Mr. Mortoun," she replied.

The next witness called (and here as an old police-constable I may remark upon the unbusiness-like way in which the witnesses were arranged)—the next witness called was the doctor.

His evidence was as follows, omitting the purely professional points. "I was called to the deceased on Tuesday morning, at near upon six in the morning. I recognized the body as that of Mr. Petleigh junior. Life was quite extinct. He had been dead about seven or eight hours, as well as I could judge. That would bring his death about ten or eleven on the previous night. Death had been caused by a stab, which had penetrated the left lung. The deceased had bled inwardly. The instrument which had caused death had remained in the wound, and stopped what little effusion of blood there would otherwise have been. Deceased literally died from suffocation, the blood leaking into the lungs and filling them. All the other organs of the body were in a healthy condition. The instrument by which death was produced is one with which I have no acquaintance. It is a kind of iron arrow, very roughly made, and with a shaft. It must have been fixed in some kind of handle when it was used, and which must have yielded and loosed the barb when an attempt was made to withdraw it—an attempt which had been made, because I found that one of the flanges of the arrow had caught behind a rib. I repeat that I am totaly unacquainted with the instrument with which death was effected. It is remarkably coarse and rough. The deceased might have lived a quarter of a minute after the wound had been inflicted. He would not in all probability have called out. There is no evidence of the least struggle having taken place—not a particle of evidence can I find to show that the deceased had exhibited even any knowledge of danger. And yet, nevertheless, supposing the deceased not to have been asleep at the time of the murder, for murder it undoubtedly was, or manslaughter, he must have seen his assailant, who, from the position of the weapon, must have been more before than behind him. Assuredly the death was the result of either murder or accident, and not the result of suicide, because I will stake my professional reputation that it would be quite impossible for any man to thrust such an instrument into his body with such a force as in this case has been used, as is proved by the cutting of a true bone-formed rib. Nor could a suicide, under such circumstances as those of the present catastrophe, have thrust the dart in the direction which this took. To sum up, it is my opinion that the deceased was murdered without, on his part, any knowledge of the murderer."

Mr. Mortoun cross-examined the doctor:

To this gentleman's inquiries he answered willingly.

"Do you think, Dr. Pitcherley, that no blood flowed externally?"

"Of that I am quite sure."

"How?"

"There were no marks of blood on the clothes."

"Then the inference stands that no blood stained the place of the murder?"

"Certainly."

"Then the body may have been brought an immense way, and no spots of blood would form a clue to the road?"

"Not one."

"Is it your impression that the murder was committed far away from the spot, or near the place where the body was found?"

"This question is one which it is quite out of my power to answer, Mr. Mortoun, my duty here being to give evidence as to my being called to the deceased, and as to the cause of death. But I need not tell you that I have formed my own theory of the catastrophe, and if the jury desire to have it, I am ready to offer it for their consideration."

Here there was a consultation, from which it resulted that the jury expressed themselves very desirous of obtaining the doctor's impression.

[I have no doubt the following words led the jury to their decision.]

The medical gentleman said:

"It is my impression that this death resulted out of a poaching—I will not say affray—but accident. It is thoroughly well-known in these districts, and at such a juncture as the present I need feel no false delicacy, Mr. Petleigh, in making this statement, that young Petleigh was much given to poaching. I believe that he and his companions were out poaching—I myself on two separate occasions, being called out to nightcases, saw the young gentleman under very suspicious circumstances—and that one of the party was armed with the weapon which caused the death, and which may have been carried at the end of such a heavy stick as is frequently used for flinging at rabbits. I suppose that by some frightful accident—we all know how dreadful are the surgical accidents which frequently arise when weapons are in use—the young man was wounded mortally, and so died, after the frightened companion had hurriedly attempted to withdraw the arrow, only to leave the barb sticking in the body and hooked behind a rib, while the force used in the resistance of the bone caused the weapon to part company from the haft. The discovery of the body outside the father's house can then readily be accounted for. His companions knowing who he was, and dreading their identification with an act which could but result in their own condemnation of character, carried the body to the threshold of his father's house, and there left it. This," the doctor concluded, "appears to me the most rational mode I can find of accounting for the circumstances of this remarkable and deplorable case. I apologize to Mr. Petleigh for the slur to which I may have committed myself in referring to the character of that gentleman's son, the deceased, but my excuse must rest in this fact, that where a crime or catastrophe is so obscure that the criminal, or guilty person, may be in one of many directions, it is but just to narrow the circle of inquiry as much as possible, in order to avoid the resting of suspicion upon the greater number of individuals. If, however, any one can suggest a more lucid explanation of the catastrophe than mine, I shall indeed be glad to admit I was wrong."

[There can be little question, I repeat, that Dr. Pitcherley's analysis fitted in very satisfactorily and plausibly with the facts of the case.]

Mr. Mortoun asked Dr. Pitcherley no more questions.

The next witness called was the police-constable of Tram, a stupid, hopeless dolt, as I found to my cost, who was good at a rustic publichouse row, but who as a detective was not worth my dog Dart.

It appeared that he gave his flat evidence with a stupidity which called even for the rebuke of the coroner.

All he could say was, that he was called, and that he went, and that he saw whose body it "be'd." That was "arl" he could say.

Mr. Mortoun took him in hand, but even he could do nothing with the man.

"Had many persons been on the spot where the body was found before he arrived?"

"Noa."

"How was that?"

"Whoy, 'cos Toom Broown, the gard'ner, coomed t'him at wuncet, and 'cos Toom Broown coomed t'him furst, 'cas he's cot wur furst coomed too."

This was so, as I found when I went down to Tram. The gardener, Brown, panic-stricken, after calling to, and obtaining the attention of the housekeeper, had rushed off to the village for that needless help which all panic-stricken people will seek, and the constable's cottage happening to be the first dwelling he reached, the constable obtained the first alarm. Now, had the case been conducted properly, the constable being the first man to get the alarm, would have obtained such evidence as would at once have put the detectives on the right scent.

The first two questions put by the lawyerlike juryman showed that he saw how important the evidence might have been which this witness, Joseph Higgins by name, should have given had he but known his business.

The first question was——

"It had rained, hadn't it, on the Monday night?"

[That previous to the catastrophe.]

"Ye-es t'had rained," Higgins replied.

Then followed this important question:

"You were on the spot one of the very first. Did you notice if there were any footsteps about?"

It appears to me very clear that Mr. Mortoun was here following up the theory of the catastrophe offered by the doctor. It would be clear that if several poaching companions had carried the young squire, after death, to the hall-door, that, as rain had fallen during the night, there would inevitably be many boot-marks on the soft ground.

This question put, the witness asked, "Wh-a-at?"

The question was repeated.

"Noa," he replied; "ah didn't see noa foot ma-arks."

"Did you look for any?"

"Noa; ah didn't look for any."

"Then you don't know your business," said Mr. Mortoun.

And the juryman was right; for I may tell the reader that boot-marks have sent more men to the gallows, as parts of circumstantial evidence, than any other proof whatever; indeed, the evidence of the boot-mark is terrible. A nail fallen out, or two or three put very close together, a broken nail, or all the nails perfect, have, times out of number, identified the boot of the suspected man with the boot-mark near the murdered, and has been the first link of the chain of evidence which has dragged a murderer to the gallows, or a minor felon to the hulks.

Indeed, if I were advising evil-doers on the best means of avoiding detection, I would say by all means take a second pair of boots in your pocket, and when you near the scene of your work change those you have on for those you have in your pocket, and do your wickedness in these latter; flee from the scene in these latter, and when you have "made" some distance, why return to your other boots, and carefully hide the tell-tale pair. Then the boots you wear will rather be a proof of your innocence than presumable evidence of your guilt.

Nor let any one be shocked at this public advice to rascals; for I flatter myself I have a counter-mode of foiling such a felonious arrangement as this one of two pairs of boots. And as I have disseminated the mode amongst the police, any attempt to put the suggestions I have offered actually into action, would be attended with greater chances of detection than would be incurred by running the ordinary risk.

To return to the subject in hand.

The constable of Tram, the only human being in the town, Mortoun apart perhaps, who should have known, in the ordinary course of his duty, the value of every foot-mark near the dead body, had totally neglected a precaution which, had he observed it, must have led to a discovery (and an immediate one), which in consequence of his dullness was never publicly made.

Nothing could be more certain than this, that what is called foot-mark evidence was totally wanting.

The constable taking no observations, not the cutest detective in existence could have obtained any evidence of this character, for the news of the catastrophe spreading, as news only spreads in villages, the rustics tramped up in scores, and so obliterated what foot-marks might have existed.

To be brief, Mr. Josh. Higgins could give no evidence worth hearing.

And now the only depositions which remained to be given were those of Dinah Yarton.

She came into court "much reduced," said the paper from which I gain these particulars, "from the effects of the succession of fits which she had fallen into and struggled out of."

She was so stupid that every question had to be repeated in half-a-dozen shapes before she could offer a single reply. It took four inquiries to get at her name, three to know where she lived, five to know what she was; while the coroner and the jury, after a score of questions, gave over trying to ascertain whether she knew the nature of an oath. However, as she stated that she was quite sure she would go to a "bad place" if she did not speak the truth, she was declared to be a perfectly competent witness, and I have no doubt she was badgered accordingly.

And as Mr. Mortoun got more particulars out of her than all

the rest of the questioners put together, perhaps it will not be amiss, as upon her evidence turned the whole of my actions so far as I was concerned, to give that gentleman's questions and her answers in full, precisely as they were quoted in the greedy county paper, which doubtless looked upon the whole case as a publishing godsend, the proprietors heartily wishing that the inquest might be adjourned a score of times for further evidence.

"Well now, Dinah," said Mr. Mortoun, "what time did you go to bed on Monday?"

[The answers were generally got after much hammering in on the part of the inquirist. I will simply return them at once as ultimately given.]

"Ten."

"Did you go to sleep?"

"Noa—Ise didunt goa to sleep."

"Why not?"

"Caize Ise couldn't."

"But why?"

"Ise wur thinkin'."

"What of?"

"Arl manner o' thing'."

"Tell us one of them?"

[No answer—except symptoms of another fit.]

"Tut—tut! Well, did you go to sleep at last?"

"Ise did."

"Well, when did you wake?"

"Ise woke when missus ca'd I."

"What time?"

"Doant know clock."

"Was it daylight?"

"E-es, it wur day."

"Did you wake during the night?"

"E-es, wuncet."

"How did that happen?"

"Doant knaw."

"Did you hear anything?"

"Noa."

"Did you think you heard anything?"

"E-es."

"What?"

"Whoy, it movin'."

"What was moving?"

"Whoy, the box."

"Box—tut, tut," said the lawyer, "answer me properly."

Now here he raised his voice, and I have no doubt Dinah had to thank the juryman for the return of her fits.

"Do you hear?—answer me properly."

"E-es."

"When you woke up did you hear any noise?"

"Noa."

"But you thought you heard a noise?"

"E-es, in the——"

"Tut, tut. Never mind the box—where was it?"

"Ter box? In t' hall!"

"No—no, the noise."

"In t' hall, zur!"

"What—the noise was?"

"Noa, zur, ter box."

"There, my good girl," says the Tram oracle, "never mind the box, I want you to think of this—did you hear any noise *outside the house?*"

"Noa."

"But you said you heard a noise?"

"No, zur, I didunt."

"Well, but you said you thought you heard a noise?"

"E-es."

"Well—where?"

"In ter box——"

Here, said the county paper, the lawyer, striking his hand on the table before him, continued—

"Speak of the box once more, my girl, and to prison you go."

"Prizun!" says the luckless witness.

"Yes, jail and bread and water!"

And thereupon the unhappy witness without any further remarks plunged into a fit, and had to be carried out, battling with that strength which convulsions appear to bring with them, and in the arms of three men, who had quite their work to do to keep her moderately quiet.

"I don't think, gentlemen," said the coroner, "that this witness is material. In the first place, it seems doubtful to me whether she is capable of giving evidence; and, in the second, I believe she has little evidence to give—so little that I doubt the policy of adjourning the inquest till her recovery. It appears to me that it would be cruelty to force this poor young woman again into the position she has just endured, unless you are satisfied that she is a material witness. I think she has said enough to show that she is not. It appears certain, from her own statement, that she retired to rest with Mrs. Quinion, and knows nothing more of what occurred till the housekeeper awoke her in the morning, after she herself had received the alarm. I suggest, therefore, that what evidence she could give is included in that already before the jury, and given by the housekeeper."

The jury coincided in the remarks made by the coroner, Mr. Mortoun, however, adding that he was at a loss to comprehend the girl's frequent reference to the box. Perhaps Mrs. Quinion could help to elucidate the mystery.

The housekeeper immediately rose.

"Mrs. Quinion," said Mr. Mortoun, "can you give any explanation as to what the young person meant by referring to a box?"

"No."

"There are of course boxes at Petleighcote?"

"Beyond all question."

"Any box in particular?"

"No box in particular."

"No box which is spoken of as *the* box?"

"Not any."

"The girl said it was in the hall. Is there a box in the hall?"

"Yes, several."

"What are they?"

"There is a clog and boot box, a box on the table in which letters for the post are placed when the family is at home, and from which they are removed every day at four; and also a box fixed to the wall, the use of which I have never been able to discover, and of the removal of which I have several times spoken to Mr. Petleigh."

"How large is it?"

"About a foot-and-a-half square and three feet deep."

"Locked?"

"No, the flap is always open."

"Has the young woman ever betrayed any fear of this box?"

"Never."

"You have no idea to what box in the hall she referred in her evidence?"

"Not the least idea."

"Do you consider the young woman weak in her head?"

"She is decidedly not of strong intellect."

"And you suppose this box idea a mere fancy?"

"Of course."

"And a recent one?"

"I never heard her refer to a box before."

"That will do."

The paper whence I take my evidence describes Mrs. Quinion as a woman of very great self-possession, who gave what she had to say with perfect calmness and slowness of speech.

This being all the evidence, the coroner was about to sum up, when the Constable Higgins remembered that he had forgotten something, and came forward in a great hurry to repair his error.

He had not produced the articles found on the deceased.

These articles were a key and a *black crape mask*.

The squire being recalled, and the key shown to him, he identified the key as (he believed) one of his "household keys." It was of no particular value, and it did not matter if it remained in the hands of the police.

The report continued: "The key is now in the custody of the constable."

With regard to the crape mask the squire could offer no explanation concerning it.

The coroner then proceeded to sum up, and in doing so he paid many well-termed compliments to the doctor for that gentleman's view of the matter (which I have no doubt threw off all interest in the matter on the part of the public, and slackened the watchfulness of the detective force, many of whom, though very clever, are equally simple, and accept a plain and straightforward statement with extreme willingness)—and urged that the discovery of the black crape mask appeared to be very much like corroborative proof of the doctor's suggestion. "The young man," said the coroner, "would, if poaching, be exceedingly desirous of hiding his face, considering his position in the county, and then the finding of this black crape mask upon the body would, if the poaching explanation were accepted, be a very natural discovery. But——"

And then the coroner proceeded to explain to the jury that they had to decide not upon suppositions but facts. They might all be convinced that Dr. Pitcherley's explanation was the true one, but in law it could not be accepted. Their verdict must be in accordance with facts, and the simple facts of the case were these:—A man was found dead, and the causes of his death were such that it was impossible to believe that the deceased had been guilty of suicide. They would therefore under the circumstances feel it was their duty to return an open verdict of murder.

The jury did not retire, but at the expiration of a consultation of three minutes, in which (I learnt) the foreman, Mr. Mortoun, had all the talking to himself, the jury gave in a verdict of wilful murder against some person or persons unknown.

Thus ended the inquest.

And I have little hesitation in saying it was one of the weakest inquiries of that kind which had ever taken place. It was characterized by no order, no comprehension, no common sense.

The facts of the case made some little stir, but the plausible explanations offered by the doctor, and the several coinciding circumstances, deprived the affair of much of its interest, both to the public and the detective force; to the former, because they had little room for ordinary conjecture; to the latter, because I need not say the general, the chief motive power in the detective is gain, and here the probabilities of profit were almost annihilated by the possibility that a true explanation of the facts of this affair had been offered, while it was such as promised little hope of substantial reward.

But the mere fact of my here writing this narrative will be sufficient to show that *I* did not coincide with the general view taken of the business.

That I was right the following pages will I think prove.

Of course the Government offered the usual reward, £ 100, of which proclamation is published in all cases of death where presumably foul play has taken place.

But it was not the ordinary reward which tempted me to choose this case for investigation. It was several peculiar circumstances which attracted me.

They were as follows:

1. Why did the father refuse to offer a reward?

2. Why did the deceased have one of the household keys with him at the time of his death, and how came he to have it at all?

3. What did the box mean?

1. It seemed to me that the refusal by the father to offer a reward must arise from one of three sources. Either he did not believe a murder had been committed, and therefore felt the offer was needless; or he knew murder was committed, and did not wish to accelerate the action of the police; or, thirdly, whether he believed or disbelieved in the murder, knew or did not know it to be a murder, that he was too sordid to offer a reward by the payment of which he would lose without gaining any corresponding benefit.

2. How came the deceased to have one of the keys of his father's establishment in his pocket? Such a possession was extremely unusual, and more inexplicable. How came he to possess it? Why did he possess it? What was he going to do with it?

3. What did the box mean? Did the unhappy girl Dinah Yarton refer to any ordinary or extraordinary box? It appeared to me that if she referred to any ordinary box it must be an ordinary box under extraordinary circumstances. But fools have very rarely any imagination, and knowing this I was not disposed to accredit Dinah with any ability to invest the box ordinary with any extraordinary attributes. And then remembering that there was nobody in the house to play tricks with her but a grave housekeeper who would not be given to that kind of thing, I came to the conclusion that the box in question was an extraordinary box. "*It was in the hall.*" Now if the box were no familiar box, and it

was in the hall, the inference stood that it had just arrived there. Did I at this time associate the box intimately with the case? I think not.

At all events I determined to go down to Tram and investigate the case, and as with us detectives action is as nearly simultaneous with determination to act as it can be, I need not say that, making up my mind to visit Tram, I was soon nearing that station by the first train which started after I had so determined.

Going down I arranged mentally the process with which I was to go through.

Firstly, I must see the constable.

Secondly, I must talk to the girl Dinah.

Thirdly, I must examine the place of the murder.

All this would be easy work.

But what followed would be more difficult.

This was to apply what I should discover to any persons whom my discoveries might implicate, and see what I could make of it all.

Arrived at Tram at once I found out the constable, and I am constrained to say—a greater fool I never indeed did meet.

He was too stupid to be anything else than utterly, though idiotically, honest.

Under my corkscrew-like qualities as a detective he had no more chance than a tender young cork with a corkscrew proper. I believe that to the end of the chapter he never comprehended that I was a detective. His mind could not grasp the idea of a police officer in petticoats.

I questioned him as the shortest way of managing him, smoothing his suspicions and his English with shillings of the coin of this realm.

Directly I came face to face with him I knew what I had to do. I had simply to question him. And here I set out my questions and his answers as closely as I can recollect them, together with a narrative of the actions which resulted out of both.

I told him at once I was curious to know all I could about the affair; and as I illustrated this statement with the exhibition of the first shilling, in a moment I had the opportunity of seeing every tooth he had in his head—thirty-two. Not one was missing.

"There was found on the body a key and a mask—where are they?"

"War be they—why, in my box, sin' I be coonstubble!"

"Will you show them me?"

"Oh, Ise show they ye!"

And thereupon he went to a box in the corner of the room, and unlocked it solemnly.

As the constable of Tram it was perfectly natural that he should keep possession of these objects, since a verdict of wilful murder had been given, and at any time, therefore, inquiries might have to be made.

From this box he took out a bundle; this opened, a suit of clothes came to view, and from the middle of these he produced a key and a mask.

I examined the key first. It was a well-made—a beautifully-made key, and very complicated. We constables learn in the course of our experience a good deal about keys, and therefore I saw at a glance that it was the key to a complicated and more than ordinarily valuable lock.

On the highly-polished loop of the key a carefully-cut number was engraved—No. 13.

Beyond all question this key was no ordinary key to an ordinary lock.

Now, extraordinary locks and keys guard extraordinary treasures.

The first inference I arrived at, therefore, from my interview with the Tram constable was this—that the key found upon the body opened a lock put upon something valuable.

Then I examined the mask.

It was of black crape, stretched upon silver wire. I had never seen anything like it before, although as a detective I had been much mixed up with people who wore masks, both at masquerades and on other occasions even less satisfactory.

I therefore inferred that the mask was of foreign manufacture.

[I learnt ultimately that I was right, and no great credit to me either, for that which is not white may fairly be guessed to be of some other colour. The mask was what is called abroad a *masque de luxe*, a mask which, while it changes the countenance sufficiently to prevent recognition, is made so delicately that the material, crape, admits of free perspiration—a condition which inferior masks will not admit.]

"Anything else found on the body?"

"Noa."

"No skeleton keys?"

"Noa; on'y wan key."

So, if the constable were right, and *if the body had remained as it fell*, when found by the gardener, Brown, the only materials found were a key and mask.

But, surely, there was something else in the pockets.

"Was there no purse found?" I asked.

"Noa; noa poorse."

"No handkerchief?"

"Ooh, 'ees; thar war a kerchiefer."

"Where is it?"

He went immediately to the bundle.

"Are these the clothes in which he was found?"

"Ees, they be."

So far, so good, I felt.

The constable, stupid and honest as he appeared, and as he existed, was very suspicious, and therefore I felt that he had to be managed most carefully.

Having hooked the handkerchief out from some recess in the bundle with the flattest forefinger I think I ever remarked, he handed it to me.

It was a woman's handkerchief.

It was new; had apparently never been used; there was no crease nor dirt upon it, as there would have been had it been carried long in the pocket; and it was marked in the corner "Freddy"—undoubtedly the diminutive of Frederica.

"Was the 'kerchiefer,'" I asked, using the word the constable had used—"was it wrapped in anything?"

"Noa."

"What pocket was it in?"

"Noa poockut."

"Where was it, then?"

"In 's weskit, agin 's hart, an' joost aboove th' ole made in 'um."

Now, what was the inference of the handkerchief?

It was a woman's; it was not soiled; it had not been worn long; it was thrust in his breast; it was marked.

The inference stood thus:

This handkerchief belonged to a woman, in all probability young, whose Christian name was Frederica; as it was not soiled, and as it was not blackened by wear, it had recently been given to, or taken, by him; and as the handkerchief was found in the breast of his shirt, it appeared to have been looked upon with favour. Suppose then we say that it was a gift by a young woman to the deceased about the time when he was setting out on his expedition?

Now, the deceased had left London within eighteen hours of his death; had the handkerchief been given him in London or after he left town?

Again, had the mask anything to do with this woman?

Taking it up again and re-examining it, the delicacy of the fabric struck me more than before, and raising it close to my eyes to make a still narrower examination I found that it was scented.

The inference stood, upon the whole, that this mask had belonged to a woman.

Again I began to question Joseph Higgins, constable.

"I should be glad to look at the clothes," I said.

"Lard, thee may look," said the constable.

They were an ordinary suit of clothes, such as a middle-class man would wear of a morning, but not so good or fashionable as one might have expected to find in wear by the son of a wealthy squire.

[This apparent incongruity was soon explained away by my learning, as I did in the evening of my arrival, that the squire was mean and even parsimonious.]

There was nothing in the pockets, but my attention was called to the *fluffy* state of the cloth, which was a dark grey, and which therefore in a great measure hid this fluffiness.

"You have not been taking care of these clothes, I am afraid."

"They be joost as they coomed arf him!"

"What, was all this fluff about the cloth?"

"Yoa."

[Yoa was a new version of "e-es," and both meant "yes."]

"They look as though they had been rolled about a bed."

"Noa."

The clothes in question were stained on their underside with gravel-marks, and they were still damp on these parts.

The remarking of this fact, recalled to my mind something which came out at the inquest, and which now I remembered and kept in mind while examining the state of the clothes.

On the Monday night, as the body was discovered on the Tuesday morning, it had rained.

Now the clothes were not damp all over, for the fluff was quite wavy, and flew about in the air. It was necessary to know what time it left off raining on the Monday night, or Tuesday morning.

It was very evident that the clothes had not been exposed to rain between the time of their obtaining the fluffiness and the discovery of the body. Therefore ascertain at what hour the rain ceased, and I had the space of time (the hour at which the body was discovered being half-past five) within which the body had been deposited.

The constable knew nothing about the rain, and I believe it was at this point, in spite of the shillings, that the officer began to show rustic signs of impatience.

I may add here that I found the rain had only ceased at three o'clock on the Tuesday morning. It was therefore clear that the body had been deposited between three and half-past five—*two hours and a-half.*

This discovery I made that same evening of my landlady, a most useful person.

Now, does it not strike the reader that three o'clock on a May morning, and when the morning had almost come, was an extraordinarily late hour at which to be poaching?

This indisputable fact, taken into consideration with the needlessness of the mask (for poachers do not wear masks), and the state of the clothes, to say nothing of the kind of clothes found on the deceased, led me to throw over Mr. Mortoun's theory that the young squire had met his death in a poaching affray, or rather while out on a poaching expedition.

I took a little of the fluff from the clothes and carefully put it away in my pocket-book.

The last thing I examined was the barb which had caused the death.

And here I admit I was utterly foiled—completely, positively foiled. I had never seen anything of the kind before—never.

It was a very coarse iron barb, shaped something like a queen's broad arrow, only that the flanges widened from their point, so that each appeared in shape like the blade of a much-worn penknife. The shaft was irregular and perhaps even coarser than the rest of the work. The weapon was made of very poor iron, for I turned its point by driving it, not by any means heavily, against the frame of the window—to the intense disgust of the constable, whose exclamation, I remember thoroughly well, was "Woa."

Now what did I gain by my visit to the constable? This series of suppositions:

That the deceased was placed where he was found between three and half-past five A.M. on the Tuesday; that he was not killed from any result of a poaching expedition; and that he had visited a youngish woman named Frederica a few hours before death, and of whom he had received a handkerchief and possibly a mask.

The only troublesome point was the key, which, by the way, had been found in a small fob-pocket in the waist of the coat.

While taking my tea at the inn at which I had set down, I need not say I asked plenty of questions, and hearing a Mrs. Green frequently referred to, I surmised she was a busybody, and getting her address, as that of a pleasant body who let lodgings, I may at once add that that night I slept in the best room of the pleasant body's house.

She was the most incorrigible talker ever I encountered. Nor was she devoid of sharpness; indeed, with more circumspection than she possessed, or let me say, with ordinary circumspection, she would have made a good ordinary police officer, and had she possessed that qualification I might have done something for her. As it was the idea could not be entertained for any part of a moment.

She was wonderful, this Mrs. Green.

You only had to put a question on any point, and she abandoned the subject in which she had been indulging, and sped away on a totally new tack.

She was ravenous to talk of the murder; for it was her foregone conclusion that murder had been committed.

In a few words, all the information afforded to this point, which has not arisen out of my own seeking, or came by copy from the county newspaper (and much of that information which is to follow) all proceeded from the same gushing source—Mrs. Green.

All I had to do was to put another question when I thought we had exhausted the previous one, and away she went again at score, and so we continued from seven to eleven. It was half-past eight or nine before she cleared away the long-since cold and sloppy tea-things.

"And what has become of Mrs. Quinion?" I asked, in the course of this to me valuable entertainment on the part of Mrs. Green, throughout the whole of which she never asked me my business in these parts (though I felt quite sure so perfect a busybody was dying to know my affairs), because any inquiry would have called for a reply, and this was what she could not endure while I was willing to listen to her. Hence she chose the less of two evils.

"And what became of the girl?"

"What gal?"

"Dinah."

"Dinah Yarton?"

"Yes. I believe that *was* her name."

"Lor' bless 'ee! it's as good and as long as a blessed big book to tell 'ee all about Dinah Yarton. She left two days after, and they not having a bed for she at the Lamb and Flag, and I having a bed, her came here—the Lamb and Flag people always sending me their over beds, bless 'em, bless 'ee! and that's how I comes to know arl about it, bless 'ee, and the big box!"

[The box—now this was certainly what I did want Mrs. Green to come to. The reader will remember that I laid some stress upon the girl's frequent reference to the trunk.]

"Bless 'ee! the big box caused arl the row, because Mrs. Quinion said she were a fool to have been frightened by a big box; but so Dinah would be, and so her did, being probable in the nex' county at this time, at Little Pocklington, where her mother lives making lace, and her father a farmer, and where her was born—Dinah, and not her mother—on the 1st o'April, 1835, being now twenty years old. What art thee doing? bless 'ee!"

[I was making a note of Little Pocklington.]

Nor will I here make any further verbatim notes of Mrs. Green's remarks, but use them as they are required in my own way, and as in actuality really I did turn them to account.

I determined to see the girl at once; that is, after I had had a night's rest. And therefore next morning, after carefully seeing my box and bag were locked, I made a quick breakfast, and sallied out. Reaching the station, there was Mrs. Green. She had obviously got the start of me by crossing Goose Green fields, as in fact she told me.

She said she thought I must have dropped that, and had come to see.

"That" was a purse so old that it was a curiosity.

"Bless 'ee!" she says, "isn't yourn? Odd, beant it? But, bless 'ee! ye'll have to wait an hour for a train. There beant a train to anywhere for arl an hour."

"Then I'll take a walk," said I.

"Shall I come, and tark pleasant to 'ee?" asked Mrs. Green.

"No," I replied; "I've some business to transact."

I had an hour to spare, and remembering that I had seen the things at Higgins's by a failing evening light, I thought I would again visit that worthy, and make a second inspection.

It was perhaps well I did so.

Not that I discovered anything of further importance, but the atom of novelty of which I made myself master, helped to confirm me in my belief that the deceased had visited a young woman, probably a lady, a very short time before his death.

Higgins, a saddler by trade, was not at all delighted at my reappearance, and really I was afraid I should have to state what I was in order to get my way, and then civilly bully him into secrecy. But happily his belief in me as a mild mad woman overcame his surliness, and so with the help of a few more shillings I examined once more the clothes found on the unfortunate young squire.

And now, in the full blazing spring morning sunlight, I saw what had missed my view on the previous evening. This was nothing less than a bright crimson scrap of silk braid, such as ladies use in prosecuting their embroidery studies.

This bit of braid had been wound round and round a breast button, and then tied in a natty bow at the top.

"She is a lady," I thought; "and she was resting her head against his breast when she tied that bit of braid there. She is innocent, I should think, or she never would have done such a childish action as that."

Higgins put away the dead youth's clothes with a discontented air.

"Look ye yere—do 'ee think ye'l want 'em wuncet more?"

"No."

"Wull, if 'ee do, 'ee wunt have 'un."

"Oh, very well," I said, and went back to the station.

Of course there was Mrs. Green on the watch, though in the morning I had seen about the house symptoms of the day being devoted to what I have heard comic Londoners describe as "a water party"—in other words, a grand wash.

That wash Mrs. Green had deserted.

"Bless 'ee, I'm waitin' for a dear fren'!"

"Oh, indeed, Mrs. Green."

"Shall I take ticket for 'ee, dear?"

"Yes, if you like. Take it for Stokeley," said I.

"Four mile away," says Mrs. Green. "*I've* got a fren' at Stokeley. I wounds if your fren' be *my* fren'! Who *be* your fren', bless 'ee?"

"Mrs. Blotchley."

"What, her as lives near th' peump?" (pump)

"Yes."

"Oh, I don't know *she*."

It seemed to me Mrs. Green was awed—I never learnt by what, because as I never knew Mrs. Blotchley, and dropped upon her name by chance, and indeed never visited Stokeley, why Green had all the benefit of the discovery.

"And, Mrs. Green, if I am not home by nine, do not sit up for me."

"*Oh!*—goin' maybe to sleep at *her* hoose?"

"Very likely."

"*Oh!*"

And as Mrs. Green here dropped me a curtsey I have remained under the impression that Mrs. B. was a lady of consequence whose grandeur Mrs. Green saw reflected upon me.

I have no doubt the information she put at once in circulation helped to screen the actual purpose for which I had arrived at Tram from leaking out.

When the train reached Stokeley I procured another ticket on to Little Pocklington, and reached that town about two in the afternoon. It was not more than sixty miles from Tram.

The father of this Dinah Yarton was one of those small few-acre farmers who throughout the country are gradually but as certainly vanishing.

I may perhaps at once say that the poor girl Dinah had no less than three fits over the cross-examination to which I submitted her, and here (to the honour of rustic human nature) let it be recorded that actually I had to use my last resource, and show myself to be a police officer, by the production of my warrant in the presence of the Little Pocklington constable, who was brought into the affair, before I could overcome the objections of the girl's father. He with much justifiable reason urged that the "darned" business had already half-killed his wench, and he would be "darned" if I should altogether send her out of the "warld."

As I have said, the unhappy girl had three fits, and I have no doubt the family were heartily glad when I had turned my back upon the premises.

The unhappy young woman had to make twenty struggles before she could find one reply.

Here I need not repeat her evidence to that point past which it was not carried when she stood before the coroner and jury, but I will commence from that point.

"Dinah," I inquired in a quiet tone, and I believe the fussiness betrayed by the girl's mother tended as much to the fits as the girl's own nervousness—"Dinah, what was all that about the big box?"

"Darn the box," said the mother.

And here it was that the unfortunate girl took her second fit.

"There, she's killed my Dinah now," said the old woman, and it must be confessed Dinah was horribly convulsed, and indeed looked frightful in the extreme. The poor creature was quite an hour fighting with the fit, and when she came to and opened her eyes, the first object they met made her shut them again, for that object was myself.

However, I had my duty to perform, and therein lies the excuse for my torture.

"What—oh—o-o-oh wha-at did thee say?"

"What about the big box?"

"Doa noa." [This was the mode in those part of saying "I do not know."]

"Where was it?"

"In th' hall."

"Where did it come from?"

"Doa noa."

"How long had it been there?"

"Sin' the day afore."

"Who brought it?"

"Doa noa."

"Was it a man?"

"Noa."

"What then?"

"Two men."

"How did they come?"

"They coomed in a great big waggoon."

"And did they bring the box in the waggon?"

"Yoa." [This already I knew meant "Yes."]

"And they left the box at the hall?"

"Yoa."

"What then?"

"Whoa?" [This I guessed meant "What."]

"What did they say?"

"Zed box wur for squoire."

"Did they both carry it?"

"Yoa."

"How?"

"Carefool loike." [Here there were symptoms of another convulsion.]

"What became of the big box?"

"Doa noa."

"Did they come for it again?"

"Doa noa."

"Is it there now?"

"Noa."

"Then it went away again?"

"Yoa."

"You did not see it taken away?"

"Noa."

"Then how do you know it is not there now?"

"Doa noa."

"But you say it is not at the hall—how do you know that?"

"Mrs. Quanyan (Quinion) told I men had been for it."

"When was that?"

"After I'd been garne to bed."

"Was it there the next morning?"

"Whoa?"

"Was it there the morning when they found the young squire dead outside the door?"

And now "Diney," as her mother called her, plunged into the third fit, and in the early throes of that convulsion I was forced to leave her, for her father, an honest fellow, told me to leave his house, "arficer or no arficer," and that if I did not do so he would give me what he called a "sta-a-art."

Under the circumstances I thought that perhaps it was wise to go, and did depart accordingly.

That night I remained in Little Pocklington in the hope, in which I was so grievously disappointed, of discovering further particulars which the girl might have divulged to her companions. But in the first place Diney had no companions, and in the second all attempts to draw people out, for the case had been copied into that county paper which held sway at Little Pocklington, all attempts signally failed.

Upon my return to Tram, Mrs. Green received me with all the honours, clearly as a person who had visited Mrs. Blotchley, and I noticed that the parlour fire-place was decorated with a new stove-ornament in paper of a fiery and flaring description.

I thanked Mrs. Green, and in answer to that lady's inquiries I was happy to say Mrs. Blotchley was well—except a slight cold. Yes, I had slept there. What did I have for dinner at Mrs. Blotchley's? Well, really I had forgotten. "Dear heart," said Mrs. Green, " 'ow unfortnet."

After seeing "Diney," and in coming home by the train (and indeed I can always think well while travelling), I turned over all that I had pinched out of Dinah Yarton in reference to the big box.

Did that box, or did it not, in any way relate to the death?

It was large; it had been carried by two men; and according to Dinah's information it had been removed again from the hall.

At all events I must find out what the box meant.

The whole affair was still so warm—not much more than a fortnight had passed since the occurrence—that I still felt sure all particulars about that date which had been noticed would be remembered.

I set Mrs. Green to work, for nobody could better suit my purpose.

"Mrs. Green, can you find out whether any strange carrier's cart or waggon, containing a very big box, was seen in Tram on the Monday, and the day before young Mr. Petleigh's body was found?"

I saw happiness in Mrs. Green's face; and having thus set her to work, I put myself in the best order, and went up to Petleighcote Hall.

The door was opened (with suspicious slowness) by a servant-woman, who closed it again before she took my message and a card to Mrs. Quinion. The message consisted of a statement that I had come after the character of a servant.

A few moments passed, and I was introduced into the house-keeper's presence.

I found her a calm-looking, fine, portly woman, with much quiet determination in her countenance. She was by no means badly featured.

She was quite self-possessed.

The following conversation took place between us. The reader will see that not the least reference was made by me to the real object of my visit—the prosecution of an inquiry as to the mode by which young Mr. Petleigh had met his death. And if the reader complains that there is much falsity in what I state, I would urge that as evil-doing is a kind of lie levelled at society, if it is to be conquered it must be met on the side of society, through its employés, by similar false action.

Here is the conversation.

"Mrs. Quinion, I believe?"

"Yes, as I am usually termed—but let that pass. You wish to see me?"

"Yes; I have called about the character of a servant."

"Indeed—who?"

"I was passing through Tram, where I shall remain some days, on my way from town to York, and I thought it would be wise to make a personal inquiry, which I find much the best plan in all affairs relating to my servants."

"A capital plan; but as you came from town, why did you not apply to the town housekeeper, since I have no doubt you take the young person from the town house?"

"There is the difficulty. I should take the young person, if her character were to answer, from a sort of charity. She has never been in town, and here's my doubt. However, if you give me any hope of the young person—"

"What is her name?"

"Dinah—Dinah—you will allow me to refer to my pocket-book."

"Don't take that trouble," said she, and I thought she looked pale; but her pallor might have been owing, I thought at the time, to the deep mourning she was wearing; "you mean Dinah Yarton."

"Yarton—that is the name. Do you think she will suit?"

"Much depends upon what she is wanted for."

"An under nurserymaid."

"Your own family?"

"Oh, dear no—a sister's."

"In town?"

[She asked this question most calmly.]

"No—abroad."

"Abroad?" and I remarked that she uttered the word with an

energy which, though faint in itself, spoke volumes when compared with her previous serenity.

"Yes," I said, "my sister's family are about leaving England for Italy, where they will remain for years. Do you think this girl would do?"

"Well—yes. She is not very bright, it is true, but she is wonderfully clean, honest, and extremely fond of children."

Now, it struck me then and there that the experience of the housekeeper at childless Petleighcote as to Dinah's love of children must have been extremely limited.

"What I most liked in Dinah," continued Mrs. Quinion, "was her frankness and trustworthiness. There can be no doubt of her gentleness with children."

"May I ask why you parted with her?"

"She left me of her own free will. We had, two or three weeks since, a very sad affair here. It operated much upon her; she wished to get away from the place; and indeed I was glad she determined to go."

"Has she good health?"

"Very fair health."

Not a word about the fits.

It struck me Mrs. Qunion relished the idea of Dinah Yarton's going abroad.

"I think I will recommend her to my sister. She tells me she would have no objection to go abroad."

"Oh! you have seen her?"

"Yes—the day before yesterday, and before leaving for town, whence I came here. I will recommend the girl. Good morning."

"Good morning, ma'am; but before you go, will you allow me to take the liberty of asking you, since you are from London, if you can recommend me a town servant, or at all events a young person who comes from a distance. When the family is away I require only one servant here, and I am not able to obtain this one now that the hall has got amongst the scandal-mongers, owing to the catastrophe to which I have already referred. The young person I have with me is intolerable; she has only been here four days, and I am quite sure she must not remain fourteen."

"Well, I think I can recommend you a young person, strong and willing to please, and who only left my sister's household on the score of followers. Shall I write to my sister's housekeeper and see what is to be done?"

"I should be most obliged," said Mrs. Quinion; "but where may I address a letter to you in event of my having to write?"

"Oh!" I replied, "I shall remain at Tram quite a week. I have received a telegraphic message which makes my journey to the north needless; and as I have met here in Tram with a person who is a friend of an humble friend of mine, I am in no hurry to quit the place."

"Indeed! may I ask who?"

"Old Mrs. Green, at the corner of the Market Place, and her friend is Mrs. Blotchley of Stokeley."

"Oh, thank you. I know neither party."

"I may possibly see you again," I continued.

"Most obliged," continued Mrs. Quinion; "shall be most happy."

"Good morning."

She returned the salute, and there was an end of the visit.

And then it came about that upon returning to the house of old Mrs. Green, I said in the most innocent manner in the world, and in order to make all my acts and words in the place as consistent as possible, for in a small country town if you do not do your falsehood deftly you will very quickly be discovered—I said to that willing gossip——

"Why, Mrs. Green, I find you are a friend of Mrs. Blotchley of Stokeley!"

"E-es," she said in a startled manner, "Ise her fren', bless 'ee."

"And I'm gratified to hear it, for as her friend you are mine, Mrs. Green."

And here I took her hand.

No wonder after our interview was over that she went out in her best bonnet, though it was only Wednesday. I felt sure it was quite out of honour to Mrs. Blotchley and her friend, who had claimed her friendship, and the history of which she was taking out to tea with her.

Of the interview with Mrs. Green I must say a few words, and in her own expressions.

"Well, Mrs. Green, have you heard of any unusual cart having been seen in Tram on the day before Mr. Petleigh was found dead?"

"Lardy, lardy, e-es," said Mrs. Green; "but bless 'ee, whaty want to know for?"

"I want to know if it was Mrs. Blotchley's brother's cart, that's all."

"Des say it war. I've been arl over toon speering aboot that waggoon. I went to Jones the baker, and Willmott, who married Mary Sprinters—which wur on'y fair; the grocer, an' him knowed nought about it; an' the bootcher in froont street, and bootcher in back street; and Mrs. Macnab, her as mangles, and no noos, bless 'ee, not even of Tom Hatt the milkman, but, lardy, lardy! when Ise tarking for a fren' o' my fren's Ise tark till never. 'Twur draper told I arl aboot the ca-art."

"What?" I said, I am afraid too eagerly for a detective who knew her business thoroughly.

"Why, draper White wur oot for stroll loike, an' looking about past turning to the harl (hall), and then he sees coming aloong a cart him guessed wur coming to him's shop; but, bless 'ee, 'twarnt comin' to his shop at ARL!"

"Where was it going?"

"Why the cart turned right arf to harl, and that moost ha' been wher they cart went to; and, bless 'ee, that's arl."

Then Mrs. Green, talking like machinery to the very threshold, went, and I guess put on her new bonnet instanter, for she wore it before she went out, and when she brought in my chop and potatoes.

Meanwhile I was ruminating the news of the box, if I may be allowed the figure, and piecing it together.

It was pretty clear to me that a box had been taken to the hall, for the evidence of the girl Dinah and that which Mrs. Green brought together coincided in supporting a supposition to that effect.

The girl said a big box (which must have been large, seeing it took two men to carry it) had been brought to the hall in a large cart on the day previous to the finding of the body.

It was on that day the draper, presumably, had seen a large cart turn out of the main road towards Petleighcote.

Did that cart contain the box the girl Dinah referred to?

If so, had it anything to do with the death?

If so, where was it?

If hidden, who had hidden it?

These were the questions which flooded my mind, and which the reader will see were sufficiently important and equally embarrassing.

The first question to be decided was this,——

Had the big box anything to do with the matter?

I first wrote my letter to headquarters putting things in train to plant one of our people as serving woman at Petleighcote, and then I sallied out to visit Mr. White, the draper.

He was what men would call a "jolly" man, one who took a good deal of gin-and-water, and the world as it came. He was a man to be hail met with the world, but to find it rather a thirsty sphere, and diligently to spirit-and-water that portion of it contained within his own suit of clothes.

He was a man to be rushed at and tilted over with confidence.

"Mr. White," said I, "I want an umbrella, and also a few words with you."

"Both, mum," said he; and I would have bet, for though a woman I am fond of a little wager now and then,—yes, I would have bet that before his fourth sentence he would drop the "mum."

"Here are what we have in umberellers, mum."

"Thank you. Do you remember meeting a strange cart on the day, a Monday, before Mr. Petleigh—Petleigh—what was his name?—was found dead outside the hall? I mention that horrid circumstance to recall the day to your mind."

"Well, yes, I do, mum. I've been hearing of this from Mary Green."

"What kind of cart was it?"

"Well, mum, it was a wholesale fancy article manufacturer's van."

"Ah, such as travel from drapers to drapers with samples, and sometimes things for sale."

"Yes; that were it."

[He dropped the mum at the fourth sentence.]

"A very large van, in which a man could almost stand upright?"

"A man, my dear!" He was just the kind of man to "my dear" a customer, though by so doing he should offend her for life. "Half-a-dozen of 'em, and filled with boxes of samples, in each of which you might stow away a long—what's the matter, eh? What do you want to find out about the van for, eh?"

"Oh, pray don't ask me, White," said I, knowing the way to such a man's confidence is the road of familiarity. "Don't, don't inquire what. But tell me, how many men were there on the van?"

"Two, my dear."

"What were they like?"

"Well, I didn't notice."

"Did you know them, or either of them?"

"Ha! *I* see," said White; and I am afraid I allowed him to infer that he had surprised a personal secret. "No; I knew neither of 'em, if *I* know it. Strangers to me. Of course *I* thought they were coming with samples to *my* shop; for I am the only one in the village. But they DIDN'T."

"No; they went to the hall, I believe?"

"Yes. *I* thought they had turned wrong, and I hollered after them, but it was no use. I wish I could describe them for you, my dear, but I can't. However, I believe they looked like gentlemen. Do you think *that* description will answer?"

"Did they afterwards come into the town, Mr. White?"

"Well, my dear, they did, and baited at the White Horse, and then it was I was so surprised they did not call. And then—in fact, my dear, if you would like to know all——"

"Oh, don't keep anything from me, White."

"Well, then, my dear, I went over as they were making ready to go, and I asked them if they were looking for a party of the name of White? And then——"

"Oh, pray, pray continue."

"Well, then, one of them told me to go to a place, to repeat which before you, my dear, I would not; from which it seemed to me that they did *not* want a person of the name of White."

"And, Mr. White, did they quit Tram by the same road as that by which they entered it?"

"No, they did *not*; they drove out at the other end of the town."

"Is it possible? And tell me, Mr. White, if they wanted to get back to the hall, could they have done so by any other means than by returning through the village?"

"No, not without—let me see, me dear—not without going thirty miles round by the heath, which," added Mr. White, "and no offence, my dear, I am bound to submit they were not men who seemed likely to take any unnecessary trouble; or why—why in fact did they tell me to go to where in fact they told me to go to?"

"True; but they may have returned, and you not know anything about it, Mr. White."

"There you have it, my dear. You go to the gateman, and as it's only three weeks since, you take his word, for Tom remembers every vehicle that passes his 'pike—there are not many of them, for business is woundily slack. Tom remembers 'em all for a good quarter."

"Oh, thank you, Mr. White. I think I'll take the green umbrella. How much is it?"

"Now look here, my dear," the draper continued, leaning over the counter, and dropping his voice; "I know the umbereller is the excuse, and though business *is* bad, I'm sure I don't want you to take it; unless, indeed, you want it," he added, the commercial spirit struggling with the spirit proper of the man.

"Thank you," said I. "I'll take the green—you will kindly let me call upon you again?"

"With pleasure, my dear; as often as you like; the more the better. And look here, you need not buy any more umberellers or things. You just drop in in a friendly way, you know. *I* see it all."

"Thank you," I said; and making an escape I was rather desirous of obtaining, I left the shop, which, I regret to say, I was ungrateful enough not to revisit. But, on the other hand, I met White several and at most inconvenient times.

Tom the 'pikeman's memory for vehicles was, I found, a proverb in the place; and when I went to him, he remembered the vehicle almost before I could explain its appearance to him.

As for the question—"Did the van return?"—he treated the "Are you sure of it?" with which I met his shake of the head—he treated my doubt with such violent decision that I became confident he was right.

Unless he was bribed to secrecy?

But the doubt was ridiculous; for could all the town be bribed to secrecy?

I determined that doubt at once. And indeed it is the great gain and drawback to our profession that we have to doubt so imperiously. To believe every man to be honest till he is found out to be a thief, is a motto most self-respecting men cling to; but we detectives on the contrary would not gain salt to our bread, much less the bread itself, if we adopted such a belief. We have to believe every man a rogue till, after turning all sorts of evidence inside out, we can only discover that he is an honest man. And even then I am much afraid we are not quite sure of him.

I am aware this is a very dismal way of looking upon society, but the more thinking amongst my profession console themselves with the knowledge that our system is a necessary one (under the present condition of society), and that therefore in conforming to the melancholy rules of this system, however repulsive we may feel them, we are really doing good to our brother men.

Returning home after I left the 'pikeman—from whom I ascertained that the van had passed his gate at half-past eight in the evening, I turned over all my new information in my mind.

The girl Dinah must have seen the box in the hall as she went to bed. Say this was half-past nine; at half-past five, at the time the alarm was given, the box was gone.

This made eight hours.

Now, the van had left Tram at half-past eight, and to get round to the hall it had to go thirty miles by night over a heath. (By a reference to my almanack I found there was no moon that night.) Now, take it that a heavy van travelling by night-time could not go more than five miles an hour, and allowing the horse an hour's rest when half the journey was accomplished, we find that seven hours would be required to accomplish that distance.

This would bring the earliest time at which the van could arrive at the hall at half-past three, assuming no impediments to arise.

There would be then just two hours before the body was discovered, and actually as the dawn was breaking.

Such a venture was preposterous even in the contemplation.

In the first place, why should the box be left if it were to be called for again?

In the second, why should it be called for so early in the morning as half-past three?

And yet at half-past five it had vanished, and Mrs. Quinion had said to the girl (I assumed the girl's evidence to be true) that the box had been taken away again.

From my investigation of these facts I inferred—firstly:

That the van which brought the box had not taken it away.

Secondly: That Mrs. Quinion, for some as yet unexplained purpose, had wished the girl to suppose the box had been removed.

Thirdly: That the box was still in the house.

Fourthly: That as Mrs. Quinion had stated the box was gone, while it was still on the premises, she had some purpose (surely important) in stating that it had been taken away.

It was late, but I wanted to complete my day's work as far as it lay in my power.

I had two things to do.

Firstly, to send the "fluff" which I had gathered from the clothes to a microscopic chemist; and secondly, to make some inquiry at the inn where the van-attendants had baited, and ascertain what they were.

Therefore I put the "fluff" in a tin box, and directed it to the gentleman who is good enough to control these kind of investigations for me, and going out I posted my communication. Then I made for the tavern, with the name of which Mrs. Green had readily furnished me, and asked for the landlady.

The interest she exhibited showed me in a moment that Mrs. Green's little remarks and Mr. White's frank observations had got round to that quarter.

And here let me break off for a moment to show how nicely people will gull themselves. I had plainly made no admission which personally identified me with the van, and yet people had already got up a very sentimental feeling in my favour in reference to that vehicle.

For this arrangement I was unfeignedly glad. It furnished a motive for my remaining in Tram, which was just what I wanted.

And furthermore, the tale I told Mrs. Quinion about my remaining in Tram because I had found a friend of my own friend, would, if it spread (which it did not, from which I inferred that Mrs. Quinion had no confidences with the Tram maiden at that hour with her, and that this latter did not habitually listen) do me no harm, as I might ostensibly be supposed to invent a fib which might cover my supposed tribulation. Here is a condensation of the conversation I had with the landlady.

"Ah! I know; I'm glad to see you. Pray sit down. Take that chair—it's the easiest. And how are you, my poor dear?"

"Not strong," I had to say.

"Ah! and well you may not be."

"I came to ask, did two persons, driving a van—a large black van, picked out with pale blue (this description I had got from the 'pikeman)—stop here on the day before Mr.——I've forgotten his name—the young squire's death?"

"Yes, my poor dear, an' a tall gentleman with auburn whiskers, and the other shorter, without whiskers."

"Dear me; did you notice anything peculiar in the tall gentleman?"

"Well, my poor dear, I noticed that every now and then his upper lip flitched a bit, like a dog's asleep will sometimes go."

Here I sighed.

"And the other?" I continued.

"Oh! all that seemed odd in him was that he broke out into bits of song, something like birds more nor English Christian singing; which the words, if words there were, I could not understand."

"Italian scraps," I thought; and immediately I associated this evidence of the man with the foreign mask.

If they were commercial travellers, one of them was certainly an unusual one, operatic accomplishments not being usually one of the tendencies of commercial men.

"Were they nice people?"

"Oh!" says the landlady, concessively and hurriedly; "they were every inch gentlemen; and I said to mine, said I—'they aint like most o' the commercial travellers that stop here'; and mine answers me back, 'No,' says he, 'for commercials prefers beers to sherries, and whiskies after dinner to both!'"

"Oh! did they only drink wine?"

"Nothing but sherry, my dear; and says they to mine—'Very good wine,'—those were their very words—'whatever you do, bring it dry'; and said mine—I saying his very words—'Gents, I will.'"

Some more conversation ensued, with which I need not trouble the reader, though I elicited several points which were of minor importance.

I was not permitted to leave the hotel without "partaking,"—I use the landlady's own verb—without partaking of a warmer and stronger comfort than is to be found in mere words.

And the last inference I drew, before satisfactorily I went to bed that night, was to the effect that the apparent commercial travellers were not commercial travellers, but men leading the lives of gentlemen.

And now as I have set out a dozen inferences which rest upon very good evidence, before I go to the history of the work of the following days, I must recapitulate these inferences—if I may use so pompous a word.

They are as follow:

1. That the key found on the body opened a receptacle containing treasure.

2. That the mask found on the body was of foreign manufacture.

3. That the handkerchief found on the body had very recently belonged to a young lady named Frederica, and to whom the deceased was probably deeply attached.

4. That the circumstances surrounding the deceased showed that he had been engaged in no poaching expedition, nor in any housebreaking attempt, notwithstanding the presence of the mask, because no house-breaking implements were found upon him.

5. [Omitted by the author. E.F.B.]

6. That the young lady was innocent of participation in whatever evil work the deceased may have been engaged upon. [This inference, however, was solely based upon the discovery of the embroidery braid round the button of the deceased's coat. This inference is the least supported by evidence of the whole dozen.]

7. That a big box had been taken to the hall on the day previous to that on which the deceased was found dead outside the hall.

8. That the box was not removed again in the van in which it had been brought to the house.

9. That whatever the box contained that something was heavy, as it took the two men to carry it into the house.

10. That Mrs. Quinion, for some so far unexplainable reason, had endeavoured to make the witness Dinah Yarton believe that the box had been removed; while, in fact, the box was still in the house.

11. That as Mrs. Quinion had stated the box was gone while it was still on the premises, she had some important motive for saying it had been taken away.

12. That the van-attendants, who were apparent commercial travellers, were not commercial travellers, and were in the habit of living the lives of gentlemen.

And what was the condensed inference of all these inferences?

Why—THAT THE FIRST PROBABLE MEANS BY WHICH THE SOLUTION OF THE MYSTERY WAS TO BE ARRIVED AT WAS THE FINDING OF THE BOX.

To hunt for this box it was necessary that I should obtain free admission to Petleighcote, and by the most extraordinary chance Mrs. Quinion had herself thrown the opportunity in my way by asking me to recommend her a town servant.

Of course, beyond any question, she had made this request with the idea of obtaining a servant who, being a stranger to the district, would have little or not any of that interest in the catastrophe of the young squire's death which all felt who, by belonging to the neighbourhood, had more or less known him.

I had now to wait two days before I could move in the matter—those two days being consumed in the arrival of the woman police officer who was to play the part of servant up at the hall, and in her being accepted and installed at that place.

On the morning of that second day the report came from my microscopic chemist.

He stated that the fluff forwarded him for inspection consisted of two different substances; one, fragments of feathers, the other, atoms of nap from some linen material, made of black and white stuff, and which, from its connexion with the atoms of feather, he should take to be the fluff of a bed-tick.

For a time this report convinced me that the clothes had been covered with this substance, in consequence of the deceased having lain down in his clothes to sleep at a very recent time before he was found dead.

And now came the time to consider the question—"What was my own impression regarding the conduct of the deceased immediately preceding the death?"

My impression was this—that he was about to commit some illegal action, but that he had met with his death before he could put his intention into execution.

This impression arose from the fact that the mask showed a secret intention, while the sound state of the clothes suggested that no struggle had preceded the bloody death—struggle, however brief, generally resulting in clothes more or less damaged, as any soldier who has been in action will tell you (and perhaps tell you wonderingly), to the effect that though he himself may have come out of the fight without a scratch, his clothes were one vast rip.

The question that chiefly referred to the body was, who placed it where it was found between three o'clock (the time when the rain ceased, before which hour the body could not have been deposited, since the clothes, where they did not touch the ground, were dry) and half-past five?

Had it been brought from a distance?

Had it been brought from a vicinity?

The argument against distance was this one, which bears in all cases of the removal of dead bodies—that if it is dangerous to move them a yard, it is a hundred times more dangerous to move them a hundred yards.

Granted the removal of young Petleigh's body, in a state which would at once excite suspicion, and it is clear that a great risk was run by those who carried that burden.

But was there any apparent advantage to compensate that risk?

No, there was not.

The only rational way of accounting for the deposition of the body where it was found, lay in the supposition that those who were mixed up with his death were just enough to carry the body to a spot where it would at once be recognised and cared for.

But against this argument it might be held, the risk was so great that the ordinary instinct of self-preservation natural to man would prevent such a risk being encountered. And this impression becomes all the deeper when it is remembered that the identification of the body could have been secured by the slipping of a piece of paper in the pocket bearing his address.

Then, when it is remembered that it must have been quite dawn at the time of the assumed conveyance, the improbability becomes the greater that the body was brought any great distance.

Then this probability became the greater, that the young man had died in the vicinity of the spot where he was found.

Then followed the question, how close?

And in considering this point, it must not be forgotten that if it were dangerous to bring the body to the hall, it would be equally dangerous to remove the body *from the hall*; *supposing* the murder (if murder it were) had been committed within the hall.

Could this be the case?

Beyond all question, the only people known to be at the hall on the night of the death were Mrs. Quinion and Dinah.

Now we have closed in the space within which the murder (as we will call it) had been done, as narrowly circumscribing the hall. Now was the place any other than the hall, and yet near it?

The only buildings near the hall, within a quarter of a mile, were the gardener's cottage, and the cottage of the keeper.

The keeper was ill at the time, and it was the gardener who had discovered the body. To consider the keeper as implicated in the affair, was quite out of the question; while as to the gardener, an old man, and older servant of the family (for he had entered the service of the family as a boy), it must be remembered that he was the discoverer of the dead body.

Now is it likely that if he was implicated in the affair that he would have identified himself with the discovery? Such a supposition is hardly holdable.

Very well; then, as the doctor at six A.M. declared death had taken place from six to eight hours; and as the body, from the dry state of the clothes, had *not* been exposed during the night's rain, which ceased at three, it was clear either that the murder had been committed within doors, or that the body had been sheltered for some hours after death beneath a roof of some kind.

Where was that roof?

Apart from the gardener's cottage and the keeper's, there was no building nearer than a quarter of a mile; and if therefore the body had been carried after three to where it was found, it was evident that those cognizant of the affair had carried it a furlong at or after dawn.

To suppose such an amount of moral courage in evil-doers was to suppose an improbability, against which a detective, man or woman, cannot too thoroughly be on his or her guard.

But what of the supposition that the body had been removed from the hall, and placed where it was found?

So far, all the external evidences of the case leant in favour of this theory.

But the theory was at total variance with the ordinary experience of life.

In the first place, what apparent motive could Mrs. Quinion have for taking the young heir's life? Not any apparently.

What motive had the girl?

She had not sufficient strength of mind to hold a fierce motive. I doubt if the poor creature could ever have imagined active evil.

I may here add I depended very much upon what that girl said, because it was consistent, was told under great distress of mind, and was in many particulars borne out by other evidence.

I left Dinah Yarton quite out of my list of suspects.

But in accepting her evidence I committed myself to the belief that no one had been at Petleighcote on the night of the catastrophe beyond the girl and the housekeeper.

Then how could I support the supposition that the young man had passed the night and met his death at the hall?

Very easily.

Because a weak-headed woman like Dinah did not know of the

presence of the heir at Petleighcote, it did not follow he could not be there—his presence being known only to the housekeeper.

But was there any need for such secrecy?

Yes.

I found out that fact before the town servant arrived.

Mrs. Quinion's express orders were not to allow the heir to remain at the hall while the family were in town.

Then here was a good reason why the housekeeper should maintain his presence a secret from a stupid blurting servant maid.

But I have said motive for murder on the part of the housekeeper could scarcely be present.

Then suppose the death was accidental (though certainly no circumstance of the catastrophe justified such a supposition), and suppose Mrs. Quinion the perpetratress, what was the object in exposing the body outside the house?

Such an action was most unwomanly, especially where an accident had happened.

I confess that at this point of the case (and up to the time when my confederate arrived) I was completely foiled. All the material evidence was in favour of the murder or manslaughter having been committed under the roof of Petleighcote Hall, while the mass of the evidence of probability opposed any such belief.

Up to this time I had in no way identified the death with the "big box," although I identified that box with the clearing up of the mystery. This identification was the result of an ordinary detective law.

The law in question is as follows:

In all cases which are being followed up by the profession, a lie is a suspicious act, whether it has relation or no relation, apparent or beyond question, with the matter in hand. As a lie it must be followed to its source, its meaning cleared up, and its value or want of value decided upon. The probability stands good always that a lie is part of a plot.

So as Mrs. Quinion had in all probability lied in reference to the removal of the box, it became necessary to find out all about it, and hence my first directions to Martha—as she was always called (she is now in Australia and doing well) at our office, and I doubt if her surname was known to any of us—hence my first instruction to Martha was to look about for a big box.

"What kind of box?"

"That I don't know," said I.

"Well there will be plenty of boxes in a big house—is it a new box?"

"I can't tell; but keep an eye upon boxes, and tell me if you find one that is more like a new one than the rest."

Martha nodded.

But by the date of our first interview after her induction at Petleighcote, and when Quinion sent her down upon a message to a tradesman, I had learnt from the polished Mr. White that boxes such as drapers' travellers travelled with were invariably painted black.

This information I gave her. Martha had not any for me in return—that is of any importance. I heard, what I had already inferred, that Quinion was a very calm, self-possessed woman, "whom it would take," said Martha, "one or two good collisions to drive off the rails."

"You mark my words," said Matty, "she'd face a judge as cool as she faces herself in a looking-glass, and that I can tell you she does face cool, for I've seen her do it twice."

Martha's opinion was, that the housekeeper was all right, and I am bound to say that I was unable to suppose that she was all wrong, for the suspicion against her was of the faintest character.

She visited me the day after Martha's arrival, thanked me coolly enough for what I had done, said she believed the young person would do, and respectfully asked me up to the hall.

Three days passed, and in that time I had heard nothing of value from my aide-de-camp, who used to put her written reports twice a day in a hollow tree upon which we had decided.

It was on the fourth day that I got a fresh clue to feel my way by.

Mrs. Lamb, the publican's wife, who had shown such a tender interest in my welfare on the night when I had inquired as to the appearance of the two persons who baited the van-horses at their stables on the night of the death—Mrs. Lamb in reluctantly letting me leave her (she was a most sentimental woman, who I much fear increased her tendencies by a too ready patronage of her own liquors) intreated me to return, "like a poor dear as I was"—for I had said I should remain at Tram—"and come and take a nice cup of tea" with her.

In all probability I never should have taken that nice cup of tea, had I not learnt from my Mrs. Green that young Petleigh had been in the habit of smoking and drinking at Lamb's house.

That information decided me.

I "dropped in" at Mrs. Lamb's that same afternoon, and I am bound to say it was a nice cup of tea.

During that refreshment I brought the conversation round to young Petleigh, and thus I heard much of him told to his credit from a publican's point of view, but which did not say much for him from a social standing-place.

"And this, my poor dear, is the very book he would sit in this very parlour and read from for an hour together, and—coming!"

For here there was a tap-tap on the metal counter with a couple of halfpence.

Not thinking much of the book, for it was a volume of a very ordinary publication, which has been in vogue for many years amongst cheap literature devotees, I let it fall open, rather than opened it, and I have no doubt that I did not once cast my eyes upon the page during the spirting of the beer-engine and the return of Mrs. Lamb.

"Bless me!" said she, in a moved voice, for she was one of the most sentimental persons ever I encountered. "Now that's very odd!—poor dear."

"What's odd, Mrs. Lamb?" I asked.

"Why if you haven't got the book open at his fav'rite tale!"

"Whose, Mrs. Lamb?"

"Why that poor dear young Graham Petleigh."

I need not say I became interested directly.

"Oh! did he read this tale?"

"Often; and very odd it is, my own dear, as you should be about to read it too; though true it is that that there book do always open at that same place, which I take to be his reading it so often the place is worn and—coming!"

Here Mrs. Lamb shot away once more, while I, it need not be said, looked upon the pages before me.

And if I say that, before Mrs. Lamb had done smacking at the beer-engine, and ending her long gossip with the customer, I had got the case by the throat—I suppose I should astonish most of my readers.

And yet there is nothing extraordinary in the matter.

Examine most of the great detected cases on record, and you will find a little accident has generally been the clue to success.

So with great discoveries. One of the greatest improvements in the grinding of flour, and by which the patentee has made many thousands of pounds, was discovered by seeing a miller blow some flour out of a nook; and all the world knows that the cause which led the great Newton to discover the great laws of the universe was the fall of an apple.

So it frequently happens in these days of numberless newspapers that a chance view of a man will identify him with the description of a murderer.

Chance!

In the history of crime and its detection chance plays the chief character.

Why, as I am writing a newspaper is near me, in which there is the report of a trial for attempt to murder, where the woman who was shot at was only saved by the intervention of a piece of a ploughshare, which was under her shawl, and which she had *stolen* only a few minutes before the bullet struck the iron!

Why, compared with that instance of chance, what was mine when, by reading a tale which had been pointed out to me as one frequently read by the dead young man, I discovered the mystery which was puzzling me?

The tale told of how, in the north of England, a pedlar had left a pack at a house, and how a boy saw the top of it rise up and down; how they supposed a man must be *in* it who intended to rob the house; and how the boy shot at the pack, and killed a man.*

I say, before Mrs. Lamb returned to her "poor dear" I had the mystery by heart.

The young man had been attracted by the tale, remembered it, and put it in form for some purpose. What?

* This story was probably "The Long Pack" by James Hogg. E.F.B.

In a moment I recalled the mania of the squire for plate, and, remembering how niggardly he was to the boy, it flashed upon me that the youth had in all probability formed a plan for robbing his father of a portion of his plate.

It stood true that it was understood the plate went up to town with the family. But was this so?

Now see how well the probabilities of the case would tell in with such a theory.

The youth was venturesome and daring, as his poaching affrays proved.

He was kept poor.

He knew his father to possess plate.

He was not allowed to be at Petleighcote when the father was away.

He had read a tale which coincided with my theory.

A large box had been left by strangers at the hall.

The young squire's body had been found under such circumstances, that the most probable way of accounting for its presence where it was found was by supposing that it had been removed there from the hall itself.

Such a plot explained the presence of the mask.

Finally, there was the key, a key opening, beyond all question, an important receptacle—a supposition very clear, seeing the character of the key.

Indeed, by this key might be traced the belief of treasure in the house.

Could this treasure really exist?

Before Mrs. Lamb had said "Good night, dear," to a female customer who had come for a pint of small beer and a gallon of more strongly brewed scandal, I had come to the conclusion that plate might be in the house.

For miserly men are notoriously suspicious and greedy. What if there were some of the family plate which was not required at the town house then at Petleighcote, and which the squire, relying for its security upon the habitual report of his taking all his plate to town, had not lodged at the county bank, because of that natural suspiciousness which might lead him to believe more in his own strong room than a banker's?

Accept this supposition, and the youth's motive was evident.

Accept young Petleigh's presence in the house under these circumstances, and then we have to account for the death.

Here, of course, I was still at fault.

If Mrs. Quinion and the girl only were in the house, and the girl was innocent, then the housekeeper alone was guilty.

Guilty—what of? Murder or manslaughter?

Had the tale young Petleigh used to read been carried out to the end?

Had he been killed without any knowledge of who he was?

That I should have discovered the real state of the case without Mrs. Lamb's aid I have little doubt, for even that very evening, after leaving Mrs. Lamb, and promising to bear in mind the entreaty to "come again, you *dear* dear," my confederate brought me a piece of information which must have put me on the track.

It appeared that morning Mrs. Quinion had received a letter which much discomposed her. She went out directly after breakfast, came down to the village, and returned in about an hour. My confederate had picked the pocket (for, alas! we police officers have sometimes to turn thieves—for the good of society of course) of the housekeeper while she slept that afternoon, and while the new maid was supposed to be putting Mrs. Quinion's stockings in wearable order, and she had made a mental copy of that communication. It was from a Joseph Spencer, and ran as follows:

> "My dear Margaret,—For God's sake look all over the place for key 13. There's such a lot of 'em I never missed it; and if the governor finds it out I'm as good as ruined. It must be somewhere about. I can't tell how it ever come orf the ring. So no more at present. It's post time. With dear love, from your own
>
> "JOSEPH SPENCER"

Key 13!

Why, it was the same number as that on the key found on the dead man.

A letter was despatched that night to town, directing the police to find out who Joseph Spencer was, and giving the address heading the letter—a printed one.

Mrs. Green then came into operation.

No, she could not tell who lived at the address I mentioned. Thank the blessed stars *she* knowed nought o' Lunnon. What! Where had Mrs. Quinion been that morning? Why, to Joe Higgins's. What for? Why, to look at the young squire's clothes and things. What did she want with them? Why, she "actially" wanted to take " 'em arl oop" to the Hall. No, Joe Higgins wouldn't.

Of course I now surmised that Joseph Spencer was the butler.

And my information from town showed I was right.

Now, certain as to my preliminaries, I knew that my work lay within the walls of the Hall.

But how was I to reach that place?

Alas! the tricks of detective police officers are infinite. I am afraid many a kindly-disposed advertisement hides the hoof of detection. At all events I know mine did.

It appeared in the second column of the *Times*, and here is an exact copy of it. By the way, I had received the *Times* daily, as do most detectives, during the time I had been in Tram:

"Wanted, to hear of Margaret Quinion, or her heirs-at-law. She was known to have left the South of England (that she was a Southerner I had learnt by her accent) about the year 1830 to become housekeeper to a married foster-sister, who settled in a midland county (this information, and especially the date, Mrs. Green had to answer for). Address,——" Here followed that of my own solicitors, who had their instructions to keep the lady hanging about the office several days, and until they heard from me.

I am very much afraid I intended that should the case appear as black against her as I feared it would, she was to be arrested at the offices of the gentlemen to whom she was to apply in order to hear of something to her advantage. And furthermore, I am quite sure that many an unfortunate has been arrested who has been enticed to an office under the promise of something to his or her special benefit.

For of such misrepresentations is this deplorable world.

When this advertisement came out, the least acute reader is already aware of the use I made of it.

I pointed out the news to Mrs. Green, and I have no doubt she digited the intelligence to every soul she met, or rather overtook, in the course of the day. And indeed before evening (when I was honoured with a visit from Mrs. Quinion herself), it was stated with absolute assurance that Mrs. Quinion had come in for a good twenty-two thousand pounds, and a house in Dyot Street, Bloomsbury Square, Lunnun.

It was odd, and yet natural, that Mrs. Quinion should seek me out. I was the only stranger with whom she was possibly acquainted in the district, and my strangeness to the neighbourhood she had already, from her point of view, turned to account. Therefore (human nature considered) I did not wonder that she tried to turn me to account again. My space is getting contracted, but as the following is the last conversation I had with Mrs. Quinion, I may perhaps be pardoned for here quoting it. Of course I abridge it very considerably. After the usual salutations, and an assurance that Martha suited very fairly, she said,——

"I have a favour to ask you."

"Indeed; pray what is it?"

"I have received some news which necessarily takes me from home."

"I think," said I, smiling, "I know what that news is," and I related how I had myself seen the advertisement in the morning.

I am afraid I adopted this course the more readily to attract her confidence.

I succeeded.

"Indeed," said she, "then since you have identified yourself with that news, I can the more readily ask you the favour I am about to——"

"And what is that?"

"I am desirous of going up to town—to London—for a few hours, to see what this affair of the advertisement means, but I hesitate to leave Martha alone in the house. You have started, and perhaps you feel offended that I should ask a stranger such a favour, but the fact is, I do not care to let anyone belonging to the neighbourhood know that I have left the Hall—it will be for only twenty-four hours. The news might reach Mr. Petleigh's ears, and I desire that he should hear nothing about it. You see the position in which I am placed. If, my dear lady, you can oblige me I shall be most grateful; and, as you are staying here, it seemed—to—me——"

Here she trailed off into silence.

The cunning creature! How well she hid her real motive—the desire to keep those who knew of the catastrophe out of the Hall, because she feared their curiosity.

Started! Yes, indeed I had started. At best I had expected that I should have to divulge who I was to the person whom she would leave in the place did the advertisement take, and here by the act of what she thought was her forethought, she was actually placing herself at my mercy, while I still remained screened in all my actions referring to her. For I need not say that had I had to declare who I was, and had I failed, all further slow-trapping in this affair would have been at an end—the "game" would have taken the alarm, and there would have been an end to the business.

To curtail here needless particulars, that same evening at nine I was installed in the housekeeper's parlour, and she had set out for the first station past Tram, to which she was going to walk across the fields in order to avoid all suspicion.

She had not got a hundred yards away from the house, before I had turned up my cuffs, and I and Martha (a couple of detectives) were hard at work, trying to find that box.

Her keys we soon found, in a work-basket, and lightly covered with a handkerchief.

Now, this mode of hiding should have given me a clue.

But it did not.

For three hours—from nine till midnight, we hunted for that box, and unsuccessfully.

In every room that, from the absence of certain dusty evidences, we knew must have been recently opened—in every passage, cellar, corridor, and hall we hunted.

No box.

I am afraid that we even looked in places where it could not have gone—such as under beds.

But we found it at last, and then the turret-clock had gone twelve about a quarter of an hour.

It was in her bedroom; and what is more, it formed her dressing-table.

And I have no doubt I should have missed it had it not been that she had been imperfect in her concealment.

Apparently she comprehended the value of what I may call "audacity hiding"—that is, such concealment that an ordinary person searching would never dream of looking for the object where it was to be found.

For instance, the safest hiding-place in a drawing-room for a bank note, would be the bottom of a loosely-filled card-basket. Nobody would dream of looking for it in such a place.

The great enigma-novelist, Edgar Poe, illustrates this style of concealment where he makes the holder of a letter place it in a card-rack over the mantelpiece, when he knows his house will be ransacked, and every inch of it gone over to find the document.

Mrs. Quinion was evidently acquainted with this mode of concealment.

Indeed, I believe I should not have found the box had it not been that she had overdone her unconcealed-concealment. For she had used a bright pink slip with a white flounce over it to complete the appearance of a dressing-table, having set the box up on one side.

And therefore the table attracted my notice each time I passed and saw it. As it was Martha, in passing between me and the box, swept the drapery away with her petticoats, and showed a *black corner.*

The next moment the box was discovered.

I have no doubt that being a strong-minded woman she could not endure to have the box out of her sight while waiting for an opportunity to get rid of it.

It was now evident that my explanation of the case, to the effect that young Petleigh had been imitating the action of the tale, was correct.

The box was quite large enough to contain a man lying with his legs somewhat up; there was room to turn in the box; and, finally, there were about two dozen holes round the box, about the size of a crown piece, and which were hidden by the coarse black canvas with which the box was covered.

Furthermore, the box was closeable from within by means of a bolt, and therefore openable from within by the same means.

Furthermore, if any further evidence were wanting, there was a pillow at the bottom of the box (obviously for the head to rest on), and from a hole the feathers had escaped over the bottom of the box, which was lined with black and white striped linen bed-tick, this material being cut away from the holes.

I was now at no loss to comprehend the fluff upon the unhappy young man's coat.

And, finally, there was the most damnifying evidence of all.

For in the black canvas over one of the holes *there was a jagged cut.*

"Lie down, Martha," said I, "in the box, with your head at this end."

"Why, whatever——"

"Tut—tut,—girl; do as I tell you."

She did; and using the stick of a parasol which lay on the dressing-table, I found that by passing it through the hole its end reached the officer in exactly the region by a wound in which young Mr. Petleigh had been killed.

Of course the case was now clear.

After the young woman, Dinah, had gone to bed, the housekeeper must have had her doubts about the chest, and have inspected it.

Beyond all question, the young man knew the hour at which the housekeeper retired, and was waiting perhaps for eleven o'clock to strike by the old turret-clock before he ventured out—to commit what?

It appeared to me clear, bearing in mind the butler's letter, to rob the plate-chest No. 13, which I inferred had been left behind, a fact of which the young fellow might naturally be aware.

The plan doubtless was to secure the plate without any alarm, to let himself out of the Hall by some mode long-since well-known to him, and then to meet his confederates, and share with them the plunder, leaving the chest to tell the tale of the robbery, and to exculpate the housekeeper.

It struck me as a well-executed scheme, and one far beyond the ordinary run of robbery plots.

What had caused that scheme to fail?

I could readily comprehend that a strong-minded woman like Quinion would rely rather upon her own than any other assistance.

I could comprehend her discovery; perhaps a low-muttered blasphemy on the part of the young man; or maybe she may have heard his breathing.

Then, following out her action, I could readily suppose that once aware of the danger near her she would prepare to meet it.

I could follow her, silent and self-possessed, in the hall, asking herself what she should do.

I could mark her coming to the conclusion that there must be holes in the box through which the evil-doer could breathe, and I apprehended readily enough that she had little need to persuade herself that she had a right to kill one who might be there to kill her.

Then in my mind's eye I could follow her seeking the weapon, and feeling all about the box for a hole.

She finds it.

She fixes the point for a thrust.

A movement—and the manslaughter is committed.

That the unhappy wretch had time to open the box is certain, and doubtless it was at that moment the fierce woman, still clutching the shaft of the arrow, or barb—call it what you will—leant back, and so withdrew the shaft from the rankling iron.

Did the youth recognise her? Had he tried to do so?

From the peacefulness of the face, as described at the inquest, I imagined that he had, after naturally unbolting the lid, fallen back, and in a few moments died.

Then must have followed her awful discovery, succeeded by her equally awful determination to hide the fault of her master's, and perhaps of her own sister's son.

And so it came to pass that she dragged the youth's dead body out into the cold morning atmosphere, as the bleak dawn was filling the air, and the birds were fretfully awaking.

No doubt, had a sharp detective been at once employed, she would not have escaped detection.

As it was she had so far avoided discovery.

And I could easily comprehend that a powerfully-brained woman like herself would feel no compunction and little grief for what she had done—no compunction, because the act was an accident; little grief, because she must have felt she had saved the youth from a life of misery—for a son who at twenty robs a father, however bad, is rarely at forty, if he lives so long, an honest man.

But though I had made this discovery I could do nothing so far against the housekeeper, whom of course it was my duty to arrest, if I could convince myself she had committed manslaughter. I was not to be ruled by any feeling of screening the family—the motive indirectly which had actuated Quinion, for, strong-minded as she was, it appeared to me that she would not have hesitated to admit the commission of the act which she had completed had the burglar, as I may call the young man, been an ordinary felon, and unknown to her.

No, the box had no identification with the death, because it exhibited no unanswerable signs of its connexion with that catastrophe.

So far, how was it identifiable (beyond my own circumstantial evidence, known only to myself) with the murder?

The only particle of evidence was that given by the girl, who could or could not swear to the box having been brought on the previous day, and to the housekeeper saying that it had been taken away again—a suspicious circumstance certainly, but one which, without corroborative evidence, was of little or indeed no value.

As to the jagged cut in the air-hole, in the absence of all bloodstain it was not mentionable.

Corroborative evidence I must have, and that corroborative evidence would best take the shape of the discovery of the shaft of the weapon which had caused death, or a weapon of similar character.

This, the box being found, was now my work.

"Is there any armoury in the house, Martha?"

"No; but there's lots of arms in the library."

We had not searched in the library for the box, because I had taken Martha's assurance that no boxes were there.

When we reached the place, I remarked immediately—"What a damp place."

As I said so I observed that there were windows on each side of the room, and that the end of the chamber was circular.

"Well it may be," said Martha, "for there's water all round it—a kind of fountain-pond, with gold fish in it. The library," continued Martha, who was more sharp than educated, "butts out of the house."

Between each couple of book-cases there was fixed a handsome stand of arms, very picturesque and taking to the eyes.

There were modern arms, antique armour, and foreign arms of many kinds; but I saw no arrows, though in the eagerness of my search I had the chandelier, which still held some old yellow wax-candles, lighted up.

No arrow.

But my guardian angel, if there be such good creatures, held tight on to my shoulder that night, and by a strange chance, yet not a tithe so wonderful as that accident by which the woman was saved from a bullet by a piece of just stolen iron, the origin of the weapon used by Quinion came to light.

We had been searching amongst the stands of arms for some minutes, when I had occasion suddenly to cry——

"Hu-u-sh! what are you about?"

For my confederate had knocked off its hook a large drum, which I had noticed very coquettishly finished off a group of flags, and cymbals, and pikes.

"I'm very sorry," she said, as I ran to pick up the still reverberating drum with that caution which, even when useless, generally stands by the detective, when——

There, sticking through the drum, and hooked by its barbs, was the point of such a weapon—the exact counterpart—as had been used to kill young Petleigh.

Had a ghost, were there such a thing, appeared I had not been more astounded.

The drum was ripped open in a moment, and there came to light an iron arrow with a wooden shaft about eighteen inches long, this shaft being gaily covered with bits of tinsel and coloured paper.

[I may here at once state, what I ultimately found out—for in spite of our danger I kept hold of my prize and brought it out of battle with me—that this barb was one of such as are used by picadors in Spanish bull-fights for exciting the bull. The barbs cause the darts to stick in the flesh and skin. The cause of the decoration of the haft can now readily be comprehended. Beyond all doubt the arrow used by Quinion and the one found by me were a couple placed as curiosities amongst the other arms. The remaining one the determined housekeeper had used as suiting best her purpose, the other (which I found) had doubtless at some past time been used by an amateur picador, perhaps the poor dead youth himself, with the drum for an imaginary bull, and within it the dart had remained till it was to reappear as a witness against the guilty and yet guiltless housekeeper.

I had barely grasped my prize when Martha said—"What a smell of burning!"

"Good God!" I cried, "we have set the house on fire!"

The house was on fire, but we were not to blame.

We ran to the door.

We were locked in!

What brought her back I never learnt, for I never saw or heard of her again. I guess that the motion of the train quickened her thought (it does mine), that she suspected—that she got out at the station some distance from Tram, and that she took a post-chaise back to Petleighcote.

All this, however, is conjecture.

But if not she, who locked us in? We could not have done it ourselves.

We were locked in, and I attribute the act to her—though how she entered the house I never learnt.

The house was on fire, and we were surrounded by water.

This tale is the story of the "Unknown Weapon," and therefore I cannot logically here go into any full explanation of our escape. Suffice it to our honour as detectives to say, that we did not lose our presence of mind, and that by the aid of the library tables, chairs, big books, &c., we made a point of support on one side the narrow pond for the library ladder to rest on, while the other end reached shallow water.

Having made known the history of the "Unknown Weapon," my tale is done; but my reader might fancy my work incomplete did I not add a few more words.

I have no doubt that Quinion returning, her quick mind in but a few moments came to the conclusion that the only way to save her master's honour was the burning of the box by the incendiarism of the Hall.

The Petleighs were an old family, I learnt, with almost Spanish notions of family honour.

Effectually did she complete her work.

I acknowledge she conquered me. She might have burnt the same person to a cinder into the bargain; and, upon my word, I think she would have grieved little had she achieved that purpose.

For my part in the matter—I carried it no further.

At the inquiry, I appeared as the lady who had taken care of the house while Mrs. Quinion went to look after her good fortune; and I have no doubt her disappearance was unendingly connected with my advertisement in the *Times*.

I need not say that had I found Quinion I would have done my best to make her tremble.

I have only one more fact to relate—and it is an important one. It is this——

The squire had the ruins carefully examined, and two thousand ounces of gold and silver plate, melted into shapelessness of course, were taken out of the rubbish.

From this fact it is pretty evident that the key No. 13, found upon the poor, unhappy, ill-bred, and neglected boy, was the "Open Sesamè" to the treasure which was afterwards taken from the ruins—perhaps worth £4000, gold and silver together.

Beyond question he had stolen the key from the butler, gone into a plot with his confederates—and the whole had resulted in his death and the conflagration of Petleighcote, one of the oldest, most picturesque, and it must be admitted dampest seats in the midland counties.

And, indeed, I may add that I found out who was the "tall gentleman with the auburn whiskers and the twitching of the face"; I discovered who was the short gentleman with no whiskers at all; and finally I have seen the young lady (she was very beautiful) called Frederica, and for whose innocent sake I have no doubt the unhappy young man acted as he did.

As for me, I carried the case no further.

I had no desire to do so—had I had, I doubt if I possessed any further evidence than would have sufficed to bring me into ridicule.

I left the case where it stood.

C. L. PIRKIS

(1841–1910)

The astute and courageous Loveday Brooke seems to have been the first female detective created by a female author. For this and other reasons, Catherine Louisa Pirkis's character stands out among the characters in this anthology. "Emerging at a historical moment when understandings of women, criminality, and law enforcement were rapidly changing in Britain," writes scholar Elizabeth Carolyn Miller, "Pirkis's stories offer an interpretation of these intersecting cultural shifts that is surprisingly different from that of her contemporaries."

Throughout the series, Brooke is a respected professional investigator. Unlike Mrs. Paschal, she doesn't act subservient in order to curry favor with her superior; frequently Brooke verbally spars with her boss, Ebenezer Dyer. She is socially mobile, moving constantly between train and cab, princess and housemaid, village and city. Occasionally she must walk alone at night unaccompanied by a man, which instantly places her in the suspect category of a likely prostitute. Unlike, say, Hugh Weir about Madelyn Mack, Pirkis doesn't claim that her heroine is blessed with ultrafeminine charms and intuition to offset her allegedly masculine job. In fact, she is pointedly described as "neither handsome nor ugly." Perhaps most significant of all, she doesn't wind up married in the last story.

Pirkis's was the era of criminologist Cesare Lombroso, who argued that criminal inclinations resulted from hereditary atavism that was literally visible in features such as large chins and fleshy lips; and of sexologist Havelock Ellis, who insisted that female criminals exhibit a degenerate abundance of body hair and other masculine traits, as well as "pathological" sexual organs. (Elizabeth Carolyn Miller explores these background issues in detail in her article cited in Further Reading.) Pirkis resists both trendy and traditional notions of appearance; her characters defy Victorian categories such as the beautiful damsel and the roughneck immigrant.

She also demonstrates a more sympathetic and clearheaded view of class relations than many of her contemporaries. Pirkis doesn't merely disguise Brooke as a servant; she knows that doing so almost affords Brooke a cloak of invisibility as she spies for clues behind the scenes. Pirkis was fully aware of the irony that a society in which well-connected women were not permitted to work was built upon the unseen backroom labor of less privileged women. Again and again, when theft or violence disturbs the Victorian home, suspicion turns toward the servants—especially if they also embody another suspect group: foreigners. Each year the Victorian legal system prosecuted a great many offenders in the separate category of "larceny by servants."

C. L. Pirkis published several romantic melodramas, including a lead story in *All the Year Round*, the weekly periodical that Charles Dickens launched after he bailed out of *Household Words* because of conflicts with its publisher. By the time that Pirkis appeared in its pages, it was published by Dickens's eldest son, Charles Jr. Pirkis published her first book in 1877 and wrote thirteen more, including *In a World of His Own* and *Disappeared from Her Home*. The Loveday Brooke stories were gathered into her last book. She retired from fiction writing in 1894. Three years earlier, she had cofounded—with her husband, retired naval officer Fred E. Pirkis—the organization to which she devoted much of her time until her death in 1910: the National Canine Defence League. This hugely influential animal-welfare group is still active and in 2003 renamed itself the Dogs Trust. The NCDL campaigned against vivisection, abuse, muzzling, and later even the use of dogs such as Laika in early space exploration. Not surprisingly, in Loveday Brooke stories animal abuse is a clue to other kinds of brutality.

It's interesting to note that Brooke's quietly subversive adventures appeared in the *Ludgate Monthly*. Founded only two years earlier, *Ludgate* called itself a "family magazine," which meant that proper young women could read it without blushing; magazine publishers were beginning to target market to female readers. Pirkis published six Brooke stories between February and July 1893 in consecutive issues of the *Ludgate Monthly*. A couple of months after the sixth Brooke story, the magazine joined the new trend of emphasizing visuals and renamed itself *The Ludgate Illustrated Magazine*. It was under this new title that it published a seventh Brooke outing in March 1894. At the same time, Hutchinson & Company published all seven stories in a collection entitled *The Experiences of Loveday Brooke, Lady Detective*, with ink-and-wash drawings by the unaccountably popular illustrator Bernard Higham. The first story was "The Black Bag Left on a Door-Step," from which comes the opening description of Brooke below. "Drawn Daggers" was the fifth published adventure and appeared fifth in the collection. Unlike many Victorian detective series, the Brooke stories were not a novel-like cycle that built toward a unifying denouement. Each stood alone, like the cases of Sherlock Holmes.

DRAWN DAGGERS

Loveday Brooke, at this period of her career, was a little over thirty years of age, and could be best described in a series of negations.

She was not tall, she was not short; she was not dark, she was not fair; she was neither handsome nor ugly. Her features were altogether nondescript; her one noticeable trait was a habit she had, when absorbed in thought, of dropping her eyelids over her eyes till only a line of eyeball showed, and she appeared to be looking out at the world through a slit, instead of through a window.

Her dress was invariably black, and was almost Quaker-like in its neat primness.

Some five or six years previously, by a jerk of Fortune's wheel, Loveday had been thrown upon the world penniless and all but friendless. Marketable accomplishments she had found she had none, so she had forthwith defied convention, and had chosen for herself a career that had cut her off sharply from her former associates and her position in society. For five or six years she drudged away patiently in the lower walks of her profession; then chance, or, to speak more precisely, an intricate criminal case, threw her in the way of the experienced head of the flourishing detective agency in Lynch Court. He quickly enough found out the stuff she was made of, and threw her in the way of better-class work—work, indeed, that brought increase of pay and of reputation alike to him and to Loveday.

Ebenezer Dyer was not, as a rule, given to enthusiasm; but he would at times wax eloquent over Miss Brooke's qualifications for the profession she had chosen.

"Too much of a lady, do you say?" he would say to anyone who chanced to call in question those qualifications. "I don't care twopence-halfpenny whether she is or is not a lady. I only know she is the most sensible and practical woman I ever met. In the first place, she has the faculty—so rare among women—of carrying out orders to the very letter: in the second place, she has a clear, shrewd brain, unhampered by any hard-and-fast theories; thirdly, and most important item of all, she has so much common sense that it amounts to genius—positively to genius, sir."

"I admit that the dagger business is something of a puzzle to me, but as for the lost necklace—well, I should have thought a child would have understood that," said Mr. Dyer irritably. "When a young lady loses a valuable article of jewellery and wishes to hush the matter up, the explanation is obvious."

"Sometimes," answered Miss Brooke calmly, "the explanation that is obvious is the one to be rejected, not accepted."

Off and on these two had been, so to speak, "jangling" a good deal that morning. Perhaps the fact was in part to be attributed to the biting east wind which had set Loveday's eyes watering with the gritty dust, as she had made her way to Lynch Court, and which was, at the present moment, sending the smoke, in aggravating gusts, down the chimney into Mr. Dyer's face. Thus it was, however. On the various topics that had chanced to come up for discussion that morning between Mr. Dyer and his colleague, they had each taken up, as if by design, diametrically opposite points of view.

His temper altogether gave way now.

"If," he said, bringing his hand down with emphasis on his writing table, "you lay it down as a principle that the obvious is to be rejected in favour of the abstruse, you'll soon find yourself launched in the predicament of having to prove that two apples added to two other apples do not make four. But there, if you don't choose to see things from my point of view, that is no reason why you should lose your temper!"

"Mr. Hawke wishes to see you, sir," said a clerk, at that moment entering the room.

It was a fortunate diversion. Whatever might be the differences of opinion in which these two might indulge in private, they were careful never to parade those differences before their clients.

Mr. Dyer's irritability vanished in a moment.

"Show the gentleman in," he said to the clerk. Then he turned to Loveday. "This is the Rev. Anthony Hawke, the gentleman at whose house I told you that Miss Monroe is staying temporarily. He is a clergyman of the Church of England, but gave up his living some twenty years ago when he married a wealthy lady. Miss Monroe has been sent over to his guardianship from Pekin by her father, Sir George Monroe, in order to get her out of the way of a troublesome and undesirable suitor."

The last sentence was added in a low and hurried tone, for Mr. Hawke was at that moment entering the room.

He was a man close upon sixty years of age, white-haired, clean shaven, with a full, round face, to which a small nose imparted a somewhat infantine expression. His manner of greeting was urbane but slightly flurried and nervous. He gave Loveday the impression of being an easy-going, happy-tempered man who, for the moment, was unusually disturbed and perplexed.

He glanced uneasily at Loveday. Mr. Dyer hastened to explain that this was the lady by whose aid he hoped to get to the bottom of the matter now under consideration.

"In that case there can be no objection to my showing you this," said Mr. Hawke; "it came by post this morning. You see my enemy still pursues me."

As he spoke he took from his pocket a big, square envelope, from which he drew a large-sized sheet of paper.

On this sheet of paper were roughly drawn, in ink, two daggers, about six inches in length, with remarkably pointed blades.

Mr. Dyer looked at the sketch with interest.

"We will compare this drawing and its envelope with those you previously received," he said, opening a drawer of his writing-table and taking thence a precisely similar envelope. On the sheet of paper, however, that this envelope enclosed, there was drawn one dagger only.

He placed both envelopes and their enclosures side by side, and in silence compared them. Then, without a word, he handed them to Miss Brooke, who, taking a glass from her pocket, subjected them to a similar careful and minute scrutiny.

Both envelopes were of precisely the same make, and were each addressed to Mr. Hawke's London address in a round, schoolboyish, copy-book sort of hand—the hand so easy to write and so difficult to being home to any writer on account of its want of individuality. Each envelope likewise bore a Cork and a London postmark.

The sheet of paper, however, that the first envelope enclosed bore the sketch of one dagger only.

Loveday laid down her glass.

"The envelopes," she said, "have, undoubtedly, been addressed by the same person, but these last two daggers have not been drawn by the hand that drew the first. Dagger number one was, evidently, drawn by a timid, uncertain and inartistic hand—see how the lines wave and how they have been patched here and there. The person who drew the other daggers, I should say, could do better work; the outline, though rugged, is bold and free. I should like to take these sketches home with me and compare them again at my leisure."

"Ah, I felt sure what your opinion would be!" said Mr. Dyer complacently.

Mr. Hawke seemed much disturbed.

"Good gracious!" he ejaculated; "you don't mean to say I have two enemies pursuing me in this fashion! What does it mean? Can it be—is it possible, do you think, that these things have been sent to me by the members of some Secret Society in Ireland—under error, of course—mistaking me for someone else? They can't be meant for me; I have never, in my whole life, been mixed up with any political agitation of any sort."

Mr. Dyer shook his head. "Members of secret societies generally make pretty sure of their ground before they send out missives of this kind," he said. "I have never heard of such an error being made. I think, too, we mustn't build any theories on the Irish postmark; the letters may have been posted in Cork for the whole and sole purpose of drawing off attention from some other quarter."

"Will you mind telling me a little about the loss of the necklace?" here said Loveday, bringing the conversation suddenly round from the daggers to the diamonds.

"I think," interposed Mr. Dyers, turning towards her, "that the episode of the drawn daggers—drawn in a double sense—should be treated entirely on its own merits, considered as a thing apart from the loss of the necklace. I am inclined to believe that when we have gone a little further into the matter we shall find that each circumstance belongs to a different group of facts. After all, it is possible that these daggers may have been sent by way of a joke—a rather foolish one, I admit—by some harum-scarum fellow bent on causing a sensation."

Mr. Hawke's face brightened.

"Ah! now, do you think so—really think so?" he ejaculated. "It would lift such a load from my mind if you could bring the thing home, in this way, to some practical joker. There are a lot of such fellows knocking about the world. Why, now I come to think of it, my nephew, Jack, who is a good deal with us just now, and is not quite so steady a fellow as I should like him to be, must have a good many such scamps among his acquaintances."

"A good many such scamps among his acquaintances," echoed Loveday; "that certainly gives plausibility to Mr. Dyer's supposition. At the same time, I think we are bound to look at the other side of the case, and admit the possibility of these daggers being sent in right-down sober earnest by persons concerned in the robbery, with the intention of intimidating you and preventing full investigation of the matter. If this be so, it will not signify which thread we take up and follow. If we find the sender of the daggers we are safe to come upon the thief; or, if we follow up and find the thief, the sender of the daggers will not be far off."

Mr. Hawke's face fell once more.

"It's an uncomfortable position to be in," he said slowly. "I suppose, whoever they are, they will do the regulation thing, and next time will send an instalment of three daggers, in which case I may consider myself a doomed man. It did not occur to me before, but I remember now that I did not receive the first dagger until after I had spoken very strongly to Mrs. Hawke, before the servants, about my wish to set the police to work. I told her I felt bound, in honour to Sir George, to do so, as the necklace had been lost under my roof."

"Did Mrs. Hawke object to your calling in the aid of the police?" asked Loveday.

"Yes, most strongly. She entirely supported Miss Monroe in her wish to take no steps in the matter. Indeed, I should not have come round as I did last night to Mr. Dyer, if my wife had not been suddenly summoned from home by the serious illness of her sister. At least," he corrected himself with a little attempt at self-assertion, "my coming to him might have been a little delayed. I hope you understand, Mr. Dyer; I do not mean to imply that I am not master in my own house."

"Oh, quite so, quite so," responded Mr. Dyer. "Did Mrs. Hawke or Miss Monroe give any reasons for not wishing you to move in the matter?"

"All told, I should think they gave about a hundred reasons—I can't remember them all. For one thing, Miss Monroe said it might necessitate her appearing in the police courts, a thing she would not consent to do; and she certainly did not consider the necklace was worth the fuss I was making over it. And that necklace, sir, has been valued at over nine hundred pounds, and has come down to the young lady from her mother."

"And Mrs. Hawke?"

"Mrs. Hawke supported Miss Monroe in her views in her presence. But privately to me afterwards, she gave other reasons for not wishing the police called in. Girls, she said, were always careless with their jewellery, she might have lost the necklace in Pekin, and never have brought it to England at all."

"Quite so," said Mr. Dyer. "I think I understood you to say that no one had seen the necklace since Miss Monroe's arrival in England. Also, I believe it was she who first discovered it to be missing?"

"Yes. Sir George, when he wrote apprising me of his daughter's visit, added a postscript to his letter, saying that his daughter was bringing her necklace with her and that he would feel greatly obliged if I would have it deposited with as little delay as possible at my bankers', where it could be easily got at if required. I spoke to Miss Monroe about doing this two or three times, but she did not seem at all inclined to comply with her father's wishes. Then my wife took the matter in hand—Mrs. Hawke, I must tell you, has a very firm, resolute manner—she told Miss Monroe plainly that she would not have the responsibility of those diamonds in the house, and insisted that there and then they should be sent off to the bankers. Upon this Miss Monroe went up to her room, and presently returned, saying that her necklace had disappeared. She herself, she said, had placed it in her jewel-case and the jewel-case in her wardrobe, when her boxes were unpacked. The jewel-case was in the wardrobe right enough, and no other article of jewellery appeared to have been disturbed, but the little padded niche in which the necklace had been deposited was empty. My wife and her maid went upstairs immediately, and searched every corner of the room, but, I'm sorry to say, without any result."

"Miss Monroe, I suppose, has her own maid?"

"No, she has not. The maid—an elderly native woman—who left Pekin with her, suffered so terribly from sea-sickness that, when they reached Malta, Miss Monroe allowed her to land and remain there in charge of an agent of the P. and O. Company till an outward bound packet could take her back to China. It seems the poor woman thought she was going to die, and was in a terrible state of mind because she hadn't brought her coffin with her. I dare say you know the terror these Chinese have of being buried in foreign soil. After her departure, Miss Monroe engaged one of the steerage passengers to act as her maid for the remainder of the voyage."

"Did Miss Monroe make the long journey from Pekin accompanied only by this native woman?"

"No; friends escorted her to Hong Kong—by far the roughest part of the journey. From Hong Kong she came on in *The Colombo*, accompanied only by her maid. I wrote and told her father I would meet her at the docks in London; the young lady, however, preferred landing at Plymouth, and telegraphed to me from there that she was coming on by rail to Waterloo, where, if I liked, I might meet her."

"She seems to be a young lady of independent habits. Was she brought up and educated in China?"

"Yes; by a succession of French and American governesses. After her mother's death, when she was little more than a baby, Sir George could not make up his mind to part with her, as she was his only child."

"I suppose you and Sir George Monroe are old friends?"

"Yes; he and I were great chums before he went out to China—now about twenty years ago—and it was only natural, when he wished to get his daughter out of the way of young Danvers's impertinent attentions, that he should ask me to take charge of her till he could claim his retiring pension and set up his tent in England."

"What was the chief objection to Mr. Danvers's attentions?"

"Well, he is only a boy of one-and-twenty, and has no money into the bargain. He has been sent out to Pekin by his father to study the language, in order to qualify for a billet in the customs, and it may be a dozen years before he is in a position to keep a wife. Now, Miss Monroe is an heiress—will come into her mother's large fortune when she is of age—and Sir George, naturally, would like her to make a good match."

"I suppose Miss Monroe came to England very reluctantly?"

"I imagine so. No doubt it was a great wrench for her to leave her home and friends in that sudden fashion and come to us, who are, one and all, utter strangers to her. She is very quiet, very shy and reserved. She goes nowhere, sees no one. When some old China friends of her father's called to see her the other day, she immediately found she had a headache, and went to bed. I think, on the whole, she gets on better with my nephew than with anyone else."

"Will you kindly tell me of how many persons your household consists at the present moment?"

"At the present moment we are one more than usual, for my nephew, Jack, is home with his regiment from India, and is staying with us. As a rule, my household consists of my wife and myself, butler, cook, housemaid and my wife's maid, who just now is doing double duty as Miss Monroe's maid also."

Mr. Dyer looked at his watch.

"I have an important engagement in ten minutes' time," he said, "so I must leave you and Miss Brooke to arrange details as to how and when she is to begin her work inside your house, for, of course, in a case of this sort we must, in the first instance at any rate, concentrate attention within your four walls."

"The less delay the better," said Loveday. "I should like to attack the mystery at once—this afternoon."

Mr. Hawke thought for a moment.

"According to present arrangements," he said, with a little hesitation, "Mrs. Hawke will return next Friday, that is the day after to-morrow, so I can only ask you to remain in the house till the morning of that day. I'm sure you will understand that there might be some—some little awkwardness in—"

"Oh, quite so," interrupted Loveday. "I don't see at present that there will be any necessity for me to sleep in the house at all. How would it be for me to assume the part of a lady house decorator in the employment of a West-end firm, and sent by them to survey your house and advise upon its re-decoration? All I should have to do, would be to walk about your rooms with my head on one side, and a pencil and note-book in my hand. I should interfere with no one, your family life would go on as usual, and I could make my work as short or as long as necessity might dictate."

Mr. Hawke had no objection to offer to this. He had, however, a request to make as he rose to depart, and he made it a little nervously.

"If," he said, "by any chance there should come a telegram from Mrs. Hawke, saying she will return by an earlier train, I suppose—I hope, that is, you will make some excuse, and—and not get me into hot water, I mean."

To this, Loveday answered a little evasively that she trusted no such telegram would be forthcoming, but that, in any case, he might rely upon her discretion.

Four o'clock was striking from a neighbouring church clock as Loveday lifted the old-fashioned brass knocker of Mr. Hawke's house in Tavistock Square. An elderly butler admitted her and showed her into the drawing-room on the first floor. A single glance round showed Loveday that if her rôle had been real instead of assumed, she would have found plenty of scope for her talents. Although the house was in all respects comfortably furnished, it bore unmistakably the impress of those early Victorian days when aesthetic surroundings were not deemed a necessity of existence; an impress which people past middle age, and growing increasingly indifferent to the accessories of life, are frequently careless to remove.

"Young life here is evidently an excrescence, not part of the home; a troop of daughters turned into this room would speedily set going a different condition of things," thought Loveday, taking stock of the faded white and gold wall paper, the chairs covered with lilies and roses in cross-stitch, and the knick-knacks of a past generation that were scattered about on tables and mantelpiece.

A yellow damask curtain, half-festooned, divided the back drawing-room from the front in which she was seated. From the other side of this curtain there came to her the sound of voices—those of a man and a girl.

"Cut the cards again, please," said the man's voice. "Thank you. There you are again—the queen of hearts, surrounded with diamonds, and turning her back on a knave. Miss Monroe, you can't do better than make that fortune come true. Turn your back on the man who let you go without a word and—"

"Hush!" interrupted the girl with a little laugh: "I heard the next room door open—I'm sure someone came in."

The girl's laugh seemed to Loveday utterly destitute of that echo of heart-ache that in the circumstances might have been expected.

At this moment Mr. Hawke entered the room, and almost simultaneously the two young people came from the other side of the yellow curtain and crossed towards the door.

Loveday took a survey of them as they passed.

The young man—evidently "my nephew, Jack"—was a good-looking young fellow, with dark eyes and hair. The girl was small, slight and fair. She was perceptibly less at home with Jack's uncle than she was with Jack, for her manner changed and grew formal and reserved as she came face to face with him.

"We're going downstairs to have a game of billiards," said Jack, addressing Mr. Hawke, and throwing a look of curiosity at Loveday.

"Jack," said the old gentleman, "what would you say if I told you I was going to have the house re-decorated from top to bottom, and that this lady had come to advise on the matter."

This was the nearest (and most Anglicé) approach to a fabrication that Mr. Hawke would allow to pass his lips.

"Well," answered Jack promptly, "I should say, 'not before its time.' That would cover a good deal."

Then the two young people departed in company.

Loveday went straight to her work.

"I'll begin my surveying at the top of the house, and at once, if you please," she said. "Will you kindly tell one of your maids to show me through the bed-rooms? If it is possible, let that maid be the one who waits on Miss Monroe and Mrs. Hawke."

The maid who responded to Mr. Hawke's summons was in perfect harmony with the general appearance of the house. In addition, however, to being elderly and faded, she was also remarkably sour-visaged, and carried herself as if she thought that Mr. Hawke had taken a great liberty in thus commanding her attendance.

In dignified silence she showed Loveday over the topmost story, where the servants' bed-rooms were situated, and with a somewhat supercilious expression of countenance, watched her making various entries in her note-book.

In dignified silence, also, she led the way down to the second floor, where were the principal bed-rooms of the house.

"This is Miss Monroe's room," she said, as she threw back a door of one of these rooms, and then shut her lips with a snap, as if they were never going to open again.

The room that Loveday entered was, like the rest of the house, furnished in the style that prevailed in the early Victorian period. The bedstead was elaborately curtained with pink lined upholstery; the toilet-table was befrilled with muslin and tarlatan out of all likeness to a table. The one point, however, that chiefly attracted Loveday's attention was the extreme neatness that prevailed throughout the apartment—a neatness, however, that was carried out with so strict an eye to comfort and convenience that it seemed to proclaim the hand of a first-class maid. Everything in the room was, so to speak, squared to the quarter of an inch, and yet everything that a lady could require in dressing lay ready to hand. The dressing-gown lying on the back of a chair had footstool and slippers beside it. A chair stood in front of the toilet table, and on a small Japanese table to the right of the chair were placed hair-pin box, comb and brush, and hand mirror.

"This room will want money spent upon it," said Loveday, letting her eyes roam critically in all directions. "Nothing but Moorish wood-work will take off the squareness of those corners. But what a maid Miss Monroe must have. I never before saw a room so orderly and, at the same time, so comfortable."

This was so direct an appeal to conversation that the sour-visaged maid felt compelled to open her lips.

"I wait on Miss Monroe, for the present," she said snappishly; "but, to speak the truth, she scarcely requires a maid. I never before in my life had dealings with such a young lady."

"She does so much for herself, you mean—declines much assistance."

"She's like no one else I ever had to do with." (This was said even more snappishly than before.) "She not only won't be helped in dressing, but she arranges her room every day before leaving it, even to placing the chair in front of the looking glass."

"And to opening the lid of the hair-pin box, so that she may have the pins ready to her hand," added Loveday, for a moment bending over the Japanese table, with its toilet accessories.

Another five minutes were all that Loveday accorded to the inspection of this room. Then, a little to the surprise of the dignified maid, she announced her intention of completing her survey of the bed-rooms some other time, and dismissed her at the drawing-room door, to tell Mr. Hawke that she wished to see him before leaving.

Mr. Hawke, looking much disturbed and with a telegram in his hand, quickly made his appearance.

"From my wife, to say she'll be back to-night. She'll be at Waterloo in about half an hour from now," he said, holding up the brown envelope. "Now, Miss Brooke, what are we to do? I told you how much Mrs. Hawke objected to the investigation of this matter, and she is very—well—firm when she once says a thing, and—and—"

"Set your mind at rest," interrupted Loveday; "I have done all I wished to do within your walls, and the remainder of my investigation can be carried on just as well at Lynch Court or at my own private rooms."

"Done all you wished to do!" echoed Mr. Hawke in amazement; "why, you've not been an hour in the house, and do you mean to tell me you've found out anything about the necklace or the daggers?"

"Don't ask me any questions just yet; I want you to answer one or two instead. Now, can you tell me anything about any letters

Miss Monroe may have written or received since she has been in your house?"

"Yes, certainly, Sir George wrote to me very strongly about her correspondence, and begged me to keep a sharp eye on it, so as to nip in the bud any attempt to communicate with Danvers. So far, however, she does not appear to have made any such attempt. She is frankness itself over her correspondence. Every letter that has come addressed to her, she has shown either to me or to my wife, and they have one and all been letters from old friends of her father's, wishing to make her acquaintance now that she is in England. With regard to letter-writing, I am sorry to say she has a marked and most peculiar objection to it. Every one of the letters she has received, my wife tells, me, remain unanswered still. She has never once been seen, since she came to the house, with a pen in her hand. And if she wrote on the sly, I don't know how she would get her letters posted—she never goes outside the door by herself, and she would have no opportunity of giving them to any of the servants to post except Mrs. Hawke's maid, and she is beyond suspicion in such a matter. She has been well cautioned, and, in addition, is not the sort of person who would assist a young lady in carrying on a clandestine correspondence."

"I should imagine not! I suppose Miss Monroe has been present at the breakfast table each time that you have received your daggers through the post—you told me, I think, that they had come by the first post in the morning?"

"Yes; Miss Monroe is very punctual at meals, and has been present each time. Naturally, when I received such unpleasant missives, I made some sort of exclamation and then handed the thing round the table for inspection, and Miss Monroe was very much concerned to know who my secret enemy could be."

"No doubt. Now, Mr. Hawke, I have a very special request to make to you, and I hope you will be most exact in carrying it out."

"You may rely upon my doing so to the very letter."

"Thank you. If, then, you should receive by post to-morrow morning one of those big envelopes you already know the look of, and find that it contains a sketch of three, not two, drawn daggers—"

"Good gracious! what makes you think such a thing likely?" exclaimed Mr. Hawke, greatly disturbed. "Why am I to be persecuted in this way? Am I to take it for granted that I am a doomed man?"

He began to pace the room in a state of great excitement.

"I don't think I would if I were you," answered Loveday calmly. "Pray let me finish. I want you to open the big envelope that may come to you by post to-morrow morning just as you have opened the others—in full view of your family at the breakfast-table—and to hand round the sketch it may contain for inspection to your wife, your nephew and to Miss Monroe. Now, will you promise me to do this?"

"Oh, certainly; I should most likely have done so without any promising. But—but—I'm sure you'll understand that I feel myself to be in a peculiarly uncomfortable position, and I shall feel so very much obliged to you if you'll tell me—that is if you'll enter a little more fully into an explanation."

Loveday looked at her watch. "I should think Mrs. Hawke would be just at this moment arriving at Waterloo; I'm sure you'll be glad to see the last of me. Please come to me at my rooms in Gower Street to-morrow at twelve—here is my card. I shall then be able to enter into fuller explanations I hope. Good-bye."

The old gentleman showed her politely downstairs, and, as he shook hands with her at the front door, again asked, in a most emphatic manner, if she did not consider him to be placed in a "peculiarly unpleasant position."

Those last words at parting were to be the first with which he greeted her on the following morning when he presented himself at her rooms in Gower Street. They were, however, repeated in considerably more agitated a manner.

"Was there ever a man in a more miserable position!" he exclaimed, as he took the chair that Loveday indicated. "I not only received the three daggers for which you prepared me, but I got an additional worry, for which I was totally unprepared. This morning, immediately after breakfast, Miss Monroe walked out of the house all by herself, and no one knows where she has gone. And the girl has never before been outside the door alone. It seems the servants saw her go out, but did not think it necessary to tell either me or Mrs. Hawke, feeling sure we must have been aware of the fact."

"So Mrs. Hawke has returned," said Loveday. "Well, I suppose you will be greatly surprised if I inform you that the young lady, who has so unceremoniously left your house, is at the present moment to be found at the Charing Cross Hotel, where she has engaged a private room in her real name of Miss Mary O'Grady."

"Eh! What! Private room! Real name O'Grady! I'm all bewildered!"

"It is a little bewildering; let me explain. The young lady whom you received into your house as the daughter of your old friend, was in reality the person engaged by Miss Monroe to fulfill the duties of her maid on board ship, after her native attendant had been landed at Malta. Her real name, as I have told you, is Mary O'Grady, and she has proved herself a valuable coadjutor to Miss Monroe in assisting her to carry out a programme, which she must have arranged with her lover, Mr. Danvers, before she left Pekin."

"Eh! what!" again ejaculated Mr. Hawke; "how do you know all this? Tell me the whole story."

"I will tell you the whole story first, and then explain to you how I came to know it. From what has followed, it seems to me that Miss Monroe must have arranged with Mr. Danvers that he was to leave Pekin within ten days of her so doing, travel by the route by which she came, and land at Plymouth, where he was to receive a note from her, apprising him of her whereabouts. So soon as she was on board ship, Miss Monroe appears to have set her wits to work with great energy; every obstacle to the carrying-out of her programme she appears to have met and conquered. Step number one was to get rid of her native maid, who, perhaps, might have been faithful to her master's interests and have proved troublesome. I have no doubt the poor woman suffered terribly from sea-sickness, as it was her first voyage, and I have equally no doubt that Miss Monroe worked on her fears, and persuaded her to land at Malta, and return to China by the next packet. Step number two was to find a suitable person, who for a consideration, would be willing to play the part of the Pekin heiress among the heiress's friends in England, while the young lady herself arranged her private affairs to her own liking. That person was quickly found among the steerage passengers of the *Colombo* in Miss Mary O'Grady, who had come on board with her mother at Ceylon, and who, from the glimpse I had of her, must, I should conjecture, have been absent many years from the land of her birth. You know how cleverly this young lady has played her part in your house—how, without attracting attention to the matter, she has shunned the society of her father's old Chinese friends, who might be likely to involve her in embarrassing conversations; how she has avoided the use of pen and ink lest—"

"Yes, yes," interrupted Mr. Hawke; "but, my dear Miss Brooke, wouldn't it be as well for you and me to go at once to the Charing Cross Hotel, and get all the information we can out of her respecting Miss Monroe and her movements—she may be bolting, you know?"

"I do not think she will. She is waiting there patiently for an answer to a telegram she dispatched more than two hours ago to her mother, Mrs. O'Grady, at 14, Woburn Place, Cork."

"Dear me! dear me! How is it possible for you to know all this."

"Oh, that last little fact was simply a matter of astuteness on the part of the man whom I have deputed to watch the young lady's movements to-day. Other details, I assure you, in this somewhat intricate case, have been infinitely more difficult to get at. I think I have to thank those 'drawn daggers,' that caused you so much consternation, for having, in the first instance, put me on the right track."

"Ah—h," said Mr. Hawke, drawing a long breath; "now we come to the daggers! I feel sure you are going to set my mind at rest on that score."

"I hope so. Would it surprise you very much to be told that it was I who sent to you those three daggers this morning?"

"You! Is it possible?"

"Yes, they were sent by me, and for a reason that I will presently explain to you. But let me begin at the beginning. Those roughly-drawn sketches, that to you suggested terrifying ideas of blood-shedding and violence, to my mind were open to a more peaceful and commonplace explanation. They appeared to me to suggest the herald's office rather than the armoury; the cross fitchée of the knight's shield rather than the poniard with which the members of secret societies are supposed to render their recalcitrant brethren familiar. Now, if you will look at these sketches again, you will see what I mean."

Here Loveday produced from her writing-table the missives which had so greatly disturbed Mr. Hawke's peace of mind. "To begin with, the blade of the dagger of common life is, as a rule, at least two-thirds of the weapon in length; in this sketch, what you would call the blade, does not exceed the hilt in length. Secondly, please note the absence of guard for the hand. Thirdly, let me draw your attention to the squareness of what you considered the hilt of the weapon, and what, to my mind, suggested the upper portion of a crusader's cross. No hand could grip such a hilt as the one outlined here. After your departure yesterday, I drove to the British Museum, and there consulted a certain valuable work on heraldry, which has more than once done me good service. There I found my surmise substantiated in a surprising manner. Among the illustrations of the various crosses borne on armorial shields, I found one that had been taken by Henri d'Anvers from his own armorial bearings, for his crest when he joined the Crusaders under Edward I., and which has since been handed down as the crest of the Danvers family. This was an important item of information to me. Here was someone in Cork sending to your house, on two several occasions, the crest of the Danvers family; with what object it would be difficult to say, unless it were in some sort a communication to someone in your house. With my mind full of this idea, I left the Museum and drove next to the office of the P. and O. Company, and requested to have given me the list of the passengers who arrived by the *Colombo*. I found this list to be a remarkably small one; I suppose people, if possible, avoid crossing the Bay of Biscay during the Equinoxes. The only passengers who landed at Plymouth besides Miss Monroe, I found, were a certain Mrs. and Miss O'Grady, steerage passengers who had gone on board at Ceylon on their way home from Australia. Their name, together with their landing at Plymouth, suggested the possibility that Cork might be their destination. After this I asked to see the list of the passengers who arrived by the packet following the *Colombo*, telling the clerk who attended to me that I was on the look-out for the arrival of a friend. In that second list of arrivals I quickly found my friend—William Wentworth Danvers by name."

"No! The effrontery! How dared he! In his own name, too!"

"Well, you see, a plausible pretext for leaving Pekin could easily be invented by him—the death of a relative, the illness of a father or mother. And Sir George, though he might dislike the idea of the young man going to England so soon after his daughter's departure, and may, perhaps, write to you by the next mail on the matter, was utterly powerless to prevent his so doing. This young man, like Miss Monroe and the O'Gradys, also landed at Plymouth. I had only arrived so far in my investigation when I went to your house yesterday afternoon. By chance, as I waited a few minutes in your drawing-room, another important item of information was acquired. A fragment of conversation between your nephew and the supposed Miss Monroe fell upon my ear, and one word spoken by the young lady convinced me of her nationality. That one word was the monosyllable 'Hush.' "

"No! You surprise me!"

"Have you never noted the difference between the 'hush' of an Englishman and that of an Irishman? The former begins his 'hush' with a distinct aspirate, the latter with as distinct a W. That W is a mark of his nationality which he never loses. The unmitigated 'whist' may lapse into a 'whish' when he is transplanted to another soil, and the 'whish' may in course of time pass into a 'whush,' but to the distinct aspirate of the English 'hush,' he never attains. Now Miss O'Grady's was as pronounced a 'whush' as it was possible for the lips of a Hibernian to utter.' "

"And from that you concluded that Mary O'Grady was playing the part of Miss Monroe in my house?"

"Not immediately. My suspicions were excited, certainly; and when I went up to her room, in company with Mrs. Hawke's maid, those suspicions were confirmed. The orderliness of that room was something remarkable. Now, there is the orderliness of a lady in the arrangement of her room, and the orderliness of a maid, and the two things, believe me, are widely different. A lady, who has no maid, and who has the gift of orderliness, will put things away when done with, and so leave her room a picture of neatness. I don't think, however, it would for a moment occur to her to pull things so as to be conveniently ready for her to use the next time she dresses in that room. This would be what a maid, accustomed to arrange a room for her mistress's use, would do mechanically. Miss Monroe's room was the neatness of a maid—not of a lady, and I was assured by Mrs. Hawke's maid that it was a neatness accomplished by her own hands. As I stood there, looking at that room, the whole conspiracy—if I may so call it—little by little pieced itself together, and became plain to me. Possibilities quickly grew into probabilities, and these probabilities once admitted, brought other suppositions in their train. Now, supposing that Miss Monroe and Mary O'Grady had agreed to change places, the Pekin heiress, for the time being, occupying Mary O'Grady's place in the humble home at Cork and vice versa, what means of communicating with each other had they arranged? How was Mary O'Grady to know when she might lay aside her assumed rôle and go back to her mother's house. There was no denying the necessity for such communication; the difficulties in its way must have been equally obvious to the two girls. Now, I think we must admit that we must credit these young women with having hit upon a very clever way of meeting those difficulties. An anonymous and startling missive sent to you would be bound to be mentioned in the house, and in this way a code of signals might be set up between them that could not direct suspicion to them. In this connection, the Danvers crest, which it is possible that they mistook for a dagger, suggested itself naturally, for no doubt Miss Monroe had many impressions of it on her lover's letters. As I thought over these things, it occurred to me that possibly dagger (or cross) number one was sent to notify the safe arrival of Miss Monroe and Mrs. O'Grady at Cork. The two daggers or crosses you subsequently received were sent on the day of Mr. Danvers's arrival at Plymouth, and were, I should say, sketched by his hand. Now, was it not within the bounds of likelihood that Miss Monroe's marriage to this young man, and the consequent release of Mary O'Grady from the onerous part she was playing, might be notified to her by the sending of three such crosses or daggers to you. The idea no sooner occurred to me than I determined to act upon it, forestall the sending of this latest communication, and watch the result. Accordingly, after I left your house yesterday, I had a sketch made of three daggers of crosses exactly similar to those you had already received, and had it posted to you so that you would get it by the first post. I told off one of our staff at Lynch Court to watch your house, and gave him special directions to follow and report on Miss O'Grady's movements throughout the day. The results I anticipated quickly came to pass. About half-past nine this morning the man sent a telegram to me from your house to the Charing Cross Hotel, and furthermore had ascertained that she had since despatched a telegram, which (possibly by following the hotel servant who carried it to the telegraph office), he had overheard was addressed to Mrs. O'Grady, at Woburn Place, Cork. Since I received this information an altogether remarkable cross-firing of telegrams has been going backwards and forwards along the wires to Cork."

"A cross-firing of telegrams! I do not understand."

"In this way. So soon as I knew Mrs. O'Grady's address I telegraphed to her, in her daughter's name, desiring her to address her reply to 1154 Gower Street, not to Charing Cross Hotel. About three-quarters of an hour afterwards I received in reply this telegram, which I am sure you will read with interest.

Here Loveday handed a telegram—one of several that lay on her writing-table—to Mr. Hawke.

He opened it and read aloud as follows:

"Am puzzled. Why such hurry? Wedding took place this morning. You will receive signal as agreed to-morrow. Better return to Tavistock Square for the night."

"The wedding took place this morning," repeated Mr. Hawke blankly. "My poor old friend! It will break his heart."

"Now that the thing is done past recall we must hope he will make the best of it," said Loveday. "In reply to this telegram," she went on, "I sent another, asking as to the movements of the bride and bridegroom, and got in reply this":

Here she read aloud as follows:

"They will be at Plymouth to-morrow night; at Charing Cross Hotel and next day, as agreed."

"So, Mr. Hawke," she added, "if you wish to see your old friend's daughter and tell her what you think of the part she has played, all you will have to do will be to watch the arrival of the Plymouth trains."

"Miss O'Grady has called to see a lady and gentleman," said a maid at that moment entering.

"Miss O'Grady!" repeated Mr. Hawke in astonishment.

"Ah, yes, I telegraphed to her, just before you came in, to come here to meet a lady and gentlemen, and she, no doubt thinking that she would find here the newly-married pair, has, you see, lost no time in complying with my request. Show the lady in."

"It's all so intricate—so bewildering," said Mr. Hawke, as he lay back in his chair. "I can scarcely get it all into my head."

His bewilderment, however, was nothing compared with that of Miss O'Grady, when she entered the room and found herself face to face with her late guardian, instead of the radiant bride and bridegroom whom she had expected to meet.

She stood silent in the middle of the room, looking the picture of astonishment and distress.

Mr. Hawke also seemed a little at a loss for words, so Loveday took the initiative.

"Please sit down," she said, placing a chair for the girl. "Mr. Hawke and I have sent to you in order to ask you a few questions. Before doing so, however, let me tell you that the whole of your conspiracy with Miss Monroe has been brought to light, and the best thing you can do, if you want your share in it treated leniently, will be to answer our questions as fully and truthfully as possible."

The girl burst into tears. "It was all Miss Monroe's fault from beginning to end," she sobbed. "Mother didn't want to do it—I didn't want to—to go into a gentleman's house and pretend to be what I was not. And we didn't want her hundred pounds—"

Here sobs checked her speech.

"Oh," said Loveday contemptuously, "so you were to have a hundred pounds for your share in this fraud, were you?"

"We didn't want to take it," said the girl, between hysterical bursts of tears; "but Miss Monroe said if we didn't help her someone else would, and so I agreed to—"

"I think," interrupted Loveday, "that you can tell us very little that we do not already know about what you agreed to do. What we want you to tell us is what has been done with Miss Monroe's diamond necklace—who has possession of it now?"

The girl's sobs and tears redoubled. "I've had nothing to do with the necklace—it has never been in my possession," she sobbed. "Miss Monroe gave it to Mr. Danvers two or three months before she left Pekin, and he sent it on to some people he knew in Hong Kong, diamond merchants, who lent him money on it. Decastro, Miss Monroe said, was the name of these people."

"Decastro, diamond merchant, Hong Kong. I should think that would be sufficient address," said Loveday, entering it in a ledger; "and I suppose Mr. Danvers retained part of that money for his own use and travelling expenses, and handed the remainder to Miss Monroe to enable her to bribe such creatures as you and your mother, to practice a fraud that ought to land both of you in jail."

The girl grew deadly white. "Oh, don't do that—don't send us to prison!" she implored, clasping her hands together. "We haven't touched a penny of Miss Monroe's money yet, and we don't want to touch a penny, if you'll only let us off! Oh, pray, pray, pray be merciful!"

Loveday looked at Mr. Hawke.

He rose from his chair. "I think the best thing you can do," he said, "will be to get back home to your mother at Cork as quickly as possible, and advise her never to play such a risky game again. Have you any money in your purse? No—well then here's some for you, and lose no time in getting home. It will be best for Miss Monroe—Mrs. Danvers I mean—to come to my house and claim her own property there. At any rate, there it will remain until she does so."

As the girl, with incoherent expressions of gratitude, left the room, he turned to Loveday.

"I should like to have consulted Mrs. Hawke before arranging matters in this way," he said a little hesitatingly; "but still, I don't see that I could have done otherwise."

"I feel sure Mrs. Hawke will approve what you have done when she hears all the circumstance of the case," said Loveday.

"And," continued the old clergyman, "when I write to Sir George, as, of course, I must immediately, I shall advise him to make the best of a bad bargain, now that the thing is done. 'Past cure should be past care'; eh, Miss Brooke? And, think! what a narrow escape my nephew, Jack, has had!"

MARY E. WILKINS

(1852–1930)

Mary E. Wilkins was a popular and respected author in her time who also published under her married name, Mary Wilkins Freeman. A 1903 book entitled *Women Authors of Our Day in Their Homes* describes her as "the most delicate and appreciative delineator of rural New England characters who has written within a generation." While this encomium may sound precious, Mark Twain was also a vocal fan of Wilkins and she was the first recipient of the William Dean Howells Medal for distinction in fiction, awarded by the American Academy of Arts and Letters. Naturally she was later slighted by male critics for writing about home and family rather than about manly pursuits such as war and politics.

Wilkins started writing at a young age. While still a teenager, she began publishing poems and stories for children, and her later books included *Pembroke* and *Jerome, a Poor Man*. She wrote while also serving as private secretary to author and medical reformer Oliver Wendell Holmes Sr. Ghost-story fans remember Wilkins for her 1903 collection *The Wind in the Rosebush and Other Stories of the Supernatural*, which includes American Gothic classics such as "The Lost Ghost" and "Luella Miller"—the latter a superb tale of a psychic vampire. It is interesting that, born on Halloween, she retained a lifelong interest in spirits and hauntings. She lost both parents and a sister in her youth, and many abandoned and abused children wander through her writings. She survived the rigid code of a Congregationalist childhood but, although she began college at Mount Holyoke, she finished within the more conservative confines of West Brattleboro Seminary.

"The Long Arm" first appeared in the August 1895 issue of *Chapman's Magazine of Fiction* and took the title position in an anthology published the same year by the British publishers Chapman and Hall, this time in the Chapman's Story Series. *The Long Arm and Other Detective Stories* also included one of the infrequent tales by American educator and scholar Brander Matthews. Sarah Fairbanks, the protagonist of "The Long Arm," is not a professional detective and does not appear in any other story, although she is certainly resourceful enough to have pursued a career in such work. A male detective joins Fairbanks but does not diminish her own contributions to the investigation that leads to a rather helpfully detailed confession from the killer.

THE LONG ARM

CHAPTER I

The Tragedy

(From notes written by Miss Sarah Fairbanks immediately after the report of the Grand Jury.)

As I take my pen to write this, I have a feeling that I am in the witness-box—for, or against myself, which? The place of the criminal in the dock I will not voluntarily take. I will affirm neither my innocence nor my guilt. I will present the facts of the case as impartially and as coolly as if I had nothing at stake. I will let all who read this judge me as they will.

This I am bound to do, since I am condemned to something infinitely worse than the life-cell or the gallows. I will try my own self in lieu of judge and jury; my guilt or my innocence I will prove to you all, if it be in mortal power. In my despair I am tempted to say, I care not which it may be, so something be proved. Open condemnation could not overwhelm me like universal suspicion.

Now, first, as I have heard is the custom in the courts of law, I will present the case. I am Sarah Fairbanks, a country school teacher, twenty-nine years of age. My mother died when I was twenty-three. Since then, while I have been teaching at Digby, a cousin of my father's, Rufus Bennett, and his wife have lived with my father. During the long summer vacation they returned to their little farm in Vermont, and I kept house for my father.

For five years I have been engaged to be married to Henry Ellis, a young man whom I met in Digby. My father was very much opposed to the match, and has told me repeatedly that if I insisted upon marrying him in his lifetime he would disinherit me. On this account Henry never visited me at my own home; while I could not bring myself to break off my engagement. Finally, I wished to avoid an open rupture with my father. He was quite an old man, and I was the only one he had left of a large family.

I believe that parents should honour their children, as well as children their parents; but I had arrived at this conclusion: in nine-tenths of the cases wherein children marry against their parents' wishes, even when the parents have no just grounds for opposition, the marriages are unhappy.

I sometimes felt that I was unjust to Henry, and resolved that, if ever I suspected that his fancy turned toward any other girl, I would not hinder it, especially as I was getting older and, I thought, losing my good looks.

A little while ago, a young and pretty girl came to Digby to teach the school in the south district. She boarded in the same house with Henry. I heard that he was somewhat attentive to her, and I made up my mind I would not interfere. At the same time it seemed to me that my heart was breaking. I heard her people had money, too, and she was an only child. I had always felt that Henry ought to marry a wife with money, because he had nothing himself, and was not very strong.

School closed five weeks ago, and I came home for the summer vacation. The night before I left, Henry came to see me, and urged me to marry him. I refused again; but I never before had felt that my father was so hard and cruel as I did that night. Henry said that he should certainly see me during the vacation, and when I replied that he must not come, he was angry, and said—but such foolish things are not worth repeating. Henry has really a very sweet temper, and would not hurt a fly.

The very night of my return home Rufus Bennett and my father had words about some maple sugar which Rufus made on his Vermont farm and sold to father, who made a good trade for it to some people in Boston. That was father's business. He had once kept a store, but had given it up, and sold a few articles that he could make a large profit on here and there at wholesale. He used to send to New Hampshire and Vermont for butter, eggs, and cheese. Cousin Rufus thought father did not allow him enough profit on the maple sugar, and in the dispute father lost his temper, and said that Rufus had given him underweight. At that, Rufus swore an oath, and seized father by the throat. Rufus's wife screamed, "Oh, don't! don't! oh, he'll kill him!"

I went up to Rufus and took hold of his arm.

"Rufus Bennett," said I, "you let my father go!"

But Rufus's eyes glared like a madman's, and he would not let go. Then I went to the desk-drawer where father had kept a pistol since some houses in the village were broken into; I got out the pistol, laid hold of Rufus again, and held the muzzle against his forehead.

"You let go of my father," said I, "or I'll fire!"

Then Rufus let go, and father dropped like a log. He was purple in the face. Rufus's wife and I worked a long time over him to bring him to.

"Rufus Bennett," said I, "go to the well and get a pitcher of water." He went, but when father had revived and got up, Rufus gave him a look that showed he was not over his rage.

"I'll get even with you yet, Martin Fairbanks, old man as you are!" he shouted out, and went into the outer room.

We got father to bed soon. He slept in the bedroom downstairs, out of the sitting-room. Rufus and his wife had the north chamber, and I had the south one. I left my door open that night, and did not sleep. I listened; no one stirred in the night. Rufus and his wife were up very early in the morning, and before nine o'clock left for Vermont. They had a day's journey, and would reach home about nine in the evening. Rufus's wife bade father good-bye, crying, while Rufus was getting their trunk downstairs, but Rufus did not go near father nor me. He ate no breakfast; his very back looked ugly when he went out of the yard.

That very day about seven in the evening, after tea, I had just washed the dishes and put them away, and went out on the north doorstep, where father was sitting, and sat down on the lowest step. There was a cool breeze there; it had been a very hot day.

"I want to know if that Ellis fellow has been to see you any lately?" said father all at once.

"Not a great deal," I answered.

"Did he come to see you the last night you were there?" said father.

"Yes, sir," said I, "he did come."

"If you ever have another word to say to that fellow while I live, I'll kick you out of the house like a dog, daughter of mine though you be," said he. Then he swore a great oath and called God to witness. "Speak to that fellow again, if you dare, while I live!" said he.

I did not say a word; I just looked up at him as I sat there. Father turned pale and shrank back, and put his hand to his throat, where Rufus had clutched him. There were some purple finger-marks there.

"I suppose you would have been glad if he had killed me," father cried out.

"I saved your life," said I.

"What did you do with that pistol?" he asked.

"I put it back in the desk-drawer."

I got up and went around and sat on the west doorstep, which is the front one. As I sat there, the bell rang for the Tuesday evening meeting, and Phœbe Dole and Maria Woods, two old maiden ladies, dressmakers, our next-door neighbours, went past on their way to meeting. Phœbe stopped and asked if Rufus and his wife were gone. Maria went around the house. Very soon they went on, and several other people passed. When they had all gone, it was as still as death.

I sat alone a long time, until I could see by the shadows that the full moon had risen. Then I went to my room and went to bed.

I lay awake a long time, crying. It seemed to me that all hope of marriage between Henry and me was over. I could not expect him to wait for me. I thought of that other girl; I could see her pretty face wherever I looked. But at last I cried myself to sleep.

At about five o'clock I awoke and got up. Father always wanted his breakfast at six o'clock, and I had to prepare it now.

When father and I were alone, he always built the fire in the kitchen stove, but that morning I did not hear him stirring as usual, and I fancied that he must be so out of temper with me, that he would not build the fire.

I went to my closet for a dark blue calico dress which I wore to do housework in. It had hung there during all the school term.

As I took it off the hook, my attention was caught by something strange about the dress I had worn the night before. This dress was made of thin summer silk; it was green in colour, sprinkled over with white rings. It had been my best dress for two summers, but now I was wearing it on hot afternoons at home, for it was the coolest dress I had. The night before, too, I had thought of the possibility of Henry's driving over from Digby and passing the house. He had done this sometimes during the last summer vacation, and I wished to look my best if he did.

As I took down the calico dress I saw what seemed to be a stain on the green silk. I threw on the calico hastily, and then took the green silk and carried it over to the window. It was covered with spots—horrible great splashes and streaks down the front. The right sleeve, too, was stained, and all the stains were wet.

"What have I got on my dress?" said I.

It looked like blood. Then I smelled of it, and it was sickening in my nostrils, but I was not sure what the smell of blood was like. I thought I must have got the stains by some accident the night before.

"If that is blood on my dress," I said, "I must do something to get it off at once, or the dress will be ruined."

It came to my mind that I had been told that blood-stains had been removed from cloth by an application of flour paste on the wrong side. I took my green silk, and ran down the back stairs, which lead—having a door at the foot—directly into the kitchen.

There was no fire in the kitchen stove, as I had thought. Everything was very solitary and still, except for the ticking of the clock on the shelf. When I crossed the kitchen to the pantry, however, the cat mewed to be let in from the shed. She had a little door of her own by which she could enter or leave the shed at will, an aperture just large enough for her Maltese body to pass at ease beside the shed door. It had a little lid, too, hung upon a leathern hinge. On my way I let the cat in; then I went into the pantry and got a bowl of flour. This I mixed with water into a stiff paste, and applied to the under surface of the stains on my dress. I then hung the dress up to dry in the dark end of a closet leading out of the kitchen, which contained some old clothes of father's.

Then I made up the fire in the kitchen stove. I made coffee, baked biscuits, and poached some eggs for breakfast.

Then I opened the door into the sitting-room and called, "Father, breakfast is ready." Suddenly I started. There was a red stain on the inside of the sitting-room door. My heart began to beat in my ears. "Father!" I called out—"father!"

There was no answer.

"Father!" I called again, as loud as I could scream. "Why don't you speak? What is the matter?"

The door of his bedroom stood open. I had a feeling that I saw a red reflection in there. I gathered myself together and went across the sitting-room to father's bedroom door. His little looking-glass hung over his bureau opposite his bed, which was reflected in it.

That was the first thing I saw, when I reached the door. I could see father in the looking-glass and the bed. Father was dead there; he had been murdered in the night.

CHAPTER II

The Knot of Ribbon

I think I must have fainted away, for presently I found myself on the floor, and for a minute I could not remember what had happened. Then I remembered, and an awful, unreasoning terror seized me. "I must lock all the doors quick," I thought; "quick, or the murderer will come back."

I tried to get up, but I could not stand. I sank down again. I had to crawl out of the room on my hands and knees.

I went first to the front door; it was locked with a key and a bolt. I went next to the north door, and that was locked with a key and bolt. I went to the north shed door, and that was bolted. Then I went to the little-used east door in the shed, beside which the cat had her little passage-way, and that was fastened with an iron hook. It has no latch.

The whole house was fastened on the inside. The thought struck me like an icy hand, "The murderer is in this house!" I rose to my feet then; I unhooked that door, and ran out of the house, and out of the yard, as for my life.

I took the road to the village. The first house, where Phœbe Dole and Maria Woods live, is across a wide field from ours. I did not intend to stop there, for they were only women, and could do nothing; but seeing Phœbe looking out of the window, I ran into the yard.

She opened the window.

"What is it?" said she. "What is the matter, Sarah Fairbanks?"

Maria Woods came and leaned over her shoulder. Her face looked almost as white as her hair, and her blue eyes were dilated. My face must have frightened her.

"Father—father is murdered in his bed!" I said.

There was a scream, and Maria Woods's face disappeared from over Phœbe Dole's shoulder—she had fainted. I do not know whether Phœbe looked paler—she is always very pale—but I saw in her black eyes a look which I shall never forget. I think she began to suspect me at that moment.

Phœbe glanced back at Maria, but she asked me another question.

"Has he had words with anybody?" said she.

"Only with Rufus," I said; "but Rufus is gone."

Phœbe turned away from the window to attend to Maria, and I ran on to the village.

A hundred people can testify what I did next—can tell how I called for the doctor and the deputy-sheriff; how I went back to my own home with the horror-stricken crowd; how they flocked in and looked at poor father; but only the doctor touched him, very carefully, to see if he were quite dead; how the coroner came, and all the rest.

The pistol was in the bed beside father, but it had not been fired; the charge was still in the barrel. It was blood-stained, and there was one bruise on father's head which might have been inflicted by the pistol, used as a club. But the wound which caused his death was in his breast, and made evidently by some cutting instrument, though the cut was not a clean one; the weapon must have been dull.

They searched the house, lest the murderer should be hidden away. I heard Rufus Bennett's name whispered by one and another. Everybody seemed to know that he and father had had words the night before; I could not understand how, because I had told nobody except Phœbe Dole, who had had no time to spread the news, and I was sure that no one else had spoken of it.

They looked in the closet where my green silk dress hung, and pushed it aside to be sure nobody was concealed behind it, but they did not notice anything wrong about it. It was dark in the closet, and besides, they did not look for anything like that until later.

All these people—the deputy-sheriff, and afterwards the high sheriff, and other out-of-town officers, for whom they had telegraphed, and the neighbours—all hunted their own suspicion, and that was Rufus Bennett. All believed he had come back, and killed my father. They fitted all the facts to that belief. They made him do the deed with a long, slender screw-driver, which he had recently borrowed from one of the neighbours and had not returned. They made his finger-marks, which were still on my father's throat, fit the red prints of the sitting-room door. They made sure that he had returned and stolen into the house by the east door shed, while father and I sat on the doorsteps the evening before; that he had hidden himself away, perhaps in that very closet where my dress hung, and afterwards stolen out and killed my father, and then escaped.

They were not shaken when I told them that every door was bolted and barred that morning. They themselves found all the windows fastened down, except a few which were open on account of the heat, and even these last were raised only the width of the sash, and fastened with sticks, so that they could be raised no higher. Father was very cautious about fastening the house, for he sometimes had considerable sums of money by him. The officers saw all these difficulties in the way, but they fitted them somehow to their theory, and two deputy-sheriffs were at once sent to apprehend Rufus.

They had not begun to suspect me then, and not the slightest watch was kept on my movements. The neighbours were very kind, and did everything to help me, relieving me altogether of all those last offices—in this case so much sadder than usual.

An inquest was held, and I told freely all I knew, except about the blood-stains on my dress. I hardly knew why I kept that back. I had no feeling then that I might have done the deed myself, and I could not bear to convict myself, if I was innocent.

Two of the neighbours, Mrs. Holmes and Mrs. Adams, remained with me all that day. Towards evening, when there were very few in the house, they went into the parlour to put it in order for the funeral, and I sat down alone in the kitchen. As I sat there by the window I thought of my green silk dress, and wondered if the stains were out. I went to the closet and brought the dress out to the light. The spots and streaks had almost disappeared. I took the dress out into the shed, and scraped off the flour paste, which was quite dry; I swept up the paste, burned it in the stove, took the dress upstairs to my own closet, and hung it in its old place. Neighbours remained with me all night.

At three o'clock in the afternoon of the next day, which was Thursday, I went over to Phœbe Dole's to see about a black dress to wear at the funeral. The neighbours had urged me to have my black silk dress altered a little, and trimmed with crape.

I found only Maria Woods at home. When she saw me she gave a little scream, and began to cry. She looked as if she had already been weeping for hours. Her blue eyes were bloodshot.

"Phœbe's gone over to—Mrs. Whitney's to—try on her dress," she sobbed.

"I want to get my black silk dress fixed a little," said I.

"She'll be home—pretty soon," said Maria.

I laid my dress on the sofa and sat down. Nobody ever consults Maria about a dress. She sews well, but Phœbe does all the planning.

Maria Woods continued to sob like a child, holding her little soaked handkerchief over her face. Her shoulders heaved. As for me, I felt like a stone; I could not weep.

"Oh," she gasped out finally, "I knew—I knew! I told Phœbe—I knew just how it would be, I—knew!"

I roused myself at that.

"What do you mean?" said I.

"When Phœbe came home Tuesday night and said she heard your father and Rufus Bennett having words, I knew how it would be," she choked out. "I knew he had a dreadful temper."

"Did Phœbe Dole know Tuesday night that father and Rufus Bennett had words?" said I.

"Yes," said Maria Woods.

"How did she know?"

"She was going through your yard, the short cut to Mrs. Ormsby's, to carry her brown alpaca dress home. She came right home and told me; and she overheard them."

"Have you spoken of it to anybody but me?" said I.

Maria said she didn't know; she might have done so. Then she remembered hearing Phœbe herself speak of it to Harriet Sargent when she came in to try on her dress. It was easy to see how people knew about it.

I did not say any more, but I thought it was strange that Phœbe Dole had asked me if father had had words with anybody when she knew it all the time.

Phœbe came in before long. I tried on my dress, and she made her plan about the alterations, and the trimming. I made no suggestions. I did not care how it was done, but if I had cared it would have made no difference. Phœbe always does things her own way. All the women in the village are in a manner under Phœbe Dole's thumb. The garments are visible proofs of her force of will.

While she was taking up my black silk on the shoulder seams, Phœbe Dole said—

"Let me see—you had a green silk dress made at Digby three summers ago, didn't you?"

"Yes," I said.

"Well," said she, "why don't you have it dyed black? those thin silks dye quite nice. It would make you a good dress."

I scarcely replied, and then she offered to dye it for me herself. She had a recipe which she used with great success. I thought it was very kind of her, but did not say whether I would accept her offer or not. I could not fix my mind upon anything but the awful trouble I was in.

"I'll come over and get it to-morrow morning," said Phœbe.

I thanked her. I thought of the stains, and then my mind seemed to wander again to the one subject.

All the time Maria Woods sat weeping. Finally Phœbe turned to her with impatience. "If you can't keep calmer, you'd better go upstairs, Maria," said she. "You'll make Sarah sick. Look at her! she doesn't give way—and think of the reason she's got."

"I've got reason, too," Maria broke out; then, with a piteous shriek, "Oh, I've got reason."

"Maria Woods, go out of the room!" said Phœbe. Her sharpness made me jump, half dazed as I was.

Maria got up without a word, and went out of the room, bending almost double with convulsive sobs.

"She's been dreadfully worked up over your father's death," said Phœbe calmly, going on with the fitting. "She's terribly nervous. Sometimes I have to be real sharp with her, for her own good."

I nodded. Maria Woods has always been considered a sweet, weakly, dependent woman, and Phœbe Dole is undoubtedly very fond of her. She has seemed to shield her, and take care of her nearly all her life. The two have lived together since they were young girls.

Phœbe is tall, and very pale and thin; but she never had a day's illness. She is plain, yet there is a kind of severe goodness and faithfulness about her colourless face, with the smooth bands of white hair over her ears.

I went home as soon as my dress was fitted. That evening Henry Ellis came over to see me. I do not need to go into details concerning that visit. It seemed enough to say that he tendered the fullest sympathy and protection, and I accepted them. I cried a little, for the first time, and he soothed and comforted me.

Henry had driven over from Digby and tied his horse in the yard. At ten o'clock he bade me good-night on the doorstep, and was just turning his buggy around, when Mrs. Adams came running to the door.

"Is this yours?" said she, and she held out a knot of yellow ribbon.

"Why, that's the ribbon you have around your whip, Henry," said I.

He looked at it.

"So it is," he said. "I must have dropped it." He put it into his pocket and drove away.

"He didn't drop that ribbon to-night!" said Mrs. Adams. "I found it Wednesday morning out in the yard. I thought I remembered seeing him have a yellow ribbon on his whip."

CHAPTER III

Suspicion Is Not Proof

When Mrs. Adams told me she had picked up Henry's whip-ribbon Wednesday morning, I said nothing, but thought that Henry must have driven over Tuesday evening after all, and even come up into the yard, although the house was shut up and I in bed, to get a little nearer to me. I felt conscience-stricken because I could not help a thrill of happiness, when my father lay dead in the house.

My father was buried as privately and as quietly as we could bring it about. But it was a terrible ordeal. Meantime word came from Vermont that Rufus Bennett had been arrested on his farm. He was perfectly willing to come back with the officers, and indeed, had not the slightest trouble in proving that he was at his home in Vermont when the murder took place. He proved by several witnesses that he was out of the State long before my father and I sat on the steps together that evening, and that he proceeded directly to his home as fast as the train and stage-coach could carry him.

The screw-driver with which the deed was supposed to have been committed was found, by the neighbour from whom it had been borrowed, in his wife's bureau drawer. It had been returned, and she had used it to put a picture-hook in her chamber. Bennett was discharged and returned to Vermont.

Then Mrs. Adams told of the finding of the yellow ribbon from Henry Ellis's whip, and he was arrested, since he was held to have a motive for putting my father out of the world. Father's opposition to our marriage was well known, and Henry was suspected also of having had an eye to his money. It was found, indeed, that my father had more money than I had known myself.

Henry owned to having driven into the yard that night, and to having missed the ribbon from his whip on his return; but one of the hostlers in the livery stables in Digby, where he kept his horse and buggy, came forward and testified to finding the yellow ribbon in the carriage-room that Tuesday night before Henry returned from his drive. There were two yellow ribbons in evidence, therefore, and the one produced by the hostler seemed to fit Henry's whip-stock the more exactly.

Moreover, nearly the exact minute of the murder was claimed to be proved by the post-mortem examination; and by the testimony of the stableman as to the hour of Henry's return and the speed of his horse, he was further cleared of suspicion; for, if the opinion of the medical experts was correct, Henry must have returned to the livery stable too soon to have committed the murder.

He was discharged, at any rate, although suspicion still clung to him. Many people believe now in his guilt—those who do not, believe in mine; and some believe we were accomplices.

After Henry's discharge, I was arrested. There was no one else left to accuse. There must be a motive for the murder; I was the only person left with a motive. Unlike the others, who were discharged after preliminary examination, I was held to the grand jury and taken to Dedham, where I spent four weeks in jail, awaiting the meeting of the grand jury.

Neither at the preliminary examination, nor before the grand jury, was I allowed to make the full and frank statement that I am making here. I was told simply to answer the questions that were put to me, and to volunteer nothing, and I obeyed.

I know nothing about law. I wished to do the best I could—to act in the wisest manner, for Henry's sake and my own. I said nothing about the green silk dress. They searched the house for all manner of things, at the time of my arrest, but the dress was not there—it was in Phœbe Dole's dye-kettle. She had come over after it one day when I was picking beans in the garden, and had taken it out of the closet. She brought it back herself, and told me this, after I had returned from Dedham.

"I thought I'd get it and surprise you," said she. "It's taken a beautiful black."

She gave me a strange look—half as if she would see into my very soul, in spite of me, half as if she were in terror of what she would see there, as she spoke. I do not know just what Phœbe Dole's look meant. There may have been a stain left on that dress after all, and she may have seen it.

I suppose if it had not been for that flour-paste which I had learned to make, I should have hung for the murder of my father. As it was, the grand jury found no bill against me because there was absolutely no evidence to convict me; and I came home a free woman. And if people were condemned for their motives, would there be enough hangmen in the world?

They found no weapon with which I could have done the deed. They found no blood-stains on my clothes. The one thing which told against me, aside from my ever-present motive, was the fact that on the morning after the murder the doors and windows were fastened. My volunteering this information had of course weakened its force as against myself.

Then, too, some held that I might have been mistaken in my terror and excitement, and there was a theory, advanced by a few, that the murderer had meditated making me also a victim, and had locked the doors that he might not be frustrated in his designs, but had lost heart at the last, and had allowed me to escape, and then fled himself. Some held that he had intended to force me to reveal the whereabouts of father's money, but his courage had failed him.

Father had quite a sum in a hiding-place which only he and I knew. But no search for money had been made, as far as any one could see—not a bureau drawer had been disturbed, and father's gold watch was ticking peacefully under his pillow; even his wallet in his vest pocket had not been opened. There was a small roll of bank-notes in it, and some change; father never carried much money. I suppose if father's wallet and watch had been taken, I should not have been suspected at all.

I was discharged, as I have said, from lack of evidence, and have returned to my home—free, indeed, but with this awful burden of suspicion on my shoulders. That brings me up to the present day. I returned yesterday evening. This evening Henry Ellis has been over to see me; he will not come again, for I have forbidden him to do so. This is what I said to him:

"I know you are innocent, you know I am innocent. To all the world beside we are under suspicion—I more than you, but we are both under suspicion. If we are known to be together that suspicion is increased for both of us. I do not care for myself, but I do care for you. Separated from me the stigma attached to you will soon fade away, especially if you should marry elsewhere."

Then Henry interrupted me.

"I will never marry elsewhere," said he.

I could not help being glad that he said it, but I was firm.

"If you should see some good woman whom you could love, it will be better for you to marry elsewhere," said I.

"I never will!" he said again. He put his arms around me, but I had strength to push him away.

"You never need, if I succeed in what I undertake before you meet the other," said I. I began to think he had not cared for that pretty girl who boarded in the same house after all.

"What is that?" he said. "What are you going to undertake?"

"To find my father's murderer," said I.

Henry gave me a strange look; then, before I could stop him, he took me fast in his arms and kissed my forehead.

"As God is my witness, Sarah, I believe in your innocence," he said; and from that minute I have felt sustained and fully confident of my power to do what I had undertaken.

My father's murderer I will find. To-morrow I begin my search. I shall first make an exhaustive examination of the house, such as no officer in the case has yet made, in the hope of finding a clue. Every room I propose to divide into square yards, by line and measure, and every one of these square yards I will study as if it were a problem in algebra.

I have a theory that it is impossible for any human being to enter any house, and commit in it a deed of this kind, and not leave behind traces which are the known quantities in an algebraic equation to those who can use them.

There is a chance that I shall not be quite unaided. Henry has promised not to come again until I bid him, but he is to send a detective here from Boston—one whom he knows. In fact, that man is a cousin of his, or else there would be small hope of our securing him, even if I were to offer him a large price.

The man has been remarkably successful in several cases, but his health is not good; the work is a severe strain upon his nerves, and he is not driven to it from any lack of money. The physicians have forbidden him to undertake any new case, for a year at least, but Henry is confident that we may rely upon him for this.

I will now lay this aside and go to bed. To-morrow is Wednesday; my father will have been dead seven weeks. To-morrow morning I commence the work, in which, if it be in human power, aided by a higher wisdom, I shall succeed.

CHAPTER IV

The Box of Clues

(The pages which follow are from Miss Fairbanks' journal, begun after the conclusion of the notes already given to the reader.)

Wednesday night.—I have resolved to record carefully each day the progress I make in my examination of the house. I began today at the bottom—that is, with the room least likely to contain any clue, the parlour. I took a chalk-line and a yard-stick, and divided the floor into square yards, and every one of these squares I examined on my hands and knees. I found in this way literally nothing on the carpet but dust, lint, two common white pins, and three inches of blue sewing-silk.

At last I got the dustpan and brush, and yard by yard swept the floor. I took the sweepings in a white pasteboard box out into the yard in the strong sunlight, and examined them. There was nothing but dust and lint and five inches of brown woollen thread—evidently a ravelling of some dress material. The blue silk and the brown thread are the only possible clues which I found to-day, and they are hardly possible. Rufus's wife can probably account for them. I have written to her about them.

Nobody has come to the house all day. I went down to the store this afternoon to get some necessary provisions, and people stopped talking when I came in. The clerk took my money as if it were poison.

Thursday night.—To-day I have searched the sitting-room, out of which my father's bedroom opens. I found two bloody footprints on the carpet which no one had noticed before—perhaps because the carpet itself is red and white. I used a microscope which I had in my school work. The footprints, which are close to the bedroom door, pointing out into the sitting-room, are both from the right foot; one is brighter than the other, but both are faint. The foot was evidently either bare or clad only in a stocking—the prints are so widely spread. They are wider than my father's shoes. I tried one in the brightest print.

I found nothing else new in the sitting-room. The blood-stains on the doors which have been already noted are still there. They had not been washed away, first by order of the sheriff, and next by mine. These stains are of two kinds; one looks as if made by a bloody garment brushing against it; the other, I should say, was made in the first place by the grasp of a bloody hand, and then brushed over with a cloth. There are none of these marks upon the door leading to the bedroom—they are on the doors leading into the front entry and the china closet. The china closet is really a pantry, although I use it only for my best dishes and preserves.

Friday night.—To-day I searched the closet. One of the shelves, which is about as high as my shoulders, was blood-stained. It looked to me as if the murderer might have caught hold of it to steady himself. Did he turn faint after his dreadful deed? Some tumblers of jelly were ranged on that shelf and they had not been disturbed. There was only that bloody clutch on the edge.

I found on this closet floor, under the shelves, as if it had been rolled there by a careless foot, a button, evidently from a man's clothing. It is an ordinary black enamelled metal trousers-button: it had evidently been worn off and clumsily sewn on again, for a quantity of stout white thread is still clinging to it. This button must have belonged either to a single man or to one with an idle wife.

If one black button had been sewn on with white thread, another is likely to be. I may be wrong, but I regard this button as a clue.

The pantry was thoroughly swept—cleaned, indeed, by Rufus's wife, the day before she left. Neither my father nor Rufus could have dropped it there, and they never had occasion to go to that closet. The murderer dropped the button.

I have a white pasteboard box which I have marked "clues." In it I have put the button.

This afternoon Phœbe Dole came in. She is very kind. She had re-cut the dyed silk, and she fitted it to me. Her great shears clicking in my ears made me nervous. I did not feel like stopping to think about clothes. I hope I did not appear ungrateful, for she is the only soul beside Henry who has treated me as she did before this happened.

Phœbe asked me what I found to busy myself about, and I replied, "I am searching for my father's murderer." She asked me if I thought I should find a clue, and I replied, "I think so." I had found the button then, but I did not speak of it. She said Maria was not very well.

I saw her eyeing the stains on the doors, and I said I had not washed them off, for I thought they might yet serve a purpose in detecting the murderer. She looked closely at those on the entry-door—the brightest ones—and said she did not see how they could help, for there were no plain finger-marks there, and she should think they would make me nervous.

"I'm beyond being nervous," I replied.

Saturday.—To-day I have found something which I cannot understand. I have been at work in the room where my father came to his dreadful end. Of course some of the most startling evidences have been removed. The bed is clean, and the carpet washed, but the worst horror of it all clings to that room. The spirit of murder seemed to haunt it. It seemed to me at first that I could not enter that room, but in it I made a strange discovery.

My father, while he carried little money about his person, was in the habit of keeping considerable sums in the house; there is no bank within ten miles. However he was wary; he had a hiding-place which he had revealed to no one but myself. He had a small stand in his room near the end of his bed. Under this stand, or rather under the top of it, he had tacked a large leather wallet. In this he kept all his spare money. I remember how his eyes twinkled when he showed it to me.

"The average mind thinks things have either got to be in or on," said my father. "They don't consider there's ways of getting around gravitation and calculation."

In searching my father's room I called to mind that saying of his, and his peculiar system of concealment, and then I made my discovery. I have argued that in a search of this kind I ought not only to search for hidden traces of the criminal, but for everything which had been for any reason concealed. Something which my father himself had hidden, something from his past history, may furnish a motive for someone else.

The money in the wallet under the table, some five hundred dollars, had been removed and deposited in the bank. Nothing more was to be found there. I examined the bottom of the bureau, and the undersides of the chair seats. There are two chairs in the room, besides the cushioned rocker—green-painted wooden chairs, with flag seats. I found nothing under the seats.

Then I turned each of the green chairs completely over, and examined the bottoms of the legs. My heart leaped when I found a bit of leather tacked over one. I got the tack-hammer and drew the tacks. The chair-leg had been hollowed out, and for an inch the hole was packed tight with cotton. I began picking out the cotton, and soon I felt something hard. It proved to be an old-fashioned gold band, quite wide and heavy, like a wedding-ring.

I took it over to the window and found this inscription on the inside: "Let love abide for ever." There were two dates—one in August, forty years ago, and the other in August of the present year.

I think the ring had never been worn; while the first part of the inscription is perfectly clear, it looks old, and the last is evidently freshly cut.

This could not have been my mother's ring. She had only her wedding-ring, and that was buried with her. I think my father must have treasured up this ring for years; but why? What does it mean? This can hardly be a clue; this can hardly lead to the discovery of a motive, but I will put it in the box with the rest.

Sunday night.—To-day, of course, I did not pursue my search. I did not go to church. I could not face old friends that could not face me. Sometimes I think that everybody in my native village believes in my guilt. What must I have been in my general appearance and demeanour all my life? I have studied myself in the glass, and tried to discover the possibilities of evil that they must see in my face.

This afternoon, about three o'clock, the hour when people here have just finished their Sunday dinner, there was a knock on the north door. I answered it, and a strange young man stood there with a large book under his arm. He was thin and cleanly shaved, with a clerical air.

"I have a work here to which I would like to call your attention," he began; and I stared at him in astonishment, for why should a book agent be peddling his wares upon the Sabbath?

His mouth twitched a little.

"It's a Biblical Cyclopædia," said he.

"I don't think I care to take it," said I.

"You are Miss Sarah Fairbanks, I believe?"

"That is my name," I replied stiffly.

"Mr. Henry Ellis, of Digby, sent me here," he said next. "My name is Dix—Francis Dix."

Then I knew it was Henry's first cousin from Boston—the detective who had come to help me. I felt the tears coming to my eyes.

"You are very kind to come," I managed to say.

"I am selfish, not kind," he returned, "but you had better let me come in, or any chance of success in my book agency is lost, if the neighbours see me trying to sell it on a Sunday. And, Miss Fairbanks, this is a bona fide agency. I shall canvass the town."

He came in. I showed him all that I have written, and he read it carefully. When he had finished he sat still for a long time, with his face screwed up in a peculiar meditative fashion.

"We'll ferret this out in three days at the most," said he finally, with a sudden clearing of his face and a flash of his eyes at me.

"I had planned for three years, perhaps," said I.

"I tell you, we'll do it in three days," he repeated. "Where can I get board while I canvass for this remarkable and interesting book under my arm? I can't stay here, of course, and there is no hotel. Do you think the two dressmakers next door, Phœbe Dole and the other one, would take me in?"

I said they had never taken boarders.

"Well, I'll go over and enquire," said Mr. Dix; and he had gone, with his book under his arm, almost before I knew it.

Never have I seen any one act with the strange noiseless soft speed that this man does. Can he prove me innocent in three days? He must have succeeded in getting board at Phœbe Dole's, for I saw him go past to meeting with her this evening. I feel sure he will be over very early to-morrow morning.

CHAPTER V

The Evidence Points to One

Monday night.—The detective came as I expected. I was up as soon as it was light, and he came across the dewy fields, with his Cyclopædia under his arm. He had stolen out from Phœbe Dole's back door.

He had me bring my father's pistol; then he bade me come with him out into the back yard. "Now, fire it," he said, thrusting the pistol into my hands. As I have said before, the charge was still in the barrel.

"I shall arouse the neighbourhood," I said.

"Fire it," he ordered.

I tried; I pulled the trigger as hard as I could.

"I can't do it," I said.

"And you are a reasonably strong woman, too, aren't you?"

I said I had been considered so. Oh, how much I heard about the strength of my poor woman's arms, and their ability to strike that murderous weapon home!

Mr. Dix took the pistol himself, and drew a little at the trigger.

"I could do it," he said, "but I won't. It would arouse the neighbourhood."

"This is more evidence against me," I said despairingly. "The murderer had tried to fire the pistol and failed."

"It is more evidence against the murderer," said Mr. Dix.

We went into the house, where he examined my box of clues long and carefully. Looking at the ring, he asked whether there was a jeweller in this village, and I said there was not. I told him that my father oftener went on business to Acton, ten miles away, than elsewhere.

He examined very carefully the button which I had found in the closet, and then asked to see my father's wardrobe. That was soon done. Beside the suit in which father was laid away there was one other complete one in the closet in his room. Besides that, there were in this closet two overcoats, an old black frock coat, a pair of pepper-and-salt trousers, and two black vests. Mr. Dix examined all the buttons; not one was missing. There was still another old suit in the closet off the kitchen. This was examined, and no button found wanting.

"What did your father do for work the day before he died?" he then asked.

I reflected and said that he had unpacked some stores which had come down from Vermont, and done some work out in the garden.

"What did he wear?"

"I think he wore the pepper-and-salt trousers and the black vest. He wore no coat, while at work."

Mr. Dix went quietly back to father's room and his closet, I following. He took out the grey trousers and the black vest, and examined them closely.

"What did he wear to protect these?" he asked.

"Why, he wore overalls!" I said at once. As I spoke I remembered seeing father go around the path to the yard, with those blue overalls drawn up high under his arms.

"Where are they?"

"Weren't they in the kitchen closet?"

"No."

We looked again, however, in the kitchen closet; we searched the shed thoroughly. The cat came in through her little door, as we stood there, and brushed around our feet. Mr. Dix stooped and stroked her. Then he went quickly to the door, beside which her little entrance was arranged, unhooked it, and stepped out. I was following him, but he motioned me back.

"None of my boarding mistress's windows command us," he said, "but she might come to the back door."

I watched him. He passed slowly around the little winding footpath, which skirted the rear of our house and extended faintly through the grassy fields to the rear of Phœbe Dole's. He stopped, searched a clump of sweetbriar, went on to an old well, and stopped there. The well had been dry many a year, and was choked up with stones and rubbish. Some boards are laid over it, and a big stone or two, to keep them in place.

Mr. Dix, glancing across at Phœbe Dole's back door, went down on his knees, rolled the stones away, then removed the boards and peered down the well. He stretched far over the brink, and reached down. He made many efforts; then he got up and came to me, and asked me to get for him an umbrella with a crooked handle, or something that he could hook into clothing.

I brought my own umbrella, the silver handle of which formed an exact hook. He went back to the well, knelt again, thrust in the umbrella and drew up, easily enough, what he had been fishing for. Then he came bringing it to me.

"Don't faint," he said, and took hold of my arm. I gasped when I saw what he had—my father's blue overalls, all stained and splotched with blood!

I looked at them, then at him.

"Don't faint," he said again. "We're on the right track. This is where the button came from—see, see!" He pointed to one of the straps of the overalls, and the button was gone. Some white thread clung to it. Another black metal button was sewed on roughly with the same white thread that I found on the button in my box of clues.

"What does it mean?" I gasped out. My brain reeled.

"You shall know soon," he said. He looked at his watch. Then he laid down the ghastly bundle he carried. "It has puzzled you to know how the murderer went in and out and yet kept the doors locked, has it not?" he said.

"Yes."

"Well, I am going out now. Hook that door after me."

He went out, still carrying my umbrella. I hooked the door. Presently I saw the lid of the cat's door lifted, and his hand and arm thrust through. He curved his arm up towards the hook, but it came short by half a foot. Then he withdrew his arm, and thrust in my silver-handled umbrella. He reached the door-hook easily enough with that.

Then he hooked it again. That was not so easy. He had to work a long time. Finally he accomplished it, unhooked the door again, and came in.

"That was how!" I said.

"No, it was not," he returned. "No human being, fresh from such a deed, could have used such patience as that to fasten the door after him. Please hang your arm down by your side."

I obeyed. He looked at my arm, then at his own.

"Have you a tape measure?" he asked.

I brought one out of my work-basket. He measured his arm, then mine, and then the distance from the cat-door to the hook.

"I have two tasks for you to-day and to-morrow," he said. "I shall come here very little. Find all your father's old letters, and read them. Find a man or woman in this town whose arm is six inches longer than yours. Now I must go home, or my boarding-mistress will get curious."

He went through the house to the front door, looked all ways to be sure no eyes were upon him, made three strides down the yard, and was pacing soberly up the street, with his Cyclopædia under his arm.

I made myself a cup of coffee, then I went about obeying his instructions. I read old letters all the forenoon; I found packages in trunks in the garret; there were quantities in father's desk. I have selected several to submit to Mr. Dix. One of them treats of an old episode in father's youth, which must have years since ceased to interest him. It was concealed after his favourite fashion—tacked under the bottom of his desk. It was written forty years ago, by Maria Woods, two years before my father's marriage—and it was a refusal of an offer of his hand. It was written in the stilted fashion of that day; it might have been copied from a "Complete Letter-writer."

My father must have loved Maria Woods as dearly as I love Henry, to keep that letter so carefully all these years. I thought he cared for my mother. He seemed as fond of her as other men of their wives, although I did use to wonder if Henry and I would ever get to be quite so much accustomed to each other.

Maria Woods must have been as beautiful as an angel when she was a girl. Mother was not pretty; she was stout, too, and awkward, and I suppose people would have called her rather slow and dull. But she was a good woman, and tried to do her duty.

Tuesday night.—This evening was my first opportunity to obey the second of Mr. Dix's orders. It seemed to me the best way to compare the average length of arms was to go to the prayer-meeting. I could not go about the town with my tape measure, and demand of people that they should hold out their arms. Nobody knows how I dreaded to go to the meeting, but I went, and I looked not at my neighbours' cold altered faces, but at their arms.

I discovered what Mr. Dix wished me to, but the discovery can avail nothing, and it is one he could have made himself. Phœbe Dole's arm is fully seven inches longer than mine. I never noticed it before, but she has an almost abnormally long arm. But why should Phœbe Dole have unhooked that door?

She made a prayer—a beautiful prayer. It comforted even me a little. She spoke of the tenderness of God in all the troubles of life, and how it never failed us.

When we were all going out I heard several persons speak of Mr. Dix and his Biblical Cyclopædia. They decided that he was a theological student, book-canvassing to defray the expenses of his education.

Maria Woods was not at the meeting. Several asked Phœbe how she was, and she replied, "Not very well."

It is very late. I thought Mr. Dix might be over to-night, but he has not been here.

Wednesday.—I can scarcely believe what I am about to write. Our investigations seem to point all to one person, and that person—It is incredible! I will not believe it.

Mr. Dix came as before, at dawn. He reported, and I reported. I showed Maria Woods' letter. He said he had driven to Acton, and found that the jeweller there had engraved the last date in the ring about six weeks ago.

"I don't want to seem rough, but your father was going to get married again," said Mr. Dix.

"I never knew him to go near any woman since mother died," I protested.

"Nevertheless, he had made arrangements to be married," persisted Mr. Dix.

"Who was the woman?"

He pointed at the letter in my hand.

"Maria Woods!"

He nodded.

I stood looking at him—dazed. Such a possibility had never entered my head.

He produced an envelope from his pocket, and took out a little card with blue and brown threads neatly wound upon it.

"Let me see those threads you found," he said.

I got the box and we compared them. He had a number of pieces of blue sewing-silk and brown woollen ravellings, and they matched mine exactly.

"Where did you find them?" I asked.

"In my boarding-mistress's piece-bag."

I stared at him.

"What does it mean?" I gasped out.

"What do you think?"

"It is impossible!"

CHAPTER VI

The Revelation

Wednesday, continued.—When Mr. Dix thus suggested to me the absurd possibility that Phœbe Dole had committed the murder, he and I were sitting in the kitchen. He was near the table; he laid a sheet of paper upon it, and began to write. The paper is before me.

"First," said Mr. Dix, and he wrote rapidly as he talked, "Whose arm is of such length that it might unlock a certain door of this house from the outside?—Phœbe Dole's.

"Second, who had in her piece-bag bits of the same threads and ravellings found upon your parlour floor, where she had not by your knowledge entered?—Phœbe Dole.

"Third, who interested herself most strangely in your blood-stained green silk dress, even to dyeing it?—Phœbe Dole.

"Fourth, who was caught in a lie, while trying to force the guilt of the murder upon an innocent man?—Phœbe Dole."

Mr. Dix looked at me. I had gathered myself together. "That proves nothing," I said. "There is no motive in her case."

"There is a motive."

"What is it?"

"Maria Woods shall tell you this afternoon."

He then wrote—

"Fifth, who was seen to throw a bundle down the old well, in the rear of Martin Fairbanks's house, at one o'clock in the morning?—Phœbe Dole."

"Was she—seen?" I gasped.

Mr. Dix nodded. Then he wrote.

"Sixth, who had a strong motive, which had been in existence many years ago?—Phœbe Dole."

Mr. Dix laid down his pen, and looked at me again.

"Well, what have you to say?" he asked.

"It is impossible!"

"Why?"

"She is a woman."

"A man could have fired that pistol, as she tried to do."

"It would have taken a man's strength to kill with the kind of weapon that was used," I said.

"No, it would not. No great strength is required for such a blow."

"But she is a woman!"

"Crime has no sex."

"But she is a good woman—a church member. I heard her pray yesterday afternoon. It is not in character."

"It is not for you, nor for me, nor for any mortal intelligence, to know what is or is not in character," said Mr. Dix.

He arose and went away. I could only stare at him in a half-dazed manner.

Maria Woods came this afternoon, taking advantage of Phœbe's absence on a dressmaking errand. Maria has aged ten years in the last few weeks. Her hair is white, her cheeks are fallen in, her pretty colour is gone.

"May I have the ring he gave me forty years ago?" she faltered.

I gave it to her; she kissed it and sobbed like a child. "Phœbe took it away from me before," she said; "but she shan't this time."

Maria related with piteous sobs the story of her long subordination to Phœbe Dole. This sweet child-like woman had always been completely under the sway of the other's stronger nature. The subordination went back beyond my father's original proposal to her; she had, before he made love to her as a girl, promised Phœbe she would not marry; and it was Phœbe who, by representing to her that she was bound by this solemn promise, had led her to write a letter to my father declining his offer, and sending back the ring.

"And after all, we were going to get married, if he had not died," she said. "He was going to give me this ring again, and he had had the other date put in. I should have been so happy!"

She stopped and stared at me with horror-stricken enquiry.

"What was Phœbe Dole doing in your backyard at one o'clock that night?" she cried.

"What do you mean?" I returned.

"I saw Phœbe come out of your back shed-door at one o'clock that very night. She had a bundle in her arms. She went along the path about as far as the old well, then she stooped down, and seemed to be working at something. When she got up she didn't have the bundle. I was watching at our back-door. I thought I heard her go out a little while before, and went downstairs, and found that door unlocked. I went in quick, and up to my chamber, and into my bed, when she started home across the fields. Pretty soon I heard her come in, then I heard the pump going. She slept downstairs; she went on to her bedroom. What was she doing in your back-yard that night?"

"You must ask her," said I. I felt my blood running cold.

"I've been afraid to," moaned Maria Woods. "She's been dreadful strange lately. I wish that book agent was going to stay at our house."

Maria Woods went home in about an hour. I got a ribbon for her, and she has my poor father's ring concealed in her withered bosom. Again I cannot believe this.

Thursday.—It is all over, Phœbe Dole has confessed! I do not know now in exactly what way Mr. Dix brought it about—how he accused her of her crime. After breakfast I saw them coming across the fields; Phœbe came first, advancing with rapid strides like a man, Mr. Dix followed, and my father's poor old sweetheart tottered behind, with her handkerchief at her eyes. Just as I noticed them the front-door bell rang; I found several people there, headed by the high sheriff. They crowded into the sitting-room just as Phœbe Dole came rushing in, with Mr. Dix and Maria Woods.

"I did it!" Phœbe cried out to me. "I am found out, and I have made up my mind to confess. She was going to marry your father—I found it out. I stopped it once before. This time I knew I couldn't unless I killed him. She's lived with me in that house for over forty years. There are other ties as strong as the marriage one, that are just as sacred. What right had he to take her away from me and break up my home?

"I overheard your father and Rufus Bennett having words. I thought folks would think he did it. I reasoned it all out. I had watched your cat go in that little door, I knew the shed door hooked, I knew how long my arm was; I thought I could undo it. I stole over here a little after midnight. I went all around the house to be sure nobody was awake. Out in the front yard I happened to think my shears were tied on my belt with a ribbon, and I untied them. I thought I put the ribbon in my pocket—it was a piece of yellow ribbon—but I suppose I didn't, because they found it afterwards, and thought it came off your young man's whip.

"I went round to the shed-door, unhooked it, and went in. The moon gave light enough. I got out your father's overalls from the kitchen closet; I knew where they were. I went through the sitting-room to the parlour. In there I slipped off my dress and skirts and put on the overalls. I put a handkerchief over my face, leaving only my eyes exposed. I crept out then into the sitting-room; there I pulled off my shoes and went into the bedroom.

"Your father was fast asleep; it was such a hot night, the clothes were thrown back and his chest was bare. The first thing I saw was that pistol on the stand beside his bed. I suppose he had had some fear of Rufus Bennett coming back, after all. Suddenly I thought I'd better shoot him. It would be surer and quicker; and if you were aroused I knew that I could get away, and everybody would suppose that he had shot himself.

"I took up the pistol and held it close to his head. I had never fired a pistol, but I knew how it was done. I pulled, but it would not go off. Your father stirred a little—I was mad with horror—I struck at his head with the pistol. He opened his eyes and cried out; then I dropped the pistol, and took these"—Phœbe Dole pointed to the great shining shears hanging at her waist—"for I am strong in my wrists. I only struck twice, over his heart.

"Then I went back into the sitting-room. I thought I heard a noise in the kitchen—I was full of terror then—and slipped into the sitting-room closet. I felt as if I were fainting, and clutched the shelf to keep from falling.

"I felt that I must go upstairs to see if you were asleep, to be sure you had not waked up when your father cried out. I thought if you had I should have to do the same by you. I crept upstairs to your chamber. You seemed sound asleep, but, as I watched, you stirred a little; but instead of striking at you I slipped into your closet. I heard nothing more from you. I felt myself wet with blood. I caught something hanging in your closet, and wiped myself over with it. I knew by the feeling it was your green silk. You kept quiet, and I saw you were asleep, so crept out of the closet, and down the stairs, got my clothes and shoes, and, out in the shed, took off the overalls and dressed myself. I rolled up the overalls, and took a board away from the old well and threw them in as I went home. I thought if they were found it would be no clue to me. The handkerchief, which was not much stained, I put to soak that night, and washed it out next morning, before Maria was up. I washed my hands and arms carefully that night, and also my shears.

"I expected Rufus Bennett would be accused of the murder, and, maybe, hung. I was prepared for that, but I did not like to think I had thrown suspicion upon you by staining your dress. I had nothing against you. I made up my mind I'd get hold of that dress—before anybody suspected you—and dye it black. I came in and got it, as you know. I was astonished not to see any more stains on it. I only found two or three little streaks that scarcely anybody would have noticed. I didn't know what to think. I suspected, of course, that you had found the stains and got them off, thinking they might bring suspicion upon you.

"I did not see how you could possibly suspect me in any case. I was glad when your young man was cleared. I had nothing against him. That is all I have to say."

I think I must have fainted away then. I cannot describe the dreadful calmness with which that woman told this—that woman with the good face, whom I had last heard praying like a saint in meeting. I believe in demoniacal possession after this.

When I came to, the neighbours were around me, putting camphor on my head, and saying soothing things to me, and the old friendly faces had returned. But I wish I could forget!

They have taken Phœbe Dole away—I only know that. I cannot bear to talk any more about it when I think there must be a trial, and I must go!

Henry has been over this evening. I suppose we shall be happy after all, when I have had a little time to get over this. He says I have nothing more to worry about. Mr. Dix has gone home. I hope Henry and I may be able to repay his kindness some day.

A month later: I have just heard that Phœbe Dole has died in prison. This is my last entry. May God help all other innocent women in hard straights as He has helped me!

ANNA KATHARINE GREEN

(1846–1935)

Anna Katharine Green is one of the towering figures in the history of the detective story. Her primary detective, the tireless and sardonic Ebenezer Gryce of the New York City Police Department, is one of the great creations in the early days of the genre and deserves more attention than he usually receives nowadays. Green also created two female detectives—the highly amusing Amelia Butterworth, who appears in this chapter from her debut adventure, and a moody young socialite named Violet Strange, who appears later in this anthology.

Some critics cite an 1866 dime novel entitled *The Dead Letter*, by Seeley Regester, whose real name was Metta Victoria Fuller Victor, as the first detective story by a woman. But Regester's detective, Mr. Burton, often relies upon the psychic visions of his long-suffering daughter—whose gift he callously exploits despite the trances' toll on her already poor health—and this paranormal element alone disqualifies the book for consideration as a legitimate detective novel. Regester also has a very loose conception of plot and depends heavily upon coincidence. From similarities in key elements, such as the male narrator's romantic interest in one of the victim's beautiful daughters, it seems likely that Green was influenced by Regester's novel.

However, when Green published her first book, *The Leavenworth Case*, in 1878, she greatly surpassed Regester in plot, characterization, wit, and sheer authorial style. She had worked on the novel for six years in secret before showing it to her father, the lawyer whose experiences helped inspire the book, and she was dumbfounded when it became a huge bestseller. This first case for Ebenezer Gryce even became required reading at Yale Law School, as an example of the dangers of circumstantial evidence. Green grew up in Brooklyn and Buffalo and set most of her three dozen books in New York City or elsewhere in the state.

Not until 1897, two decades into her career, did Green introduce a second detective, Miss Amelia Butterworth, who herself narrates the three cases that she shares with Ebenezer Gryce. Butterworth's courage and intelligence paved the way for female detectives from Miss Marple to Veronica Mars. Although two other novels about her followed this debut, the strongest in terms of both plot and character is the first, *That Affair Next Door.* Later in this book, when Butterworth first meets the famous police detective Ebenezer Gryce, he mistakenly concludes that she is merely a busybody. His mistake is in assuming "merely." In time he develops great respect for her, and in subsequent adventures they evolve into something of an unofficial team.

(For more about Anna Katharine Green, see the introduction to "The Second Bullet.")

THAT AFFAIR NEXT DOOR

CHAPTER I

A Discovery

I am not an inquisitive woman, but when, in the middle of a certain warm night in September, I heard a carriage draw up at the adjoining house and stop, I could not resist the temptation of leaving my bed and taking a peep through the curtains of my window.

First: because the house was empty, or supposed to be so, the family still being, as I had every reason to believe, in Europe; and secondly: because, not being inquisitive, I often miss in my lonely and single life much that it would be both interesting and profitable for me to know.

Luckily I made no such mistake this evening. I rose and looked out, and though I was far from realizing it at the time, took, by so doing, my first step in a course of inquiry which has ended—

But it is too soon to speak of the end. Rather let me tell you what I saw when I parted the curtains of my window in Gramercy Park, on the night of September 17, 1895.

Not much at first glance, only a common hack drawn up at the neighboring curb-stone. The lamp which is supposed to light our part of the block is some rods away on the opposite side of the street, so that I obtained but a shadowy glimpse of a young man and woman standing below me on the pavement. I could see, however, that the woman—and not the man—was putting money into the driver's hand. The next moment they were on the stoop of this long-closed house, and the coach rolled off.

It was dark, as I have said, and I did not recognize the young people,—at least their figures were not familiar to me; but when, in another instant, I heard the click of a night-key, and saw them, after a rather tedious fumbling at the lock, disappear from the stoop, I took it for granted that the gentleman was Mr. Van Burnam's eldest son Franklin, and the lady some relative of the family; though why this, its most punctilious member, should bring a guest at so late an hour into a house devoid of everything necessary to make the least exacting visitor comfortable, was a mystery that I retired to bed to meditate upon.

I did not succeed in solving it, however, and after some ten minutes had elapsed, I was settling myself again to sleep when I was re-aroused by a fresh sound from the quarter mentioned. The door I had so lately heard shut, opened again, and though I had to rush for it, I succeeded in getting to my window in time to catch a glimpse of the departing figure of the young man hurrying away towards Broadway. The young woman was not with him, and as I realized that he had left her behind him in the great, empty house, without apparent light and certainly without any companion, I began to question if this was like Franklin Van Burnam. Was it not more in keeping with the recklessness of his more easy-natured and less reliable brother, Howard, who, some two or three years back, had married a young wife of no very satisfactory antecedents, and who, as I had heard, had been ostracized by the family in consequence?

Whichever of the two it was, he had certainly shown but little consideration for his companion, and thus thinking, I fell off to sleep just as the clock struck the half hour after midnight.

Next morning as soon as modesty would permit me to approach the window, I surveyed the neighboring house minutely. Not a blind was open, nor a shutter displaced. As I am an early riser, this did not disturb me at the time, but when after breakfast I looked again and still failed to detect any evidences of life in the great barren front beside me, I began to feel uneasy. But I did nothing till noon, when going into my rear garden and observing that the back windows of the Van Burnam house were as closely shuttered as the front, I became so anxious that I stopped the next policeman I saw going by, and telling him my suspicions, urged him to ring the bell.

No answer followed the summons.

"There is no one here," said he.

"Ring again!" I begged.

And he rang again but with no better result.

"Don't you see that the house is shut up?" he grumbled. "We have had orders to watch the place, but none to take the watch off."

"There is a young woman inside," I insisted. "The more I think over last night's occurrence, the more I am convinced that the matter should be looked into."

He shrugged his shoulders and was moving away when we both observed a common-looking woman standing in front looking at us. She had a bundle in her hand, and her face, unnaturally ruddy though it was, had a scared look which was all the more remarkable from the fact that it was one of those wooden-like countenances which under ordinary circumstances are capable of but little expression. She was not a stranger to me; that is, I had seen her before in or about the house in which we were at that moment so interested; and not stopping to put any curb on my excitement, I rushed down to the pavement and accosted her.

"Who are you?" I asked. "Do you work for the Van Burnams, and do you know who the lady was who came here last night?"

The poor woman, either startled by my sudden address or by my manner which may have been a little sharp, gave a quick bound backward, and was only deterred by the near presence of the policeman from attempting flight. As it was, she stood her ground, though the fiery flush, which made her face so noticeable, deepened till her cheeks and brow were scarlet.

"I am the scrub-woman," she protested. "I have come to open the windows and air the house,"—ignoring my last question.

"Is the family coming home?" the policeman asked.

"I don't know; I think so," was her weak reply.

"Have you the keys?" I now demanded, seeing her fumbling in her pocket.

She did not answer; a sly look displaced the anxious one she had hitherto displayed, and she turned away.

"I don't see what business it is of the neighbors," she muttered, throwing me a dissatisfied scowl over her shoulder.

"If you've got the keys, we will go in and see that things are all right," said the policeman, stopping her with a light touch.

She trembled; I saw that she trembled, and naturally became excited. Something was wrong in the Van Burnam mansion, and I was going to be present at its discovery. But her next words cut my hopes short.

"I have no objection to your going in," she said to the policeman, "but I will not give up my keys to her. What right has she in our house any way." And I thought I heard her murmur something about a meddlesome old maid.

The look which I received from the policeman convinced me that my ears had not played me false.

"The lady's right," he declared; and pushing by me quite disrespectfully, he led the way to the basement door, into which he and the so-called cleaner presently disappeared.

I waited in front. I felt it to be my duty to do so. The various passers-by stopped an instant to stare at me before proceeding on their way, but I did not flinch from my post. Not till I had heard that the young woman whom I had seen enter these doors at midnight was well, and that her delay in opening the windows was entirely due to fashionable laziness, would I feel justified in returning to my own home and its affairs. But it took patience and some courage to remain there. Several minutes elapsed before I perceived the shutters in the third story open, and a still longer time before a window on the second floor flew up and the policeman looked out, only to meet my inquiring gaze and rapidly disappear again.

Meantime three or four persons had stopped on the walk near me, the nucleus of a crowd which would not be long in collecting, and I was beginning to feel I was paying dearly for my virtuous resolution, when the front door burst violently open and we caught sight of the trembling form and shocked face of the scrubwoman.

"She's dead!" she cried, "she's dead! Murder!" and would have said more had not the policeman pulled her back, with a growl which sounded very much like a suppressed oath.

He would have shut the door upon me had I not been quicker

than lightning. As it was, I got in before it slammed, and happily too; for just at that moment the house-cleaner, who had grown paler every instant, fell in a heap in the entry, and the policeman, who was not the man I would want about me in any trouble, seemed somewhat embarrassed by this new emergency, and let me lift the poor thing up and drag her farther into the hall.

She had fainted, and should have had something done for her, but anxious though I always am to be of help where help is needed, I had no sooner got within range of the parlor door with my burden, than I beheld a sight so terrifying that I involuntarily let the poor woman slip from my arms to the floor.

In the darkness of a dim corner (for the room had no light save that which came through the doorway where I stood) lay the form of a woman under a fallen piece of furniture. Her skirts and distended arms alone were visible; but no one who saw the rigid outlines of her limbs could doubt for a moment that she was dead.

At a sight so dreadful, and, in spite of all my apprehensions, so unexpected, I felt a sensation of sickness which in another moment might have ended in my fainting also, if I had not realized that it would never do for me to lose my wits in the presence of a man who had none too many of his own. So I shook off my momentary weakness, and turning to the policeman, who was hesitating between the unconscious figure of the woman outside the door and the dead form of the one within I cried sharply:

"Come, man, to business! The woman inside there is dead, but this one is living. Fetch me a pitcher of water from below if you can, and then go for whatever assistance you need. I'll wait here and bring this woman to. She is a strong one, and it won't take long."

"You'll stay here alone with that—" he began.

But I stopped him with a look of disdain.

"Of course I will stay here; why not? Is there anything in the dead to be afraid of? Save me from the living, and I undertake to save myself from the dead."

But his face had grown very suspicious.

"You go for the water," he cried. "And see here! Just call out for some one to telephone to Police Headquarters for the Coroner and a detective. I don't quit this room till one or the other of them comes."

Smiling at a caution so very ill-timed, but abiding by my invariable rule of never arguing with a man unless I see some way of getting the better of him, I did what he bade me, though I hated dreadfully to leave the spot and its woful mystery, even for so short a time as was required.

"Run up to the second story," he called out, as I passed by the prostrate figure of the cleaner. "Tell them what you want from the window, or we will have the whole street in here."

So I ran up-stairs,—I had always wished to visit this house, but had never been encouraged to do so by the Misses Van Burnam,—and making my way into the front room, the door of which stood wide open, I rushed to the window and hailed the crowd, which by this time extended far out beyond the curb-stone.

"An officer!" I called out, "a police officer! An accident has occurred and the man in charge here wants the Coroner and a detective from Police Headquarters."

"Who's hurt?" "Is it a man?" "Is it a woman?" shouted up one or two; and "Let us in!" shouted others; but the sight of a boy rushing off to meet an advancing policeman satisfied me that help would soon be forthcoming, so I drew in my head and looked about me for the next necessity—water.

I was in a lady's bed-chamber, probably that of the eldest Miss Van Burnam; but it was a bed-chamber which had not been occupied for some months, and naturally it lacked the very articles which would have been of assistance to me in the present emergency. No eau de Cologne on the bureau, no camphor on the mantel-shelf. But there was water in the pipes (something I had hardly hoped for), and a mug on the wash-stand; so I filled the mug and ran with it to the door, stumbling, as I did so, over some small object which I presently perceived to be a little round pincushion. Picking it up, for I hate anything like disorder, I placed it on a table near by, and continued on my way.

The woman was still lying at the foot of the stairs. I dashed the water in her face and she immediately came to.

Sitting up, she was about to open her lips when she checked herself; a fact which struck me as odd, though I did not allow my surprise to become apparent.

Meantime I stole a glance into the parlor. The officer was standing where I had left him, looking down on the prostrate figure before him.

There was no sign of feeling in his heavy countenance, and he had not opened a shutter, nor, so far as I could see, disarranged an object in the room.

The mysterious character of the whole affair fascinated me in spite of myself, and leaving the now fully aroused woman in the hall, I was half-way across the parlor floor when the latter stopped me with a shrill cry:

"Don't leave me! I have never seen anything before so horrible. The poor dear! The poor dear! Why don't he take those dreadful things off her?"

She alluded not only to the piece of furniture which had fallen upon the prostrate woman, and which can best be described as a cabinet with closets below and shelves above, but to the various articles of bric-à-brac which had tumbled from the shelves, and which now lay in broken pieces about her.

"He will do so; they will do so very soon," I replied. "He is waiting for some one with more authority than himself; for the Coroner, if you know what that means."

"But what if she's alive! Those things will crush her. Let us take them off. I'll help. I'm not too weak to help."

"Do you know who this person is?" I asked, for her voice had more feeling in it than I thought natural to the occasion, dreadful as it was.

"I?" she repeated, her weak eyelids quivering for a moment as she tried to sustain my scrutiny. "How should I know? I came in with the policeman and haven't been any nearer than I now be. What makes you think I know anything about her? I'm only the scrub-woman, and don't even know the names of the family."

"I thought you seemed so very anxious," I explained, suspicious of her suspiciousness, which was of so sly and emphatic a character that it changed her whole bearing from one of fear to one of cunning in a moment.

"And who wouldn't feel the like of that for a poor creature lying crushed under a heap of broken crockery!"

Crockery! those Japanese vases worth hundreds of dollars! that ormulu clock and those Dresden figures which must have been more than a couple of centuries old!

"It's a poor sense of duty that keeps a man standing dumb and staring like that, when with a lift of his hand he could show us the like of her pretty face, and if it's dead she be or alive."

As this burst of indignation was natural enough and not altogether uncalled for from the standpoint of humanity, I gave the woman a nod of approval, and wished I were a man myself that I might lift the heavy cabinet or whatever it was that lay upon the poor creature before us. But not being a man, and not judging it wise to irritate the one representative of that sex then present, I made no remark, but only took a few steps farther into the room, followed, as it afterwards appeared, by the scrub-woman.

The Van Burnam parlors are separated by an open arch. It was to the right of this arch and in the corner opposite the doorway that the dead woman lay. Using my eyes, now that I was somewhat accustomed to the semi-darkness enveloping us, I noticed two or three facts which had hitherto escaped me. One was, that she lay on her back with her feet pointing towards the hall door, and another, that nowhere in the room, save in her immediate vicinity, were there to be seen any signs of struggle or disorder. All was as set and proper as in my own parlor when it has been undisturbed for any length of time by guests; and though I could not see far into the rooms beyond, they were to all appearance in an equally orderly condition.

Meanwhile the cleaner was trying to account for the overturned cabinet.

"Poor dear! poor dear! she must have pulled it over on herself! But however did she get into the house? And what was she doing in this great empty place?"

The policeman, to whom these remarks had evidently been addressed, growled out some unintelligible reply, and in her perplexity the woman turned towards me.

But what could I say to her? I had my own private knowledge of the matter, but she was not one to confide in, so I stoically shook my head. Doubly disappointed, the poor thing shrank back, after looking first at the policeman and then at me in an odd, appealing way, difficult to understand. Then her eyes fell again on the dead girl at her feet, and being nearer now than before, she evidently saw something that startled her, for she sank on her knees with a little cry and began examining the girl's skirts.

"What are you looking at there?" growled the policeman. "Get up, can't you! No one but the Coroner has right to lay hand on anything here."

"I'm doing no harm," the woman protested, in an odd, shaking voice. "I only wanted to see what the poor thing had on. Some blue stuff, isn't it?" she asked me.

"Blue serge," I answered; "store-made, but very good; must have come from Altman's or Stern's."

"I—I'm not used to sights like this," stammered the scrub-woman, stumbling awkwardly to her feet, and looking as if her few remaining wits had followed the rest on an endless vacation. "I—I think I shall have to go home." But she did not move.

"The poor dear's young, isn't she?" she presently insinuated, with an odd catch in her voice that gave to the question an air of hesitation and doubt.

"I think she is younger than either you or myself," I deigned to reply. "Her narrow pointed shoes show she has not reached the years of discretion."

"Yes, yes, so they do!" ejaculated the cleaner, eagerly—too eagerly for perfect ingenuousness. "That's why I said 'Poor dear!' and spoke of her pretty face. I am sorry for young folks when they get into trouble, aint you? You and me might lie here and no one be much the worse for it, but a sweet lady like this—"

This was not very flattering to me, but I was prevented from rebuking her by a prolonged shout from the stoop without, as a rush was made against the front door, followed by a shrill peal of the bell.

"Man from Headquarters," stolidly announced the policeman. "Open the door, ma'am; or step back into the further hall if you want me to do it."

Such rudeness was uncalled for; but considering myself too important a witness to show feeling, I swallowed my indignation and proceeded with all my native dignity to the front door.

GEORGE R. SIMS

(1847–1922)

In 1922, when George Robert Sims died in London two days after his seventy-fifth birthday, the *Times* declaimed that "no other journalist has ever occupied quite the same place in the affections not only of the great public but also of people of more discriminating taste." Discounted for hyperbole, this remark still testifies to the high profile of this versatile and prolific writer. He was born in 1847 in London, on almost the same day as the future outlaw Jesse James was born in Missouri—a reminder of the panoply of characters untidily crammed into the mental folder we label "the Victorian era." He grew up to become a quotable bon vivant, a bestselling novelist and popular playwright, and a crusader against social ills.

Sims was a lively and memorable fellow, as one would expect from his noble surname. Photographs of him in midlife show an elegantly waistcoated man-about-town with a Prince Albert beard and a corsage in his lapel. The author of numerous successful books, Sims earned a lot of royalties in his lifetime and didn't salt them away in a bank. When he wasn't boxing or playing badminton, he was frittering away his money on horse races.

Yet Sims also donated considerable sums to charity. The eldest of six children, he was named after his socially progressive father, an affluent businessman, but he acquired many of his interests in life from his mother, Louisa Amelia Ann Stevenson. As president of the organization that would evolve into the Women's Trade Union League, she introduced young George to suffragettes, actors, and musicians. His awareness of feminist and other social issues shows up throughout his writings. Like Arthur Conan Doyle, who interfered in real-world criminal cases now and then—most famously in his defense of wrongly accused George Edalji—Sims even left his mark on legal history. He fought to secure the pardon of Adolph Beck, a mistakenly jailed Norwegian immigrant. Together, Sims and Conan Doyle greatly influenced the movement that culminated in the establishment of the English Court of Criminal Appeal in 1907.

Sims began his career with satirical jibes for the Victorian weekly *Fun,* a cheaper rival of the omnipresent *Punch.* He was in good company. *Fun*'s contributions to history range from serving as the cradle of William S. Gilbert's nonsensical verse—the ancestors of his comic operas—to publishing the now famous cartoon of Darwin as a long-tailed monkey studiously examining a woman's bustle for clues to her evolutionary ancestry. Sims loved the theater. Most of his thirty-plus plays he adapted from French farces and other European sources. His autobiography dwells on his theatrical and journalistic work rather than on his novels and other fiction; crime fiction was such a small percentage of his literary output that he barely mentioned it.

However, he made a notable contribution to the field. In 1897 he published *Dorcas Dene, Detective: Her Life and Adventures.* She proved popular enough for Sims to write a second collection the next year, and several silent film adaptations appeared during his lifetime. "The Man with the Wild Eyes" comprised chapters 3 and 4 of the original volume. The first story, "The Council of Four," is not the strongest in the series, but it opens with a lively account of how Dorcas Dene became a detective. In the following version of "The Man with the Wild Eyes," this background material appears as an overture; the story actually begins at the first break.

Dorcas Dene may remind you of Sherlock Holmes. Like Conan Doyle, Sims tended to start a story with an outrageous situation, the cause of which shows up only after both ratiocination and legwork. In her talent for impersonation and tireless pursuit of an antagonist, her attention to footprints and inconsistencies, Dene is reminiscent of the great man himself; she even grants her doting Watson permission to chronicle their adventures. Again like Conan Doyle, Sims didn't hesitate to stack the deck in favor of his protagonist, enabling her to overhear muttered words and glimpse telling details.

Dene first appeared three years after a bored Arthur Conan Doyle sent his famous brainchild to grapple with Moriarty above the Reichenbach Falls and tumble to his death. (Badgered by fans and journalists, Conan Doyle finally surrendered to fate in 1903 and revealed that Holmes hadn't died during his fall.) Dene begins her career of impersonation, not surprisingly, as an actress; her Watson is a dramatist named Saxon, who knew Miss Lester the actress before she became Mrs. Dean the detective. Like Holmes, Dene is a professional detective and also a passionate vigilante in the cause of justice. Her world is one of tragedy and misfortune, drunken violence and family betrayal. In one story, she rescues a millionaire's caged and drugged first wife from the hideaway in which she is slowly dying of poison. Other than occasionally ignoring the letter of the law, Dene herself commits only one crime. She names her bulldog Toddlekins.

THE MAN WITH THE WILD EYES

(1897)

When I first knew Dorcas Dene she was Dorcas Lester. She came to me with a letter from a theatrical agent, and wanted one of the small parts in a play we were then rehearsing at a West End Theatre.

She was quite unknown in the profession. She told me that she wanted to act, and would I give her a chance? She was engaged for a maid-servant who had about two lines to speak. She spoke them exceedingly well, and remained at the theatre for nearly twelve months, never getting beyond "small parts," but always playing them exceedingly well.

The last part she had played was that of an old hag. We were all astonished when she asked to be allowed to play it, as she was a young and handsome woman, and handsome young women on the stage generally like to make the most of their appearance.

As the hag, Dorcas Lester was a distinct success. Although she was only on the stage for about ten minutes in one act and five minutes in another, everybody talked about her realistic and well-studied impersonation.

In the middle of the run of the play she left, and I understood that she had married and quitted the profession.

It was eight years before I met her again. I had business with a well-known West End solicitor. The clerk, thinking his employer was alone, ushered me at once into his room. Mr. —— was engaged in earnest conversation with a lady. I apologised. "It's all right," said Mr. ——, "the lady is just going." The lady, taking the hint, rose, and went out.

I saw her features as she passed me, for she had not then lowered her veil, and they seemed familiar to me.

"Who do you think that was?" said Mr. —— mysteriously, as the door closed behind his visitor.

"I don't know," I said; "but I think I've seen her before somewhere. Who is she?"

"That, my dear fellow, is Dorcas Dene, the famous lady detective. *You* may not have heard of her; but with our profession and with the police, she has a great reputation."

"Oh! Is she a private inquiry agent, or a female member of the Criminal Investigation Department?"

"She holds no official position," replied my friend, "but works entirely on her own account. She has been mixed up in some of the most remarkable cases of the day—cases that sometimes come into court, but which are far more frequently settled in a solicitor's office."

"If it isn't an indiscreet question, what is she doing for you? You are not in the criminal business."

"No, I am only an old-fashioned, humdrum family solicitor, but I have a very peculiar case in hand just now for one of my clients. I am not revealing a professional secret when I tell you that young Lord Helsham, who has recently come of age, has mysteriously disappeared. The matter has already been guardedly referred to in the gossip column of the society papers. His mother, Lady Helsham, who is a client of mine, has been to me in the greatest distress of mind. She is satisfied that her boy is alive and well. The poor lady is convinced that it is a case of *cherchez la femme*, and she is desperately afraid that her son, perhaps in the toils of some unprincipled woman, may be induced to contract a disastrous *mésalliance*. That is the only reason she can suggest to me for his extraordinary conduct."

"And the famous lady detective who has just left your office is to unravel the mystery—is that it?"

"Yes. All our own inquiries having failed, I yesterday decided to place the case in her hands, as it was Lady Helsham's earnest desire that no communication should be made to the police.

She is most anxious that the scandal shall not be made a public one. To-day Dorcas Dene has all the facts in her possession, and she has just gone to see Lady Helsham. And now, my dear fellow, what can I do for you?"

My business was a very trifling matter. It was soon discussed and settled, and then Mr. —— invited me to lunch with him at a neighbouring restaurant. After lunch I strolled back with him as far as his office. As we approached, a cab drove up to the door and a lady alighted.

"By Jove! it's your lady detective again," I exclaimed.

The lady detective saw us, and came towards us.

"Excuse me," she said to Mr. ——, "I want just a word or two with you."

Something in her voice struck me then, and suddenly I remembered where I had seen her before.

"I beg your pardon," I said, "but are we not old friends?"

"Oh, yes," replied the lady detective with a smile; "I knew you at once, but thought you had forgotten me. I have changed a good deal since I left the theatre."

"You have changed your name and your profession, but hardly your appearance—I ought to have known you at once. May I wait for you here while you discuss your business with Mr. ——? I should like to have a few minutes' chat with you about old times."

Dorcas Lester—or rather Dorcas Dene, as I must call her now—gave a little nod of assent, and I walked up and down the street smoking my cigar for fully a quarter of an hour before she reappeared.

"I'm afraid I've kept you waiting a long time," she said pleasantly, "and now if you want to talk to me you will have to come home with me. I'll introduce you to my husband. You needn't hesitate or think you'll be in the way, because, as a matter of fact, directly I saw you I made up my mind you could be exceedingly useful to me."

She raised her umbrella and stopped a taxi, and before I quite appreciated the situation, we were making our way to St. John's Wood.

On the journey Dorcas Dene was confidential. She told me that she had taken to the stage because her father, an artist, had died suddenly and left her and her mother nothing but a few unmarketable pictures.

"Poor dad!" she said. "He was very clever, and he loved us very dearly, but he was only a great big boy to the last. When he was doing well he spent everything he made, and enjoyed life—when he was doing badly he did bills and pawned things, and thought it was rather fun. At one time he would be treating us to dinner at the Café Royal and the theatre afterwards, and at another time he would be showing us how to live as cheaply as he used to do in his old Paris days in the Quartier Latin, and cooking our meals himself at the studio fire.

"Well, when he died I got on to the stage, and at last—as I daresay you remember—I was earning two guineas a week. On that my mother and I lived in two rooms in St. Paul's Road, Camden Town.

"Then a young artist, a Mr. Paul Dene, who had been our friend and constant visitor in my father's lifetime, fell in love with me. He had risen rapidly in his profession, and was making money. He had no relatives, and his income was seven or eight hundred a year, and promised to be much larger. Paul proposed to me, and I accepted him. He insisted that I should leave the stage, and he would take a pretty little house, and mother should come and live with us, and we could all be happy together.

"We took the house we are going to now—a sweet little place with a lovely garden in Elm Tree Road, St. John's Wood—and for two years we were very happy. Then a terrible misfortune happened. Paul had an illness and became blind. He would never be able to paint again.

"When I had nursed him back to health I found that the interest of what we had saved would barely pay the rent of our house. I did not want to break up our home—what was to be done? I thought of the stage again, and I had just made up my mind to see if I could not get an engagement, when chance settled my future for me and gave me a start in a very different profession.

"In the next house to us there lived a gentleman, a Mr. Johnson, who was a retired superintendent of police. Since his retirement he had been conducting a high-class private inquiry business, and was employed in many delicate family matters by a well-known firm of solicitors who are supposed to have the secrets of half the aristocracy locked away in their strong room.

"Mr. Johnson had been a frequent visitor of ours, and there was nothing which delighted Paul more in our quiet evenings than a chat and a pipe with the genial, good-hearted ex-superintendent of police. Many a time have I and my husband sat till the small hours by our cosy fireside listening to the strange tales of crime, and the unravelling of mysteries which our kind neighbour had to tell. There was something fascinating to us in following the slow and cautious steps with which our friend—who looked more like a jolly sea captain than a detective—had threaded his way through the Hampton Court maze in the centre of which lay the truth which it was his business to discover.

"He must have thought a good deal of Paul's opinion, for after a time he would come in and talk over cases which he had in hand—without mentioning names when the business was confidential—and the view which Paul took of the mystery more than once turned out to be the correct one. From this constant association with a private detective we began to take a kind of interest in his work, and when there was a great case in the papers which seemed to defy the efforts of Scotland Yard, Paul and I would talk it over together, and discuss it and build up our own theories around it.

"After my poor Paul lost his sight Mr. Johnson, who was a widower, would come in whenever he was at home—many of his cases took him out of London for weeks together—and help to cheer my poor boy up by telling him all about the latest romance or scandal in which he had been engaged.

"On these occasions my mother, who is a dear, old-fashioned, simple-minded woman, would soon make an excuse to leave us. She declared that to listen to Mr. Johnson's stories made her nervous. She would soon begin to believe that every man and woman she met had a guilty secret, and the world was one great Chamber of Horrors with living figures instead of waxwork ones like those of Madame Tussaud's.

"I had told Mr. Johnson of our position when I found that it would be necessary for me to do something to supplement the hundred a year which was all that Paul's money would bring us in, and he had agreed with me that the stage afforded the best opening.

"One morning I made up my mind to go to the agent's. I had dressed myself in my best and had anxiously consulted my looking-glass. I was afraid that my worries and the long strain of my husband's illness might have left their mark upon my features and spoilt my 'market value' in the managerial eye.

"I had taken such pains with myself, and my mind was so concentrated upon the object I had in view, that when I was quite satisfied with my appearance I ran into our little sitting-room, and, without thinking, said to my husband, 'Now I'm off! How do you think I look, dear?'"

"My poor Paul turned his sightless eyes towards me, and his lip quivered. Instantly I saw what my thoughtlessness had done. I flung my arms round him and kissed him, and then, the tears in my eyes, I ran out of the room and went down the front garden. When I opened the door Mr. Johnson was outside with his hand on the bell.

" 'Where are you going?' he said.

" 'To the agent, to see about an engagement.'

" 'Come back; I want to talk to you.'

"I led the way into the house, and we went into the dining-room, which was empty.

" 'What do you think you could get on the stage?' he said.

" 'Oh, if I'm lucky I may get what I had before—two guineas a week.'

" 'Well, then, put off the stage for a little and I can give you something that will pay you a great deal better. I've just got a case in which I must have the assistance of a lady. The lady who has worked for me the last two years has been idiot enough to get married, with the usual consequences, and I'm in a fix.'

" 'You—you want me to be a lady detective—to watch people?' I gasped. 'Oh, I couldn't!'

" 'My dear Mrs. Dene,' Mr. Johnson said gently, 'I have too much respect for you and your husband to offer you anything that you need be afraid of accepting. I want you to help me to rescue an unhappy man who is being so brutally blackmailed that he has run away from his broken-hearted wife and his sorrowing children. That is surely a business transaction in which an angel could engage without soiling its wings.'

"'But I'm not clever at—at that sort of thing!'

"'You are cleverer than you think. I have formed a very high opinion of your qualifications for our business. You have plenty of shrewd common sense, you are a keen observer, and you have been an actress. Come, the wife's family are rich, and I am to have a good round sum if I save the poor fellow and get him home again. I can give you a guinea a day and your expenses, and you have only to do what I tell you.'

"I thought everything over, and then I accepted—on one condition. I was to see how I got on before Paul was told anything about it. If I found that being a lady detective was repugnant to me—if I found that it involved any sacrifice of my womanly instincts—I should resign, and my husband would never know that I had done anything of the sort.

"Mr. Johnson agreed, and we left together for his office.

"That was how I first became a lady detective. I found that the work interested me, and that I was not so awkward as I had expected to be. I was successful in my first undertaking, and Mr. Johnson insisted on my remaining with him and eventually we became partners. A year ago he retired, strongly recommending me to all his clients, and that is how you find me to-day a professional lady detective."

"And one of the best in England," I said, with a bow. "My friend Mr. —— has told me of your great reputation."

Dorcas Dene smiled.

"Never mind about my reputation," she said. "Here we are at my house—now you've got to come in and be introduced to my husband and to my mother and to Toddlekins."

"Toddlekins—I beg pardon—that's the baby, I suppose?"

A shade crossed Dorcas Dene's pretty womanly face, and I thought I saw her soft grey eyes grow moist.

"No—we have no family. Toddlekins is a dog."

I had become a constant visitor at Elm Tree Road. I had conceived a great admiration for the brave and yet womanly woman who, when her artist husband was stricken with blindness, and the future looked dark for both of them, had gallantly made the best of her special gifts and opportunities and nobly undertaken a profession which was not only a harassing and exhausting one for a woman, but by no means free from grave personal risks.

Dorcas Dene was always glad to welcome me for her husband's sake. "Paul has taken to you immensely," she said to me one afternoon, "and I hope you will call in and spend an hour or two with him whenever you can. My cases take me away from home so much—he cannot read, and my mother, with the best intentions in the world, can never converse with him for more than five minutes without irritating him. Her terribly matter of fact views of life are, to use his own expression, absolutely 'rasping' to his dreamy, artistic temperament."

I had plenty of spare time on my hands, and so it became my custom to drop in two or three times a week, and smoke a pipe, and chat with Paul. His conversation was always interesting, and the gentle resignation with which he bore his terrible affliction won my heart. But I am not ashamed to confess that my frequent journeys to Elm Tree Road were also largely influenced by my desire to see Dorcas Dene, and hear more of her strange adventures and experiences.

From the moment she knew that her husband valued my companionship she treated me as one of the family, and when I was fortunate enough to find her at home, she discussed her professional affairs openly before me. I was grateful for this confidence, and I was sometimes able to assist her by going about with her in cases where the presence of a male companion was a material advantage to her. I had upon one occasion laughingly dubbed myself her "assistant," and by that name I was afterwards generally known. There was only one drawback to the pleasure I felt at being associated with Dorcas Dene in her detective work. I saw that it would be quite impossible for me to avoid reproducing my experiences in some form or other. One day I broached the subject to her cautiously.

"Are you not afraid of the assistant one day revealing the professional secrets of his chief?" I said.

"Not at all," replied Dorcas—everybody called her Dorcas, and

I fell into the habit when I found that she and her husband preferred it to the formal "Mrs. Dene"—"I am quite sure that you will not be able to resist the temptation."

"And you don't object?"

"Oh, no, but with this stipulation, that you will use the material in such a way as not to identify any of the cases with the real parties concerned."

That lifted a great responsibility from my shoulders, and made me more eager than ever to prove myself a valuable "assistant" to the charming lady who honoured me with her confidence.

We were sitting in the dining-room one evening after dinner. Mrs. Lester was looking contemptuously over the last number of the *Tatler*, and wondering out loud what on earth young women were coming to. Paul was smoking the old briar-root pipe which had been his constant companion in the studio when he was able to paint, poor fellow, and Dorcas was lying down on the sofa. Toddlekins, nestled up close to her, was snoring gently after the manner of his kind.

Dorcas had had a hard and exciting week, and had not been ashamed to confess that she felt a little played out. She had just succeeded in rescuing a young lady of fortune from the toils of an unprincipled Russian adventurer, and stopping the marriage almost at the altar rails by the timely production of the record of the would-be bridegroom, which she obtained with the assistance of the head of the French detective police. It was a return compliment. Dorcas had only a short time previously undertaken for the Chef de la Sureté a delicate investigation, in which the son of one of the noblest houses in France was involved, and had nipped in the bud a scandal which would have kept the Boulevards chattering for a month.

Paul and I were conversing below our voices, for Dorcas's measured breathing showed us that she had fallen into a doze.

Suddenly Toddlekins opened his eyes and uttered an angry growl. He had heard the front gate bell.

A minute later the servant entered and handed a card to her mistress, who, with her eyes still half closed, was sitting up on the sofa.

"The gentleman says he must see you at once, ma'am, on business of the greatest importance."

Dorcas looked at the card. "Show the gentleman into the dining-room," she said to the servant, "and say that I will be with him directly."

Then she went to the mantel-glass and smoothed away the evidence of her recent forty winks. "Do you know him at all?" she said, handing me the card.

"Colonel Hargreaves, Orley Park, near Godalming." I shook my head, and Dorcas, with a little tired sigh, went to see her visitor.

A few minutes later the dining-room bell rang, and presently the servant came into the drawing-room. "Please, sir," she said, addressing me, "mistress says will you kindly come to her at once?"

When I entered the dining-room I was astonished to see an elderly, soldierly looking man lying back unconscious in the easy chair, and Dorcas Dene bending over him.

"I don't think it's anything but a faint," she said. "He's very excited and overwrought, but if you'll stay here I'll go and get some brandy. You had better loosen his collar—or shall we send for a doctor?"

"No, I don't think it is anything serious," I said, after a hasty glance at the invalid.

As soon as Dorcas had gone I began to loosen the Colonel's collar, but I had hardly commenced before, with a deep sigh, he opened his eyes and came to himself.

"You're better now," I said. "Come—that's all right."

The Colonel stared about him for a moment, and then said, "I—I—where is the lady?"

"She'll be here in a moment. She's gone to get some brandy."

"Oh, I'm all right now, thank you. I suppose it was the excitement, and I've been travelling, had nothing to eat, and I'm so terribly upset. I don't often do this sort of thing, I assure you."

Dorcas returned with the brandy. The Colonel brightened up directly she came into the room. He took the glass she offered him and drained the contents.

"I'm all right now," he said. "Pray let me get on with my story.

I hope you will be able to take the case up at once. Let me see—where was I?"

He gave a little uneasy glance in my direction. "You can speak without reserve before this gentleman," said Dorcas. "It is possible he may be able to assist us if you wish me to come to Orley Park at once. So far you have told me that your only daughter, who is five-and-twenty, and lives with you, was found last night on the edge of the lake in your grounds, half in the water and half out. She was quite insensible, and was carried into the house and put to bed. You were in London at the time, and returned to Orley Park this morning in consequence of a telegram you received. That is as far as you had got when you became ill."

"Yes—yes!" exclaimed the Colonel, "but I am quite well again now. When I arrived at home this morning shortly before noon I was relieved to find that Maud—that is my poor girl's name—was quite conscious, and the doctor had left a message that I was not to be alarmed, and that he would return and see me early in the afternoon.

"I went at once to my daughter's room and found her naturally in a very low, distressed state. I asked her how it had happened, as I could not understand it, and she told me that she had gone out in the grounds after dinner and must have turned giddy when by the edge of the lake and fallen in."

"Is it a deep lake?" asked Dorcas.

"Yes, in the middle, but shallow near the edge. It is a largish lake, with a small fowl island in the centre, and we have a boat upon it."

"Probably it was a sudden fainting fit—such as you yourself have had just now. Your daughter may be subject to them."

"No, she is a thoroughly strong, healthy girl."

"I am sorry to have interrupted you," said Dorcas; "pray go on, for I presume there is something more than a fainting fit behind this accident, or you would not have come to engage my services in the matter."

"There is a great deal more behind it," replied Colonel Hargreaves, pulling nervously at his grey moustache. "I left my daughter's bedside devoutly thankful that Providence had preserved her from such a dreadful death, but when the doctor arrived he gave me a piece of information which caused me the greatest uneasiness and alarm."

"He didn't believe in the fainting fit?" said Dorcas, who had been closely watching the Colonel's features.

The Colonel looked at Dorcas Dene in astonishment. "I don't know how you have divined that," he said, "but your surmise is correct. The doctor told me that he had questioned Maud himself, and she had told him the same story—sudden giddiness and a fall into the water. But he had observed that on her throat there were certain marks, and that her wrists were bruised.

"When he told me this I did not at first grasp his meaning. 'It must have been the violence of the fall,' I said.

"The doctor shook his head and assured me that no accident would account for the marks his experienced eye had detected. The marks round the throat must have been caused by the clutch of an assailant. The wrists could only have been bruised in the manner they were by being held in a violent and brutal grip."

Dorcas Dene, who had been listening apparently without much interest, bent forward as the Colonel made this extraordinary statement. "I see," she said. "Your daughter told you that she had fallen into the lake, and the doctor assures you that she must have told you an untruth. She had been pushed or flung in by some one else after a severe struggle."

"Yes!"

"And the young lady, when you questioned her further, with this information in your possession, what did she say?"

"She appeared very much excited, and burst into tears. When I referred to the marks on her throat, which were now beginning to show discoloration more distinctly, she declared that she had invented the story of the faint in order not to alarm me—that she had been attacked by a tramp who must have got into the grounds, and that he had tried to rob her, and that in the struggle, which took place near the edge of the lake, he had thrown her down at the water's edge and then made his escape."

"And that explanation you *do* accept?" said Dorcas, looking at the Colonel keenly.

"How can I? Why should my daughter try to screen a tramp?

Why did she tell the doctor an untruth? Surely the first impulse of a terrified woman rescued from a terrible death would have been to have described her assailant in order that he might have been searched for and brought to justice."

"And the police, have they made any inquiries? Have they learned if any suspicious persons were seen about that evening?"

"I have not been to the police. I talked the matter over with the doctor. He says that the police inquiries would make the whole thing public property, and it would be known everywhere that my daughter's story, which has now gone all over the neighbourhood, was untrue. But the whole affair is so mysterious, and to me so alarming, that I could not leave it where it is. It was the doctor who advised me to come to you and let the inquiry be a private one."

"You need employ no one if your daughter can be persuaded to tell the truth. Have you tried?"

"Yes. But she insists that it was a tramp, and declares that until the bruises betrayed her she kept to the fainting-fit story in order to make the affair as little alarming to me as possible."

Dorcas Dene rose. "What time does the last train leave for Godalming?"

"In an hour," said the Colonel, looking at his watch. "At the station my carriage will be waiting to take us to Orley Court. I want you to stay at the Court until you have discovered the key to the mystery."

"No," said Dorcas, after a minute's thought. "I could do no good to-night, and my arrival with you would cause talk among the servants. Go back by yourself. Call on the doctor. Tell him to say his patient requires constant care during the next few days, and that he has sent for a trained nurse from London. The trained nurse will arrive about noon to-morrow."

"And you?" exclaimed the Colonel, "won't you come?"

Dorcas smiled. "Oh, yes; I shall be the trained nurse."

The Colonel rose. "If you can discover the truth and let me know what it is my daughter is concealing from me I shall be eternally grateful," he said. "I shall expect you to-morrow at noon."

"To-morrow at noon you will expect the trained nurse for whom the doctor has telegraphed. Good evening."

I went to the door with Colonel Hargreaves, and saw him down the garden to the front gate.

When I went back to the house Dorcas Dene was waiting for me in the hall. "Are you busy for the next few days?" she said.

"No—I have practically nothing to do."

"Then come to Godalming with me to-morrow. You are an artist, and I must get you permission to sketch that lake while I am nursing my patient indoors."

It was past noon when the fly, hired from the station, stopped at the lodge gates of Orley Park, and the lodge-keeper's wife opened them to let us in.

"You are the nurse for Miss Maud, I suppose, miss?" she said, glancing at Dorcas's neat hospital nurse's costume.

"Yes."

"The Colonel and the doctor are both at the house expecting you, miss—I hope it isn't serious with the poor young lady."

"I hope not," said Dorcas, with a pleasant smile.

A minute or two later the fly pulled up at the door of a picturesque old Elizabethan mansion. The Colonel, who had seen the fly from the window, was on the steps waiting for us, and at once conducted us into the library. Dorcas explained my presence in a few words. I was her assistant, and through me she would be able to make all the necessary inquiries in the neighbourhood.

"To your people Mr. Saxon will be an artist to whom you have given permission to sketch the house and the grounds—I think that will be best."

The Colonel promised that I should have free access at all hours to the grounds, and it was arranged that I should stay at a pretty little inn which was about half a mile from the park. Having received full instructions on the way down from Dorcas, I knew exactly what to do, and bade her good-bye until the evening, when I was to call at the house to see her.

The doctor came into the room to conduct the new nurse to the patient's bedside, and I left to fulfil my instructions.

At "The Chequers," which was the name of the inn, it was no sooner known that I was an artist, and had permission to sketch in the grounds of Orley Park, than the landlady commenced to entertain me with accounts of the accident which had nearly cost Miss Hargreaves her life.

The fainting-fit story, which was the only one that had got about, had been accepted in perfect faith.

"It's a lonely place, that lake, and there's nobody about the grounds, you see, at night, sir—it was a wonder the poor young lady was found so soon."

"Who found her?" I asked.

"One of the gardeners who lives in a cottage in the park. He'd been to Godalming for the evening, and was going home past the lake."

"What time was it?"

"Nearly ten o'clock. It was lucky he saw her, for it had been dark nearly an hour then, and there was no moon."

"What did he think when he found her?"

"Well, sir, to tell you the truth, he thought at first it was suicide, and that the young lady hadn't gone far enough in and had lost her senses."

"Of course, he couldn't have thought it was murder or anything of that sort," I said, "because nobody could get in at night—without coming through the lodge gates."

"Oh! yes, they could at one place, but it 'ud have to be somebody who knew the dogs or was with some one who did. There's a couple of big mastiffs have got a good run there, and no stranger 'ud try to clamber over—it's a side gate used by the family, sir—after they'd started barking."

"Did they bark that night at all, do you know?"

"Well, yes," said the landlady. "Now I come to think of it, Mr. Peters—that's the lodge-keeper—heard 'em, but they was quiet in a minute, so he took no more notice."

That afternoon the first place I made up my mind to sketch was the Lodge. I found Mr. Peters at home, and my pass from the Colonel secured his good graces at once. His wife had told him of the strange gentleman who had arrived with the nurse, and I explained that there being only one fly at the station and our destination the same, the nurse had kindly allowed me to share the vehicle with her.

I made elaborate pencil marks and notes in my new sketching

book, telling Mr. Peters I was only doing something preliminary and rough, in order to conceal the amateurish nature of my efforts, and keep the worthy man gossiping about the "accident" to his young mistress.

I referred to the landlady's statement that he had heard dogs bark that night.

"Oh, yes, but they were quiet directly."

"Probably some stranger passing down by the side gate, eh?"

"Most likely, sir. I was a bit uneasy at first, but when they quieted down I thought it was all right."

"Why were you uneasy?"

"Well, there'd been a queer sort of a looking man hanging about that evening. My missus saw him peering in at the lodge gates about seven o'clock."

"A tramp?"

"No, a gentlemanly sort of man, but he gave my missus a turn, he had such wild, staring eyes. But he spoke all right. My missus asked him what he wanted, and he asked her what was the name of the big house he could see, and who lived there. She told him it was Orley Park, and Colonel Hargreaves lived there, and he thanked her and went away. A tourist, maybe, sir, or perhaps an artist gentleman, like yourself."

"Staying in the neighbourhood and studying its beauties, perhaps."

"No; when I spoke about it the next day in the town I heard as he'd come by the train that afternoon; the porters had noticed him, he seemed so odd."

I finished my rough sketch and then asked Mr. Peters to take me to the scene of the accident. It was a large lake and answered the description given by the Colonel.

"That there's the place where Miss Maud was found," said Mr. Peters. "You see it's shallow there, and her head was just on the bank here out of the water."

"Thank you. That's a delightful little island in the middle. I'll smoke a pipe here and sketch. Don't let me detain you."

The lodge-keeper retired, and obeying the instructions received from Dorcas Dene, I examined the spot carefully.

The marks of hobnailed boots were distinctly visible in the mud at the side, near the place where the struggle, admitted by Miss Hargreaves, had taken place. They might be the tramp's—they might be the gardener's; I was not skilled enough in the art of footprints to determine. But I had obtained a certain amount of information, and with that, at seven o'clock, I went to the house and asked for the Colonel.

I had, of course, nothing to say to him, except to ask him to let Dorcas Dene know that I was there. In a few minutes Dorcas came to me with her bonnet and cloak on.

"I'm going to get a walk while it is light," she said; "come with me."

Directly we were outside I gave her my information, and she at once decided to visit the lake.

She examined the scene of the accident carefully, and I pointed out the hobnailed boot marks.

"Yes," she said, "those are the gardener's probably—I'm looking for some one else's."

"Whose?"

"These," she said, suddenly stooping and pointing to a series of impressions in the soil at the edge. "Look—here are a woman's footprints, and here are larger ones beside them—now close to—now a little way apart—now crossing each other. Do you see anything particular in these footprints?"

"No—except that there are no nails in them."

"Exactly—the footprints are small, but larger than Miss Hargreaves'—the shape is an elegant one: you see the toes are pointed, and the sole is a narrow one. No tramp would have boots like those. Where did you say Mrs. Peters saw that strange-looking gentleman?"

"Peering through the lodge gates."

"Let us go there at once."

Mrs. Peters came out and opened the gates for us.

"What a lovely evening," said Dorcas. "Is the town very far?"

"Two miles, miss."

"Oh, that's too far for me to-night."

She took out her purse and selected some silver.

"Will you please send down the first thing in the morning and buy me a bottle of Wood Violet scent at the chemist's. I always use it, and I've come away without any."

She was just going to hand some silver to Mrs. Peters, when she dropped her purse in the roadway, and the money rolled in every direction.

We picked most of it up, but Dorcas declared there was another half-sovereign. For fully a quarter of an hour she peered about in every direction outside the lodge gates for that missing half-sovereign, and I assisted her. She searched for quite ten minutes in one particular spot, a piece of sodden, loose roadway close against the right-hand gate.

Suddenly she exclaimed that she had found it, and, slipping her hand into her pocket, rose, handed Mrs. Peters a five-shilling piece for the scent, beckoned me to follow her, and strolled down the road.

"How came you to drop your purse? Are you nervous to-night?" I said.

"Not at all," replied Dorcas, with a smile. "I dropped my purse that the money might roll and give me an opportunity of closely examining the ground outside the gates."

"Did you really find your half-sovereign?"

"I never lost one; but I found what I wanted."

"And that was?"

"The footprints of the man who stood outside the gates that night. They are exactly the same shape as those by the side of the lake. The person Maud Hargreaves struggled with that night, the person who flung her into the lake and whose guilt she endeavoured to conceal by declaring she had met with an accident, was the man who wanted to know the name of the place, and asked who lived there—*the man with the wild eyes*."

"You are absolutely certain that the footprints of the man with the wild eyes, who frightened Mrs. Peters at the gate, and the footprints which are mixed up with those of Miss Hargreaves by the side of the lake, are the same?" I said to Dorcas Dene.

"Absolutely certain."

"Then perhaps, if you describe him, the Colonel may be able to recognize him."

"No," said Dorcas Dene, "I have already asked him if he knew any one who could possibly bear his daughter a grudge, and he declares that there is no one to his knowledge. Miss Hargreaves has scarcely any acquaintances."

"And has had no love affair?" I asked.

"None, her father says, but of course he can only answer for the last three years. Previously to that he was in India, and Maud—who was sent home at the age of fourteen, when her mother died—had lived with an aunt at Norwood."

"Who do you think this man was who managed to get into the grounds and meet or surprise Miss Hargreaves by the lake—a stranger to her?"

"No; had he been a stranger, she would not have shielded him by inventing the fainting fit story."

We had walked some distance from the house, when an empty station fly passed us. We got in, Dorcas telling the man to drive us to the station.

When we got there, she told me to go and interview the porter and try and find out if a man of the description of our suspect had left on the night of the "accident."

I found the man who had told Mr. Peters that he had seen such a person arrive, and had noticed the peculiar expression of his eyes. This man assured me that no such person had left from that station. He had told his mates about him, and some of them would be sure to have seen him. The stranger brought no luggage, and gave up a single ticket from Waterloo.

Dorcas was waiting for me outside, and I gave her my information.

"No luggage," she said; "then he wasn't going to an hotel or to stay at a private house."

"But he might be living somewhere about."

"No; the porter would have recognized him if he had been in the habit of coming here."

"But he must have gone away after flinging Miss Hargreaves into the water. He might have got out of the grounds again and walked to another station, and caught a train back to London."

"Yes, he might," said Dorcas, "but I don't think he did. Come, we'll take the fly back to Orley Park."

Just before we reached the park Dorcas stopped the driver, and we got out and dismissed the man.

"Whereabouts are those dogs—near the private wooden door in the wall used by the family, aren't they?" she said to me.

"Yes, Peters pointed the spot out to me this afternoon."

"Very well, I'm going in. Meet me by the lake to-morrow morning about nine. But watch me now as far as the gates. I'll wait outside five minutes before ringing. When you see I'm there, go to that portion of the wall near the private door. Clamber up and peer over. When the dogs begin to bark, and come at you, notice if you could possibly drop over and escape them without some one they knew called them off. Then jump down again and go back to the inn."

I obeyed Dorcas's instructions; and when I had succeeded in climbing to the top of the wall, the dogs flew out of their kennel, and commenced to bark furiously. Had I dropped I must have fallen straight into their grip. Suddenly I heard a shout, and I recognized the voice—it was the lodge-keeper. I dropped back into the road and crept along in the shadow of the wall. In the distance I could hear Peters talking to some one, and I knew what had happened. In the act of letting Dorcas in, he had heard the dogs, and had hurried off to see what was the matter. Dorcas had followed him.

At nine o'clock next morning I found Dorcas waiting for me.

"You did your work admirably last night," she said. "Peters was in a terrible state of alarm. He was very glad for me to come with him. He quieted the dogs, and we searched about everywhere in the shrubbery to see if any one was in hiding. That man wasn't let in at the door that night by Miss Hargreaves; he dropped over. I found the impression of two deep footprints close together, exactly as they would be made by a drop or jump down from a height."

"Did he go back that way—*were there return footsteps?*"

I thought I had made a clever suggestion, but Dorcas smiled, and shook her head. "I didn't look. How could he return past the dogs when Miss Hargreaves was lying in the lake? They'd have torn him to pieces."

"And you still think this man with the wild eyes is guilty! Who can he have been?"

"His name was Victor."

"You have discovered that!" I exclaimed. "Has Miss Hargreaves been talking to you?"

"Last night I tried a little experiment. When she was asleep, and evidently dreaming, I went quietly in the dark and stood just behind the bed, and in the gruffest voice I could assume, I said, bending down to her ear, 'Maud!'

"She started up, and cried out, 'Victor!'

"In a moment I was by her side, and found her trembling violently. 'What's the matter, dear?' I said, 'have you been dreaming?'

" 'Yes—yes,' she said. 'I—I was dreaming.'

"I soothed her, and talked to her a little while, and finally she lay down again and fell asleep."

"That's something," I said, "to have got the man's Christian name."

"Yes, it's a little, but I think we shall have the surname to-day. You must go up to town and do a little commission for me presently. In the meantime, pull that boat in and row me across to the fowl island. I want to search it."

"You don't imagine the man's hiding there," I said. "It's too small."

"Pull me over," said Dorcas, getting into the boat.

I obeyed, and presently we were on the little island.

Dorcas carefully surveyed the lake in every direction. Then she walked round and examined the foliage and the reeds that were at the edge and drooping into the water.

Suddenly pushing a mass of close over-hanging growth aside, she thrust her hand deep down under it into the water and drew out a black, saturated, soft felt hat.

"I thought if anything drifted that night, this is where it would get caught and entangled," said Dorcas.

"If it is that man's hat, he must have gone away bareheaded."

"Quite so," replied Dorcas, "but first let us ascertain if it is his. Row ashore at once."

She wrung the water from the hat, squeezed it together and wrapped it up in her pocket-handkerchief and put it under her cloak.

When we were ashore, I went to the lodge and got Mrs. Peters on to the subject of the man with the wild eyes. Then I asked what sort of a hat he had on, and Mrs. Peters said it was a soft felt hat with a dent in the middle, and I knew that our find was a good one.

When I told Dorcas she gave a little smile of satisfaction.

"We've got his Christian name and his hat," she said; "now we want the rest of him. You can catch the 11.20 easily."

"Yes."

She drew an envelope from her pocket and took a small photograph from it.

"That's the portrait of a handsome young fellow," she said. "By the style and size I should think it was taken four or five years ago. The photographers are the London Stereoscopic Company—the number of the negative is 111,492. If you go to them, they will search their books and give you the name and address of the original. Get it, and come back here."

"Is that the man?" I said.

"I think so."

"How on earth did you get it?"

"I amused myself while Miss Hargreaves was asleep by looking over the album in her boudoir. It was an old album, and filled with portraits of relatives and friends. I should say there were over fifty, some of them being probably her schoolfellows. I thought I *might* find something, you know. People have portraits given them, put them in an album, and almost forget they are there. I fancied Miss Hargreaves might have forgotten.

"But how did you select this from fifty? There were other male portraits, I suppose?"

"Oh, yes, but I took out every portrait and examined the back and the margin."

I took the photo from Dorcas and looked at it. I noticed that a portion of the back had been rubbed away and was rough.

"That's been done with an ink eraser," said Dorcas. "That made me concentrate on this particular photo. There has been a name written there or some word the recipient didn't want other eyes to see."

"That is only surmise."

"Quite so—but there's a certainty in the photo itself. Look closely at that little diamond scarf-pin in the necktie. What shape is it?"

"It looks like a small V."

"Exactly. It was fashionable a few years ago for gentlemen to wear a small initial pin. V stands for Victor—take that and the erasure together, and I think it's worth a return fare to town to find out what name and address are opposite the negative number in the books of the London Stereoscopic Company."

Before two o'clock I was interviewing the manager of the Stereoscopic Company, and he readily referred to the books. The photograph had been taken six years previously, and the name and address of the sitter were "Mr. Victor Dubois, Anerley Road, Norwood."

Following Dorcas Dene's instructions, I proceeded at once to the address given, and made inquiries for a Mr. Victor Dubois. No one of that name resided there. The present tenants had been in possession for three years.

As I was walking back along the road I met an old postman. I thought I would ask him if he knew the name anywhere in the neighbourhood. He thought a minute, then said, "Yes—now I come to think of it, there was a Dubois here at No. —, but that was five years ago or more. He was an oldish, white-haired gentleman."

"An old gentleman—Victor Dubois!"

"Ah, no—the old gentleman's name was Mounseer Dubois, but there was a Victor. I suppose that must have been his son as lived with him. I know the name. There used to be letters addressed there for Mr. Victor most every day—sometimes twice a day—always in the same hand-writing, a lady's—that's what made me notice it."

"And you don't know where M. Dubois and his son went to?"

"No, I did hear as the old gentleman went off his head, and was put in a lunatic asylum; but they went out o' my round."

"You don't know what he was, I suppose?"

"Oh, it said on the brass plate, 'Professor of Languages.' "

I went back to town and took the first train to Godalming, and hastened to Orley Court to report the result of my inquiries to Dorcas.

She was evidently pleased, for she complimented me. Then she rang the bell—we were in the dining-room—and the servant entered.

"Will you let the Colonel know that I should like to see him?" said Dorcas, and the servant went to deliver the message.

"Are you going to tell him everything?" I said.

"I am going to tell him nothing yet," replied Dorcas. "I want him to tell me something."

The Colonel entered. His face was worn, and he was evidently worrying himself a great deal.

"Have you anything to tell me?" he said eagerly. "Have you found out what my poor girl is hiding from me?"

"I'm afraid I cannot tell you yet. But I want to ask you a few questions."

"I have given you all the information I can already," replied the Colonel a little bitterly.

"All you recollect, but now try and think. Your daughter, before you came back from India, was with her aunt at Norwood. Where was she educated from the time she left India?"

"She went to school at Brighton at first, but from the time she was sixteen she had private instruction at home."

"She had professors, I suppose, for music, French, etc.?"

"Yes, I believe so. I paid bills for that sort of thing. My sister sent them out to me in India."

"Can you remember the name of Dubois?"

The Colonel thought a little while.

"Dubois? Dubois? Dubois?" he said. "I have an idea there was such a name among the accounts my sister sent to me, but whether it was a dressmaker or a French master I really can't say."

"Then I think we will take it that your daughter had lessons at Norwood from a French professor named Dubois. Now, in any letters that your late sister wrote you to India, did she ever mention anything that had caused her uneasiness on Maud's account?"

"Only once," replied the Colonel, "and everything was satisfactorily explained afterwards. She left home one day at nine o'clock in the morning, and did not return until four in the afternoon. Her aunt was exceedingly angry, and Maud explained that she had met some friends at the Crystal Palace—she attended the drawing class there—had gone to see one of her fellow students off at the station, and sitting in the carriage, the train had started before she could get out and she had to go on to London. I expect my sister told me that to show me how thoroughly I might reply upon her as my daughter's guardian."

"Went on to London?" said Dorcas to me under her voice, "and she could have got out in three minutes at the next station to Norwood!" Then turning to the Colonel, she said, "Now, Colonel, when your wife died, what did you do with her wedding ring?"

"Good heavens, madam!" exclaimed the Colonel, rising and pacing the room. "What can my poor wife's wedding ring have to do with my daughter's being flung into the lake yonder?"

"I am sorry if my question appears absurd," replied Dorcas quietly, "but will you kindly answer it?"

"My wife's wedding ring is on my dead wife's finger in her coffin in the graveyard at Simla," exclaimed the Colonel, "and now perhaps you'll tell me what all this means!"

"Tomorrow," said Dorcas. "Now, if you will excuse me, I'll take a walk with Mr. Saxon. Miss Hargreaves' maid is with her, and she will be all right until I return."

"Very well, very well!" exclaimed the Colonel, "but I beg—I pray of you to tell me what you know as soon as you can. I am setting spies upon my own child, and to me it is monstrous—and yet—and yet—what can I do? She won't tell me, and for her sake I must know—I must know."

The old Colonel grasped the proffered hand of Dorcas Dene.

"Thank you," he said, his lips quivering.

Directly we were in the grounds Dorcas Dene turned eagerly to me.

"I'm treating you very badly," she said, "but our task is nearly over. You must go back to town tonight. The first thing tomorrow morning go to Somerset House. You will find an old fellow named Daddy Green, a searcher in the inquiry room. Tell him you come from me, and give him this paper. When he has searched, telegraph the result to me, and come back by the next train."

I looked at the paper, and found written on it in Dorcas's hand:

"*Search wanted.*

Marriage—Victor Dubois and Maud Eleanor Hargreaves—probably between the years 1905 and 1908—London."

I looked up from the paper at Dorcas Dene.

"Whatever makes you think she is a married woman?" I said.

"This," exclaimed Dorcas, drawing an unworn wedding-ring from her purse. "I found it among a lot of trinkets at the bottom of a box her maid told me was her jewel-case. I took the liberty of trying all her keys till I opened it. A jewel-box tells many secrets to those who know how to read them."

"And you concluded from that——?"

"That she wouldn't keep a wedding-ring without it had belonged to some one dear to her or had been placed on her own finger. It is quite unworn, you see, so it was taken off immediately after the ceremony. It was only to make doubly sure that I asked the Colonel where his wife's was."

I duly repaired to Somerset House, and soon after midday the searcher brought a paper and handed it to me. It was a copy of the certificate of the marriage of Victor Dubois, bachelor, aged twenty-six, and Maud Eleanor Hargreaves, aged twenty-one, in London, in the year 1906. I telegraphed the news, wording the message simply "Yes," and the date, and I followed my wire by the first train.

When I arrived at Orley Park I rang several times before any one came. Presently Mrs. Peters, looking very white and excited, came from the grounds and apologized for keeping me waiting.

"Oh, sir—such a dreadful thing!" she said—"a body in the lake!"

"A body!"

"Yes, sir—a man. The nurse as came with you here that day, she was rowing herself on the lake, and she must have stirred it pushing with her oar, for it come up all tangled with weeds. It's a man sir, and I do believe it's the man I saw at the gate that night."

"*The man with the wild eyes!*" I exclaimed.

"Yes, sir! Oh, it is dreadful—Miss Maud first, and then this. Oh, what can it mean!"

I found Dorcas standing at the edge of the lake, and Peters and two of the gardeners lifting the drowned body of a man into the boat which was alongside.

Dorcas was giving instructions. "Lay it in the boat, and cover it with a tarpaulin," she said. "Mind, nothing is to be touched till the police come. I will go and find the Colonel."

As she turned away I met her.

"What a terrible thing! Is it Dubois?"

"Yes," replied Dorcas. "I suspected he was there yesterday, but I wanted to find him myself instead of having the lake dragged."

"Why?"

"Well, I didn't want any one else to search the pockets. There might have been papers or letters, you know, which would have been read at the inquest, and might have compromised Miss Hargreaves. But there was nothing——"

"What—you searched!"

"Yes, after I'd brought the poor fellow to the surface with the oars."

"But how do you think he got in?"

"Suicide—insanity. The father was taken to a lunatic asylum—you learned that at Norwood yesterday. Son doubtless inherited tendency. Looks like a case of homicidal mania—he attacked Miss Hargreaves, whom he had probably tracked after years of separation, and after he had as he thought killed her, he drowned himself. At any rate, Miss Hargreaves is a free woman. She was evidently terrified of her husband when he was alive, and so——"

I guessed what Dorcas was thinking as we went together to the house. At the door she held out her hand. "You had better go to the inn and return to town to-night," she said. "You can do no more good, and had better keep out of it. I shall be home to-morrow. Come to Elm Tree Road in the evening."

The next evening Dorcas told me all that had happened after I left. Paul had already heard it, and when I arrived was profuse in his thanks for the assistance I had rendered his wife. Mrs. Lester, however, felt compelled to remark that she never thought a daughter of hers would go gadding about the country fishing up corpses for a living.

Dorcas had gone to the Colonel and told him everything. The Colonel was in a terrible state, but Dorcas told him that the only way in which to ascertain the truth was for them to go to the unhappy girl together, and attempt, with the facts in their possession, to persuade her to divulge the rest.

When the Colonel told his daughter that the man she had married had flung her into the lake that night, she was dumbfounded, and became hysterical, but when she learned that Dubois had been found in the lake she became alarmed and instantly told all she knew.

She had been in the habit of meeting Victor Dubois constantly when she was at Norwood, at first with his father—her French master—and afterwards alone. He was handsome, young, romantic, and they fell madly in love. He was going away for some time to an appointment abroad, and he urged her to marry him secretly. She foolishly consented, and they parted at the church, she returning to her home and he going abroad the same evening.

She received letters from him clandestinely from time to time. Then he wrote that his father had become insane and had to be removed to a lunatic asylum, and he was returning. He had only time to see to his father's removal and return to his appointment. She did not hear from him for a long time, and then through a friend at Norwood who knew the Dubois and their relatives she made inquiries. Victor had returned to England, and met with an accident which had injured his head severely. He had become insane and had been taken to a lunatic asylum.

Then the poor girl resolved to keep her marriage a secret for ever, especially as her father had returned from India, and she knew how bitterly it would distress him to learn that his daughter was the wife of a madman.

On the night of the affair Maud was in the grounds by herself. She was strolling by the lake after dinner, when she heard a sound, and the dogs began to bark. Looking up, she saw Victor Dubois scaling the wall. Fearful that the dogs would bring Peters or some one on the scene, she ran to them and silenced them, and her husband leapt down and stood by her.

"Come away!" she said, fearing the dogs might attack him or begin to bark again, and she led him round by the lake which was out of sight of the house and the lodge.

She forgot for the moment in her excitement that he had been mad. At first he was gentle and kind. He told her he had been ill and in an asylum, but had recently been discharged cured. Directly he regained his liberty he set out in search of his wife, and ascertained from an old Norwood acquaintance that Miss Hargreaves was now living with her father at Orley Park, near Godalming.

Maud begged him to go away quietly, and she would write to him. He tried to take her in his arms and kiss her, but instinctively she shrank from him. Instantly he became furious. Seized with a sudden mania, he grasped her by the throat. She struggled and freed herself.

They were at the edge of the lake. Suddenly the maniac got her by the throat again, and hurled her down into the water. She fell in up to her waist, but managed to drag herself towards the edge, but before she emerged she fell senseless—fortunately with her head on the bank just out of the water.

The murderer, probably thinking that she was dead, must have waded out into the deep water and drowned himself.

Before she left Orley Park Dorcas advised the Colonel to let the inquest be held without any light being thrown on the affair by him. Only he was to take care that the police received information that a man answering the description of the suicide had recently been discharged from a lunatic asylum.

We heard later that at the inquest an official from the asylum attended, and the local jury found that Victor Dubois, a lunatic, got into the grounds in some way, and drowned himself in the lake while temporarily insane. It was suggested by the coroner that probably Miss Hargreaves, who was too unwell to attend, had not seen the man, but might have been alarmed by the sound of his footsteps, and that this would account for her fainting away near the water's edge. At any rate, the inquest ended in a satisfactory verdict, and the Colonel shortly afterwards took his daughter abroad with him on a Continental tour for the benefit of her health.

But of this, of course, we knew nothing on the evening after the eventful discovery, when I met Dorcas once more beneath her own roof-tree.

Paul was delighted to have his wife back again, and she devoted herself to him, and that evening had eyes and ears for no one else—not even for her faithful "assistant."

GRANT ALLEN

(1848–99)

"The Adventure of the Cantankerous Old Lady" is not the most mysterious story in this anthology, nor does its young heroine need great detective skills. Yet it's difficult to imagine a more concise and entertaining portrait of the late nineteenth-century New Woman than this opening story in what would become Grant Allen's 1899 book *Miss Cayley's Adventures*. It first appeared in *The Strand* in March 1898.

A recent graduate of Girton, which not four decades earlier had opened its doors as Cambridge University's first residential college for women, Lois Cayley is twenty-one, bright, well-read, and—like a number of her colleagues in this anthology—suddenly impoverished. Her friends nickname her Brownie in reference to the tricky household spirits in the folklore of northern England and Scotland. Like them, Cayley is notorious for her inexplicable ways and talent for mischief.

Grant Allen was a friend of everyone from Charles Darwin to Arthur Conan Doyle, who completed *Hilda Wade* after Allen dictated a draft of the last chapter from his deathbed. Wade's motivation as a detective is to solve and revenge her father's death; Lois Cayley is simply seeking adventure and a job. A versatile writer, Allen wrote scientific and philosophical books such as *Evolutionist at Large, Story of the Plants, The Evolution of the Idea of God,* and *Physiological Aesthetics,* but he also wrote many popular novels and story collections, including *The White Man's Foot* and *The Desire of the Eyes.* Two of his novels appeared under female pen names. His time-travel novel, *The British Barbarians*, appeared in 1895, the same year as H. G. Wells's *The Time Machine.* In his own time, the progressive Allen was notorious for a different novel from that productive year: *The Woman Who Did*, about a young woman who decides to openly have a child out of wedlock. However, he is remembered now mostly for one of the great characters of Victorian crime fiction, Colonel Clay, the ingenious con artist who robs the same millionaire twelve times in the clever and stylish 1897 story cycle *An African Millionaire.*

Allen's diverse interests reflected his cosmopolitan life. Born in Ontario to an Irish father and a Scottish-French-Canadian mother, raised partly in the United States, he attended college in England and France and then taught in Jamaica before settling in London to write. Allen was a friend of Herbert Spencer, the British polymath who, five years after Darwin's *Origin of Species*, coined the term *survival of the fittest*; Allen wrote a perceptive critique of Spencer. His mind always seems to be playing over a topic, whether in his brief biography of Charles Darwin in the English Worthies series or in this tale of a high-spirited young woman testing herself in the world.

THE ADVENTURE OF THE CANTANKEROUS OLD LADY

On the day when I found myself with twopence in my pocket, I naturally made up my mind to go round the world.

It was my stepfather's death that drove me to it. I had never seen my stepfather. Indeed, I never even thought of him as anything more than Colonel Watts-Morgan. I owed him nothing, except my poverty. He married my dear mother when I was a girl at school in Switzerland; and he proceeded to spend her little fortune, left at her sole disposal by my father's will, in paying his gambling debts. After that, he carried my dear mother off to Burma; and when he and the climate between them had succeeded in killing her, he made up for his appropriations at the cheapest rate by allowing me just enough to send me to Girton. So, when the Colonel died, in the year I was leaving college, I did not think it necessary to go into mourning for him. Especially as he chose the precise moment when my allowance was due, and bequeathed me nothing but his consolidated liabilities.

"Of course you will teach," said Elsie Petheridge, when I explained my affairs to her. "There is a good demand just now for high-school teachers."

I looked at her, aghast. "*Teach!* Elsie," I cried. (I had come up to town to settle her in at her unfurnished lodgings.) "Did you say *teach*? That's just like you dear good schoolmistresses! You go to Cambridge, and get examined till the heart and life have been examined out of you; then you say to yourselves at the end of it all, "Let me see; what am I good for now? I'm just about fit to go away and examine other people!" That's what our Principal would call "a vicious circle"—if one could ever admit there was anything vicious at all about *you*, dear. No, Elsie, I do *not* propose to teach. Nature did not cut me out for a high-school teacher. I couldn't swallow a poker if I tried for weeks. Pokers don't agree with me. Between ourselves, I am a bit of a rebel."

"You are, Brownie," she answered, pausing in her papering, with her sleeves rolled up—they called me "Brownie," partly because of my dark complexion, but partly because they could never understand me. "We all knew that long ago."

I laid down the paste-brush and mused.

"Do you remember, Elsie," I said, staring hard at the paper-board, "when I first went to Girton, how all you girls wore your hair quite straight, in neat smooth coils, plaited up at the back about the size of a pancake; and how of a sudden I burst in upon you, like a tropical hurricane, and demoralised you; and how, after three days of me, some of the dear innocents began with awe to cut themselves artless fringes, while others went out in fear and trembling and surreptitiously purchased a pair of curling-tongs? I was a bomb-shell in your midst in those days; why, you yourself were almost afraid at first to speak to me."

"You see, you had a bicycle," Elsie put in, smoothing the half-papered wall; "and in those days, of course, ladies didn't bicycle. You must admit, Brownie, dear, it *was* a startling innovation. You terrified us so. And yet, after all, there isn't much harm in you."

"I hope not," I said devoutly. "I was before my time, that was all; at present, even a curate's wife may blamelessly bicycle."

"But if you don't teach," Elsie went on, gazing at me with those wondering big blue eyes of hers, "whatever will you do, Brownie?" Her horizon was bounded by the scholastic circle.

"I haven't the faintest idea," I answered, continuing to paste. "Only, as I can't trespass upon your elegant hospitality for life, whatever I mean to do, I must begin doing this morning, when we've finished the papering. I couldn't teach" (teaching, like mauve, is the refuge of the incompetent); "and I don't, if possible, want to sell bonnets."

"As a milliner's girl?" Elsie asked, with a face of red horror.

"As a milliner's girl; why not? 'Tis an honest calling. Earls' daughters do it now. But you needn't look so shocked. I tell you, just at present, I am not contemplating it."

"Then what *do* you contemplate?"

I paused and reflected. "I am here in London," I answered, gazing rapt at the ceiling; "London, whose streets are paved with gold—though it *looks* at first sight like muddy flagstones; London, the greatest and richest city in the world, where an adventurous soul ought surely to find some loophole for an adventure. (That piece is hung crooked, dear; we shall have to take it down again.) I devise a Plan, therefore. I submit myself to fate; or, if you prefer it, I leave my future in the hands of Providence. I shall stroll out this morning, as soon as I've 'cleaned myself,' and embrace the first stray enterprise that offers. Our Bagdad teems with enchanted carpets. Let one but float my way, and, hi, presto, I seize it. I go where glory or a modest competence waits me. I snatch at the first offer, the first hint of an opening."

Elsie stared at me, more aghast and more puzzled than ever. "But, how?" she asked. "Where? When? You *are* so strange! What will you do to find one?"

"Put on my hat and walk out," I answered. "Nothing could be simpler. This city bursts with enterprises and surprises. Strangers from east and west hurry through it in all directions. Omnibuses traverse it from end to end—even, I am told, to Islington and Putney; within, folk sit face to face who never saw one another before in their lives, and who may never see one another again, or, on the contrary, may pass the rest of their days together."

I had a lovely harangue all pat in my head, in much the same strain, on the infinite possibilities of entertaining angels unawares, in cabs, on the Underground, in the aërated bread shops; but Elsie's widening eyes of horror pulled me up short like a hansom in Piccadilly when the inexorable upturned hand of the policeman checks it. "Oh, Brownie," she cried, drawing back, "you *don't* mean to tell me you're going to ask the first young man you meet in an omnibus to marry you?"

I shrieked with laughter, "Elsie," I cried, kissing her dear yellow little head, "you are *impayable*. You never will learn what I mean. You don't understand the language. No, no; I am going out, simply in search of adventure. What adventure may come, I have not at this moment the faintest conception. The fun lies in the search, the uncertainty, the toss-up of it. What is the good of being penniless—with the trifling exception of twopence—unless you are prepared to accept your position in the spirit of a masked ball at Covent Garden?"

"I have never been to one," Elsie put in.

"Gracious heavens, neither have I! What on earth do you take me for? But I mean to see where fate will lead me."

"I may go with you?" Elsie pleaded.

"Certainly *not*, my child," I answered—she was three years older than I, so I had the right to patronise her. "That would spoil all. Your dear little face would be quite enough to scare away a timid adventure." She knew what I meant. It was gentle and pensive, but it lacked initiative.

So, when we had finished that wall, I popped on my best hat, and popped out by myself into Kensington Gardens.

I am told I ought to have been terribly alarmed at the straits in which I found myself—a girl of twenty-one, alone in the world, and only twopence short of penniless, without a friend to protect, a relation to counsel her. (I don't count Aunt Susan, who lurked in ladylike indigence at Blackheath, and whose counsel, like her tracts, was given away too profusely to everybody to allow of one's placing any very high value upon it.) But, as a matter of fact, I must admit I was not in the least alarmed. Nature had endowed me with a profusion of crisp black hair, and plenty of high spirits. If my eyes had been like Elsie's—that liquid blue which looks out upon life with mingled pity and amazement—I might have felt as a girl ought to feel under such conditions; but having large dark eyes, with a bit of a twinkle in them, and being as well able to pilot a bicycle as any girl of my acquaintance, I have inherited or acquired an outlook on the world which distinctly leans rather towards cheeriness than despondency. I croak with difficulty. So I accepted my plight as an amusing experience, affording full scope for the congenial exercise of courage and ingenuity.

How boundless are the opportunities of Kensington Gardens—the Round Pond, the winding Serpentine, the mysterious seclusion of the Dutch brick Palace! Genii swarm there. One jostles possibilities. It is a land of romance, bounded on the north by the Abyss of Bayswater, and on the south by the Amphitheatre of the Albert Hall. But for a centre of adventure I choose the Long Walk; it beckoned me somewhat as the North-West Passage beckoned my seafaring ancestors—the buccaneering mariners of Elizabethan Devon. I sat down on a chair at the foot of an old elm with a poetic hollow, prosaically filled by a utilitarian plate of galvanised iron. Two ancient ladies were seated on the other side already—very grand-looking dames, with the haughty and exclusive ugliness of the English aristocracy in its later stages. For frank hideousness, commend me to the noble dowager. They were talking confidentially as I sat down; the trifling episode of my approach did not suffice to stem the full stream of their conversation. The great ignore the intrusion of their inferiors.

"Yes, it's a terrible nuisance," the eldest and ugliest of the two observed—she was a high-born lady, with a distinctly cantankerous cast of countenance. She had a Roman nose, and her skin was wrinkled like a wilted apple; she wore coffee-coloured point-lace in her bonnet, with a complexion to match. "But what could I do, my dear? I simply *couldn't* put up with such insolence. So I looked her straight back in the face—oh, she quailed, I can tell you; and I said to her, in my iciest voice—you know how icy I can be when occasion demands it"—the second old lady nodded an ungrudging assent, as if perfectly prepared to admit her friend's rare gift of iciness—"I said to her, 'Célestine, you can take your month's wages, and half an hour to get out of this house.' And she dropped me a deep reverence, and she answered: "*Oui, madame; merci beaucoup, madame; je ne desire pas mieux, madame.*" And out she flounced. So there was the end of it."

"Still, you go to Schlangenbad on Monday?"

"That's the point. On Monday. If it weren't for the journey, I should have been glad enough to be rid of the minx. I'm glad as it is, indeed; for a more insolent, upstanding, independent, answer-you-back-again young woman, with a sneer of her own, *I* never saw, Amelia—but I *must* get to Schlangenbad. Now, there the difficulty comes in. On the one hand, if I engage a maid in London, I have the choice of two evils. Either I must take a trapesing English girl—and I know by experience that an English girl on the

Continent is a vast deal worse than no maid at all: *you* have to wait upon *her*, instead of her waiting upon you; she gets seasick on the crossing, and when she reaches France or Germany, she hates the meals, and she detests the hotel servants, and she can't speak the language, so that she's always calling you in to interpret for her in her private differences with the *fille-de-chambre* and the landlord; or else I must pick up a French maid in London, and I know equally by experience that the French maids one engages in London are invariably dishonest—more dishonest than the rest even; they've come here because they have no character to speak of elsewhere, and they think you aren't likely to write and enquire of their last mistress in Toulouse or St. Petersburg. Then, again, on the other hand, I can't wait to get a Gretchen, an unsophisticated little Gretchen of the Taunus at Schlangenbad— I suppose there *are* unsophisticated girls in Germany still—made in Germany—they don't make 'em any longer in England, I'm sure—like everything else, the trade in rustic innocence has been driven from the country. I can't wait to get a Gretchen, as I should like to do, of course, because I simply *daren't* undertake to cross the Channel alone and go all that long journey by Ostend or Calais, Brussels and Cologne, to Schlangenbad."

"You could get a temporary maid," her friend suggested, in a lull of the tornado.

The Cantankerous Old Lady flared up. "Yes, and have my jewel-case stolen! Or find she was an English girl without one word of German. Or nurse her on the boat when I want to give my undivided attention to my own misfortunes. No, Amelia, I call it positively unkind of you to suggest such a thing. You're *so* unsympathetic! I put my foot down there. I will *not* take any temporary person."

I saw my chance. This was a delightful idea. Why not start for Schlangenbad with the Cantankerous Old Lady?

Of course, I had not the slightest intention of taking a lady's-maid's place for a permanency. Nor even, if it comes to that, as a passing expedient. But *if* I wanted to go round the world, how could I do better than set out by the Rhine country? The Rhine leads you on to the Danube, the Danube to the Black Sea, the Black Sea to Asia; and so, by way of India, China, and Japan, you reach the Pacific and San Francisco; whence one returns quite easily by New York and the White Star Liners. I began to feel like a globe-trotter already; the Cantankerous Old Lady was the thin end of the wedge—the first rung of the ladder! I proceeded to put my foot on it.

I leaned around the corner of the tree and spoke. "Excuse me," I said, in my suavest voice, "but I think I see a way out of your difficulty."

My first impression was that the Cantankerous Old Lady would go off in a fit of apoplexy. She grew purple in the face with indignation and astonishment, that a casual outsider should venture to address her; so much so, indeed, that for a second I almost regretted my well-meant interposition. Then she scanned me up and down, as if I were a girl in a mantle shop, and she contemplated buying either me or the mantle. At last, catching my eye, she thought better of it, and burst out laughing.

"What do you mean by this eavesdropping?" she asked.

I flushed up in turn. "This is a public place," I replied, with dignity; "and you spoke in a tone which was hardly designed for the strictest privacy. If you don't wish to be overheard, you oughtn't to shout. Besides, I desired to do you a service."

The Cantankerous Old Lady regarded me once more from head to foot. I did not quail. Then she turned to her companion. "The girl has spirit," she remarked, in an encouraging tone, as if she were discussing some absent person. "Upon my word, Amelia, I rather like the look of her. Well, my good woman, what do you want to suggest to me?"

"Merely this," I replied, bridling up and crushing her. "I am a Girton girl, an officer's daughter, no more a good woman than most others of my class; and I have nothing in particular to do for the moment. I don't object to going to Schlangenbad. I would convoy you over, as companion, or lady-help, or anything else you choose to call it; I would remain with you there for a week, till you could arrange with your Gretchen, presumably unsophisticated; and then I would leave you. Salary is unimportant; my fare suffices. I accept the chance as a cheap opportunity of attaining Schlangenbad."

The yellow-faced old lady put up her long-handled tortoise-shell eyeglasses and inspected me all over again. "Well, I declare," she murmured. "What are girls coming to, I wonder? Girton, you say; Girton! That place at Cambridge! You speak Greek, of course; but how about German?"

"Like a native," I answered, with cheerful promptitude. "I was at school in Canton Berne; it is a mother tongue to me."

"No, no," the old lady went on, fixing her keen small eyes on my mouth. "Those little lips could never frame themselves to 'schlecht' or 'wunderschön'; they were not cut out for it."

"Pardon me," I answered, in German. "What I say, that I mean. The never-to-be-forgotten music of the Fatherland's-speech has on my infant ear from the first-beginning impressed itself."

The old lady laughed aloud.

"Don't jabber it to me, child," she cried. "I hate the lingo. It's the one tongue on earth that even a pretty girl's lips fail to render attractive. You yourself make faces over it. What's your name, young woman?"

"Lois Cayley."

"Lois! *What* a name! I never heard of any Lois in my life before, except Timothy's grandmother. *You're* not anybody's grandmother, are you?"

"Not to my knowledge," I answered, gravely.

She burst out laughing again.

"Well, you'll do, I think," she said, catching my arm. "That big mill down yonder hasn't ground the originality altogether out of you. I adore originality. It was clever of you to catch at the suggestion of this arrangement. Lois Cayley, you say; any relation of a madcap Captain Cayley whom I used once to know, in the Forty-second Highlanders?"

"His daughter," I answered, flushing. For I was proud of my father.

"Ha! I remember; he died, poor fellow; he was a good soldier—and his"—I felt she was going to say "his fool of a widow," but a glance from me quelled her; "his widow went and married that good-looking scapegrace, Jack Watts-Morgan. Never marry a man, my dear, with a double-barrelled name and no visible means of subsistence; above all, if he's generally known by a nickname. So you're poor Tom Cayley's daughter, are you? Well, well, we can settle this little matter between us. Mind, I'm a person who always expects to have my own way. If you come with *me* to Schlangenbad, you must do as I tell you."

"I *think* I could manage it—for a week," I answered, demurely.

She smiled at my audacity. We passed on to terms. They were quite satisfactory. She wanted no references. "Do I look like a woman who cares about a reference? What are called *characters* are usually essays in how not to say it. You take my fancy; that's the point! And poor Tom Cayley! But, mind, I will *not* be contradicted."

"I will not contradict your wildest misstatement," I answered, smiling. "*And* your name and address?" I asked, after we had settled preliminaries.

A faint red spot rose quaintly in the centre of the Cantankerous Old Lady's sallow cheek. "My dear," she murmured, "my name is the one thing on earth I'm really ashamed of. My parents chose to inflict upon me the most odious label that human ingenuity ever devised for a Christian soul; and I've not had courage enough to burst out and change it."

A gleam of intuition flashed across me. "You don't mean to say," I exclaimed, "that you're called Georgina?"

The Cantankerous Old Lady gripped my arm hard. "What an unusually intelligent girl!" she broke in. "How on earth did you guess? It *is* Georgina."

"Fellow-feeling," I answered. "So is mine, Georgina Lois. But as I quite agree with you as to the atrocity of such conduct, I have suppressed the Georgina. It ought to be made penal to send innocent girls into the world so burdened."

"My opinion to a T! You are really an exceptionally sensible young woman. There's my name and address; I start on Monday."

I glanced at her card. The very copperplate was noisy. "Lady Georgina Fawley, 49 Fortescue Crescent, W."

It had taken us twenty minutes to arrange our protocols. As I walked off, well pleased, Lady Georgina's friend ran after me quickly.

"You must take care," she said, in a warning voice. "You've caught a Tartar."

"So I suspect," I answered. "But a week in Tartary will be at least an experience."

"She has an awful temper."

"That's nothing. So have I. Appalling, I assure you. And if it comes to blows, I'm bigger and younger and stronger than she is."

"Well, I wish you well out of it."

"Thank you. It is kind of you to give me this warning. But I think I can take care of myself. I come, you see, of a military family."

I nodded my thanks, and strolled back to Elsie's. Dear little Elsie was in transports of surprise when I related my adventure.

"Will you really go? And what will you do, my dear, when you get there?"

"I haven't a notion," I answered; "that's where the fun comes in. But, anyhow, I shall have got there."

"Oh, Brownie, you might starve!"

"And I might starve in London. In either place, I have only two hands and one head to help me."

"But, then, here you are among friends. You might stop with me for ever."

I kissed her fluffy forehead. "You good, generous little Elsie," I cried; "I won't stop here one moment after I have finished the painting and papering. I came here to help you. I couldn't go on eating your hard-earned bread and doing nothing. I know how sweet you are; but the last thing I want is to add to your burdens. Now let us roll up our sleeves again and hurry on with the dado."

"But, Brownie, you'll want to be getting your own things ready. Remember, you're off to Germany on Monday."

I shrugged my shoulders. "'Tis a foreign trick I picked up in Switzerland. What have I got to get ready?" I asked. "I can't go out and buy a complete summer outfit in Bond Street for twopence. Now, don't look at me like that: be practical, Elsie, and let me help you paint the dado." For unless I helped her, poor Elsie could never have finished it herself. I cut out half her clothes for her; her own ideas were almost entirely limited to differential calculus. And cutting out a blouse by differential calculus is weary, uphill work for a high-school teacher.

By Monday I had papered and furnished the rooms, and was ready to start on my voyage of exploration. I met the Cantankerous Old Lady at Charing Cross, by appointment, and proceeded to take charge of her luggage and tickets.

Oh my, how fussy she was! "You will drop that basket! I hope you have got through tickets, *viâ* Malines, *not* by Brussels— I won't go by Brussels. You have to change there. Now, mind you notice how much the luggage weighs in English pounds, and make the man at the office give you a note of it to check those horrid Belgian porters. They'll charge you for double the weight, unless you reduce it at once to kilogrammes. *I* know their ways. Foreigners have no consciences. They just go to the priest and confess, you know, and wipe it all out, and start fresh again on a career of crime next morning. I'm sure I don't know why I *ever* go abroad. The only country in the world fit to live in is England. No mosquitoes, no passports, no—goodness gracious, child, don't let that odious man bang about my hat-box! Have you no immortal soul, porter, that you crush other people's property as if it was blackbeetles? No, I will not let you take this, Lois; this is my jewel-box—it contains all that remains of the Fawley family jewels. I positively decline to appear at Schlangenbad without a diamond to my back. This never leaves my hands. It's hard enough nowadays to keep body and skirt together. *Have* you secured that *coupé* at Ostend?"

We got into our first-class carriage. It was clean and comfortable; but the Cantankerous Old Lady made the porter mop the floor, and fidgeted and worried till we slid out of the station. Fortunately, the only other occupant of the compartment was a most urbane and obliging Continental gentleman—I say Continental, because I couldn't quite make out whether he was French, German, or Austrian—who was anxious in every way to meet Lady Georgina's wishes. Did madame desire to have the window open? Oh, certainly, with pleasure; the day was so sultry. Closed a little more? *Parfaitement*, there *was* a current of air, *il faut l'admettre*. Madame would prefer the corner? No? Then perhaps she would like this valise for a footstool? *Permettez*—just thus. A cold draught runs so often along the floor in railway carriages. This is Kent that we traverse; ah, the garden of England! As a diplomat, he knew every nook of Europe, and he echoed the *mot* he had accidentally heard drop from madame's lips on the platform: no country in the world so delightful as England!

"Monsieur is attached to the Embassy in London?" Lady Georgina inquired, growing affable.

He twirled his grey moustache: a waxed moustache of great distinction.

"No, madame; I have quitted the diplomatic service; I inhabit London now *pour mon agrément*. Some of my compatriots call it *triste*; for me, I find it the most fascinating capital in Europe. What gaiety! What movement! What poetry! What mystery!"

"If mystery means fog, it challenges the world," I interposed.

He gazed at me with fixed eyes. "Yes, mademoiselle," he answered, in quite a different and markedly chilly voice. "Whatever your great country attempts—were it only a fog—it achieves consummately."

I have quick intuitions. I felt the foreign gentleman took an instinctive dislike to me. To make up for it, he talked much, and with animation, to Lady Georgina. They ferreted out friends in common, and were as much surprised at it as people always are at that inevitable experience.

"Ah yes, madame, I recollect him well in Vienna. I was there at the time, attached to our Legation. He was a charming man; you read his masterly paper on the Central Problem of the Dual Empire?"

"You were in Vienna then!" the Cantankerous Old Lady mused back. "Lois, my child, don't stare"—she had covenanted from the first to call me Lois, as my father's daughter, and I confess I preferred it to being Miss Cayley'd. "We must surely have met. Dare I ask your name, monsieur?" I could see the foreign gentleman was delighted at this turn. He had played for it, and carried his point. He meant her to ask him. He had a card in his pocket, conveniently close; and he handed it across to her. She read it, and passed it on: "M. le Comte de Laroche-sur-Loiret."

"Oh, I remember your name well," the Cantankerous Old Lady broke in. "I think you knew my husband, Sir Evelyn Fawley, and my father, Lord Kynaston."

The Count looked profoundly surprised and delighted. "What! you are then Lady Georgina Fawley!" he cried, striking an attitude. "Indeed, miladi, your admirable husband was one of the very first to exert his influence in my favour at Vienna. Do I recall him, *ce cher* Sir Evelyn? If I recall him! What a fortunate encounter! I must have seen you some years ago at Vienna, miladi, though I had not then the great pleasure of making your acquaintance. But your face had impressed itself on my sub-conscious self!" (I did not learn till later that the esoteric doctrine of the sub-conscious self was Lady Georgina's favourite hobby.) "The moment chance led me to this carriage this morning, I said to myself, 'That face, those features: so vivid, so striking: I have seen them somewhere. With what do I connect them in the recesses of my memory? A high-born family; genius; rank; the diplomatic service; some unnameable charm; some faint touch of eccentricity. Ha! I have it. Vienna, a carriage with footmen in red livery, a noble presence, a crowd of wits—poets, artists, politicians—pressing eagerly round the landau.' That was my mental picture as I sat and confronted you: I understand it all now; this is Lady Georgina Fawley!"

I thought the Cantankerous Old Lady, who was a shrewd person in her way, must surely see through this obvious patter; but I had under-estimated the average human capacity for swallowing flattery. Instead of dismissing his fulsome nonsense with a contemptuous smile, Lady Georgina perked herself up with a conscious air of coquetry, and asked for more. "Yes, they were delightful days in Vienna," she said, simpering; "I was young then, Count; I enjoyed life with a zest."

"Persons of miladi's temperament are always young," the Count retorted, glibly, leaning forward and gazing at her. "Growing old is a foolish habit of the stupid and the vacant. Men and women of *esprit* are never older. One learns as one goes on in life to admire, not the obvious beauty of mere youth and health"—he glanced across at me disdainfully—"but the profounder beauty of deep character in a face—that calm and serene beauty which is imprinted on the brow by experience of the emotions."

"I have had my moments," Lady Georgina murmured, with her head on one side.

"I believe it, miladi," the Count answered, and ogled her.

Thenceforward to Dover, they talked together with ceaseless animation. The Cantankerous Old Lady was capital company. She had a tang in her tongue, and in the course of ninety minutes she had flayed alive the greater part of London society, with keen wit and sprightliness. I laughed against my will at her ill-tempered sallies; they were too funny not to amuse, in spite of their vitriol. As for the Count, he was charmed. He talked well himself, too, and between them I almost forgot the time till we arrived at Dover.

It was a very rough passage. The Count helped us to carry our nineteen hand-packages and four rugs on board; but I noticed that, fascinated as she was with him, Lady Georgina resisted his ingenious efforts to gain possession of her precious jewel-case as she descended the gangway. She clung to it like grim death, even in the chops of the Channel. Fortunately I am a good sailor, and when Lady Georgina's sallow cheeks began to grow pale, I was steady enough to supply her with her shawl and her smelling-bottle. She fidgeted and worried the whole way over. She *would* be treated like a vertebrate animal. Those horrid Belgians had no right to stick their deck-chairs just in front of her. The impertinence of the hussies with the bright red hair—a grocer's daughters, she felt sure—in venturing to come and sit on the same bench with *her*—the bench "for ladies only," under the lee of the funnel!

"Ladies only," indeed! Did the baggages pretend they considered themselves ladies? Oh, that placid old gentleman in the episcopal gaiters was their father, was he? Well, a bishop should bring up his daughters better, having his children in subjection with all gravity. Instead of which—"Lois, my smelling-salts!" This was a beastly boat; such an odour of machinery; they had no decent boats nowadays; with all our boasted improvements, she could remember well when the cross-Channel service was much better conducted than it was at present. But *that* was before we had compulsory education. The working classes were driving trade out of the country, and the consequence was, we couldn't build a boat which didn't reek like an oil-shop. Even the sailors on board were French—jabbering idiots; not an honest British Jack-tar among the lot of them; though the stewards were English, and very inferior Cockney English at that, with their off-hand ways, and their School Board airs and graces. *She'd* School Board them if they were her servants; *she'd* show them the sort of respect that was due to people of birth and education. But the children of the lower classes never learnt their catechism nowadays; they were too much occupied with literatoor, jography, and free-' and drawrin'. Happily for my nerves, a good lurch to leeward put a stop for a while to the course of her thoughts on the present distresses.

At Ostend the Count made a second gallant attempt to capture the jewel-case, which Lady Georgina automatically repulsed. She had a fixed habit, I believe, of sticking fast to that jewel-case; for she was too overpowered by the Count's urbanity, I feel sure, to suspect for a moment his honesty of purpose. But whenever she travelled, I fancy, she clung to her case as if her life depended upon it; it contained the whole of her valuable diamonds.

We had twenty minutes for refreshments at Ostend, during which interval my old lady declared with warmth that I *must* look after her registered luggage; though, as it was booked through to Cologne, I could not even see it till we crossed the German frontier; for the Belgian *douaniers* seal up the van as soon as the through baggage for Germany is unloaded. To satisfy her, however, I went through the formality of pretending to inspect it, and rendered myself hateful to the head of the *douane* by asking various foolish and inept questions, on which Lady Georgina insisted. When I had finished this silly and uncongenial task—for I am not by nature fussy, and it is hard to assume fussiness as another person's proxy—I returned to our *coupé* which I had arranged for in London. To my great amazement, I found the Cantankerous Old Lady and the egregious Count comfortably seated there. "Monsieur has been good enough to accept a place in our carriage," she observed, as I entered.

He bowed and smiled. "Or, rather, madame has been so kind as to offer me one," he corrected.

"Would you like some lunch, Lady Georgina?" I asked, in my chilliest voice. "There are ten minutes to spare, and the *buffet* is excellent."

"An admirable inspiration," the Count murmured. "Permit me to escort you, miladi."

"You will come, Lois?" Lady Georgina asked.

"No, thank you," I answered, for I had an idea. "I am a capital sailor, but the sea takes away my appetite."

"Then you'll keep our places," she said, turning to me. "I hope you won't allow them to stick in any horrid foreigners! They will try to force them on you unless you insist. *I* know their tricky ways. You have the tickets, I trust? And the *bulletin* for the *coupé*? Well, mind you don't lose the paper for the registered luggage. Don't let those dreadful porters touch my cloaks. And if anybody attempts to get in, be sure you stand in front of the door as they mount to prevent them."

The Count handed her out; he was all high courtly politeness. As Lady Georgina descended, he made yet another dexterous effort to relieve her of the jewel-case. I don't think she noticed it, but automatically once more she waved him aside. Then she turned to me. "Here, my dear," she said, handing it to me, "you'd better take care of it. If I lay it down in the *buffet* while I am eating my soup, some rogue may run away with it. But mind, don't let it out of your hands on any account. Hold it so, on your knee; and, for Heaven's sake, don't part with it."

By this time my suspicions of the Count were profound. From the first I had doubted him; he was so blandly plausible. But as we landed at Ostend I had accidentally overheard a low whispered conversation when he passed a shabby-looking man, who had travelled in a second-class carriage from London. "That succeeds?" the shabby-looking man had muttered under his breath in French, as the haughty nobleman with the waxed moustache brushed by him.

"That succeeds admirably," the Count had answered, in the same soft undertone. "*Ça réussit à merveille!*"

I understood him to mean that he had prospered in his attempt to impose on Lady Georgina.

They had been gone five minutes at the *buffet*, when the Count came back hurriedly to the door of the *coupé* with a *nonchalant* air. "Oh, mademoiselle," he said, in an off-hand tone, "Lady Georgina has sent me to fetch her jewel-case."

I gripped it hard with both hands. "*Pardon*, M. le Comte," I answered; "Lady Georgina intrusted it to *my* safe keeping, and, without her leave, I cannot give it up to any one."

"You mistrust me?" he cried, looking black. "You doubt my honour? You doubt my word when I say that miladi has sent me?"

"*Du tout*," I answered, calmly. "But I have Lady Georgina's orders to stick to this case; and till Lady Georgina returns I stick to it."

He murmured some indignant remark below his breath, and walked off. The shabby-looking passenger was pacing up and down the platform outside in a badly-made dust-coat. As they passed their lips moved. The Count's seemed to mutter, "*C'est un coup manqué.*"

However, he did not desist even so. I saw he meant to go on with his dangerous little game. He returned to the *buffet* and rejoined Lady Georgina. I felt sure it would be useless to warn her, so completely had the Count succeeded in gulling her; but I took my own steps. I examined the jewel-case closely. It had a leather outer covering; within was a strong steel box, with stout bands of metal to bind it. I took my cue at once, and acted for the best on my own responsibility.

When Lady Georgina and the Count returned, they were like old friends together. The quails in aspic and the sparkling hock had evidently opened their hearts to one another. As far as Malines they laughed and talked without ceasing. Lady Georgina was now in her finest vein of spleen: her acid wit grew sharper and more caustic each moment. Not a reputation in Europe had a rag left to cover it as we steamed in beneath the huge iron roof of the main central junction. I had observed all the way from Ostend that the Count had been anxious lest we might have to give up our *coupé* at Malines. I assured him more than once that his fears were groundless, for I had arranged at Charing Cross that it should run right through to the German frontier. But he waved me aside, with one lordly hand. I had not told Lady Georgina of his vain attempt to take possession of her jewel-case; and the bare fact of my silence made him increasingly suspicious of me.

"Pardon me, mademoiselle," he said, coldly; "you do not understand these lines as well as I do. Nothing is more common than for those rascals of railway clerks to sell one a place in a *coupé* or a *wagon-lit*, and then never reserve it, or turn one out half way. It is very possible miladi may have to descend at Malines."

Lady Georgina bore him out by a large variety of selected stories concerning the various atrocities of the rival companies which had stolen her luggage on her way to Italy. As for *trains de luxe*, they were dens of robbers.

So when we reached Malines, just to satisfy Lady Georgina, I put out my head and inquired of a porter. As I anticipated, he replied that there was no change; we went through to Verviers.

The Count, however, was still unsatisfied. He descended, and made some remarks a little farther down the platform to an official in the gold-banded cap of a *chef-de-gare*, or some such functionary. Then he returned to us, all fuming. "It is as I said," he exclaimed, flinging open the door. "These rogues have deceived us. The *coupé* goes no farther. You must dismount at once, miladi, and take the train just opposite."

I felt sure he was wrong, and I ventured to say so. But Lady Georgina cried, "Nonsense, child! The *chef-de-gare* must know. Get out at once! Bring my bag and the rugs! Mind that cloak! Don't forget the sandwich-tin! Thanks, Count; will you kindly take charge of my umbrellas? Hurry up, Lois; hurry up! the train is just starting!"

I scrambled after her, with my fourteen bundles, keeping a quiet eye meanwhile on the jewel-case.

We took our seats in the opposite train, which I noticed was marked "Amsterdam, Bruxelles, Paris." But I said nothing. The Count jumped in, jumped about, arranged our parcels, jumped out again. He spoke to a porter; then he rushed back excitedly. "*Mille pardons*, miladi," he cried. "I find the *chef-de-gare* has cruelly deceived me. You were right, after all, mademoiselle! We must return to the *coupé*!"

With singular magnanimity, I refrained from saying, "I told you so."

Lady Georgina, very flustered and hot by this time, tumbled out once more, and bolted back to the *coupé*. Both trains were just starting. In her hurry, at last, she let the Count take possession of her jewel-case. I rather fancy that as he passed one window he handed it in to the shabby-looking passenger; but I am not certain. At any rate, when we were comfortably seated in our own compartment once more, and he stood on the footboard just about to enter, of a sudden he made an unexpected dash back, and flung himself wildly into a Paris carriage. At the self-same moment, with a piercing shriek, both trains started.

Lady Georgina threw up her hands in a frenzy of horror. "My diamonds!" she cried aloud. "Oh, Lois, my diamonds!"

"Don't distress yourself," I answered, holding her back, for I verily believe she would have leapt from the train. "He has only taken the outer shell, with the sandwich-case inside it. Here is the steel box!" And I produced it, triumphantly.

She seized it, overjoyed. "How did this happen?" she cried, hugging it, for she loved those diamonds.

"Very simply," I answered. "I saw the man was a rogue, and that he had a confederate with him in another carriage. So, while you were gone to the buffet at Ostend, I slipped the box out of the case, and put in the sandwich-tin, that he might carry it off, and we might have proofs against him. All you have to do now is to inform the conductor, who will telegraph to stop the train to Paris. I spoke to him about that at Ostend, so that everything is ready."

She positively hugged me. "My dear," she cried, "you are the cleverest little woman I ever met in my life! Who on earth could have suspected such a polished gentleman? Why, you're worth your weight in gold. What the dickens shall I do without you at Schlangenbad?"

M. McDONNELL BODKIN

(1850–1933)

When Matthias McDonnell Bodkin died in 1933, he must have been tired. Born in the middle of the nineteenth century to well-connected Irish parents, he grew up to become a prominent journalist, editor, and author, all while building a respected career as barrister, judge, King's Council, and rabid Nationalist opponent of Charles Stewart Parnell's Irish Parliamentary Party. As barrister, he defended Nationalists; as newspaper editor, he attacked Parnell. He won a seat in Parliament by a very narrow margin but abandoned it after only one term, claiming that he could not afford to forgo his legal earnings.

His many books range through history, politics, historical novels, autobiography, a volume entitled *Famous Irish Trials,* and a collection with the heinous title *Pat o' Nine Tales.* He shows up in this anthology, however, because in 1900 Chatto & Windus in London published his story collection *Dora Myrl: The Lady Detective.* The glamorous young Myrl is a professional paid detective and she is indefatigable in pursuit of clues or miscreants. "A Sherlock Holmes in petticoats," gushed the *Morning Leader* when Myrl appeared on the scene, dubbing her "pretty, refined, and piquant," as well as "adorable." The paper insisted that she was "quite a new kind of detective, and a distinct improvement on her predecessors." The *Daily News* declared the stories "spirited and vivacious." Of course, a lot of this fuss was because Myrl was more overtly feminine than some of her predecessors. Smart, efficient, and fearless, she may remind you of Grant Allen's Lois Cayley, who in one story (not reprinted in this volume) pursues a foe via bicycle. Dora Myrl is also quite the mistress of disguise. As protean as Holmes himself, she appears as a telegraph delivery boy and an oracular palmist; at one point she doubly disguises herself as male and French.

Two years earlier, in 1898, Bodkin had published *Paul Beck, the Rule of Thumb Detective.* Positioning his detective as no genius, almost an anti-Holmes, Bodkin has Beck claim modestly, "I just go by the rule of thumb, and muddle and puzzle out my cases as best I can." Beck appeared in a couple of other novels over the next few years. Then, in a 1909 novel with the coy title *The Capture of Paul Beck,* he pitted his two detectives against each other and finally married them, in a tedious love story that is one-third over before Beck and Myrl even appear. Inevitably, the two raise a child who becomes a detective, in the subsequent novel *Young Beck, a Chip off the Old Block.* Bodkin seems to have been the first major figure in the genre to write about a married couple who engage in teamwork crime solving. Many others would follow, including the charming Nick and Nora Charles, created by Dashiell Hammett in *The Thin Man;* Agatha Christie's Tommy and Tuppence Beresford; and later the unaccountably popular Mr. and Mrs. North series by Frances and Richard Lockridge.

Nowadays the story title requires some explanation; Bodkin packed two or three meanings into it. As long ago as 1899, a *New York Times* columnist explained,

> To cut his stick, in the sense of going away in a hurry, has long been a common expression, though it is not heard by any means so frequently as it was forty and fifty years ago. "He's cut his stick" equals runs away. "Now then: cut yer stick!" equals be off. In playing cricket when I was a boy, the record of runs for each player was notched on a long stick, and runs were only known as "notches" in those days. I have seen the records of bigger matches also recorded on sticks by means of notches, say, forty-five years ago.

A slang dictionary from the same era suggests an alternative origin even older: "It seems that it refers to the custom centuries ago of cutting a stout walking stick or staff—which could double as a weapon—before beginning a long journey on foot."

And yet another meaning you'll have to discover as you read.

HOW HE CUT HIS STICK

(1900)

He breathed freely at last as he lifted the small black Gladstone bag of stout calfskin, and set it carefully on the seat of the empty railway carriage close beside him.

He lifted the bag with a manifest effort. Yet he was a big powerfully built young fellow; handsome too in a way; with straw-coloured hair and moustache and a round face, placid, honest-looking but not too clever. His light blue eyes had an anxious, worried look. No wonder, poor chap! he was weighted with a heavy responsibility. That unobtrusive black bag held £5,000 in gold and notes which he—a junior clerk in the famous banking house of Gower and Grant—was taking from the head office in London to a branch two hundred miles down the line.

The older and more experienced clerk whose ordinary duty it was to convey the gold had been taken strangely and suddenly ill at the last moment.

"There's Jim Pollock," said the bank manager, looking round for a substitute, "he'll do. He is big enough to knock the head off anyone that interferes with him."

So Jim Pollock had the heavy responsibility thrust upon him. The big fellow who would tackle any man in England in a football rush without a thought of fear was as nervous as a two-year-old child. All the way down to this point his watchful eyes and strong right hand had never left the bag for a moment. But here at the Eddiscombe Junction he had got locked in alone to a single first-class carriage, and there was a clear run of forty-seven miles to the next stoppage.

So with a sigh and shrug of relief, he threw away his anxiety, lay back on the soft seat, lit a pipe, drew a sporting paper from his pocket, and was speedily absorbed in the account of the Rugby International Championship match, for Jim himself was not without hopes of his "cap" in the near future.

The train rattled out of the station and settled down to its smooth easy stride—a good fifty miles an hour through the open country.

Still absorbed in his paper he did not notice the gleam of two stealthy keen eyes that watched him from the dark shadow under the opposite seat. He did not see that long lithe wiry figure uncoil and creep out, silently as a snake, across the floor of the carriage.

He saw nothing, and felt nothing till he felt two murderous hands clutching at his throat and a knee crushing his chest in.

Jim was strong, but before his sleeping strength had time to waken, he was down on his back on the carriage floor with a handkerchief soaked in chloroform jammed close to his mouth and nostrils.

He struggled desperately for a moment or so, half rose and almost flung off his clinging assailant. But even as he struggled the dreamy drug stole strength and sense away; he fell back heavily and lay like a log on the carriage floor.

The faithful fellow's last thought as his senses left him was "The gold is gone." It was his first thought as he awoke with dizzy pain and racked brain from the deathlike swoon. The train was still at full speed; the carriage doors were still locked; but the carriage empty and the bag was gone.

He searched despairingly in the racks, under the seats—all empty. Jim let the window down with a clash and bellowed.

The train began to slacken speed and rumble into the station. Half a dozen porters ran together—the station-master following more leisurely as beseemed his dignity. Speedily a crowd gathered round the door.

"I have been robbed," Jim shouted, "of a black bag with £5,000 in it!"

Then the superintendent pushed his way through the crowd.

"Where were you robbed, sir?" he said with a suspicious look at the dishevelled and excited Jim.

"Between this and Eddiscombe Junction."

"Impossible, sir, there is no stoppage between this and Eddiscombe, and the carriage is empty."

"I thought it was empty at Eddiscombe, but there must have been a man under the seat."

"There is no man under the seat now," retorted the superintendent curtly, "you had better tell your story to the police. There is a detective on the platform."

Jim told his story to the detective, who listened gravely and told him that he must consider himself in custody pending inquiries.

A telegram was sent to Eddiscombe and it was found that communication had been stopped. This must have happened quite recently, for a telegram had gone through less than an hour before. The breakage was quickly located about nine miles outside Eddiscombe. Some of the wires had been pulled down half way to the ground, and the insulators smashed to pieces on one of the poles. All round the place the ground was trampled with heavy footprints which passed through a couple of fields out on the high road and were lost. No other clue of any kind was forthcoming.

The next day but one, a card, with the name "Sir Gregory Grant," was handed to Dora Myrl as she sat hard at work in the little drawing-room which she called her study. A portly, middle-aged, benevolent gentleman followed the card into the room.

"Miss Myrl?" he said, extending his hand, "I have heard of you from my friend, Lord Millicent. I have come to entreat your assistance. I am the senior partner of the banking firm of Gower and Grant. You have heard of the railway robbery, I suppose?"

"I have heard all the paper had to tell me."

"There is little more to tell. I have called on you personally, Miss Myrl, because, personally, I am deeply interested in the case. It is not so much the money—though the amount is, of course, serious. But the honour of the bank is at stake. We have always prided ourselves on treating our clerks well, and heretofore we have reaped the reward. For nearly a century there has not been a single case of fraud or dishonesty amongst them. It is a proud record for our bank, and we should like to keep it unbroken if possible. Suspicion is heavy on young James Pollock. I want him punished, of course, if he is guilty, but I want him cleared if he is innocent. That's why I came to you."

"The police think?"

"Oh, they think there can be no doubt about his guilt. They

have their theory pat. No one was in the carriage—no one could leave it. Pollock threw out the bag to an accomplice along the line. They even pretend to find the mark in the ground where the heavy bag fell—a few hundred yards nearer to Eddiscombe than where the wires were pulled down."

"What has been done?"

"They have arrested the lad and sent out the 'Hue and Cry' for a man with a very heavy calfskin bag—that's all. They are quite sure they have caught the principal thief anyway."

"And you?"

"I will be frank with you, Miss Myrl. I have my doubts. The case *seems* conclusive. It is impossible that anybody could have got out of the train at full speed. But I have seen the lad, and I have my doubts."

"Can I see him?"

"I would be very glad if you did."

After five minutes' conversation with Jim Pollock, Dora drew Sir Gregory aside.

"I think I see my way," she said, "I will undertake the case on one condition."

"Any fee that . . ."

"It's not the fee. I never talk of the fee till the case is over. I will undertake the case if you give me Mr. Pollock to help me. Your instinct was right, Sir Gregory: the boy is innocent."

There was much grumbling amongst the police when a *nolle prosequi* was entered on behalf of the bank, and James Pollock was discharged from custody, and it was plainly hinted the Crown would interpose.

Meanwhile Pollock was off by a morning train with Miss Dora Myrl, from London to Eddiscombe. He was brimming over with gratitude and devotion. Of course they talked of the robbery on the way down.

"The bag was very heavy, Mr. Pollock?" Dora asked.

"I'd sooner carry it one mile than ten, Miss Myrl."

"Yet you are pretty strong, I should think."

She touched his protruding biceps professionally with her finger tips, and he coloured to the roots of his hair.

"Would you know the man that robbed you if you saw him again?" Dora asked.

"Not from Adam. He had his hands on my throat, the chloroform crammed into my mouth before I knew where I was. It was about nine or ten miles outside Eddiscombe. You believe there *was* a man—don't you, Miss Myrl? You are about the only person that does. I don't blame them, for how did the chap get out of the train going at the rate of sixty miles an hour—that's what fetches me, 'pon my word," he concluded incoherently; "if I was any other chap I'd believe myself guilty on the evidence. Can you tell me how the trick was done, Miss Myrl?"

"That's my secret for the present, Mr. Pollock, but I may tell you this much, when we get to the pretty little town of Eddiscombe I will look out for a stranger with a crooked stick instead of a black bag."

There were three hotels in Eddiscombe, but Mr. Mark Brown and his sister were hard to please. They tried the three in succession, keeping their eyes about them for a stranger with a crooked stick, and spending their leisure time in exploring the town and country on a pair of capital bicycles, which they hired by the week.

As Miss Brown (alias Dora Myrl) was going down the stairs of the third hotel one sunshiny afternoon a week after their arrival, she met midway, face to face, a tall middle-aged man limping a little, a very little, and leaning on a stout oak stick, with a dark shiny varnish, and a crooked handle. She passed him without a second glance. But that evening she gossiped with the chambermaid, and learned that the stranger was a commercial traveller—Mr. McCrowder—who had been staying some weeks at the hotel, with an occasional run up to London in the train, and run round the country on his bicycle, "a nice, easily-pleased, pleasant-spoken gentleman," the chambermaid added on her own account.

Next day Dora Myrl met the stranger again in the same place on the stairs. Was it her awkwardness or his? As she moved aside to let him pass, her little foot caught in the stick, jerked it from his hand, and sent it clattering down the stairs into the hall.

She ran swiftly down the stairs in pursuit, and carried it back with a pretty apology to the owner. But not before she had seen on the inside of the crook a deep notch, cutting through the varnish into the wood.

At dinner that day their table adjoined Mr. McCrowder's. Half way through the meal she asked Jim to tell her what the hour was, as her watch had stopped. It was a curious request, for she sat facing the clock, and he had to turn round to see it. But Jim turned obediently, and came face to face with Mr. McCrowder, who started and stared at the sight of him as though he had seen a ghost. Jim stared back stolidly without a trace of recognition in his face, and Mr. McCrowder, after a moment, resumed his dinner. Then Dora set, or seemed to set and wind, her watch, and so the curious little incident closed.

That evening Dora played a musical little jingle on the piano in their private sitting-room, touching the notes abstractedly and apparently deep in thought. Suddenly she closed the piano with a bang.

"Mr. Pollock?"

"Well, Miss Myrl," said Jim, who had been watching her with the patient, honest, stupid admiration of a big Newfoundland dog.

"We will take a ride together on our bicycles to-morrow. I cannot say what hour, but have them ready when I call for them."

"Yes, Miss Myrl."

"And bring a ball of stout twine in your pocket."

"Yes, Miss Myrl."

"By the way, have you a revolver?"

"Never had such a thing in my life."

"Could you use it if you got it?"

"I hardly know the butt from the muzzle, but"—modestly—"I can fight a little bit with my fists if that's any use."

"Not the least in this case. An ounce of lead can stop a fourteen-stone champion. Besides one six-shooter is enough and I'm not too bad a shot."

"You don't mean to say, Miss Myrl, that you . . ."

"I don't mean to say one word more at present, Mr. Pollock, only have the bicycles ready when I want them and the twine."

Next morning, after an exceptionally early breakfast, Dora took her place with a book in her hand coiled up on a sofa in a bow-window of the empty drawing-room that looked out on the street. She kept one eye on her book and the other on the window from which the steps of the hotel were visible.

About half-past nine o'clock she saw Mr. McCrowder go down the steps, not limping at all, but carrying his bicycle with a big canvas bicycle-bag strapped to the handle bar.

In a moment she was down in the hall where the bicycles stood ready; in another she and Pollock were in the saddle sailing swiftly and smoothly along the street just as the tall figure of Mr. McCrowder was vanishing round a distant corner.

"We have got to keep him in sight," Dora whispered to her companion as they sped along, "or rather I have got to keep him and you to keep me in sight. Now let me go to the front; hold as far back as you can without losing me, and the moment I wave a white handkerchief—scorch!"

Pollock nodded and fell back, and in this order—each about half a mile apart—the three riders swept out of the town into the open country.

The man in front was doing a strong steady twelve miles an hour, but the roads were good and Dora kept her distance without an effort, while Pollock held himself back. For a full hour this game of follow-my-leader was played without a change. Mr. McCrowder had left the town at the opposite direction to the railway, but now he began to wheel round towards the line. Once he glanced behind and saw only a single girl cycling in the distance on the deserted road. The next time he saw no one, for Dora rode close to the inner curve.

They were now a mile or so from the place where the telegraph wires had been broken down, and Dora, who knew the lie of the land, felt sure their little bicycle trip was drawing to a close.

The road climbed a long easy winding slope thickly wooded on either side. The man in front put on a spurt; Dora answered it with another, and Pollock behind sprinted fiercely, lessening his distance from Dora. The leader crossed the top bend of the slope, turned a sharp curve, and went swiftly down a smooth decline, shaded by the interlacing branches of great trees.

Half a mile down at the bottom of the slope, he leaped suddenly from his bicycle with one quick glance back the way he had come.

There was no one in view, for Dora held back at the turn. He ran his bicycle close into the wall on the left hand side where a deep trench hid it from the casual passers by; unstrapped the bag from the handle bar, and clambered over the wall with an agility that was surprising in one of his (apparent) age.

Dora was just round the corner in time to see him leap from the top of the wall into the thick wood. At once she drew out and waved her white handkerchief, then settled herself in the saddle and made her bicycle fly through the rush of a sudden wind, down the slope.

Pollock saw the signal; bent down over his handle bar and pedalled uphill like the piston rods of a steam engine.

The man's bicycle by the roadside was a finger post for Dora. She, in her turn, over-perched the wall as lightly as a bird. Gathering her tailor-made skirt tightly around her, she peered and listened intently. She could see nothing, but a little way in front a slight rustling of the branches caught her quick ears. Moving in the underwood, stealthily and silently as a rabbit, she caught a glimpse through the leaves of a dark grey tweed suit fifteen or twenty yards off. A few steps more and she had a clear view. The man was on his knees; he had drawn a black leather bag from a thick tangle of ferns at the foot of a great old beech tree, and was busy cramming a number of small canvas sacks into his bicycle bag.

Dora moved cautiously forward till she stood in a little opening, clear of the undergrowth, free to use her right arm.

"Good morning, Mr. McCrowder!" she cried sharply.

The man started, and turned and saw a girl half a dozen yards off standing clear in the sunlight, with a mocking smile on her face.

His lips growled out a curse; his right hand left the bags and stole to his side pocket.

"Stop that!" The command came clear and sharp. "Throw up your hands!"

He looked again. The sunlight glinted on the barrel of a revolver, pointed straight at his head, with a steady hand.

"Up with your hands, or I fire!" and his hands went up over his head. The next instant Jim Pollock came crashing through the underwood, like an elephant through the jungle.

He stopped short with a cry of amazement.

"Steady!" came Dora's quiet voice; "don't get in my line of fire. Round there to the left—that's the way. Take away his revolver. It is in his right-hand coat pocket. Now tie his hands!"

Jim Pollock did his work stolidly as directed. But while he wound the strong cord round the wrists and arms of Mr. McCrowder, he remembered the railway carriage and the strangling grip at his throat, and the chloroform, and the disgrace that followed, and if he strained the knots extra tight it's hard to blame him.

"Now," said Dora, "finish his packing," and Jim crammed the remainder of the canvas sacks into the big bicycle bag.

"You don't mind the weight?"

He gave a delighted grin for answer, as he swung both bags in his hands.

"Get up!" said Dora to the thief, and he stumbled to his feet sulkily. "Walk in front. I mean to take you back to Eddiscombe with me."

When they got on the road-side Pollock strapped the bicycle bag to his own handle-bar.

"May I trouble you, Mr. Pollock, to unscrew one of the pedals of this gentleman's bicycle?" said Dora.

It was done in a twinkling. "Now give him a lift up," she said to Jim, "he is going to ride back with one pedal."

The abject thief held up his bound wrists imploringly.

"Oh, that's all right. I noticed you held the middle of your handle-bar from choice coming out. You'll do it from necessity going back. We'll look after you. Don't whine; you've played a bold game and lost the odd trick, and you've got to pay up, that's all."

There was a wild sensation in Eddiscombe when, in broad noon, the bank thief was brought in riding on a one-pedalled machine to the police barrack and handed into custody. Dora rode on through the cheering crowd to the hotel.

A wire brought Sir Gregory Grant down by the afternoon train, and the three dined together that night at his cost; the best dinner and wine the hotel could supply. Sir Gregory was brimming over with delight, like the bubbling champagne in his wine glass.

"Your health, Mr. Pollock," said the banker to the junior clerk. "We will make up in the bank to you for the annoyance you have had. You shall fix your own fee, Miss Myrl—or, rather, I'll fix it for you if you allow me. Shall we say half the salvage? But I'm dying with curiosity to know how you managed to find the money and thief."

"It was easy enough when you come to think of it, Sir Gregory. The man would have been a fool to tramp across the country with a black bag full of gold while the 'Hue and Cry' was hot on him. His game was to hide it and lie low, and he did so. The sight of Mr. Pollock at the hotel hurried him up as I hoped it would; that's the whole story."

"Oh, that's not all. How did you find the man? How did the man get out of the train going at the rate of sixty miles an hour? But I suppose I'd best ask that question of Mr. Pollock, who was there?"

"Don't ask me any questions, sir," said Jim, with a look of profound admiration in Dora's direction. "She played the game off her own bat. All I know is that the chap cut his stick after he had done for me. I cannot in the least tell how."

"Will you have pity on my curiosity, Miss Myrl."

"With pleasure, Sir Gregory. You must have noticed, as I did, that where the telegraph was broken down the line was embanked and the wires ran quite close to the railway carriage. It is easy for an active man to slip a crooked stick like this" (she held up Mr. McCrowder's stick as she spoke) "over the two or three of the wires and so swing himself into the air clear of the train. The acquired motion would carry him along the wires to the post and give him a chance of breaking down the insulators."

"By Jove! you're right, Miss Myrl. It's quite simple when one comes to think of it. But, still, I don't understand how . . ."

"The friction of the wire," Dora went on in the even tone of a lecturer, "with a man's weight on it, would bite deep into the wood of the stick, like that!" Again she held out the crook of a dark thick oak stick for Sir Gregory to examine, and he peered at it through his gold spectacles.

"The moment I saw that notch," Dora added quietly, "I knew how Mr. McCrowder had '*Cut his stick*.'"

RICHARD MARSH

(1857–1915)

Richard Bernard Heldmann began writing stories for boys when he was only twelve, and published several adventure stories under his middle and last name. But he is remembered mostly for the fiction he published after he adopted the pen name Richard Marsh in 1893. He produced about seventy books during his lifetime and was prolific enough that several of them appeared after his sudden death in 1915 at age fifty-seven. His many novels and story collections range from *The Mahatma's Pupil* to *The Romance of a Maid* to *The Confessions of a Young Lady: Her Doings and Misdoings.*

But he is best known for *The Beetle*, an atmosphere-drenched supernatural novel published by Skeffington in 1897. In its fear of the ancient and mysterious (and, apparently, irresistible) "East," Marsh's saga is reminiscent of Sax Rohmer's evil Fu Manchu and later incarnations of the Yellow Peril paranoia, including Ming the Merciless in the *Flash Gordon* serials. Published within a few weeks of Bram Stoker's *Dracula*, *The Beetle* was hugely popular and overshadowed its contemporary for decades, before fading into relative obscurity as movies promoted the evil count to a household name. Other Marsh books include the collection *Curios: Some Strange Adventures of Two Bachelors*, seven stories mixing the horrific and humorous in tales of rival antique collectors. Marsh devoted as much time as possible to sports and was known to quickly dictate his works to a secretary, often without revising a word. Perhaps this devil-may-care approach to his writing explains its wildly varying quality.

The following story, while situated in exotic psychological territory, is firmly set in the English countryside. In 1911 Marsh published the first story in a curious series about a female detective. "The Man

Who Cut off My Hair" first appeared in the August issue of *The Strand* and was reprinted as the first story in *Judith Lee, Some Pages from Her Life*, which C. Arthur Pearson published the next year.

When we meet the narrator, Judith Lee is an adult, looking back at her experiences in life. In this first story, built around a traumatic experience when she is twelve years old, we witness the origin of her unusual abilities as a detective. She learned lipreading from her deaf mother and her father, who teaches deaf-mutes. As predictably as the older James Bond movies supply 007 with an occasion on which to desperately need precisely the gadget that Q has most recently designed, so Lee finds herself in situations tailored to her unique abilities. Young Judith is intelligent and courageous, as well as a lively and observant narrator, but at times her detective abilities are overshadowed by her talent for making clues simply fall into her lap. Her story contains plenty of Marsh's signature grotesquerie, including the disturbing sexual symbolism of the cut hair.

THE MAN WHO CUT OFF MY HAIR

My name is Judith Lee. I am a teacher of the deaf and dumb. I teach them by what is called the oral system—that is, the lip-reading system. When people pronounce a word correctly they all make exactly the same movements with their lips, so that, without hearing a sound, you only have to watch them very closely to know what they are saying. Of course, this needs practice, and some people do it better and quicker than others. I suppose I must have a special sort of knack in that direction, because I do not remember a time when, by merely watching people speaking at a distance, no matter at what distance if I could see them clearly, I did not know what they were saying. In my case the gift, or knack, or whatever it is, is hereditary. My father was a teacher of the deaf and dumb—a very successful one. His father was, I believe, one of the originators of the oral system. My mother, when she was first married, had an impediment in her speech which practically made her dumb; though she was stone deaf, she became so expert at lip-reading that she could not only tell what others were saying, but she could speak herself—audibly, although she could not hear her own voice.

So, you see, I have lived in the atmosphere of lip-reading all my life. When people, as they often do, think my skill at it borders on the marvellous, I always explain to them that it is nothing of the kind, that mine is simply a case of "practice makes perfect." This knack of mine, in a way, is almost equivalent to another sense. It has led me into the most singular situations, and it has been the cause of many really extraordinary adventures. I will tell you of one which happened to me when I was quite a child, the details of which have never faded from my memory.

My father and mother were abroad, and I was staying, with some old and trusted servants, in a little cottage which we had in the country. I suppose I must have been between twelve and thirteen years of age. I was returning by train to the cottage from a short visit which I had been paying to some friends. In my compartment there were two persons beside myself—an elderly woman who sat in front of me, and a man who was at the other end of her seat. At a station not very far from my home the woman got out; a man got in and placed himself beside the one who was already there. I could see they were acquaintances—they began to talk to each other.

They had been talking together for some minutes in such low tones that you could not only not hear their words, you could scarcely tell that they were speaking. But that made no difference to me; though they spoke in the tiniest whisper I had only to look at their faces to know exactly what they were saying. As a matter of fact, happening to glance up from the magazine I was reading, I saw the man who had been there first say to the other something which gave me quite a start. What he said was this (I only saw the fag-end of the sentence):

". . . Myrtle Cottage; it's got a great, old myrtle in the front garden."

The other man said something, but as his face was turned from me I could not see what; the tone in which he spoke was so subdued that hearing was out of the question. The first man replied (whose face was to me):

"His name is Colegate. He's an old bachelor, who uses the place as a summer cottage. I know him well—all the dealers know him. He's got some of the finest old silver in England. There's a Charles II salt-cellar in the place which would fetch twenty pounds an ounce anywhere."

The other man sat up erect and shook his head, looking straight in front of him, so that I could see what he said, though he spoke only in a whisper.

"Old silver is no better than new; you can only melt it."

The other man seemed to grow quite warm.

"Only melt it! Don't be a fool; you don't know what you're talking about. I can get rid of old silver at good prices to collectors all over the world; they don't ask too many questions when they think they're getting a bargain. That stuff at Myrtle Cottage is worth to us well over a thousand; I shall be surprised if I don't get more for it."

The other man must have glanced at me while I was watching his companion speak. He was a fair-haired man, with a pair of light blue eyes, and quite a nice complexion. He whispered to his friend:

"That infernal kid is watching us as if she were all eyes."

The other said: "Let her watch. Much good may it do her; she can't hear a word—goggle-eyed brat!"

What he meant by "goggle-eyed" I didn't know, and it was true that I could not hear; but, as it happened, it was not necessary that I should. I think the other must have been suspicious, because he replied, if possible, in a smaller whisper than ever:

"I should like to twist her skinny neck and throw her out on to the line."

He looked as if he could do it too; such an unpleasant look came into his eyes that it quite frightened me. After all, I was alone with them; I was quite small; it would have been perfectly easy for him to have done what he said he would like to. So I glanced back at my magazine, and left the rest of their conversation unwatched.

But I had heard, or rather seen, enough to set me thinking. I knew Myrtle Cottage quite well, and the big myrtle tree; it was not very far from our own cottage. And I knew Mr. Colegate and his collection of old silver—particularly that Charles II salt-cellar of which he was so proud. What interest had it for these two men? Had Mr. Colegate come to the cottage? He was not there when I left. Or had Mr. and Mrs. Baines, who kept house for him—had they come? I was so young and so simple that it never occurred to me that there could be anything sinister about these two whispering gentlemen.

They both of them got out at the station before ours. Ours was a little village station, with a platform on only one side of the line; the one at which they got out served for quite an important place—our local market town. I thought no more about them, but I did think of Mr. Colegate and of Myrtle Cottage. Dickson, our housekeeper, said that she did not believe that anyone was at the cottage, but she owned that she was not sure. So after tea I went for a stroll, without saying a word to anyone—Dickson had such a troublesome habit of wanting to know exactly where you were going. My stroll took me to Myrtle Cottage.

It stood all by itself in a most secluded situation on the other side of Woodbarrow Common. You could scarcely see the house from the road—it was quite a little house. When I got into the garden and saw that the front-room window was open I jumped to the very natural conclusion that some one must be there. I went quickly to the window—I was on the most intimate terms with everyone about the place; I should never have dreamt of announcing my presence in any formal manner—and looked in. What I saw did surprise me.

In the room was the man of the train—the man who had been in my compartment first. He had what seemed to me to be Mr. Colegate's entire collection of old silver spread out on the table in front of him, and that very moment he was holding up that gem of the collection—the Charles II salt-cellar. I had moved very quietly, meaning to take Mr. Colegate—if it was he—by surprise; but I doubt if I had made a noise that that man would have heard me, he was so wrapped up in that apple of Mr. Colegate's eye.

I did not know what to make of it at all. I did not know what to think. What was that man doing there? What was I to do? Should I speak to him? I was just trying to make up my mind when some one from behind lifted me right off my feet and, putting a hand to my throat, squeezed it so tightly that it hurt me.

"If you make a sound I'll choke the life right out of you. Don't you make any mistake about it—I will!"

He said that out loudly enough, though it was not so very loud either—he spoke so close to my ear. I could scarcely breathe, but I could still see, and I could see that the man who held me so horribly by the throat was the second man of the train. The recognition seemed to be mutual.

"If it isn't that infernal brat! She seemed to be all eyes in the railway carriage, and, my word, she seems to have been all ears too."

The first man had come to the window.

"What's up?" he asked. "Who's that kid you've got hold of there?"

My captor twisted my face round for the other to look at.

"Can't you see for yourself? I felt, somehow, that she was listening."

"She couldn't have heard, even if she was; no one could have heard what we were saying. Hand her in here." I was passed through the window to the other, who kept as tight a grip on my throat as his friend had done.

"Who are you?" he asked, "I'll give you a chance to answer, but if you try to scream I'll twist your head right off you."

He loosed his grip just enough to enable me to answer if I wished. But I did not wish. I kept perfectly still. His companion said:

"What's the use of wasting time? Slit her throat and get done with it."

He took from the table a dreadful-looking knife, with a blade eighteen inches long, which I knew very well. Mr. Colegate had it in his collection because of its beautifully chased, massive silver handle. It had belonged to one of the old Scottish chieftains; Mr. Colegate would sometimes make me go all over goose-flesh by telling me of some of the awful things for which, in the old, lawless, blood-thirsty days in Scotland, it was supposed to have been used. I knew that he kept it in beautiful condition, with the edge as sharp as a razor. So you can fancy what my feelings were when that man drew the blade across my throat, so close to the skin that it all but grazed me.

"Before you cut her throat," observed his companion, "we'll tie her up. We'll make short work of her. This bit of rope will about do the dodge."

He had what looked to me like a length of clothes-line in his hand. With it, between them, they tied me to a great oak chair, so tight that it seemed to cut right into me, and, lest I should scream with the pain, the man with the blue eyes tied something across my mouth in a way which made it impossible for me to utter a sound. Then he threatened me with that knife again, and just as I made sure he was going to cut my throat he caught hold of my hair, which, of course, was hanging down my back, and with that dreadful knife sawed the whole of it from my head.

If I could have got within reach of him at that moment I believe that I should have stuck that knife into him. Rage made me half beside myself. He had destroyed what was almost the dearest thing in the world to me—not because of my own love of it, but on account of my mother's. My mother had often quoted to me, "The glory of a woman is her hair," and she would add that mine was very beautiful. There certainly was a great deal of it. She was so proud of my hair that she had made me proud of it too—for her sake. And to think that this man could have robbed me of it in so hideous a way! I do believe that at the moment I could have killed him.

I suppose he saw the fury which possessed me, because he laughed and struck me across the face with my own hair.

"I've half a mind to cram it down your throat," he said. "It didn't take me long to cut it off, but I'll cut your throat even quicker—if you so much as try to move, my little dear."

The other man said to him:

"She can't move and she can't make a sound either. You leave her alone. Come over here and attend to business."

"I'll learn her," replied the other man, and he lifted my hair above my head and let it fall all over me.

They proceeded to wrap up each piece of Mr. Colegate's collection in tissue paper, and then to pack the whole into two queer-shaped bags—pretty heavy they must have been. It was only then that I realized what they were doing—they were stealing Mr. Colegate's collection; they were going to take it away. The fury which possessed me as I sat there, helpless, and watched them! The pain was bad enough, but my rage was worse. When the man who had cut off my hair moved to the window with one of the bags held in both his hands—it was as much as he could carry—he said to his companion, with a glance towards me: "Hadn't I better cut her throat before I go?"

"You can come and do that presently," replied the other, "you'll find her waiting." Then he dropped his voice and I saw him say: "Now you quite understand?" The other nodded. "What is it?"

The face of the man who had cut my hair was turned towards me. He put his lips very close to the other, speaking in the tiniest whisper, which he never dreamed could reach my ears: "Cotterill, Cloak-room, Victoria Station Brighton Railway."

The other whispered, "That's right. You'd better make a note of it; we don't want any bungling."

"No fear, I'm not likely to forget." Then he repeated his previous words: "Cotterill, Cloak-room, Victoria Station, Brighton Railway."

He whispered this so very earnestly that I felt sure there was something about the words which was most important; by the time he had said them a second time they were printed on my brain quite as indelibly as they were on his. He got out of the window and his bag was passed to him; then he spoke a parting word to me.

"Sorry I can't take a lock of your hair with me; perhaps I'll come back for one presently."

Then he went. If he had known the passion which was blazing in my heart! That allusion to my desecrated locks only made it burn still fiercer. His companion, left alone, paid no attention to me whatever. He continued to secure his bag, searched the room, as if for anything which might have been overlooked, then, bearing the bag with the other half of Mr. Colegate's collection with him, he went through the door, ignoring my presence as if I had never existed. What he did afterwards I cannot say; I saw no more of him; I was left alone—all through the night.

What a night it was. I was not afraid; I can honestly say that I have seldom been afraid of anything—I suppose it is a matter of temperament—but I was most uncomfortable, very unhappy, and each moment the pain caused me by my bonds seemed to be growing greater. I do believe that the one thing which enabled me to keep my senses all through the night was the constant repetition of those mystic words: "Cotterill, Cloak-room, Victoria Station, Brighton Railway." In the midst of my trouble I was glad that what some people call my curious gift had enabled me to see what I was quite sure they had never meant should reach my understanding. What the words meant I had no notion; in themselves they seemed to be silly words. But that they had some hidden, weighty meaning I was so sure that I kept saying them over and over again lest they should slip through my memory.

I do not know if I ever closed my eyes; I certainly never slept. I saw the first gleams of light usher in the dawn of another morning, and I knew the sun had risen. I wondered what they were doing at home—between the repetitions of that cryptic phrase. Was Dickson looking for me? I rather wished I had let her know where I was going, then she might have had some idea of where to look. As it was she had none. I had some acquaintances three or four miles off, with whom I would sometimes go to tea and, without warning to anyone at home, stay the night. I am afraid that, even as a child, my habits were erratic. Dickson might think I was staying with them, and, if so, she would not even trouble to look for me. In that case I might have to stay where I was for days.

I do not know what time it was, but it seemed to me that it had been light for weeks, and that the day must be nearly gone, when I heard steps outside the open window. I was very nearly in a state of stupor, but I had still sense enough to wonder if it was that man who had cut my hair come back again to cut my throat. As I watched the open sash my heart began to beat more vigorously than it had for a very long time. What, then, was my relief when there presently appeared, on the other side of it, the face of Mr. Colegate, the owner of Myrtle Cottage. I tried to scream—with joy, but that cloth across my mouth prevented my uttering a sound.

I never shall forget the look which came on Mr. Colegate's face when he saw me. He rested his hands on the sill as if he wondered how the window came to be open, then when he looked in and saw me, what a jump he gave.

"Judith!" he exclaimed. "Judith Lee! Surely it is Judith Lee!"

He was a pretty old man, or he seemed so to me, but I doubt if a boy could have got through that window quicker than he did. He was by my side in less than no time; with a knife which he took from his pocket he was severing my bonds. The agony which came over me as they were loosed! It was worse than anything which had gone before. The moment my mouth was free I exclaimed—even then I was struck by the funny, hoarse voice in which I seemed to be speaking:

"Cotterill, Cloak-room, Victoria Station, Brighton Railway."

So soon as I had got those mysterious words out of my poor, parched throat I fainted; the agony I was suffering, the strain which I had gone through, proved too much for me. I knew dimly that I was tumbling into Mr. Colegate's arms, and then I knew no more.

When I came back to life I was in bed. Dickson was at my bedside, and Dr. Scott, and Mr. Colegate, and Pierce, the village policeman, and a man who I afterwards knew was a detective, who had been sent over post-haste from a neighbouring town. I wondered where I was, and then I saw I was in a room in Myrtle Cottage. I sat up in bed, put up my hands—then it all came back to me.

"He cut off my hair with MacGregor's knife!" MacGregor was the name of the Highland chieftain to whom, according to Mr. Colegate, that dreadful knife had belonged.

When it did all come back to me and I realized what had happened, and felt how strange my head seemed without its accustomed covering, nothing would satisfy me but that they should bring me a looking-glass. When I saw what I looked like, the rage which had possessed me when the outrage first took place surged through me with greater force than ever. Before they could stop me, or even guess what I was going to do, I was out of bed and facing them. That cryptic utterance came back to me as if of its own initiative; it burst from my lips.

"'Cotterill, Cloak-room, Victoria Station, Brighton Railway!' Where are my clothes? That's where the man is who cut off my hair."

They stared at me. I believe that for a moment they thought that what I had endured had turned my brain, and that I was mad. But I soon made it perfectly clear that I was nothing of the kind. I told them my story as fast as I could speak; I fancy I brought it home to their understanding. Then I told them of the words which I had seen spoken in such a solemn whisper, and how sure I was that they were pregnant with weighty meaning.

"'Cotterill, Cloak-room, Victoria Station, Brighton Railway'—that's where the man is who cut my hair off—that's where I'm going to catch him."

The detective was pleased to admit that there might be something in my theory, and that it would be worth while to go up to Victoria Station to see what the words might mean. Nothing would satisfy me but that we should go at once. I was quite convinced that every moment was of importance, and that if we were not quick we should be too late. I won Mr. Colegate over—of course, he was almost as anxious to get his collection back as I was to be quits with the miscreant who had shorn me of my locks. So we went up to town by the first train we could catch—Mr. Colegate, the detective, and an excited and practically hairless child.

When we got to Victoria Station we marched straight up to the cloak-room, and the detective said to one of the persons on the other side of the counter:

"Is there a parcel here for the name of Cotterill?"

The person to whom he had spoken did not reply, but another man who was standing by his side.

"Cotterill? A parcel for the name of Cotterill has just been taken out—a hand-bag, scarcely more than half a minute ago. You must have seen him walking off with it as you came up. He can hardly be out of sight now." Leaning over the counter, he looked along the platform.

"There he is—some one is just going to speak to him."

I saw the person to whom he referred—a shortish man in a light grey suit, carrying a brown leather hand-bag. I also saw the person who was going to speak to him; and thereupon I ceased to have eyes for the man with the bag. I broke into exclamation.

"There's the man who cut my hair!" I cried. I went rushing along the platform as hard as I could go. Whether the man heard me or not I cannot say; I dare say I had spoken loudly enough; but he gave one glance in my direction, and when he saw me I had no doubt that he remembered. He whispered to the man with the bag. I was near enough to see, though not to hear, what he said. In spite of the rapidity with which his lips were moving, I saw quite distinctly.

"Bantock, 13 Harwood Street, Oxford Street." That was what he said, and no sooner had he said it than he turned and fled—from me; I knew he was flying from me, and it gave me huge satisfaction to know that the mere sight of me had made him run. I was conscious that Mr. Colegate and the detective were coming at a pretty smart pace behind me.

The man with the bag, seeing his companion dart off without the slightest warning, glanced round to see what had caused his hasty flight. I suppose he saw me and the detective and Mr. Colegate, and he drew his own conclusions. He dropped that hand-bag as if it had been red-hot, and off he ran. He ran to such purpose that we never caught him—neither him nor the man who had cut my hair. The station was full of people—a train had just come in. The crowd streaming out covered the platform with a swarm of moving figures. They acted as cover to those two eager gentlemen—they got clean off. But we got the bag; and, one of the station officials coming on the scene, we were shown to an apartment where, after explanations had been made, the bag and its contents were examined.

Of course, we had realized from the very first moment that Mr. Colegate's collection could not possibly be in that bag, because it was not nearly large enough. When it was seen what was in it, something like a sensation was created. It was crammed with small articles of feminine clothing. In nearly every garment jewels were wrapped, which fell out of them as they were withdrawn from the bag. Such jewels! You should have seen the display they made when they were spread out upon the leather-covered table—and our faces as we stared at them.

"This does not look like my collection of old silver," observed Mr. Colegate.

"No," remarked a big, broad-shouldered man, who I afterwards learned was a well-known London detective, who had been induced by our detective to join our party.

"This does not look like your collection of old silver, sir; it looks, if you'll excuse my saying so, like something very much more worth finding. Unless I am mistaken, these are the Duchess of Datchet's jewels, some of which she wore at the last Drawing Room, and which were taken from Her Grace's bedroom after her return. The police all over Europe have been looking for them for more than a month."

"That bag has been with us nearly a month. The party who

took it out paid four-and-sixpence for cloak-room charges—twopence a day for twenty-seven days."

The person from the cloak-room had come with us to that apartment; it was he who said this. The London detective replied:

"Paid four-and-sixpence, did he? Well, it was worth it—to us. Now, if I could lay my hand on the party who put the bag in the cloak-room, I might have a word of a kind to say to him."

I had been staring, wide-eyed, as piece by piece the contents of the bag had been disclosed; I had been listening, open-eared, to what the detective said; when he made that remark about laying his hands on the party who had deposited that bag in the cloak-room, there came into my mind the words which I had seen the man who had cut my hair whisper as he fled to the man with the bag. The cryptic sentence which I had seen him whisper as I sat tied to the chair had indeed proved to be full of meaning; the words which, even in the moment of flight, he had felt bound to utter might be just as full. I ventured on an observation, the first which I had made, speaking with a good deal of diffidence.

"I think I know where he might be found—I am not sure, but I think."

All eyes were turned to me. The detective exclaimed:

"You think you know? As we haven't got so far as thinking, if you were to tell us, little lady, what you think, it might be as well, mightn't it?"

I considered—I wanted to get the words exactly right.

"Suppose you were to try"—I paused so as to make quite sure—"Bantock, 13 Harwood Street, Oxford Street."

"And who is Bantock?" the detective asked. "And what do you know about him anyhow?"

"I don't know anything at all about him, but I saw the man who cut my hair whisper to the other man just before he ran away, 'Bantock, 13 Harwood Street, Oxford Street'—I saw him quite distinctly."

"You saw him whisper? What does the girl mean by saying she saw him whisper? Why, young lady, you must have been quite fifty feet away. How, at that distance, and with all the noise of the traffic, could you hear a whisper?"

"I didn't say I heard him; I said I saw him. I don't need to hear to know what a person is saying. I just saw you whisper to the other man, 'The young lady seems to be by way of being a curiosity.'"

The London detective stared at our detective. He seemed to be bewildered.

"But I—I don't know how you heard that; I scarcely breathed the words."

Mr. Colegate explained. When they heard they all seemed to be bewildered, and they looked at me, as people do look at the present day, as if I were some strange and amazing thing. The London detective said: "I never heard the like to that. It seems to me very much like what old-fashioned people called 'black magic.'"

Although he was a detective, he could not have been a very intelligent person after all, or he would not have talked such nonsense. Then he added, with an accent on the "saw":

"What was it you said you saw him whisper?"

I bargained before I told him.

"I will tell you if you let me come with you."

"Let you come with me?" He stared still more. "What does the girl mean?"

"Her presence," struck in Mr. Colegate, "may be useful for purposes of recognition. She won't be in the way; you can do no harm by letting her come."

"If you don't promise to let me come I shan't tell you."

The big man laughed. He seemed to find me amusing; I do not know why. If he had only understood my feeling on the subject of my hair, and how I yearned to be even with the man who had wrought me what seemed to me such an irreparable injury, I dare say it sounds as if I were very revengeful. I do not think it was a question of vengeance only; I wanted justice. The detective took out a fat notebook.

"Very well; it's a bargain. Tell me what you saw him whisper, and you shall come." So I told him again, and he wrote it down. "'Bantock, 13 Harwood Street, Oxford Street.' I know Harwood Street, though I don't know Mr. Bantock, But he seems to be residing at what is generally understood to be an unlucky number. Let me get a message through to the Yard—we may want assistance. Then we'll pay a visit to Mr. Bantock—if there is such a person. It sounds like a very tall story to me."

I believe that even then he doubted if I had seen what I said I saw. When we did start I was feeling pretty nervous, because I realized that if we were going on a fool's errand, and there did turn out to be no Bantock, that London detective would doubt me more than ever. And, of course, I could not be sure that there was such a person, though it was some comfort to know that there was a Harwood Street. We went four in a cab—the two detectives, Mr. Colegate and I. We had gone some distance before the cab stopped. The London detective said:

"This is Harwood Street; I told the driver to stop at the corner—we will walk the rest of the way. A cab might arouse suspicion; you never know."

It was a street full of shops. No. 13 proved to be a sort of curiosity shop and jeweller's combined; quite a respectable-looking place, and sure enough over the top of the window was the name "Bantock."

"That looks as if, at any rate, there were a Bantock," the big man said; it was quite a weight off my own mind when I saw the name.

Just as we reached the shop a cab drew up and five men got out, whom the London detective seemed to recognize with mingled feelings.

"That's queered the show," he exclaimed. I did not know what he meant. "They rouse suspicion, if they do nothing else—so in we go."

And in we went—the detective first, and I close on his heels. There were two young men standing close together behind the counter. The instant we appeared I saw one whisper to the other:

"Give them the office—ring the alarm-bell—they're 'tecs!"

I did not quite know what he meant either, but I guessed enough to make me cry out:

"Don't let him move—he's going to ring the alarm-bell and give them the office."

Those young men were so startled—they must have been quite sure that I could not have heard—that they both stood still and stared; before they had got over their surprise a detective—they were detectives who had come in the second cab—had each by the shoulder.

There was a door at the end of the shop, which the London detective opened.

"There's a staircase here; we'd better go up and see who's above. You chaps keep yourselves handy, you may be wanted—when I call you come."

He mounted the stairs—as before, I was as close to him as I could very well get. On the top of the staircase was a landing, on to which two doors opened. We paused to listen: I could distinctly hear voices coming through one of them.

"I think this is ours," the London detective said.

He opened the one through which the voices were coming. He marched in—I was still as close to him as I could get. In it were several men, I did not know how many, and I did not care; I had eyes for only one. I walked right past the detective up to the table round which some of them were sitting, some standing, and stretching out an accusatory arm I pointed at one.

"That's the man who cut off my hair!"

It was, and well he knew it. His conscience must have smitten him; I should not have thought that a grown man could be so frightened at the sight of a child. He caught hold, with both hands, of the side of the table; he glared at me as if I were some dreadful apparition—and no doubt to him I was. It was only with an effort that he seemed able to use his voice.

"Good night!" he exclaimed, "it's that infernal kid!"

On the table, right in front of me, I saw something with which I was only too familiar. I snatched it up.

"And this is the knife," I cried, "with which he did it!"

It was; the historical blade, which had once belonged to the sanguinary and, I sincerely trust, more or less apocryphal MacGregor. I held it out towards the gaping man.

"You know that this is the knife with which you cut off my hair," I said, "You know it is."

I dare say I looked a nice young termagant with my short hair, rage in my eyes, and that frightful weapon in my hand. Apparently I did not impress him quite as I had intended—at least, his demeanour did not suggest it.

"By the living Jingo!" he shouted, "I wish I had cut her throat with it as well!"

It was fortunate for him that he did not. Probably, in the long run, he would have suffered for it more than he did—though he suffered pretty badly as it was. It was his cutting my hair that did it. Had he not done that I have little doubt that I should have been too conscious of the pains caused me by my bonds—the marks caused by the cord were on my skin for weeks after—to pay such close attention to their proceedings as I did under the spur of anger. Quite possibly that tell-tale whisper would have gone unnoticed. Absorbed by my own suffering, I should have paid very little heed to the cryptic sentence which really proved to be their undoing. It was the outrage to my locks which caused me to strain every faculty of observation I had. He had much better have left them alone.

That was the greatest capture the police had made for years. In one haul they captured practically every member of a gang of cosmopolitan thieves who were wanted by the police all over the world. The robbery of Mr. Colegate's collection of old silver shrank into insignificance before the rest of their misdeeds. And not only were the thieves taken themselves, but the proceeds of no end of robberies.

It seemed that they had met there for a sort of annual division of the common spoil. There was an immense quantity of valuable property before them on the table, and lots more about the house. Those jewels which were in the bag which had been deposited at the cloak-room at Victoria Station were to have been added to the common fund—to say nothing of Mr. Colegate's collection of old silver.

The man who called himself Bantock, and who owned the premises at 13 Harwood Street, proved to be a well-known dealer in precious stones and jewellery and bric-a-brac and all sorts of valuables. He was immensely rich; it was shown that a great deal of his money had been made by buying and selling valuable stolen property of every sort and kind. Before the police had done with him it was made abundantly clear that, under various *aliases*, in half the countries of the world, he had been a wholesale dealer in stolen goods. He was sentenced to a long term of penal servitude. I am not quite sure, but I believe that he died in jail.

All the men who were in that room were sent to prison for different terms, including the man who cut my hair—to say nothing of his companion. So far as the proceedings at the court were concerned, I never appeared at all. Compared to some of the crimes of which they had been guilty, the robbery of Mr. Colegate's silver was held to be a mere nothing. They were not charged with it at all, so my evidence was not required. But every time I looked at my scanty locks, which took years to grow to anything like a decent length—they had reached to my knees, but they never did that again—each time I stood before a looking-glass and saw what a curious spectacle I presented with my closely clipped poll, something of that old rage came back to me which had been during that first moment in my heart, and I felt—what I felt when I was tied to that chair in Myrtle Cottage. I endeavoured to console myself, in the spirit of the Old World rather than the New, that, owing to the gift which was mine, I had been able to cry something like quits with the man who, in a moment of mere wanton savagery, had deprived me of what ought to be the glory of a woman.

HUGH C. WEIR

(1884–1934)

In 1914, when the Boston-based Page Company published *Miss Madelyn Mack, Detective*, it bore a curious dedication:

> To Mary Holland,
>
> This is your book. It is you, woman detective of real life, who suggested Madelyn. It was the stories told me from your own note-book of men's knavery that suggested these exploits of Miss Mack. None should know better than you that the riddles of fiction fall ever short of the riddles of truth. What plot of the novelist could equal the grotesqueness of your affair of the mystic circle, or the subtleness of your Chicago University exploit of the Egyptian bar? I pray you, however, in the fulness of your generosity to give Madelyn welcome—not as a rival but as a student. —H. C. W.

Hugh Weir may have been imitating a predecessor in the field. Eight years earlier, Reginald Wright Kauffman had published *Miss Frances Baird, Detective: A Passage from Her Memoirs*, about her tenure at the Watkins Private Detective Agency in New York. Kauffman lends authority to his novel with a similar dedication:

> To Frances Baird
>
> My dear Frances:— You tell me that, as a detective, your professional ethics forbid me to call you by your real name in any printed record which I may make of your achievements. . . .

Whoever Kauffman may have based Baird upon, Mary Holland was not only real but well respected in her field. She and her husband, Phil, ran the Holland Detective Agency and published *The Detective*, a periodical offering to law enforcement officers all sorts of criminological supplies, including a prisoner boot designed by Mrs. Holland herself, as well as running photographs of wanted criminals. Mary Holland was also the first female fingerprint expert and first fingerprint instructor in the United States. She learned directly from Sergeant John Ferrier, the fingerprint authority who came from New Scotland Yard to help protect Queen Victoria's "Diamond Jubilee" jewels when they were displayed at the St. Louis World's Fair (officially named the Louisiana Purchase Exposition) in 1904.

A newspaper reporter and editor who started out at the *Springfield Sun* in Ohio, Hugh Cosgo Weir went on to write literally hundreds of articles and stories, and is credited with more than three hundred Hollywood screenplays. His silent film credits included *The Wolf of Debt* and *The Circus Girl's Romance*. When *Miss Madelyn Mack, Detective* was published, it included photographs of popular silent film star Alice Joyce in her role as Mack for a series produced by the Kalem Moving Picture Company. Weir's entrepreneurial versatility shows up in all sorts of historical footnotes. He ghostwrote, for example, the popular newspaper series "Great Love Stories of the Bible" for evangelist Billy Sunday, and in 1918 sued Sunday for $100,000 for contract violation.

Madelyn Mack is not much like her real-world inspiration, but she is an interesting and lively character. She claims to be an ordinary working detective, but clearly the public, the police, and her adoring Watson regard her as a genius. The series is narrated by reporter Nora Noraker, who like Mack suffers from alliteration and exclamation points. Like Sherlock Holmes, Mack turns coy about clues half glimpsed by Noraker. When bored she even consumes cola berries, as Holmes injected himself with his famous seven-percent solution of cocaine.

THE MAN WITH NINE LIVES

Now that I seek a point of beginning in the curious comradeship between Madelyn Mack and myself, the weird problems of men's knavery that we have confronted together come back to me with almost a shock.

Perhaps the events which crowd into my memory followed each other too swiftly for thoughtful digest at the time of their occurrence. Perhaps only a sober retrospect can supply a properly appreciative angle of view.

Madelyn Mack! What newspaper reader does not know the name? Who, even among the most casual followers of public events, does not recall the young woman who found the missing heiress, Virginia Denton, after a three months' disappearance; who convicted "Archie" Irwin, chief of the "firebug trust"; who located the absconder, Wolcott, after a pursuit from Chicago to Khartoum; who solved the riddle of the double Peterson murder; who—

But why continue the enumeration of Miss Mack's achievements? They are of almost household knowledge, at least that portion which, from one cause or another, have found their way into the newspaper columns. Doubtless those admirers of Miss Mack, whose opinions have been formed through the press chronicles of her exploits, would be startled to know that not one in ten of her cases has ever been recorded outside of her own file cases. And many of them—the most sensational from a newspaper viewpoint—will never be!

It is the woman, herself, however, who has seemed to me always a greater mystery than any of the problems to whose unraveling she has brought her wonderful genius. In spite of the deluge of printer's ink that she has inspired, I question if it has been given to more than a dozen persons to know the true Madelyn Mack.

I do not refer, of course, to her professional career. The salient points of that portion of her life, I presume, are more or less generally known—the college girl confronted suddenly with the necessity of earning her own living; the epidemic of mysterious "shoplifting" cases chronicled in the newspaper she was studying for employment advertisements; her application to the New York department stores, that had been victimized, for a place on their detective staffs, and their curt refusal; her sudden determination to undertake the case as a free-lance, and her remarkable success, which resulted in the conviction of the notorious Madame Bousard, and which secured for Miss Mack her first position as assistant house detective with the famous Niegel dry-goods firm. I sometimes think that this first case, and the realization which it brought her of her peculiar talent, is Madelyn's favorite—that its place in her memory is not even shared by the recovery of Mrs. Niegel's fifty-thousand-dollar pearl necklace, stolen a few months after the employment of the college girl detective at the store, and the reward for which, incidentally, enabled the ambitious Miss Mack to open her own office.

Next followed the Bergner kidnapping case, which gave Madelyn her first big advertising broadside, and which brought the beginning of the steady stream of business that resulted, after three years, in her Fifth Avenue suite in the Maddox Building, where I found her on that—to me—memorable afternoon when a sapient Sunday editor dispatched me for an interview with the woman who had made so conspicuous a success in a man's profession.

I can see Madelyn now, as I saw her then—my first close-range view of her. She had just returned from Omaha that morning, and was planning to leave for Boston on the midnight express. A suitcase and a fat portfolio of papers lay on a chair in a corner. A young woman stenographer was taking a number of letters at an almost incredible rate of dictation. Miss Mack finished the last paragraph as she rose from a flat-top desk to greet me.

I had vaguely imagined a masculine-appearing woman, curt of voice, sharp of feature, perhaps dressed in a severe, tailor-made gown. I saw a young woman of maybe twenty-five, with red and white cheeks, crowned by a softly waved mass of dull gold hair, and a pair of vivacious, grey-blue eyes that at once made one forget every other detail of her appearance. There was a quality in the eyes which for a long time I could not define. Gradually I came to know that it was the spirit of optimism, of joy in herself, and in her life, and in her work, the exhilaration of doing things. And there was something contagious in it. Almost unconsciously you found yourself *believing* in her and in her sincerity.

Nor was there a suggestion foreign to her sex in my appraisal. She was dressed in a simply embroidered white shirtwaist and white broadcloth skirt. One of Madelyn's few peculiarities is that she always dresses either in complete white or complete black. On her desk was a jar of white chrysanthemums.

"How do I do it?" she repeated, in answer to my question, in a tone that was almost a laugh. "Why—just by hard work, I suppose. Oh, there isn't anything wonderful about it! You can do almost anything, you know, if you make yourself really *think* you can! I am not at all unusual or abnormal. I work out my problems just as I would work out a problem in mathematics, only instead of figures I deal with human motives. A detective is always given certain known factors, and I keep building them up, or subtracting them, as the case may be, until I know that the answer *must* be correct.

"There are only two real rules for a successful detective, hard work and common sense—not uncommon sense such as we associate with our old friend Sherlock Holmes, but common, *business* sense. And, of course, imagination! That may be one reason why I have made what you call a success. A woman, I think, always has a more acute imagination than a man!"

"Do you then prefer women operatives on your staff?" I asked.

She glanced up with something like a twinkle from the jade paper-knife in her hands.

"Shall I let you into a secret? All of my staff, with the exception of my stenographer, are men. But I do most of my work in person. The factor of imagination can't very well be used second, or third, or fourth handed. And then, if I fail, I can only blame Madelyn Mack! Someday"—the gleam in her grey-blue eyes deepened—"someday I hope to reach a point where I can afford to do only consulting work or personal investigation. The business details of an office staff, I am afraid, are a bit too much of routine for me!"

The telephone jingled. She spoke a few crisp sentences into the receiver, and turned. The interview was over.

When I next saw her, three months later, we met across the body of Morris Anthony, the murdered bibliophile. It was a chance discovery of mine which Madelyn was good enough to say suggested to her the solution of the affair, and which brought us together in the final melodramatic climax in the grim mansion on Washington Square, when I presume my hysterical warning saved her from the fangs of Dr. Lester Randolph's hidden cobra. In any event, our acquaintanceship crystallized gradually into a comradeship, which revolutionized two angles of my life.

Not only did it bring to me the stimulus of Madelyn Mack's personality, but it gave me exclusive access to a fund of newspaper "copy" that took me from scant-paid Sunday "features" to a "space" arrangement in the city room, with an income double that which I had been earning. I have always maintained that in our relationship Madelyn gave all, and I contributed nothing. Although she invariably made instant disclaimer, and generally ended by carrying me up to the "Rosary," her chalet on the Hudson, as a cure for what she termed my attack of the "blues," she was never able to convince me that my protest was not justified!

It was at the "Rosary" where Miss Mack found haven from the stress of business. She had copied its design from an ivy-tangled Swiss chalet that had attracted her fancy during a summer vacation ramble through the Alps, and had built it on a jagged bluff of the river at a point near enough to the city to permit of fairly convenient motoring, although, during the first years of our friendship, when she was held close to the commercial grindstone, weeks often passed without her being able to snatch a day there. In the end, it was the gratitude of Chalmers Walker for her remarkable work which cleared his chorus-girl wife from the seemingly unbreakable coil of circumstantial evidence in the murder of Dempster, the theatrical broker, that enabled Madelyn to realize her long-cherished dream of setting up as a consulting expert. Although she still maintained an office in town, it was confined to one room and a small reception hall, and she limited her attendance there to two days of the week. During the remainder of the time, when not engaged directly on a case, she seldom appeared in the city at all. Her flowers and her music—she was passionately devoted to both—appeared to content her effectually.

I charged her with growing old, to which she replied with a shrug. I upbraided her as a cynic, and she smiled inscrutably. But the manner of her life was not changed. In a way I envied her. It was almost like looking down on the world and watching tolerantly its mad scramble for the rainbow's end. The days I snatched at the "Rosary," particularly in the summer, when Madelyn's garden looked like nothing so much as a Turner picture, left me with almost a repulsion for the grind of Park Row. But a workaday newspaper woman cannot indulge the dreams of a genius whom fortune has blessed. Perhaps this was why Madelyn's invitations came with a frequency and a subtleness that could not be resisted. Somehow they always reached me when I was in just the right receptive mood.

It was late on a Thursday afternoon of June, the climax of a racking five days for me under the blistering Broadway sun, that Madelyn's motor caught me at the *Bugle* office, and Madelyn insisted on bundling me into the tonneau without even a suitcase.

"We'll reach the Rosary in time for a fried chicken supper," she promised. "What you need is four or five days' rest where you can't smell the asphalt."

"You fairy godmother!" I breathed as I snuggled down on the cushions.

Neither of us knew that already the crimson trail of crime was twisting toward us—that within twelve hours we were to be pitchforked from a quiet weekend's rest into the vortex of tragedy.

We had breakfasted late and leisurely. When at length we had finished, Madelyn had insisted on having her phonograph brought to the rose garden, and we were listening to Sturveysant's matchless rendering of "The Jewel Song"—one of the three records for which Miss Mack had sent the harpist her check for two hundred dollars the day before. I had taken the occasion to read her a lazy lesson on extravagance. The beggar had probably done the work in less than two hours!

As the plaintive notes quivered to a pause, Susan, Madelyn's housekeeper, crossed the garden, and laid a little stack of letters and the morning papers on a rustic table by our bench. Madelyn turned to her correspondence with a shrug.

"From the divine to the prosaic!"

Susan sniffed with the freedom of seven years of service.

"I heard one of them Eyetalian fiddling chaps at Hammerstein's last week who could beat that music with his eyes closed!"

Madelyn stared at her sorrowfully.

"At your age—Hammerstein's!"

Susan tossed her prim rows of curls, glanced contemptuously at the phonograph by way of retaliation, and made a dignified retreat. In the doorway she turned.

"Oh, Miss Madelyn, I am baking one of your old-fashioned strawberry shortcakes for lunch!"

"Really?" Madelyn raised a pair of sparkling eyes. "Susan, you're a dear!"

A contented smile wreathed Susan's face even to the tips of her precise curls. Madelyn's gaze crossed to me.

"What are you chuckling over, Nora?"

"From a psychological standpoint, the pair of you have given me two interesting studies," I laughed. "A single sentence compensates Susan for a week of your glumness!"

Madelyn extended a hand toward her mail.

"And what is the other feature that appeals to your dissecting mind?"

"Fancy a world-known detective rising to the point of enthusiasm at the mention of strawberry shortcake!"

"Why not? Even a detective has to be human once in a while!" Her eyes twinkled. "Another point for my memoirs, Miss Noraker!"

As her gaze fell to the half-opened letter in her hand, my eyes traveled across the garden to the outlines of the chalet, and I breathed a sigh of utter content. Broadway and Park Row seemed very, very far away. In a momentary swerving of my gaze, I saw that a line as clear-cut as a pencil stroke had traced itself across Miss Mack's forehead.

The suggestion of lounging indifference in her attitude had vanished like a wind-blown veil. Her glance met mine suddenly. The twinkle I had last glimpsed in her eyes had disappeared. Silently she pushed a square sheet of close, cramped writing across the table to me.

MY DEAR MADAM:

When you read this, it is quite possible that it will be a letter from a dead man.

I have been told by no less an authority than my friend, Cosmo Hamilton, that you are a remarkable woman. While I will say at the outset that I have little faith in the analytical powers of the feminine brain, I am prepared to accept Hamilton's judgment.

I cannot, of course, discuss the details of my problem in correspondence.

As a spur to quick action, I may say, however, that, during the past five months, my life has been attempted no fewer than eight different times, and I am convinced that the ninth attempt, if made, will be successful. The curious part of it lies in the fact that I am absolutely unable to guess the reason for the persistent vendetta. So far as I know, there is no person in the world who should desire my removal. And yet I have been shot at from ambush on four occasions, thugs have rushed me once, a speeding automobile has grazed me twice, and this evening I found a cunning little dose of cyanide of potassium in my favorite cherry pie!

All of this, too, in the shadow of a New Jersey skunk farm! It is high time, I fancy, that I secure expert advice. Should the progress of the mysterious vendetta, by any chance, render me unable to receive you personally, my niece, Miss Muriel Jansen, I am sure, will endeavor to act as a substitute.

Respectfully Yours,
WENDELL MARSH

THREE FORKS JUNCTION, N. J.
JUNE 16

At the bottom of the page a lead pencil had scrawled the single line in the same cramped writing:

"For God's sake, hurry!"

Madelyn retained her curled-up position on the bench, staring across at a bush of deep crimson roses.

"Wendell Marsh?" She shifted her glance to me musingly. "Haven't I seen that name somewhere lately?" (Madelyn pays me the compliment of saying that I have a card-index brain for newspaper history!)

"If you have read the Sunday supplements," I returned drily, with a vivid remembrance of Wendell Marsh as I had last seen him, six months before, when he crossed the gangplank of his steamer, fresh from England, his face browned from the Atlantic winds. It was a face to draw a second glance—almost gaunt, self-willed, with more than a hint of cynicism. (Particularly when his eyes met the waiting press group!) Someone had once likened him to the pictures of Oliver Cromwell.

"Wendell Marsh is one of the greatest newspaper copy-makers that ever dodged an interviewer," I explained. "He hates reporters like an upstate farmer hates an automobile, and yet has a flock of them on his trail constantly. His latest exploit to catch the spotlight was the purchase of the Bainford relics in London. Just before that he published a three-volume history on 'The World's Great Cynics.' Paid for the publication himself."

Then came a silence between us, prolonging itself. I was trying, rather unsuccessfully, to associate Wendell Marsh's half-hysterical letter with my mental picture of the austere millionaire . . .

"For God's sake, hurry!"

What wrenching terror had reduced the ultra-reserved Mr. Marsh to an appeal like this? As I look back now I know that my wildest fancy could not have pictured the ghastliness of the truth!

Madelyn straightened abruptly.

"Susan, will you kindly tell Andrew to bring around the car at once? If you will find the New Jersey automobile map, Nora, we'll locate Three Forks Junction."

"You are going down?" I asked mechanically.

She slipped from the bench.

"I am beginning to fear," she said irrelevantly, "that we'll have to defer our strawberry shortcake!"

The sound eye of Daniel Peddicord, liveryman by avocation, and sheriff of Merino County by election, drooped over his florid left cheek. Mr. Peddicord took himself and his duties to the taxpayers of Merino County seriously.

Having lowered his sound eye with befitting official dubiousness, while his glass eye stared guilelessly ahead, as though it took absolutely no notice of the procedure, Mr. Peddicord jerked a fat red thumb toward the winding stairway at the rear of the Marsh hall.

"I reckon as how Mr. Marsh is still up there, Miss Mack. You see, I told 'em not to disturb the body until—"

Our stares brought the sentence to an abrupt end. Mr. Peddicord's sound eye underwent a violent agitation.

"You don't mean that you haven't—heard?"

The silence of the great house seemed suddenly oppressive. For the first time I realized the oddity of our having been received by an ill-at-ease policeman instead of by a member of the family. I was abruptly conscious of the incongruity between Mr. Peddicord's awkward figure and the dim, luxurious background.

Madelyn gripped the chief's arm, bringing his sound eye circling around to her face.

"Tell me what has happened!"

Mr. Peddicord drew a huge red handkerchief over his forehead.

"Wendell Marsh was found dead in his library at eight o'clock this morning! He had been dead for hours."

Tick-tock! Tick-tock! Through my daze beat the rhythm of a tall, gaunt clock in the corner. I stared at it dully. Madelyn's hands had caught themselves behind her back, her veins swollen into sharp blue ridges. Mr. Peddicord still gripped his red handkerchief.

"It sure is queer you hadn't heard! I reckoned as how that was what had brought you down. It—it looks like murder!"

In Madelyn's eyes had appeared a greyish glint like cold steel.

"Where is the body?"

"Upstairs in the library. Mr. Marsh had worked—"

"Will you kindly show me the room?"

I do not think we noted at the time the crispness in her tones, certainly not with any resentment. Madelyn had taken command of the situation quite as a matter of course.

"Also, will you have my card sent to the family?"

Mr. Peddicord stuffed his handkerchief back into a rear trousers' pocket. A red corner protruded in jaunty abandon from under his blue coat.

"Why, there ain't no family—at least none but Muriel Jansen." His head cocked itself cautiously up the stairs. "She's his niece, and I reckon now everything here is hers. Her maid says as how she is clear bowled over. Only left her room once since—since it happened. And that was to tell me as how nothing was to be disturbed." Mr. Peddicord drew himself up with the suspicion of a frown. "Just as though an experienced officer wouldn't know *that* much!"

Madelyn glanced over her shoulder to the end of the hall. A hatchet-faced man in russet livery stood staring at us with wooden eyes.

Mr. Peddicord shrugged.

"That's Peters, the butler. He's the chap what found Mr. Marsh."

I could feel the wooden eyes following us until a turn in the stairs blocked their range.

A red-glowing room—oppressively red. Scarlet-frescoed walls, deep red draperies, cherry-upholstered furniture, Turkish-red rugs, rows on rows of red-bound books. Above, a great, flat glass roof, open to the sky from corner to corner, through which the splash of the sun on the rich colors gave the weird semblance of a crimson pool almost in the room's exact center. Such was Wendell Marsh's library—as eccentrically designed as its master.

It was the wreck of a room that we found. Shattered vases littered the floor—books were ripped savagely apart—curtains were hanging in ribbons—a heavy leather rocker was splintered.

The wreckage might have marked the death-struggle of giants. In the midst of the destruction, Wendell Marsh was twisted on his back. His face was shriveled, his eyes were staring. There was no hint of a wound or even a bruise. In his right hand was gripped an object partially turned from me.

I found myself stepping nearer, as though drawn by a magnet. There is something hypnotic in such horrible scenes! And then I barely checked a cry.

Wendell Marsh's dead fingers held a pipe—a strangely carved red sandstone bowl, and a long, glistening stem.

Sheriff Peddicord noted the direction of my glance.

"Mr. Marsh got that there pipe in London, along with those other relics he brought home. They do say as how it was the first pipe ever smoked by a white man. The Indians of Virginia gave it to a chap named Sir Walter Raleigh. Mr. Marsh had a new stem put to it, and his butler says he smoked it every day. Queer, ain't it, how some folks' tastes do run?"

The sheriff moistened his lips under his scraggly yellow moustache.

"Must have been some fight what done this!" His head included the wrecked room in a vague sweep.

Madelyn strolled over to a pair of the ribboned curtains, and fingered them musingly.

"But that isn't the queerest part." The chief glanced at Madelyn expectantly. "There was no way for any one else to get out—or in!"

Madelyn stooped lower over the curtains. They seemed to fascinate her. "The door?" she hazarded absently. "It was locked?"

"From the inside. Peters and the footman saw the key when they broke in this morning . . . Peters swears he heard Mr. Marsh turn it when he left him writing at ten o'clock last night."

"The windows?"

"Fastened as tight as a drum—and, if they wasn't, it's a matter of a good thirty foot to the ground."

"The roof, perhaps?"

"A cat *might* get through it—if every part wasn't clamped as tight as the windows."

Mr. Peddicord spoke with a distinct inflection of triumph. Madelyn was still staring at the curtains.

"Isn't it rather odd," I ventured, "that the sounds of the struggle, or whatever it was, didn't alarm the house?"

Sheriff Peddicord plainly regarded me as an outsider. He answered my question with obvious shortness.

"You could fire a blunderbuss up here and no one would be the wiser. They say as how Mr. Marsh had the room made soundproof. And, besides, the servants have a building to themselves, all except Miss Jansen's maid, who sleeps in a room next to her at the other end of the house."

My eyes circled back to Wendell Marsh's knotted figure—his shriveled face—horror-frozen eyes—the hand gripped about the fantastic pipe. I think it was the pipe that held my glance. Of all incongruities, a pipe in the hand of a dead man!

Maybe it was something of the same thought that brought Madelyn of a sudden across the room. She stooped, straightened the cold fingers, and rose with the pipe in her hand.

A new stem had obviously been added to it, of a substance which I judged to be jessamine. At its end, teeth-marks had bitten nearly through. The stone bowl was filled with the cold ashes of half-consumed tobacco. Madelyn balanced it musingly.

"Curious, isn't it, Sheriff, that a man engaged in a life-or-death struggle should cling to a heavy pipe?"

"Why—I suppose so. But the question, Miss Mack, is what became of that there other man? It isn't natural as how Mr. Marsh could have fought with himself."

"The other man?" Madelyn repeated mechanically. She was stirring the rim of the dead ashes.

"And how in tarnation was Mr. Marsh killed?"

Madelyn contemplated a dust-covered finger.

"Will you do me a favor, Sheriff?"

"Why, er—of course."

"Kindly find out from the butler if Mr. Marsh had cherry pie for dinner last night!"

The sheriff gulped.

"Che-cherry pie?"

Madelyn glanced up impatiently.

"I believe he was very fond of it."

The sheriff shuffled across to the door uncertainly. Madelyn's eyes flashed to me.

"You might go, too, Nora."

For a moment I was tempted to flat rebellion. But Madelyn affected not to notice the fact. She is always so aggravatingly sure of her own way!—With what I tried to make a mood of aggrieved silence, I followed the sheriff's blue-coated figure. As the door closed, I saw that Madelyn was still balancing Raleigh's pipe.

From the top of the stairs, Sheriff Peddicord glanced across at me suspiciously.

"I say, what I would like to know is what became of that there other man!"

A wisp of a black-gowned figure, peering through a dormer window at the end of the second-floor hall, turned suddenly as we reached the landing. A white, drawn face, suggesting a tired child, stared at us from under a frame of dull-gold hair, drawn low from a careless part. I knew at once it was Muriel Jansen, for the time, at least, mistress of the house of death.

"Has the coroner come yet, Sheriff?"

She spoke with one of the most liquid voices I have ever heard. Had it not been for her bronze hair, I would have fancied her at once of Latin descent. The fact of my presence she seemed scarcely to notice, not with any suggestion of aloofness, but rather as though she had been drained even of the emotion of curiosity.

"Not yet, Miss Jansen. He should be here now."

She stepped closer to the window, and then turned slightly.

"I told Peters to telegraph to New York for Dr. Dench when he summoned you. He was one of Uncle's oldest friends. I—I would like him to be here when—when the coroner makes his examination."

The sheriff bowed awkwardly.

"Miss Mack is upstairs now."

The pale face was staring at us again with raised eyebrows.

"Miss Mack? I don't understand." Her eyes shifted to me.

"She had a letter from Mr. Marsh by this morning's early post," I explained. "I am Miss Noraker. Mr. Marsh wanted her to come down at once. She didn't know, of course—couldn't know—that—that he was—dead!"

"A letter from—Uncle?" A puzzled line gathered in her face.

I nodded.

"A distinctly curious letter. But—Miss Mack would perhaps prefer to give you the details."

The puzzled line deepened. I could feel her eyes searching mine intently.

"I presume Miss Mack will be down soon," I volunteered. "If you wish, however, I will tell her—"

"That will hardly be necessary. But—you are quite sure—a letter?"

"Quite sure," I returned, somewhat impatiently.

And then, without warning, her hands darted to her head, and she swayed forward. I caught her in my arms with a side-view of Sheriff Peddicord staring, open-mouthed.

"Get her maid!" I gasped.

The sheriff roused into belated action. As he took a cumbersome step toward the nearest door, it opened suddenly. A gaunt, middle-aged woman, in a crisp white apron, digested the situation with cold grey eyes. Without a word, she caught Muriel Jansen in her arms.

"She has fainted," I said rather vaguely. "Can I help you?"

The other paused with her burden.

"When I need you, I'll ask you!" she snapped, and banged the door in our faces.

In the wake of Sheriff Peddicord, I descended the stairs. A dozen question-marks were spinning through my brain. Why had Muriel Jansen fainted? Why had the mention of Wendell Marsh's letter left such an atmosphere of bewildered doubt? Why had the dragonlike maid—for such I divined her to be—faced us with such hostility? The undercurrent of hidden secrets in the dim, silent house seemed suddenly intensified.

With a vague wish for fresh air and the sun on the grass, I sought the front veranda, leaving the sheriff in the hall, mopping his face with his red handkerchief.

A carefully tended yard of generous distances stretched an inviting expanse of graded lawn before me. Evidently Wendell Marsh had provided a discreet distance between himself and his neighbors. The advance guard of a morbid crowd was already shuffling about the gate. I knew that it would not be long, too, before the press siege would begin.

I could picture frantic city editors pitchforking their star men New Jerseyward. I smiled at the thought. The *Bugle*—the slave driver that presided over my own financial destinies—was assured of a generous *beat* in advance. The next train from New York was not due until late afternoon.

From the staring line about the gate, the figure of a well-set-up young man in blue serge detached itself with swinging step.

"A reporter?" I breathed, incredulous.

With a glance at me, he ascended the steps and paused at the door, awaiting an answer to his bell. My stealthy glances failed to place him among the "stars" of New York newspaperdom. Perhaps he was a local correspondent. With smug expectancy, I awaited his discomfiture when Peters received his card. And then I rubbed my eyes. Peters was stepping back from the door, and the other was following him with every suggestion of assurance.

I was still gasping when a maid, broom in hand, zigzagged toward my end of the veranda. She smiled at me with a pair of friendly black eyes.

"Are you a detective?"

"Why?" I parried.

She drew her broom idly across the floor.

"I—I always thought detectives different from other people."

She sent a rivulet of dust through the railing, with a side-glance still in my direction.

"Oh, you will find them human enough," I laughed, "outside of detective stories!"

She pondered my reply doubtfully.

"I thought it about time Mr. Truxton was appearing!" she ventured suddenly.

"Mr. Truxton?"

"He's the man that just came—Mr. Homer Truxton. Miss Jansen is going to marry him!"

A light broke through my fog.

"Then he is not a reporter?"

"Mr. Truxton? He's a lawyer." The broom continued its dilatory course. "Mr. Marsh didn't like him—so they *say!*"

I stepped back, smoothing my skirts. I have learned the cardinal rule of Madelyn never to pretend too great an interest in the gossip of a servant.

The maid was mechanically shaking out a rug.

"For my part, I always thought Mr. Truxton far and away the pick of Miss Jansen's two steadies. I never could understand what she could see in Dr. Dench! Why, he's old enough to be her—"

In the doorway, Sheriff Peddicord's bulky figure beckoned.

"Don't you reckon as how it's about time we were going back to Miss Mack?" he whispered.

"Perhaps," I assented rather reluctantly.

From the shadows of the hall, the sheriff's sound eye fixed itself on me belligerently.

"I say, what I would like to know is what became of that there other man!"

As we paused on the second landing the well-set-up figure of Mr. Homer Truxton was bending toward a partially opened door. Beyond his shoulder, I caught a fleeting glimpse of a pale face under a border of rumpled dull-gold hair. Evidently Muriel Jansen had recovered from her faint.

The door closed abruptly, but not before I had seen that her eyes were red with weeping.

Madelyn was sunk into a red-backed chair before a huge flat-top desk in the corner of the library, a stack of Wendell Marsh's red-bound books, from a wheel-cabinet at her side, bulked before her. She finished the page she was reading—a page marked with a broad blue pencil—without a hint that she had heard us enter.

Sheriff Peddicord stared across at her with a disappointment that was almost ludicrous. Evidently Madelyn was falling short of his conception of the approved attitudes for a celebrated detective!

"Are you a student of Elizabethan literature, Sheriff?" she asked suddenly.

The sheriff gurgled weakly.

"If you are, I am quite sure you will be interested in Mr. Marsh's collection. It is the most thorough on the subject that I have ever seen. For instance, here is a volume on the inner court life of Elizabeth—perhaps you would like me to read you this random passage?"

The sheriff drew himself up with more dignity than I thought he possessed.

"We are investigating a crime, Miss Mack!"

Madelyn closed the book with a sigh.

"So we are! May I ask what is your report from the butler?"

"Mr. Marsh did *not* have cherry pie for dinner last night!" the sheriff snapped.

"You are quite confident?"

And then abruptly the purport of the question flashed to me.

"Why, Mr. Marsh, himself, mentioned the fact in his letter!" I burst out.

Madelyn's eyes turned to me reprovingly.

"You must be mistaken, Nora."

With a lingering glance at the books on the desk, she rose. Sheriff Peddicord moved toward the door, opened it, and faced about with an abrupt clearing of his throat.

"Begging your pardon, Miss Mack, have—have you found any *clues* in the case?"

Madelyn had paused again at the ribboned curtains.

"Clues? The man who made Mr. Marsh's death possible, Sheriff, was an expert chemist, of Italian origin, living for some time in London—and he died three hundred years ago!"

From the hall we had a fleeting view of Sheriff Peddicord's face, flushed as red as his handkerchief, and then it and the handkerchief disappeared.

I whirled on Madelyn sternly.

"You are carrying your absurd joke, Miss Mack, altogether too—"

I paused, gulping in my turn. It was as though I had stumbled from the shadows into an electric glare.

Madelyn had crossed to the desk, and was gently shifting the dead ashes of Raleigh's pipe into an envelope. A moment she sniffed at its bowl, peering down at the crumpled body at her feet.

"The pipe!" I gasped. "Wendell Marsh was poisoned with the pipe!"

Madelyn sealed the envelope slowly.

"Is that fact just dawning on you, Nora?"

"But the rest of it—what you told the—"

Madelyn thrummed on the bulky volume of Elizabethan history.

"Someday, Nora, if you will remind me, I will give you the material for what you call a Sunday 'feature' on the historic side of murder as a fine art!"

In a curtain-shadowed hook of the side veranda Muriel Jansen was awaiting us, pillowed back against a bronze-draped chair, whose colors almost startlingly matched the gold of her hair. Her resemblance to a tired child was even more pronounced than when I had last seen her.

I found myself glancing furtively for signs of Homer Truxton, but he had disappeared.

Miss Jansen took the initiative in our interview with a nervous abruptness, contrasting oddly with her hesitancy at our last meeting.

"I understand, Miss Mack, that you received a letter from my uncle asking your presence here. May I see it?"

The eagerness of her tones could not be mistaken.

From her wrist-bag Madelyn extended the square envelope of the morning post, with its remarkable message. Twice Muriel Jansen's eyes swept slowly through its contents. Madelyn watched her with a little frown. A sudden tenseness had crept into the air, as though we were all keying ourselves for an unexpected climax. And then, like a thunderclap, it came.

"A curious communication," Madelyn suggested. "I had hoped you might be able to add to it?"

The tired face in the bronze-draped chair stared across the lawn.

"I can. The most curious fact of your communication Miss Mack, is that *Wendell Marsh did not write it!*"

Never have I admired more keenly Madelyn's remarkable poise. Save for an almost imperceptible indrawing of her breath, she gave no hint of the shock which must have stunned her as it did me. I was staring with mouth agape. But, then, I presume you have discovered by this time that I was not designed for a detective!

Strangely enough, Muriel Jansen gave no trace of wonder in her announcement. Her attitude suggested a sense of detachment from the subject as though suddenly it had lost its interest. And yet, less than an hour ago it had prostrated her in a swoon.

"You mean the letter is a forgery?" asked Madelyn quietly.

"Quite obviously."

"And the attempts on Mr. Marsh's life to which it refers?"

"There have been none. I have been with my uncle continuously for six months. I can speak definitely."

Miss Jansen fumbled in a white crocheted bag.

"Here are several specimens of Mr. Marsh's writing. I think they should be sufficient to convince you of what I say. If you desire others—"

I was gulping like a truant schoolgirl as Madelyn spread on her lap the three notes extended to her. Casual business and personal references they were, none of more than half a dozen lines. Quite enough, however, to complete the sudden chasm at our feet—quite enough to emphasize a bold, aggressive penmanship, almost perpendicular, without the slightest resemblance to the cramped shadowy writing of the morning's astonishing communication.

Madelyn rose from her chair, smoothing her skirts thoughtfully. For a moment she stood at the railing, gazing down upon a trellis of yellow roses, her face turned from us. For the first time in our curious friendship, I was actually conscious of a feeling of pity for her! The blank wall which she faced seemed so abrupt—so final!

Muriel Jansen shifted her position slightly.

"Are you satisfied, Miss Mack?"

"Quite." Madelyn turned, and handed back the three notes. "I presume this means that you do not care for me to continue the case?"

I whirled in dismay. I had never thought of this possibility.

"On the contrary, Miss Mack, it seems to me an additional reason why you should continue!"

I breathed freely again. At least we were not to be dismissed with the abruptness that Miss Jansen's maid had shown! Madelyn bowed rather absently.

"Then if you will give me another interview, perhaps this afternoon—"

Miss Jansen fumbled with the lock of her bag. For the first time her voice lost something of its directness.

"Have—have you any explanation of this astonishing—forgery?"

Madelyn was staring out toward the increasing crowd at the gate. A sudden ripple had swept through it.

"Have you ever heard of a man by the name of Orlando Julio, Miss Jansen?"

My own eyes, following the direction of Madelyn's gaze, were brought back sharply to the veranda. For the second time, Muriel Jansen had crumpled back in a faint.

As I darted toward the servants' bell Madelyn checked me. Striding up the walk were two men with the unmistakable air of physicians. At Madelyn's motioning hand they turned toward us.

The foremost of the two quickened his pace as he caught sight of the figure in the chair. Instinctively I knew that he was Dr. Dench—and it needed no profound analysis to place his companion as the local coroner.

With a deft hand on Miss Jansen's heartbeats, Dr. Dench raised a ruddy, brown-whiskered face inquiringly toward us.

"Shock!" Madelyn explained. "Is it serious?"

The hand on the wavering breast darted toward a medicine case and selected a vial of brownish liquid. The gaze above it continued its scrutiny of Madelyn's slender figure.

Dr. Dench was of the rugged, German type, steel-eyed, confidently sure of movement, with the physique of a splendidly muscled animal. If the servant's tattle was to be credited, Muriel Jansen could not have attracted more opposite extremes in her suitors.

The coroner—a rusty-suited man of middle age, in quite obvious professional awe of his companion—extended a glass of water. Miss Jansen wearily opened her eyes before it reached her lips.

Dr. Dench restrained her sudden effort to rise.

"Drink this, please!" There was nothing but professional command in his voice. If he loved the gray-pallored girl in the chair, his emotions were under superb control.

Madelyn stepped to the background, motioning me quietly.

"I fancy I can leave now safely. I am going back to town."

"Town?" I echoed.

"I should be back the latter part of the afternoon. Would it inconvenience you to wait here?"

"But, why on earth—" I began.

"Will you tell the butler to send around the car? Thanks!"

When Madelyn doesn't choose to answer questions she ignores

them. I subsided as gracefully as possible. As her machine whirled under the porte cochere, however, my curiosity again overflowed my restraint.

"At least, who is Orlando Julio?" I demanded.

Madelyn carefully adjusted her veil.

"The man who provided the means for the death of Wendell Marsh!" And she was gone.

I swept another glance at the trio on the side veranda, and with what I tried to convince myself was a philosophical shrug, although I knew perfectly well it was merely a pettish fling, sought a retired corner of the rear drawing room, with my pad and pencil.

After all, I was a newspaper woman, and it needed no elastic imagination to picture the scene in the city room of the *Bugle*, if I failed to send a proper accounting of myself.

A few minutes later a tread of feet, advancing to the stairs, told me that the coroner and Dr. Dench were ascending for the belated examination of Wendell Marsh's body. Miss Jansen had evidently recovered, or been assigned to the ministrations of her maid. Once Peters, the wooden-faced butler, entered ghostily to inform me that luncheon would be served at one, but effaced himself almost before my glance returned to my writing.

I partook of the meal in the distinguished company of Sheriff Peddicord. Apparently Dr. Dench was still busied in his gruesome task upstairs, and it was not surprising that Miss Jansen preferred her own apartments.

However much the sheriff's professional poise might have been jarred by the events of the morning, his appetite had not been affected. His attention was too absorbed in the effort to do justice to the Marsh hospitality to waste time in table talk.

He finished his last spoonful of strawberry ice cream with a heavy sigh of contentment, removed the napkin, which he had tucked under his collar, and, as though mindful of the family's laundry bills, folded it carefully and wiped his lips with his red handkerchief. It was not until then that our silence was interrupted.

Glancing cautiously about the room, and observing that the butler had been called kitchenward, to my amazement he essayed a confidential wink.

"I say," he ventured enticingly, leaning his elbow on the table, "what I would like to know is what became of that there other man!"

"Are you familiar with the Fourth Dimension, Sheriff?" I returned solemnly. I rose from my chair, and stepped toward him confidentially in my turn. "I believe that a thorough study of that subject would answer your question."

It was three o'clock when I stretched myself in my corner of the drawing-room, and stuffed the last sheets of my copy paper into a special-delivery-stamped envelope.

My story was done. And Madelyn was not there to blue-pencil the Park Row adjectives! I smiled rather gleefully as I patted my hair and leisurely addressed the envelope. The city editor would be satisfied, if Madelyn wasn't!

As I stepped into the hall, Dr. Dench, the coroner, and Sheriff Peddicord were descending the stairs. Evidently the medical examination had been completed. Under other circumstances the three expressions before me would have afforded an interesting study in contrasts—Dr. Dench trimming his nails with professional stoicism, the coroner endeavoring desperately to copy the other's *sang-froid*, and the sheriff buried in an owllike solemnity.

Dr. Dench restored his knife to his pocket.

"You are Miss Mack's assistant, I understand?"

I bowed.

"Miss Mack has been called away. She should be back, however, shortly."

I could feel the doctor's appraising glance dissecting me with much the deliberateness of a surgical operation. I raised my eyes suddenly, and returned his stare. It was a virile, masterful face—and, I had to admit, coldly handsome!

Dr. Dench snapped open his watch.

"Very well then, Miss, Miss—"

"Noraker!" I supplied crisply.

The blond beard inclined the fraction of an inch.

"We will wait."

"The autopsy?" I ventured. "Has it—"

"The result of the autopsy I will explain to—Miss Mack!"

I bit my lip, felt my face flush as I saw that Sheriff Peddicord was trying to smother a grin, and turned with a rather unsuccessful shrug.

Now, if I had been of a vindictive nature, I would have opened my envelope and inserted a retaliating paragraph that would have returned the snub of Dr. Dench with interest. I flatter myself that I consigned the envelope to the Three Forks post office, in the rear of the Elite Dry Goods Emporium, with its contents unchanged.

As a part recompense, I paused at a corner drugstore and permitted a young man with a gorgeous pink shirt to make me a chocolate ice-cream soda. I was bent over an asthmatic straw when, through the window, I saw Madelyn's car skirt the curb.

I rushed out to the sidewalk, while the young man stared dazedly after me. The chauffeur swerved the machine as I tossed a dime to the Adonis of the fountain.

Madelyn shifted to the end of the seat as I clambered to her side. One glance was quite enough to show that her town mission, whatever it was, had ended in failure. Perhaps it was the consciousness of this fact that brought my eyes next to her blue turquoise locket. It was open. I glared accusingly.

"So you have fallen back on the cola stimulant again, Miss Mack?"

She nodded glumly, and perversely slipped into her mouth another of the dark brown berries, on which I have known her to keep up for forty-eight hours without sleep and almost without food.

For a moment I forgot even my curiosity as to her errand.

"I wish the duty would be raised so high you couldn't get those things into the country!"

She closed her locket, without deigning a response. The more volcanic my outburst, the more glacial Madelyn's coldness—particularly on the cola topic. I shrugged in resignation. I might as well have done so in the first place!

I straightened my hat, drew my handkerchief over my flushed face, and coughed questioningly. Continued silence. I turned in desperation.

"Well?" I surrendered.

"Don't you know enough, Nora Noraker, to hold your tongue?"

My pent-up emotions snapped.

"Look here, Miss Mack, I have been snubbed by Dr. Dench and the coroner, grinned at by Sheriff Peddicord, and I am not going to be crushed by you! What is your report—good, bad, or indifferent?"

Madelyn turned from her stare into the dust-yellow road.

"I have been a fool, Nora—a blind, bigoted, self-important fool!"

I drew a deep breath.

"Which means—"

From her bag Madelyn drew the envelope of dead tobacco ashes from the Marsh library, and tossed it over the side of the car. I sank back against the cushions.

"Then the tobacco after all—"

"Is nothing but tobacco—harmless tobacco!"

"But the pipe—I thought the pipe—"

"That's just it! The pipe, my dear girl, killed Wendell Marsh! But I don't know how! *I don't know how!*"

"Madelyn," I said severely, "you are a woman, even if you are making your living at a man's profession! What you need is a good cry!"

Dr. Dench, pacing back and forth across the veranda, knocked the ashes from an amber-stemmed meerschaum and advanced to meet us as we alighted. The coroner and Sheriff Peddicord were craning their necks from wicker chairs in the background. It was easy enough to surmise that Dr. Dench had parted from them abruptly in the desire for a quiet smoke to marshal his thoughts.

"Fill your pipe again if you wish," said Madelyn. "I don't mind."

Dr. Dench inclined his head, and dug the mouth of his meerschaum into a fat leather pouch. A spiral of blue smoke soon curled around his face. He was one of that type of men to whom a pipe lends a distinction of studious thoughtfulness.

With a slight gesture he beckoned in the direction of the coroner.

"It is proper, perhaps, that Dr. Williams in his official capacity should be heard first."

Through the smoke of his meerschaum, his eyes were searching

Madelyn's face. It struck me that he was rather puzzled as to just how seriously to take her.

The coroner shuffled nervously. At his elbow, Sheriff Peddicord fumbled for his red handkerchief.

"We have made a thorough examination of Mr. Marsh's body, Miss Mack, a most thorough examination—"

"Of course he was not shot, nor stabbed, nor strangled, nor sandbagged?" interrupted Madelyn crisply.

The coroner glanced at Dr. Dench uncertainly. The latter was smoking with inscrutable face.

"Nor poisoned!" finished the coroner with a quick breath.

A blue smoke curl from Dr. Dench's meerschaum vanished against the sun. The coroner jingled a handful of coins in his pocket. The sound jarred on my nerves oddly. Not poisoned! Then Madelyn's theory of the pipe—

My glance swerved in her direction. Another blank wall—the blankest in this riddle of blank walls!

But the bewilderment I had expected in her face I did not find. The black dejection I had noticed in the car had dropped like a whisked-off cloak. The tired lines had been erased as by a sponge. Her eyes shone with that tense glint which I knew came only when she saw a befogged way swept clear before her.

"You mean that you *found* no trace of poison?" she corrected.

The coroner drew himself up.

"Under the supervision of Dr. Dench, we have made a most complete probe of the various organs—lungs, stomach, heart—"

"And brain, I presume?"

"Brain? Certainly not!"

"And you?" Madelyn turned toward Dr. Dench. "You subscribe to Dr. Williams' opinion?"

Dr. Dench removed his meerschaum.

"From our examination of Mr. Marsh's body, I am prepared to state emphatically that there is no trace of toxic condition of any kind!"

"Am I to infer then that you will return a verdict of—natural death?"

Dr. Dench stirred his pipe-ashes.

"I was always under the impression, Miss Mack, that the verdict in a case of this kind must come from the coroner's jury."

Madelyn pinned back her veil, and removed her gloves.

"There is no objection to my seeing the body again?"

The coroner stared.

"Why, er—the undertaker has it now. I don't see why he should object, if you wish—"

Madelyn stepped to the door. Behind her, Sheriff Peddicord stirred suddenly.

"I say, what I would like to know, gents, is what became of that there other man!"

It was not until six o'clock that I saw Madelyn again, and then I found her in Wendell Marsh's red library. She was seated at its late tenant's huge desk. Before her were a vial of whitish-grey powder, a small rubber inked roller, a half a dozen sheets of paper, covered with what looked like smudges of black ink, and Raleigh's pipe. I stopped short, staring.

She rose with a shrug.

"Fingerprints," she explained laconically. "This sheet belongs to Miss Jansen; the next to her maid; the third to the butler, Peters; the fourth to Dr. Dench; the fifth to Wendell Marsh, himself. It was my first experiment in taking the 'prints' of a dead man. It was—interesting."

"But what has that to do with a case of this kind?" I demanded.

Madelyn picked up the sixth sheet of smudged paper.

"We have here the fingerprints of Wendell Marsh's murderer!"

I did not even cry my amazement. I suppose the kaleidoscope of the day had dulled my normal emotions. I remember that I readjusted a loose pin in my waist before I spoke.

"The murderer of Wendell Marsh!" I repeated mechanically. "Then he *was* poisoned?"

Madelyn's eyes opened and closed without answer.

I reached over to the desk, and picked up Mr. Marsh's letter of the morning post at Madelyn's elbow.

"You have found the man who forged this?"

"It was *not* forged!"

In my daze I dropped the letter to the floor.

"You have discovered then the other man in the death-struggle that wrecked the library?"

"There was no other man!"

Madelyn gathered up her possessions from the desk. From the edge of the row of books she lifted a small, red-bound volume, perhaps four inches in width, and then with a second thought laid it back.

"By the way, Nora, I wish you would come back here at eight o'clock. If this book is still where I am leaving it, please bring it to me! I think that will be all for the present."

"All?" I gasped. "Do you realize that—"

Madelyn moved toward the door.

"I think eight o'clock will be late enough for your errand," she said without turning.

The late June twilight had deepened into a somber darkness when, my watch showing ten minutes past the hour of my instructions, I entered the room on the second floor that had been assigned to Miss Mack and myself. Madelyn at the window was staring into the shadow-blanketed yard.

"Well?" she demanded.

"Your book is no longer in the library!" I said crossly.

Madelyn whirled with a smile.

"Good! And now if you will be so obliging as to tell Peters to ask Miss Jansen to meet me in the rear drawing room, with any of the friends of the family she desires to be present, I think we can clear up our little puzzle."

It was a curious group that the graceful Swiss clock in the bronze drawing room of the Marsh house stared down upon as it ticked its way past the half hour after eight. With a grave, rather insistent bow, Miss Mack had seated the other occupants of the room as they answered her summons. She was the only one of us that remained standing.

Before her were Sheriff Peddicord, Homer Truxton, Dr. Dench, and Muriel Jansen. Madelyn's eyes swept our faces for a moment in silence, and then she crossed the room and closed the door.

"I have called you here," she began, "to explain the mystery of Mr. Marsh's death." Again her glance swept our faces. "In many respects it has provided us with a peculiar, almost an unique problem.

"We find a man, in apparently normal health, dead. The observer argues at once foul play; and yet on his body is no hint of wound or bruise. The medical examination discovers no trace of poison. The autopsy shows no evidence of crime. Apparently we have eliminated all forms of unnatural death.

"I have called you here because the finding of the autopsy is incorrect, or rather incomplete. We are not confronted by natural death—but by a crime. And I may say at the outset that I am not the only person to know this fact. My knowledge is shared by one other in this room."

Sheriff Peddicord rose to his feet and rather ostentatiously stepped to the door and stood with his back against it. Madelyn smiled faintly at the movement.

"I scarcely think there will be an effort at escape, Sheriff," she said quietly.

Muriel Jansen was crumpled back into her chair, staring. Dr. Dench was studying Miss Mack with the professional frown he might have directed at an abnormality on the operating table. It was Truxton who spoke first in the fashion of the impulsive boy.

"If we are not dealing with natural death, how on earth then was Mr. Marsh killed?"

Madelyn whisked aside a light covering from a stand at her side, and raised to view Raleigh's red sandstone pipe. For a moment she balanced it musingly.

"The three-hundred-year-old death tool of Orlando Julio," she explained. "It was this that killed Wendell Marsh!"

She pressed the bowl of the pipe into the palm of her hand. "As an instrument of death, it is *almost* beyond detection. We examined the ashes, and found nothing but harmless tobacco. The organs of the victim showed no trace of foul play."

She tapped the long stem gravely.

"But the examination of the organs did *not* include the brain. And it is through the brain that the pipe strikes, killing first the mind in a nightmare of insanity, and then the body. That accounts for the wreckage that we found—the evidences apparently of *two* men engaged in a desperate struggle. The wreckage was the work of only one man—a maniac in the moment before death. The drug with which we are dealing drives its victim into an insane fury before his body succumbs. I believe such cases are fairly common in India."

"Then Mr. Marsh was poisoned after all?" cried Truxton. He was the only one of Miss Mack's auditors to speak.

"No, not poisoned! You will understand as I proceed. The pipe you will find, contains apparently but one bowl and one channel, and at a superficial glance is filled only with tobacco. In reality, there is a lower chamber concealed beneath the upper bowl, to which extends a second channel. This secret chamber is charged with a certain compound of Indian hemp and dhatura leaves, one of the most powerful brain stimulants known to science—and one of the most dangerous if used above a certain strength. From the lower chamber it would leave no trace, of course, in the ashes above.

"Between the two compartments of the pipe is a slight connecting opening, sufficient to allow the hemp beneath to be ignited gradually by the burning tobacco. When a small quantity of the compound is used, the smoker is stimulated as by no other drug, not even opium. Increase the quantity above the danger point, and mark the result. The victim is not poisoned in the strict sense of the word, but literally *smothered to death by the fumes!*"

In Miss Mack's voice was the throb of the student before the creation of the master.

"I should like this pipe, Miss Jansen, if you ever care to dispose of it!"

The girl was still staring woodenly.

"It was Orlando Julio, the medieval poisoner," she gasped, "that Uncle described—"

"In his seventeenth chapter of 'The World's Great Cynics,'" finished Madelyn. "I have taken the liberty of reading the chapter in manuscript form. Julio, however, was not the discoverer of the drug. He merely introduced it to the English public. As a matter of fact, it is one of the oldest stimulants of the East. It is easy to assume that it was not as a stimulant that Julio used it, but as a baffling instrument of murder. The mechanism of the pipe was his own invention, of course. The smoker, if not in the secret, would be completely oblivious to his danger. He might even use the pipe in perfect safety—until its lower chamber was loaded!"

Sheriff Peddicord, against the door, mopped his face with his red handkerchief, like a man in a daze. Dr. Dench was still studying Miss Mack with his intent frown. Madelyn swerved her angle abruptly.

"Last night was not the first time the hemp-chamber of Wendell Marsh's pipe had been charged. We can trace the effect of the drug on his brain for several months—hallucinations, imaginative enemies seeking his life, incipient insanity. That explains his astonishing letter to me. Wendell Marsh was not a man of nine lives, but only one. The perils which he described were merely fantastic figments of the drug. For instance, the episode of the poisoned cherry pie. There was no pie at all served at the table yesterday.

"The letter to me was not a forgery, Miss Jansen, although you were sincere enough when you pronounced it such. The complete change in your uncle's handwriting was only another effect of the drug. It was this fact, in the end, which led me to the truth. You did not perceive that the dates of your notes and mine were *six months apart!* I knew that some terrific mental shock *must* have occurred in the meantime.

"And then, too, the ravages of a drug-crazed victim were at once suggested by the curtains of the library. They were not simply torn, but fairly *chewed* to pieces!"

A sudden tension fell over the room. We shifted nervously, rather avoiding one another's eyes. Madelyn laid the pipe back on the stand. She was quite evidently in no hurry to continue. It was Truxton again who put the leading question of the moment.

"If Mr. Marsh was killed as you describe, Miss Mack, *who* killed him?"

Madelyn glanced across at Dr. Dench.

"Will you kindly let me have the red leather book that you took from Mr. Marsh's desk this evening, Doctor?"

The physician met her glance steadily.

"You think it—necessary?"

"I am afraid I must insist."

For an instant Dr. Dench hesitated. Then, with a shrug, he

reached into a coat pocket and extended the red-bound volume, for which Miss Mack had dispatched me on the fruitless errand to the library. As Madelyn opened it we saw that it was not a printed volume, but filled with several hundred pages of close, cramped writing. Dr. Dench's gaze swerved to Muriel Jansen as Miss Mack spoke.

"I have here the diary of Wendell Marsh, which shows us that he had been in the habit of seeking the stimulant of Indian hemp, or 'hasheesh' for some time, possibly as a result of his retired, sedentary life and his close application to his books. Until his purchase of the Bainford relics, however, he had taken the stimulant in the comparatively harmless form of powdered leaves or 'bhang,' as it is termed in the Orient. His acquisition of Julio's drug-pipe, and an accidental discovery of its mechanism, led him to adopt the compound of hemp and dhatura, prepared for smoking—in India called 'charas.' No less an authority than Captain E. N. Windsor, bacteriologist of the Burmese government, states that it is directly responsible for a large percentage of the lunacy of the Orient. Wendell Marsh, however, did not realize his danger, nor how much stronger the latter compound is than the form of the drug to which he had been accustomed.

"Dr. Dench endeavored desperately to warn him of his peril and free him from the bondage of the habit as the diary records, but the victim was too thoroughly enslaved. In fact, the situation had reached a point just before the final climax when it could no longer be concealed. The truth was already being suspected by the older servants. I assume this was why you feared my investigations in the case, Miss Jansen."

Muriel Jansen was staring at Madelyn in a sort of dumb appeal.

"I can understand and admire Dr. Dench's efforts to conceal the fact from the public—first, in his supervision of the inquest, which might have stumbled on the truth, and then in his removal of the betraying diary, which I left purposely exposed in the hope that it might inspire such an action. Had it *not* been removed, I might have suspected another explanation of the case—in spite of certain evidence to the contrary!"

Dr. Dench's face had gone white.

"God! Miss Mack, do you mean that after all it was not suicide?"

"It was not suicide," said Madelyn quietly. She stepped across toward the opposite door.

"When I stated that my knowledge that we are not dealing with natural death was shared by another person in this room, I might have added that it was shared by still a third person—*not in the room!*"

With a sudden movement she threw open the door before her. From the adjoining anteroom lurched the figure of Peters, the butler. He stared at us with a face grey with terror, and then crumpled to his knees. Madelyn drew away sharply as he tried to catch her skirts.

"You may arrest the murderer of Wendell Marsh, Sheriff!" she said gravely. "And I think perhaps you had better take him outside."

She faced our bewildered stares as the drawing-room door closed behind Mr. Peddicord and his prisoner. From her stand she again took Raleigh's sandstone pipe, and with it two sheets of paper, smudged with the prints of a human thumb and fingers.

"It was the pipe in the end which led me to the truth, not only as to the method but the identity of the assassin," she explained. "The hand, which placed the fatal charge in the concealed chamber, left its imprint on the surface of the bowl. The fingers, grimed with the dust of the drug, made an impression which I would have at once detected had I not been so occupied with what I might find *inside* that I forgot what I might find *outside!* I am very much afraid that I permitted myself the great blunder of the modern detective—lack of thoroughness.

"Comparison with the fingerpints of the various agents in the case, of course, made the next step a mere detail of mathematical comparison. To make my identity sure, I found that my suspect possessed not only the opportunity and the knowledge for the crime, but the motive.

"In his younger days Peters was a chemist's apprentice; a fact which he utilized in his master's behalf in obtaining the drugs which had become so necessary a part of Mr. Marsh's life. Had Wendell Marsh appeared in person for so continuous a supply, his identity would soon have made the fact a matter of common gossip. He relied on his servant for his agent, a detail which he mentions several times in his diary, promising Peters a generous bequest in his will as a reward. I fancy that it was the dream of this bequest, which would have meant a small fortune to a man in his position, that set the butler's brain to work on his treacherous plan of murder."

Miss Mack's dull gold hair covered the shoulders of her white peignoir in a great, thick braid. She was propped in a nest of pillows, with her favorite romance, *The Three Musketeers*, open at the historic siege of Porthos in the wine cellar. We had elected to spend the night at the Marsh house.

Madelyn glanced up as I appeared in the doorway of our room.

"Allow me to present a problem to your analytical skill, Miss Mack," I said humbly. "Which man does your knowledge of feminine psychology say Muriel Jansen will reward—the gravely protecting physician, or the boyishly admiring Truxton?"

"If she were thirty," retorted Madelyn, yawning, "she would be wise enough to choose Dr. Dench. But, as she is only twenty-two, it will be Truxton."

With a sigh, she turned again to the swashbuckling exploits of the gallant Porthos.

ANNA KATHARINE GREEN

(1846–1935)

More than three and a half decades after Ebenezer Gryce's debut in *The Leavenworth Case*, and almost twenty years after Amelia Butterworth first appeared in *That Affair Next Door*, the now rich and famous Anna Katharine Green launched yet another detective. In 1915 G. P. Putnam's Sons published *The Golden Slipper and Other Problems for Violet Strange*. Strange is a wealthy young New York socialite, about as far away on several spectrums from working-class policeman Gryce as it is possible to imagine, and quite some distance even from Butterworth. Strange appears in ten stories. In the first in the series, "The Golden Slipper," the head of the agency for which she occasionally works points her out at the theatre to a prospective client. The man is skeptical about her value as a detective, considering her youth and her social status:

> "And do you mean to say—"
>
> "I do—"
>
> "That yon silly little chit, whose father I know, whose fortune I know, who is seen everywhere, and who is called one of the season's belles is an agent of yours; a—a—"
>
> "No names here, please. You want a mystery solved. It is not a matter for the police—that is, as yet—and so you come to me, and when I ask for the facts, I find that women and only women are involved, and that these women are not only young but one and all of the highest society. Is it a man's work to go to the bottom of a combination like this? No. Sex against sex, and, if possible, youth against youth. Happily, I know such a person—a girl of gifts and extraordinarily well placed for the purpose. Why she uses her talents in this direction—why, with

> means enough to play the part natural to her as a successful debutante, she consents to occupy herself with social and other mysteries, you must ask her, not me. Enough that I promise you her aid if you want it. That is, if you can interest her. She will not work otherwise. . . . That's all, except this. In no event give away her secret. That's part of the compact, you remember."
>
> . . . She was a small, slight woman whose naturally quaint appearance was accentuated by the extreme simplicity of her attire. In the tier upon tier of boxes rising before his eyes, no other personality could vie with hers in strangeness, or in the illusive quality of her ever-changing expression. She was vivacity incarnate and, to the ordinary observer, light as thistledown in fibre and in feeling. But not to all. . . .

Not until the series' final story, "Violet's Own," does Green reveal the reason behind Strange's sneaking around to investigate crimes while keeping such work secret from her social equals. It turns out that long ago her sister was unjustly disinherited and young Strange is trying to raise money for her education as a musician. Thus she manages to be adventurous and heroic through numerous cases, only to prove in the end to be doing so for acceptably noble and ladylike reasons. Readers learn this only when she ceases investigative work, when she marries and reveals to her husband the origin of her seemingly illicit need for money.

"The Second Bullet," the final story in this anthology, is also perhaps the most tragic.

(For biographical information about Green, see the introduction to *That Affair Next Door*.)

THE SECOND BULLET

"You must see her."

"No. No."

"She's a most unhappy woman. Husband and child both taken from her in a moment; and now, all means of living as well, unless some happy thought of yours—some inspiration of your genius—shows us a way of re-establishing her claims to the policy voided by this cry of suicide."

But the small wise head of Violet Strange continued its slow shake of decided refusal.

"I'm sorry," she protested, "but it's quite out of my province. I'm too young to meddle with so serious a matter."

"Not when you can save a bereaved woman the only possible compensation left her by untoward fate?"

"Let the police try their hand at that."

"They have had no success with the case."

"Or you?"

"Nor I either."

"And you expect—"

"Yes, Miss Strange. I expect you to find the missing bullet which will settle the fact that murder and not suicide ended George Hammond's life. If you cannot, then a long litigation awaits this poor widow, ending, as such litigation usually does, in favour of the stronger party. There's the alternative. If you once saw her—"

"But that's what I'm not willing to do. If I once saw her I should yield to her importunities and attempt the seemingly impossible. My instincts bid me say no. Give me something easier."

"Easier things are not so remunerative. There's money in this affair, if the insurance company is forced to pay up. I can offer you—"

"What?"

There was eagerness in the tone despite her effort at nonchalance. The other smiled imperceptibly, and briefly named the sum.

It was larger than she had expected. This her visitor saw by the way her eyelids fell and the peculiar stillness which, for an instant, held her vivacity in check.

"And you think I can earn that?"

Her eyes were fixed on his in an eagerness as honest as it was unrestrained.

He could hardly conceal his amazement, her desire was so evident and the cause of it so difficult to understand. He knew she wanted money—that was her avowed reason for entering into this uncongenial work. But to want it *so much*! He glanced at her person; it was simply clad but very expensively—how expensively it was his business to know. Then he took in the room in which they sat. Simplicity again, but the simplicity of high art—the drawing-room of one rich enough to indulge in the final luxury of a highly cultivated taste, viz.: unostentatious elegance and the subjection of each carefully chosen ornament to the general effect.

What did this favoured child of fortune lack that she could be reached by such a plea, when her whole being revolted from the nature of the task he offered her? It was a question not new to him; but one he had never heard answered and was not likely to hear answered now. But the fact remained that the consent he had thought dependent upon sympathetic interest could be reached much more readily by the promise of large emolument,—and he owned to a feeling of secret disappointment even while he recognized the value of the discovery.

But his satisfaction in the latter, if satisfaction it were, was of very short duration. Almost immediately he observed a change in her. The sparkle which had shone in the eye whose depths he had never been able to penetrate, had dissipated itself in something like a tear and she spoke up in that vigorous tone no one but himself had ever heard, as she said:

"No. The sum is a good one and I could use it; but I will not waste my energy on a case I do not believe in. The man shot himself. He was a speculator, and probably had good reason for his act. Even his wife acknowledges that he has lately had more losses than gains."

"See her. She has something to tell you which never got into the papers."

"You say that? You know that?"

"On my honour, Miss Strange."

Violet pondered; then suddenly succumbed.

"Let her come, then. Prompt to the hour. I will receive her at three. Later I have a tea and two party calls to make."

Her visitor rose to leave. He had been able to subdue all evidence of his extreme gratification, and now took on a formal air. In dismissing a guest, Miss Strange was invariably the society belle and that only. This he had come to recognize.

The case (well known at the time) was, in the fewest possible words, as follows:

On a sultry night in September, a young couple living in one of the large apartment houses in the extreme upper portion of Manhattan were so annoyed by the incessant crying of a child in the adjoining suite, that they got up, he to smoke, and she to sit in the window for a possible breath of cool air. They were congratulating themselves upon the wisdom they had shown in thus giving up all thought of sleep—for the child's crying had not ceased—when (it may have been two o'clock and it may have been a little later) there came from somewhere near, the sharp and somewhat peculiar detonation of a pistol-shot.

He thought it came from above; she, from the rear, and they were staring at each other in the helpless wonder of the moment, when they were struck by the silence. The baby had ceased to cry. All was as still in the adjoining apartment as in their own—too still—much too still. Their mutual stare turned to one of horror. "It came from there!" whispered the wife. "Some accident has occurred to Mr. or Mrs. Hammond—we ought to go—"

Her words—very tremulous ones—were broken by a shout from below. They were standing in their window and had evidently been seen by a passing policeman. "Anything wrong up there?" they heard him cry. Mr. Saunders immediately looked out. "Nothing wrong here," he called down. (They were but two stories from the pavement.) "But I'm not so sure about the rear apartment. We thought we heard a shot. Hadn't you better come up, officer? My wife is nervous about it. I'll meet you at the stair-head and show you the way."

The officer nodded and stepped in. The young couple hastily donned some wraps, and, by the time he appeared on their floor, they were ready to accompany him.

Meanwhile, no disturbance was apparent anywhere else in the house, until the policeman rang the bell of the Hammond apartment. Then, voices began to be heard, and doors to open above and below, but not the one before which the policeman stood.

Another ring, and this time an insistent one;—and still no response. The officer's hand was rising for the third time when there came a sound of fluttering from behind the panels against which he had laid his ear, and finally a choked voice uttering unintelligible words. Then a hand began to struggle with the lock, and the door, slowly opening, disclosed a woman clad in a hastily donned wrapper and giving every evidence of extreme fright.

"Oh!" she exclaimed, seeing only the compassionate faces of her neighbours. "You heard it, too! a pistol-shot from there—*there* my husband's room. I have not dared to go—I—I—O, have mercy and see if anything is wrong! It is so still—so still, and only a moment ago the baby was crying. Mrs. Saunders, Mrs. Saunders, why is it so still?"

She had fallen into her neighbour's arms. The hand with which she had pointed out a certain door had sunk to her side and she appeared to be on the verge of collapse.

The officer eyed her sternly, while noting her appearance, which was that of a woman hastily risen from bed.

"Where were you?" he asked. "Not with your husband and child, or you would know what had happened there."

"I was sleeping down the hall," she managed to gasp out. "I'm not well—I—Oh, why do you all stand still and do nothing? My baby's in there. Go! go!" and, with sudden energy, she sprang upright, her eyes wide open and burning, her small well-featured face white as the linen she sought to hide.

The officer demurred no longer. In another instant he was trying the door at which she was again pointing.

It was locked.

Glancing back at the woman, now cowering almost to the floor, he pounded at the door and asked the man inside to open.

No answer came back.

With a sharp turn he glanced again at the wife.

"You say that your husband is in this room?"

She nodded, gasping faintly, "And the child!"

He turned back, listened, then beckoned to Mr. Saunders. "We shall have to break our way in," said he. "Put your shoulder well to the door. Now!"

The hinges of the door creaked; the lock gave way (this special officer weighed two hundred and seventy-five, as he found out, next day), and a prolonged and sweeping crash told the rest.

Mrs. Hammond gave a low cry; and, straining forward from where she crouched in terror on the floor, searched the faces of the two men for some hint of what they saw in the dimly-lighted space beyond.

Something dreadful, something which made Mr. Saunders come rushing back with a shout:

"Take her away! Take her to our apartment, Jennie. She must not see—"

Not see! He realized the futility of his words as his gaze fell on the young woman who had risen up at his approach and now stood gazing at him without speech, without movement, but with a glare of terror in her eyes, which gave him his first realization of human misery.

His own glance fell before it. If he had followed his instinct he would have fled the house rather than answer the question of her look and the attitude of her whole frozen body.

Perhaps in mercy to his speechless terror, perhaps in mercy to herself, she was the one who at last found the word which voiced their mutual anguish.

"Dead?"

No answer. None was needed.

"And my baby?"

O, that cry! It curdled the hearts of all who heard it. It shook the souls of men and women both inside and outside the apartment; then all was forgotten in the wild rush she made. The wife and mother had flung herself upon the scene, and, side by side with the not unmoved policeman, stood looking down upon the desolation made in one fatal instant in her home and heart.

They lay there together, both past help, both quite dead. The child had simply been strangled by the weight of his father's arm which lay directly across the upturned little throat. But the father was a victim of the shot they had heard. There was blood on his breast, and a pistol in his hand.

Suicide! The horrible truth was patent. No wonder they wanted to hold the young widow back. Her neighbour, Mrs. Saunders, crept in on tiptoe and put her arms about the swaying, fainting woman; but there was nothing to say—absolutely nothing.

At least, they thought not. But when they saw her throw herself down, not by her husband, but by the child, and drag it out from under that strangling arm and hug and kiss it and call out wildly for a doctor, the officer endeavoured to interfere and yet could not find the heart to do so, though he knew the child was dead and should not, according to all the rules of the coroner's office, be moved before that official arrived. Yet because no mother could be convinced of a fact like this, he let her sit with it on the floor and try all her little arts to revive it, while he gave orders to the janitor and waited himself for the arrival of doctor and coroner.

She was still sitting there in wide-eyed misery, alternately fondling the little body and drawing back to consult its small set features for some sign of life, when the doctor came, and, after one look at the child, drew it softly from her arms and laid it quietly in the crib from which its father had evidently lifted it but a short time before. Then he turned back to her, and found her on her feet, upheld by her two friends. She had understood his action, and without a groan had accepted her fate. Indeed, she seemed incapable of any further speech or action. She was staring down at her husband's body, which she, for the first time, seemed fully to see. Was her look one of grief or of resentment for the part he had played so unintentionally in her child's death? It was hard to tell; and when, with slowly rising finger, she pointed to the pistol so tightly clutched in the other outstretched hand, no one there—and by this time the room was full—could foretell what her words would be when her tongue regained its usage and she could speak.

What she did say was this:

"Is there a bullet gone? Did he fire off that pistol?" A question so manifestly one of delirium that no one answered it, which seemed to surprise her, though she said nothing till her glance had passed all around the walls of the room to where a window stood open to the night,—its lower sash being entirely raised. "There! look there!" she cried, with a commanding accent, and, throwing up her hands, sank a dead weight into the arms of those supporting her.

No one understood; but naturally more than one rushed to the window. An open space was before them. Here lay the fields not yet parcelled out into lots and built upon; but it was not upon these they looked, but upon the strong trellis which they found there, which, if it supported no vine, formed a veritable ladder between this window and the ground.

Could she have meant to call attention to this fact; and were her words expressive of another idea than the obvious one of suicide?

If so, to what lengths a woman's imagination can go! Or so their combined looks seemed to proclaim, when to their utter astonishment they saw the officer, who had presented a calm appearance up till now, shift his position and with a surprised grunt direct their eyes to a portion of the wall just visible beyond the half-drawn curtains of the bed. The mirror hanging there showed a star-shaped breakage, such as follows the sharp impact of a bullet or a fiercely projected stone.

"He fired two shots. One went wild; the other straight home."

It was the officer delivering his opinion.

Mr. Saunders, returning from the distant room where he had assisted in carrying Mrs. Hammond, cast a look at the shattered glass, and remarked forcibly:

"I heard but one; and I was sitting up, disturbed by that poor infant. Jennie, did you hear more than one shot?" he asked, turning toward his wife.

"No," she answered, but not with the readiness he had evidently expected. "I heard only one, but that was not quite usual in its tone. I'm used to guns," she explained, turning to the officer. "My father was an army man, and he taught me very early to load and fire a pistol. There was a prolonged sound to this shot; something like an echo of itself, following close upon the first ping. Didn't you notice that, Warren?"

"I remember something of the kind," her husband allowed.

"He shot twice and quickly," interposed the policeman, sententiously. "We shall find a spent bullet back of that mirror."

But when, upon the arrival of the coroner, an investigation was made of the mirror and the wall behind, no bullet was found either there or anywhere else in the room, save in the dead man's breast. Nor had more than one been shot from his pistol, as five full chambers testified. The case which seemed so simple had its mysteries, but the assertion made by Mrs. Saunders no longer carried weight, nor was the evidence offered by the broken mirror considered as indubitably establishing the fact that a second shot had been fired in the room.

Yet it was equally evident that the charge which had entered the dead speculator's breast had not been delivered at the close range of the pistol found clutched in his hand. There were no powder-marks to be discerned on his pajama-jacket, or on the flesh beneath. Thus anomaly confronted anomaly, leaving open but one other theory: that the bullet found in Mr. Hammond's breast came from the window and the one he shot went out of it. But this would necessitate his having shot his pistol from a point far removed from where he was found; and his wound was such as made it difficult to believe that he would stagger far, if at all, after its infliction.

Yet, because the coroner was both conscientious and alert, he caused a most rigorous search to be made of the ground overlooked by the above mentioned window; a search in which the police joined, but which was without any result save that of rousing the attention of people in the neighbourhood and leading to a story being circulated of a man seen some time the night before crossing the fields in a great hurry. But as no further particulars were forthcoming, and not even a description of the man to be had, no emphasis would have been laid upon this story had it not transpired that the moment a report of it had come to Mrs. Hammond's ears (why is there always some one to carry these reports?) she roused from the torpor into which she had fallen, and in wild fashion exclaimed:

"I knew it! I expected it! He was shot through the window and by that wretch. He never shot himself." Violent declarations which trailed off into the one continuous wail, "O, my baby! my poor baby!"

Such words, even though the fruit of delirium, merited some sort of attention, or so this good coroner thought, and as soon as opportunity offered and she was sufficiently sane and quiet to respond to his questions, he asked her whom she had meant by that wretch, and what reason she had, or thought she had, of attributing her husband's death to any other agency than his own disgust with life.

And then it was that his sympathies, although greatly roused in her favour began to wane. She met the question with a cold stare followed by a few ambiguous words out of which he could make nothing. Had she said wretch? She did not remember. They must not be influenced by anything she might have uttered in her first grief. She was well-nigh insane at the time. But of one thing they might be sure: her husband had not shot himself; he was too much afraid of death for such an act. Besides, he was too happy. Whatever folks might say he was too fond of his family to wish to leave it.

Nor did the coroner or any other official succeed in eliciting anything further from her. Even when she was asked, with cruel insistence, how she explained the fact that the baby was found lying on the floor instead of in its crib, her only answer was: "His father was trying to soothe it. The child was crying dreadfully, as you have heard from those who were kept awake by him that night, and my husband was carrying him about when the shot came which caused George to fall and overlay the baby in his struggles."

"Carrying a baby about with a loaded pistol in his hand?" came back in stern retort.

She had no answer for this. She admitted when informed that the bullet extracted from her husband's body had been found to correspond exactly with those remaining in the five chambers of the pistol taken from his hand, that he was not only the owner of this pistol but was in the habit of sleeping with it under his pillow; but, beyond that, nothing; and this reticence, as well as her manner which was cold and repellent, told against her.

A verdict of suicide was rendered by the coroner's jury, and the life-insurance company, in which Mr. Hammond had but lately insured himself for a large sum, taking advantage of the suicide clause embodied in the policy, announced its determination of not paying the same.

Such was the situation, as known to Violet Strange and the general public, on the day she was asked to see Mrs. Hammond and learn what might alter her opinion as to the justice of this verdict and the stand taken by the Shuler Life Insurance Company.

The clock on the mantel in Miss Strange's rose-coloured boudoir had struck three, and Violet was gazing in some impatience at the door, when there came a gentle knock upon it, and the maid (one of the elderly, not youthful, kind) ushered in her expected visitor.

"You are Mrs. Hammond?" she asked, in natural awe of the too black figure outlined so sharply against the deep pink of the sea-shell room.

The answer was a slow lifting of the veil which shadowed the features she knew only from the cuts she had seen in newspapers.

"You are—Miss Strange?" stammered her visitor; "the young lady who—"

"I am," chimed in a voice as ringing as it was sweet. "I am the person you have come here to see. And this is my home. But that does not make me less interested in the unhappy, or less desirous of serving them. Certainly you have met with the two greatest losses which can come to a woman—I know your story well enough to say that—; but what have you to tell me in proof that you should not lose your anticipated income as well? Something vital, I hope, else I cannot help you; something which you should have told the coroner's jury—and did not."

The flush which was the sole answer these words called forth did not take from the refinement of the young widow's expression, but rather added to it; Violet watched it in its ebb and flow and, seriously affected by it (why, she did not know, for Mrs. Hammond had made no other appeal either by look or gesture), pushed forward a chair and begged her visitor to be seated.

"We can converse in perfect safety here," she said. "When you feel quite equal to it, let me hear what you have to communicate.

It will never go any further. I could not do the work I do if I felt it necessary to have a confidant."

"But you are so young and so—so—"

"So inexperienced you would say and so evidently a member of what New Yorkers call 'society.' Do not let that trouble you. My inexperience is not likely to last long and my social pleasures are more apt to add to my efficiency than to detract from it."

With this Violet's face broke into a smile. It was not the brilliant one so often seen upon her lips, but there was something in its quality which carried encouragement to the widow and led her to say with obvious eagerness:

"You know the facts?"

"I have read all the papers."

"I was not believed on the stand."

"It was your manner—"

"I could not help my manner. I was keeping something back, and, being unused to deceit, I could not act quite naturally."

"Why did you keep something back? When you saw the unfavourable impression made by your reticence, why did you not speak up and frankly tell your story?"

"Because I was ashamed. Because I thought it would hurt me more to speak than to keep silent. I do not think so now; but I did then—and so made my great mistake. You must remember not only the awful shock of my double loss, but the sense of guilt accompanying it; for my husband and I had quarreled that night, quarreled bitterly—that was why I had run away into another room and not because I was feeling ill and impatient of the baby's fretful cries."

"So people have thought." In saying this, Miss Strange was perhaps cruelly emphatic. "You wish to explain that quarrel? You think it will be doing any good to your cause to go into that matter with me now?"

"I cannot say; but I must first clear my conscience and then try to convince you that quarrel or no quarrel, he never took his own life. He was not that kind. He had an abnormal fear of death. I do not like to say it but he was a physical coward. I have seen him turn pale at the least hint of danger. He could no more have turned that muzzle upon his own breast than he could have turned it upon his baby. Some other hand shot him, Miss Strange. Remember the open window, the shattered mirror; and *I think I know that hand.*"

Her head had fallen forward on her breast. The emotion she showed was not so eloquent of grief as of deep personal shame.

"You think you know the *man*?" In saying this, Violet's voice sunk to a whisper. It was an accusation of murder she had just heard.

"To my great distress, yes. When Mr. Hammond and I were married," the widow now proceeded in a more determined tone, "there was another man—a very violent one—who vowed even at the church door that George and I should never live out two full years together. We have not. Our second anniversary would have been in November."

"But—"

"Let me say this: the quarrel of which I speak was not serious enough to occasion any such act of despair on his part. A man would be mad to end his life on account of so slight a disagreement. It was not even on account of the person of whom I've just spoken, though that person had been mentioned between us earlier in the evening, Mr. Hammond having come across him face to face that very afternoon in the subway. Up to this time neither of us had seen or heard of him since our wedding-day."

"And you think this person whom you barely mentioned, so mindful of his old grudge that he sought out your domicile, and, with the intention of murder, climbed the trellis leading to your room and turned his pistol upon the shadowy figure which was all he could see in the semi-obscurity of a much lowered gas-jet?"

"A man in the dark does not need a bright light to see his enemy when he is intent upon revenge."

Miss Strange altered her tone.

"And your husband? You must acknowledge that he shot off his pistol whether the other did or not."

"It was in self-defence. He would shoot to save his own life—or the baby's."

"Then he must have heard or seen—"

"A man at the window."

"And would have shot there?

"Or tried to."

"Tried to?"

"Yes; the other shot first—oh, I've thought it all out—causing my husband's bullet to go wild. It was his which broke the mirror."

Violet's eyes, bright as stars, suddenly narrowed.

"And what happened then?" she asked. "Why cannot they find the bullet?"

"Because it went out of the window;—glanced off and went out of the window."

Mrs. Hammond's tone was triumphant; her look spirited and intense.

Violet eyed her compassionately.

"Would a bullet glancing off from a mirror, however hung, be apt to reach a window so far on the opposite side?"

"I don't know; I only know that it did," was the contradictory, almost absurd, reply.

"What *was* the cause of the quarrel you speak of between your husband and yourself? You see, I must know the exact truth and all the truth to be of any assistance to you."

"It was—it was about the care I gave, or didn't give, the baby. I feel awfully to have to say it, but George did not think I did my full duty by the child. He said there was no need of its crying so; that if I gave it the proper attention it would not keep the neighbours and himself awake half the night. And I—I got angry and insisted that I did the best I could; that the child was naturally fretful and that if he wasn't satisfied with my way of looking after it, he might try his. All of which was very wrong and unreasonable on my part, as witness the awful punishment which followed."

"And what made you get up and leave him?"

"The growl he gave me in reply. When I heard that, I bounded out of bed and said I was going to the spare room to sleep; and if the baby cried he might just try what he could do himself to stop it."

"And he answered?"

"This, just this—I shall never forget his words as long as I live—'If you go, you need not expect me to let you in again no matter what happens.'"

"He said that?"

"And locked the door after me. You see I could not tell all that."

"It might have been better if you had. It was such a natural quarrel and so unprovocative of actual tragedy."

Mrs. Hammond was silent. It was not difficult to see that she had no very keen regrets for her husband personally. But then he was not a very estimable man nor in any respect her equal.

"You were not happy with him," Violet ventured to remark.

"I was not a fully contented woman. But for all that he had no cause to complain of me except for the reason I have mentioned. I was not a very intelligent mother. But if the baby were living now—o, if he were living now—with what devotion I should care for him."

She was on her feet, her arms were raised, her face impassioned with feeling. Violet, gazing at her, heaved a little sigh. It was perhaps in keeping with the situation, perhaps extraneous to it, but whatever its source, it marked a change in her manner. With no further check upon her sympathy, she said very softly:

"It is well with the child."

The mother stiffened, swayed, and then burst into wild weeping.

"But not with me," she cried, "not with me. I am desolate and bereft. I have not even a home in which to hide my grief and no prospect of one."

"But," interposed Violet, "surely your husband left you something? You cannot be quite penniless?"

"My husband left nothing," was the answer, uttered without bitterness, but with all the hardness of fact. "He had debts. I shall pay those debts. When these and other necessary expenses are liquidated, there will be but little left. He made no secret of the fact that he lived close up to his means. That is why he was induced to take on a life insurance. Not a friend of his but knows his improvidence. I—I have not even jewels. I have only my determination and an absolute conviction as to the real nature of my husband's death."

"What is the name of the man you secretly believe to have shot your husband from the trellis?"

Mrs. Hammond told her.

It was a new one to Violet. She said so and then asked:

"What else can you tell me about him?"

"Nothing, but that he is a very dark man and has a club-foot."

"Oh, what a mistake you've made."

"Mistake? Yes, I acknowledge that."

"I mean in not giving this last bit of information at once to the police. A man can be identified by such a defect. Even his footsteps can be traced. He might have been found that very day. Now, what have we to go upon?"

"You are right, but not expecting to have any difficulty about the insurance money I thought it would be generous in me to keep still. Besides, this is only surmise on my part. I feel certain that my husband was shot by another hand than his own, but I know of no way of proving it. Do you?"

Then Violet talked seriously with her, explaining how their only hope lay in the discovery of a second bullet in the room which had already been ransacked for this very purpose and without the shadow of a result.

A tea, a musicale, and an evening dance kept Violet Strange in a whirl for the remainder of the day. No brighter eye nor more contagious wit lent brilliance to these occasions, but with the passing of the midnight hour no one who had seen her in the blaze of electric lights would have recognized this favoured child of fortune in the earnest figure sitting in the obscurity of an up-town apartment, studying the walls, the ceilings, and the floors by the dim light of a lowered gas-jet. Violet Strange in society was a very different person from Violet Strange under the tension of her secret and peculiar work.

She had told them at home that she was going to spend the night with a friend; but only her old coachman knew who that friend was. Therefore a very natural sense of guilt mingled with her emotions at finding herself alone on a scene whose gruesome mystery she could solve only by identifying herself with the place and the man who had perished there.

Dismissing from her mind all thought of self, she strove to think as he thought, and act as he acted on the night when he found himself (a man of but little courage) left in this room with an ailing child.

At odds with himself, his wife, and possibly with the child screaming away in its crib, what would he be apt to do in his present emergency? Nothing at first, but as the screaming continued he would remember the old tales of fathers walking the floor at night with crying babies, and hasten to follow suit. Violet, in her anxiety to reach his inmost thought, crossed to where the crib had stood, and, taking that as a start, began pacing the room in search of the spot from which a bullet, if shot, would glance aside from the mirror in the direction of the window. (Not that she was ready to accept this theory of Mrs. Hammond, but that she did not wish to entirely dismiss it without putting it to the test.)

She found it in an unexpected quarter of the room and much nearer the bed-head than where his body was found. This, which might seem to confuse matters, served, on the contrary to remove from the case one of its most serious difficulties. Standing here, he was within reach of the pillow under which his pistol lay hidden, and if startled, as his wife believed him to have been by a noise at the other end of the room, had but to crouch and reach behind him in order to find himself armed and ready for a possible intruder.

Imitating his action in this as in other things, she had herself crouched low at the bedside and was on the point of withdrawing her hand from under the pillow, when a new surprise checked her movement and held her fixed in her position, with eyes staring straight at the adjoining wall. She had seen there what he must have seen in making this same turn—the dark bars of the opposite window-frame outlined in the mirror—and understood at once what had happened. In the nervousness and terror of the moment, George Hammond had mistaken this reflection of the window for the window itself, and shot impulsively at the man he undoubtedly saw covering him from the trellis without. But while this explained the shattering of the mirror, how about the other and still more vital question, of where the bullet went afterward? Was the angle at which it had been fired acute enough to send it out of a window diagonally opposed? No; even if the pistol had been held closer to the man firing it than she had reason to believe, the angle still would be oblique enough to carry it on to the further wall.

But no sign of any such impact had been discovered on this

wall. Consequently, the force of the bullet had been expended before reaching it, and when it fell—

Here, her glance, slowly traveling along the floor, impetuously paused. It had reached the spot where the two bodies had been found, and unconsciously her eyes rested there, conjuring up the picture of the bleeding father and the strangled child. How piteous and how dreadful it all was. If she could only understand— Suddenly she rose straight up, staring and immovable in the dim light. Had the idea—the explanation—the only possible explanation covering the whole phenomena come to her at last?

It would seem so, for as she so stood, a look of conviction settled over her features, and with this look, evidences of a horror which for all her fast accumulating knowledge of life and its possibilities made her appear very small and very helpless.

A half-hour later, when Mrs. Hammond, in her anxiety at hearing nothing more from Miss Strange, opened the door of her room, it was to find, lying on the edge of the sill, the little detective's card with these words hastily written across it:

I do not feel as well as I could wish, and so have telephoned to my own coachman to come and take me home. I will either see or write you within a few days. But do not allow yourself to hope. I pray you do not allow yourself the least hope; the outcome is still very problematical.

When Violet's employer entered his office the next morning it was to find a veiled figure awaiting him which he at once recognized as that of his little deputy. She was slow in lifting her veil and when it finally came free he felt a momentary doubt as to his wisdom in giving her just such a matter as this to investigate. He was quite sure of his mistake when he saw her face, it was so drawn and pitiful.

"You have failed," said he.

"Of that you must judge," she answered; and drawing near she whispered in his ear.

"No!" he cried in his amazement.

"Think," she murmured, "think. Only so can all the facts be accounted for."

"I will look into it; I will certainly look into it," was his earnest reply. "If you are right— But never mind that. Go home and take a horseback ride in the Park. When I have news in regard to this I will let you know. Till then forget it all. Hear me, I charge you to forget everything but your balls and your parties."

And Violet obeyed him.

Some few days after this, the following statement appeared in all the papers:

> "Owing to some remarkable work done by the firm of—&—, the well-known private detective agency, the claim made by Mrs. George Hammond against the Shuler Life Insurance Company is likely to be allowed without further litigation. As our readers will remember, the contestant has insisted from the first that the bullet causing her husband's death came from another pistol than the one found clutched in his own hand. But while reasons were not lacking to substantiate this assertion, the failure to discover more than the disputed track of a second bullet led to a verdict of suicide, and a refusal of the company to pay.
>
> "But now that bullet has been found. And where? In the most startling place in the world, viz.: in the larynx of the child found lying dead upon the floor beside his father, strangled as was supposed by the weight of that father's arm. The theory is, and there seems to be none other, that the father, hearing a suspicious noise at the window, set down the child he was endeavouring to soothe and made for the bed and his own pistol, and, mistaking a reflection of the assassin for the assassin himself, sent his shot sidewise at a mirror just as the other let go the trigger which drove a similar bullet into his breast. The course of the one was straight and fatal and that of the other deflected. Striking the mirror at an oblique angle, the bullet fell to the floor where it was picked up by the crawling child, and, as was most natural, thrust at once into his mouth. Perhaps it felt hot to the little tongue; perhaps the child was simply frightened by some convulsive movement of the father who evidently spent his last moment in an endeavour to reach the child, but, whatever the cause, in the quick gasp it gave, the bullet was drawn into the larynx, strangling him.
>
> "That the father's arm, in his last struggle, should have fallen

directly across the little throat is one of those anomalies which confounds reason and misleads justice by stopping investigation at the very point where truth lies and mystery disappears.

"Mrs. Hammond is to be congratulated that there are detectives who do not give too much credence to outward appearances.

"We expect soon to hear of the capture of the man who sped home the death-dealing bullet."

THE STORY OF PENGUIN CLASSICS

Before 1946 . . . "Classics" are mainly the domain of academics and students; readable editions for everyone else are almost unheard of. This all changes when a little-known classicist, E. V. Rieu, presents Penguin founder Allen Lane with the translation of Homer's *Odyssey* that he has been working on in his spare time.

1946 Penguin Classics debuts with *The Odyssey,* which promptly sells three million copies. Suddenly, classics are no longer for the privileged few.

1950s Rieu, now series editor, turns to professional writers for the best modern, readable translations, including Dorothy L. Sayers's *Inferno* and Robert Graves's unexpurgated *Twelve Caesars*.

1960s The Classics are given the distinctive black covers that have remained a constant throughout the life of the series. Rieu retires in 1964, hailing the Penguin Classics list as "the greatest educative force of the twentieth century."

1970s A new generation of translators swells the Penguin Classics ranks, introducing readers of English to classics of world literature from more than twenty languages. The list grows to encompass more history, philosophy, science, religion, and politics.

1980s The Penguin American Library launches with titles such as *Uncle Tom's Cabin* and joins forces with Penguin Classics to provide the most comprehensive library of world literature available from any paperback publisher.

1990s The launch of Penguin Audiobooks brings the classics to a listening audience for the first time, and in 1999 the worldwide launch of the Penguin Classics Web site extends their reach to the global online community.

The 21st Century Penguin Classics are completely redesigned for the first time in nearly twenty years. This world-famous series now consists of more than 1,300 titles, making the widest range of the best books ever written available to millions—and constantly redefining what makes a "classic."

The Odyssey continues . . .

The best books ever written

PENGUIN CLASSICS

SINCE 1946

Find out more at www.penguinclassics.com

Visit www.vpbookclub.com

CLICK ON A CLASSIC

www.penguinclassics.com

The world's greatest literature at your fingertips

Constantly updated information on over 1600 titles, from Icelandic sagas to ancient Indian epics, Russian drama to Italian romance, American greats to African masterpieces

•

The latest news on recent additions to the list, updated editions and specially commissioned translations

•

Original scholarly essays by leading writers: Elaine Showalter on Zola, Laurie R King on Arthur Conan Doyle, Frank Kermode on Shakespeare, Lisa Appignanesi on Tolstoy

•

A wealth of background material, including biographies of every classic author from Aristotle to Zamyatin, plot synopses, readers' and teachers' guides, useful web links

•

Online desk and examination copy assistance for academics

•

Trivia quizzes, competitions, giveaways, news on forthcoming screen adaptations

•

eBooks available to download

Printed in the United States
by Baker & Taylor Publisher Services